Praise for the Novels of Jeane Westin

His Last Letter

"[B]eautiful scenes and a fast-moving yet easy to follow story line . . . it is a testament to Westin's writing that when we reach the end of this tale, we've become so wrapped in the story and the characters that we can feel Elizabeth's pain almost as keenly as she does. *His Last Letter* is guaranteed to be a pleasure for anyone who has even a passing interest in history or historical figures." —Fiction Addict

"This realistic, well-researched portrait of Elizabeth answers questions about her lifelong friendship with Dudley—her "Sweet Robin" and beloved "eye." Westin walks a fine line, depicting the sweetness and sadness of Elizabeth's middle years, when political turmoil supersedes personal needs. Her lively storytelling and remarkably real characters make for compelling reading." —*Romantic Times*

"Engaging, heartfelt, and touching." —Passages to the Past

"I thoroughly enjoyed this novel. . . . This book will have you smiling and crying; it grabs you, draws you in, and tears at your heartstrings. It is a joy to read and I now want to repeat the experience and read it all over again!" —The Anne Boleyn Files

continued . . .

"With hundreds of books already written about Elizabeth's life, it's a challenge for any author to come up with something new. But Jeane Westin does it with her novel about Elizabeth's affair with Robert Dudley."
—*am New York*

"A captivating and powerful love story set against the backdrop of a perilous time in Elizabeth's reign. Westin brings Elizabeth and Dudley's tempestuous relationship vividly to life. . . . I cannot recommend this book highly enough!"
—On the Tudor Trail

The Virgin's Daughters

"This is a Tudor novel not to be missed . . . well told and well researched. . . . What might have been merely two love stories truly became history brought to life. Highly recommended."
—*Historical Novels Review* (Editor's Choice)

"Takes the reader on a poignant journey into the hearts and minds of three dynamic Elizabethan women, including the queen herself . . . a compelling, unforgettable historical novel."
—Karen Harper, author of *Mistress of Mourning*

"Two well-crafted love stories set against the backdrop of the court of Elizabeth the First create high drama and at the same time paint an unforgettable portrait of the last Tudor monarch."
—Kate Emerson, author of *At the King's Pleasure*

"Vivid characters and compelling dialogue illuminate the Elizabethan court, where danger lurks in the shadows, love can be treason, and every step could be the last. You'll find yourself looking over your shoulder in this engrossing read."
—Sandra Worth, author of *The King's Daughter*

OTHER NOVELS BY JEANE WESTIN

His Last Letter

The Virgin's Daughters

The
SPYMASTER'S
DAUGHTER

❧

JEANE WESTIN

NAL NEW AMERICAN LIBRARY

NEW AMERICAN LIBRARY
Published by New American Library, a division of
Penguin Group (USA) Inc., 375 Hudson Street,
New York, New York 10014, USA
Penguin Group (Canada), 90 Eglinton Avenue East, Suite 700, Toronto,
Ontario M4P 2Y3, Canada (a division of Pearson Penguin Canada Inc.)
Penguin Books Ltd., 80 Strand, London WC2R 0RL, England
Penguin Ireland, 25 St. Stephen's Green, Dublin 2,
Ireland (a division of Penguin Books Ltd.)
Penguin Group (Australia), 250 Camberwell Road, Camberwell, Victoria 3124,
Australia (a division of Pearson Australia Group Pty. Ltd.)
Penguin Books India Pvt. Ltd., 11 Community Centre, Panchsheel Park,
New Delhi - 110 017, India
Penguin Group (NZ), 67 Apollo Drive, Rosedale, Auckland 0632,
New Zealand (a division of Pearson New Zealand Ltd.)
Penguin Books (South Africa) (Pty.) Ltd., 24 Sturdee Avenue,
Rosebank, Johannesburg 2196, South Africa

Penguin Books Ltd., Registered Offices:
80 Strand, London WC2R 0RL, England

First published by New American Library,
a division of Penguin Group (USA) Inc.

First Printing, August 2012
10 9 8 7 6 5 4 3 2 1

REGISTERED TRADEMARK—MARCA REGISTRADA

LIBRARY OF CONGRESS CATALOGING-IN-PUBLICATION DATA:
Westin, Jeane Eddy.
    The spymaster's daughter / Jeane Westin.
        p.   cm.
    ISBN 978-0-451-23702-6
    1. Courts and courtiers—Fiction.   2. Great Britain—History—Elizabeth, 1558–1603—
Fiction. I. Title.
    PS3573.E89S69 2012
    813'.54—dc23   2012013110

Set in Adobe Garamond
Designed by Ginger Legato

Printed in the United States of America

PUBLISHER'S NOTE
This is a work of fiction. Names, characters, places, and incidents either are the product of the
author's imagination or are used fictitiously, and any resemblance to actual persons, living or dead,
business establishments, events, or locales is entirely coincidental.
    The publisher does not have any control over and does not assume any responsibility for author
or third-party Web sites or their content.

ALWAYS LEARNING   PEARSON

To my husband, Gene, and my daughter, Cara.
In the end family is everything.

ACKNOWLEDGMENTS

As always I acknowledge with gratitude the help of Shirley Parenteau as first reader. Her encouragement and friendship are invaluable and I can't imagine being without them. And with thanks to Georgia Bockoven, novelist and renowned wildlife photographer, who brings me a dose of reality when I'm too high and lifts me up when I'm going in the wrong direction.

And to Lady Ashley Lucas, computer whiz, who periodically untangles my program problems on a machine that continues to mystify me after so many years.

My sincere thanks to all the antique book dealers in the U.S. and U.K. who collect and make available old books and manuscripts, without which novels like this one would be far more difficult and much less fun.

Lastly, to my ever-encouraging agent, Danielle Egan-Miller. And to the very best editor an author could have, Ellen Edwards—her fame is deserved.

The
SPYMASTER'S
DAUGHTER

CHAPTER ONE

❧

". . . the heav'n of Stella's face."

—Astrophel and Stella, *Sir Philip Sidney*

───────────────── ❧ ─────────────────

Lammas Day, August 2
In the Year of Our Lord 1585

Barn Elms, Surrey

*A*t the sound of rapid hoofbeats drawing closer, Frances, Lady Sidney, lifted her head from a forbidden cipher book. She pushed away all the paper on her writing table that she'd used to break the hidden meanings of the *Steganographia* and ran to her bedchamber window. On the road from Mortlake, dust swirled behind a royal post rider bringing mail for her father, the queen's spymaster. And perhaps for her husband, Philip.

It was the possibility of Philip's mail that urged her toward her bedchamber door. He was hiding something. She suspected the truth and had set herself to discover it no matter what the hurt. Better a short pain than a long, dark ignorance. She paused only long enough to throw her shawl over the books she had taken without permission from her father's library, books that, according to him, should never interest a lady wife.

Hurrying into the corridor above the great hall, Frances heard her aunt Jennet's angry cry from below. "Frances, your lord husband requires your presence for dinner!"

Her old, foolish hope was smothered. Philip *required*. He no longer *desired* her presence anywhere. She doubted he ever had.

Frances sank back into the shadows of the corridor outside her bedchamber. If she meant to intercept the royal post rider, she must hug the shadows until she could get away. "Anon, Aunt, I am now to the privy in some urgency," Frances called, her fingers crossed against Satan's hearing the lie. Not even her aunt Jennet could deny her the privy's comfort. And Frances knew that her aunt, who had been her nurse when she'd been young, was not so angry as she sounded, merely given to the reproachful manner that afflicted many a graying woman, unmarried and with no prospects but the continued sufferance of her powerful family.

Casting aside all other thoughts but the post, Frances sped down the back servants' stairs toward the sound of horse's hooves on the graveled carriageway approaching Barn Elms. She did regret deceiving Jennet—she knew the pain of deceit, being deceived herself by her own husband. Did one deceit justify another? The fleeting question slowed her steps for a moment, but she pushed through concern for her soul and ran on down the steep servants' stairs.

Philip had once written in his famous sonnet sequence:

> *I swear by her I love and lack, that I*
> *Was not in fault, who bend thy dazzling race*
> *Only unto the heav'n of Stella's face*
> *Counting but dust what in the way did lie.*

That particular verse haunted Frances . . . *Stella's face*. Frances knew that she was not Stella, nor ever would be. Where Philip's real inspiration was petite, blond, with o'erflowing breasts, Frances admitted to being tall, raven-haired, and small in the chest. Though some had called her a beauty, she always wondered whether their opinion was shaped by the desire to earn the favor of her father, the queen's spymaster.

Yet she refused to become the unknowing, cuckolded wife! Better to know and learn not to care.

Dashing through the flesh pantry to the surprise of sweating cooks bent over their steaming pots, she held her breath against the strong scent of hung, aging hare brought down by her father and his hounds. She ran out the open door and on down the wide path. Before her the summer sun sparkled on gravel wet with morning rain, until tall yew hedges hid her from curious eyes. A bit breathless, she waved the post rider to a stop. "I am Lady Sidney come to take the post to my father, Sir Francis Walsingham . . . and, of course, to my husband, Sir Philip."

"These are official from Whitehall Palace, my lady," he said, bowing in the saddle but not reaching toward his post bag. "I am instructed to deliver them into the lord secretary's hands."

"As my father's daughter, I am quite aware of that." Her fingers still crossed, she made her voice as arrogant as the man would expect, though arrogance was an attitude new to her and as yet not easily come by. "Would you rather I called my father and husband from council on Her Majesty's urgent business? Trust me, sir, you will receive no thanks for it." She allowed herself a half smile. "Yet, if you so command me . . ."

"My lady, I meant no command and humbly beg pardon," the rider said, hastily drawing one packet and a single letter from his bag.

Frances nodded, saying no unnecessary word, as she was learning to do. She smiled as the post rider whipped his horse back toward London, kicking his mount's flanks to speed it. She would yet make a good intelligencer for her father. A threat implied and a certain scorn were better than too many harsh words that could reveal less assurance.

Concealing the post under her tightly laced kirtle, she ran back, stopping at the privy, to turn her lie into partial truth, and raced up the back stairs to her chamber, throwing her father's packet on her bed. The writing on the single letter addressed to her husband was flowing, familiar. She sniffed at the lavender scent and sat down at her writing table. This was the same scent that she had detected on Philip's doublet after his last trip to London as a maid had taken it for brushing and airing, a mix of sweet lavender and the musk of a woman who gave her body fully and often to a man. Or, it was rumored, in the case of the Baroness Penelope Rich, to many men. *Stella!* The name seemed to have lost its haunting quality. Frances smiled at the thought.

Locking her door with a trembling key, Frances pulled one of the candles on her writing table close. She had never opened one of Philip's letters, lifting a wax seal and replacing it undetected, though she'd developed the skill on sealed letters of her own making. But these past days some secret had been on Philip's face and in his every quick glance away from her. She must not be caught unaware, only to dissolve in hot tears in front of all, to beg, to be disgraced by open pity. She was a Walsingham, and would never again expose her heart or suffer the amused sympathy she had already seen in the faces of Philip's friends.

Her hand still trembling, she passed the baroness's letter just far enough above the flame and exactly long enough to loosen the edges of the red wax seal. Frances frowned with concentration. Philip was still in love with Lady Penelope Rich, the Stella of his sonnets. She knew it, felt it with every beat of her heart, but needed only one clear proof that he was still deceiving her. All England knew that he had once been engaged to Penelope before she had rejected him for Lord Rich, a man of vast wealth. A year later, Philip had accepted Sir Walsingham's offer to be his heir and take his young daughter, Frances, to wife.

She had hoped that he would write sonnets just for her. Instead, he had learned to be considerate, treating her with only slightly less distant affection than he gave his favorite hunter carrying him faithfully through the Barn Elms deer park.

She laughed, but stopped abruptly, unable to bear the harsh sound. It would be unseemly to be jealous of a horse.

During their first year, she began to understand that Philip wanted a son of her body, but not her, nor her dreams of being the new Stella. Over that year and the next, her tears unshed, she had discarded her dream that Philip Sidney, famous throughout England as the symbol of a young man's intense love, would love her as deeply.

Frances was learning to forbid woe to assail her. Sadness must be banished from her heart or she would soon have the same tight-lipped face as Jennet, showing the world she was aging and unloved. She, a Walsingham, the daughter of one of the most powerful men in the realm, would not invite such pitiable feelings.

Philip was kind to her and furtive enough to keep her from the open humiliation visited upon other wives. She would not complain, but neither would she continue yearning for his love. She must rid herself of all such foolish hope. Her husband had most of what he wanted from her, having become her father's heir, though not yet achieving a son of his name. And someday, by the rood, she might, nay, *must* have what she desired. Someday she would prove her worth to her father and be named an intelligencer, helping him to keep England safe.

She almost laughed at herself for her girlish fancies, yet what was youth for, if not wonderful dreams. Since she was denied a soldier's sword, she would have another ambition worthy of a Walsingham.

Though she had eagerly given Philip her body and love, he

had given her what he could, and more than that she no longer expected . . . or wanted. She clenched one hand with the other and knew her girlish dreams of love's complete contentment were gone, and in their place had come a dream of achieving her father's ambition for a son to join his work. That dream now replaced everything.

Frances held the letter steady, shuffled through her cipher worksheets, and found the sharp penknife she used to trim candle wicks and quill nibs. She heated it just enough and slid it deftly under the softened wax seal. She paused to steady her hand. Was this wrong? Philip was not her enemy; he liked her well enough. Didn't he come to her bed often?

Often enough so that she now refused to be too timid to know the truth.

Covering her heart with one hand, she quieted its pounding, then carefully opened the heavy vellum page that was folded into quarters, and whispered the words on the page aloud, some deep part of her vainly hoping to prove her suspicions wrong:

> *Philip, my dearest friend, you are most welcome to*
> *visit me on the morrow in the third hour after*
> *noon so that I may wish you safe journey to the*
> *Holland war and a swift and safe return to your*
> *Stella.*

He was leaving? Going to war? And Penelope had been first to know it! Frances dropped the letter and clung to her writing table, fighting for air, her throat tight.

She took a deep, calming breath. Philip was going to war and had not told his wife. She tightened her hold on a goose quill until it broke into brittle pieces. A visit would have been bad enough, but it was not all. She was no longer a silly girl to believe in Lady Rich's innocence, or in Philip's.

The woman dared much to use that name from Philip's great love poem *Astrophel and Stella*, even if she owned it. His long sonnet sequence had not yet been published, but it had been copied and recopied in manuscript until all the court and most nobles in England boasted of owning the manuscript, and those who did not pretended to it. As every person of consequence knew, the Baroness Rich had refused many times to marry Philip throughout their long, four-year engagement. Neither would she ever quite let him go. Frances searched her heart for any residue of jealousy and, finding none, slowly folded the vellum along its original creases. Reheating the wax seal, she gently pressed the edges into the very same place.

Undetectable!

Satisfied that her work was perfect, she waved the letter in the air to cool it. She did not have her husband's love, but she had a valuable skill to ease her hurt. If only her father could see her ability, the equal, she vowed, of Arthur Gregory, an intelligencer who specialized in lifting wax seals, carefully opening dispatches meant for foreign ambassadors so that the tampering remained unknown. Was she really as good as he? She must know. And what other skills could Gregory teach her? Secret writing? That was Thomas Phelippes's special skill, along with being the chief cipher secretary for her father. How she longed to learn what she did not yet know. It would fill her life with meaning and give it great purpose. And it would be enough, or almost enough.

Somehow—her hand became a fist—somehow she must convince her father to take her to court. Once she was there, she would find her way into his work. She was his only child; she knew he loved her dearly. There would come a time when he would not refuse her.

"Frances! Anon has most assuredly come and gone." Jennet was at her door, a foot tapping impatiently.

"At once, Aunt," Frances said, grabbing the post packet for her father from her bed, carrying both packet and Philip's letter to the door with no time to smooth her skirts.

"What were you doing for so long a time?" Jennet asked, her tone scolding. "You have not changed your gown. I suppose you were at your books. Did you not hear the case clock strike the hour of noontide?" Jennet took a much-needed breath. "Well, no time for your long tale. Swiftly, now."

Frances took her aunt's hand and used her child's name. "Dearest Jenney, I am sorry for your trouble."

Jennet's face yielded up its annoyance. "I dare not think what your husband will say if you go on—"

Frances rolled her eyes. "Go on studying mathematics and ancient cipher texts. It is said Her Majesty, Queen Elizabeth, does the very same, translating Latin into Greek for an evening's relaxation." And probably for the same lonely reason, Frances thought.

Jennet's mouth was set as they approached the great stone hall. "Ah, but remember Queen Elizabeth is a virgin queen. You, my dear niece, are neither."

Frances found her temper. "Jennet, are you saying this realm has room for only one woman who loves her books?"

"I am saying, sweetest clever girl, that your father and husband expect your embroidery to improve before your games of ciphering, though I do not ignore your skill at dancing—"

Laughing, Frances pulled Jennet along the planked floor toward the table, where a dozen guests gathered from leaseholds on Walsingham land rose to greet her. This was the quarter when rents were due, and like good tenants they had come to salute the landlord who treated them well.

She curtsied low. "My lord father and lord husband, gentlemen and ladies all, I beg your indulgence. Please you, forgive me the delay."

Looking at her belly always in hopes of a grandson, her father asked, "Are you quite well, Frances? We have already read from our Bible and thanked the Lord in prayer for His bounty."

She had missed little. Reading from the Bible before meals had once been her job, but now was rightfully Philip's. She was lady of the house, and motioned to the servants to proceed serving their not quite steaming platters and bowls.

"Father, husband, I am as well as ever I have been." She smiled at Philip, since he looked worried. "Lord husband," she said, giving him a curtsy of his own. She had scoured her heart of any animus, though Lady Rich's letter had opened the old wound slightly. "You must think me a forget-me-all, Philip, but I was gathering the royal post," she said, handing the post across the wide table, first to her father and then to her husband.

She seated herself and took a dainty draft of ale, taking plea- sure in knowing her father had received the new Venetian glasses from the double spy he had planted in the Serene Republic of Venice right inside the doge's palace. A dangerous post. What would that be like? Would she have such courage?

Her head down, seeming to concentrate on the bowl of ox broth set before her, she saw Philip's eyes open wide as he recog- nized the writing on his letter and quickly slipped it inside the full slashed sleeve of his scarlet doublet worn in the court fashion over one shoulder with a sleeve hanging empty. Though his thirty-first birthday was near, his clean-shaven face was impossibly youthful under light brown, curling hair. To her own surprise, she smiled at him, and his face relaxed when he saw it. She could not, at that moment, regret her marriage. Perhaps this was the way of love outside poesy. If not, why would there be such a thirst for love son- nets? Did one ever really want what one already had? She never would, she stoutly proclaimed in her thoughts, although she was not so foolish as to completely believe herself.

Stop! Frances commanded her wandering mind. She would but

sadden herself, or a husband going to war. And she could not allow Philip to see her melancholy or he might begin to guess too
much. Now that there was no hope of winning her husband's love,
she must stay true to herself and to what she wanted: gaining a
place in her father's service and proving to him that his only child,
though not a son, was a worthy Walsingham for more than having
brought a brilliant poet into the family.

"Frances, you have not been listening," Jennet said.

"Of course I have, Aunt. You were speaking of the latest embroidery patterns from France." It was a safe guess. "I cannot wait
until I see them, all the tiny birds, flowers, and horned unicorns
guarding virgins. How exciting!"

Jennet pursed her mouth, unbelieving. "You would do well to
think so," she murmured.

Frances raised her glass, nodding to their other guests, and
motioned the servants forward with the fish course.

Her father's shadowed eyes watched her, seeming to see into
her, and she had to hold herself rigid to keep from shrinking or
blurting her every misdeed. For a moment she pitied the poor, tortured wretches in the Tower who fell under his dark, knowing gaze.
But his usually tight mouth relaxed. "Daughter, you seem almost
breathless. You should rest yourself later." He turned to Philip with
a knowing, even demanding look that said: *Give me a grandson.*

"As you wish, lord father." She bent to the fish course, motioning for her rapidly cooling broth to be taken away; then, though
she seemed to concentrate on her plate and reached for her favorite
salted radishes, she heard every word her father said.

"Philip." Walsingham turned to address his son-in-law.

"Sir," Philip said, shoulders held rigidly, as if preparing himself
for battle.

"I am assembling the greatest intelligencer network in the
world," Walsingham said, between taking bites of the deer meat
he'd knifed from the platter in the old way. "The new pope, Sixtus

the Fifth, is determined to regain all the territories lost to Protestantism, including England. Traitors are hiding everywhere in the land, thirsting for Her Majesty's blood to make a place on England's throne for that devilish woman Mary Stuart."

Philip nodded, dipping good manchet bread into his pottage. "But, sir, you capture them and give them a traitor's justice."

"Aye, but there are too many of them. Traitors in the north country, and in France . . . and especially in Spain, intent upon conquering this island nation and installing the Inquisition. Spain has now taken Portugal and her large fleet and harbors, and all the new world flies the Spanish flag and fills her treasury with endless gold and silver. Philip, they mean to root out every last believer in the true Protestant religion."

Sir Walsingham's voice had risen, and a tense muscle jumped in his cheek. "English traitors are hugger-mugger in London, and some in the court itself!" He dropped his voice to a whisper, though Frances could yet hear him. "I have them close-watched in hopes they lead me to their fellow conspirators." He picked up his knife and plunged it deep once more into the deer haunch stuffed with wren wings, as if to make sure it was quite dead.

"Sir," Philip said in his softest voice, having heard every word more than once, "you have many good intelligencers helping to keep the queen safe."

"It is true that I have good men in plenty, but never enough . . . never enough whom I trust." He put down his knife and lowered his voice so much that Frances had to read his lips. "Philip, it is my firm wish that you join me. A poet would not be suspect by Mary's agents."

Frances could see that Philip was startled into a quick response, though she suspected it was well thought out, even practiced. "I thank you, sir, for your confidence in my poor power of poesy, but my duty to the queen lies elsewhere. Within days, I will take ship for Holland in advance of my uncle the Earl of Leicester's army.

The Spanish are preparing to invade the northern provinces. You and I will be doing the same duty for the crown, Sir Walsingham, you fighting the Inquisition here and I fighting Spain on the continent."

Frances held her tongue when Philip glanced her way with a somewhat sheepish smile, since he had not told her this news. For an instant her heart slammed against her breast, as if she had not seen this information in Lady Rich's letter. It was one thing to read, another to hear the words from Philip's mouth. Now his imminent departure was made totally real.

Aware of their tenants looking on with curiosity, she raised her glass to him, acting the good, brave English wife sending her husband to war with eyes open and back straight. At least she was on his mind, for a short time. The sudden color rising in his cheeks told her that he knew he had been undutiful in not telling her earlier, and that was some recompense.

Why was he watching her? Did he think her some fainting lady? Had he forgotten her until this moment? That such thoughts still had the power to wound was maddening. She refused to survive as a broken heart, a pitiable creature to others and a burden to herself.

Walsingham nodded. "I understand a clever young man wanting to make his mark as a soldier, but I could use that man's brains and daring."

Philip smiled, shaking his head with humor. "Your pardon, sir, but I think the queen would not welcome me in her court again." He smiled slyly, like a boy caught out in a mischief. "A few years ago I made the great mistake of writing the queen my true feelings about her intended French marriage to the Duc d'Alençon. Her Majesty does not receive unwanted advice well . . . or ever forget it."

Sir Walsingham nodded without smiling. "I know that truly,

Philip. Still, it is my duty to give such advice to her grace most every day."

Frances stopped playing with her cold fish. Impatience had risen in her throughout this discourse. She could be docile no longer. "Your pardon, my lord father, but there are women with brains and courage. I am born of your blood and have skills. . . ." Before she could offer herself to her father's work, Philip laughed, and her father's dark face darkened still more.

"Women intelligencers? Nay, daughter, women are too tender-hearted, unless they be whores, and then they can too easily be turned by gold."

"But, lord father, allow me to show you—"

"I'll hear no more on this matter, daughter. Have a care for our guests, as is a woman's duty."

Fearing tears, Frances stood and curtsied to the openmouthed tenants about the table, who were rubbing their necks after straining so hard to hear.

Jennet, always alert to her charge, stood and took her arm with a hard pinch.

Frances pulled away. "I am no longer a child, Aunt."

"You do not act the lady withal, and I see the forward child come again."

Frances took a deep, consoling breath. She would have to prove herself to Jennet, too.

Lady Frances curtsied again politely to her guests and moved quickly to the stairs. Every step out of the great hall and up the stairs was accompanied by a muttered vow: "Father, you will one day have your mind changed for you by a woman . . . by this woman."

When she reached her bedchamber she threw herself on the bed, but refused to allow herself to dissolve in tears. If she did, her father would learn of it, and tears would prove to him that she was an empty-headed maid, unfit for work designed for men.

Her aunt entered but said nothing, busying herself picking up books and straightening them on the writing table with a disapproving smack of her lips.

Frances closed her eyes until the door opened and Jennet said softly, "Your lord husband is here, my lady."

Frances heard her leave.

Philip approached, removing his doublet as he came to her bed, the doublet that held a letter from Penelope Rich. She heard the vellum crinkle as he laid the garment down. He had not thought to remove the missive.

He knelt upon her soft down mattress. "Here, my dear, drink this," he said. "My physician says it is a tonic known to ensure a babe if drunk on the day of a new moon."

His voice was soft but insistent.

Frances half sat up in bed and downed the bitter brew, still warm from the mixing. She made a face.

Philip looked sympathetic. "Forgive me, wife; I should have added some carvings from the sugar loaf."

She wanted to tell him that it was not the bitter physic that near sickened her; it was the lost chance in her lifetime to adore and be adored. She had wanted desperately to love Philip, had expected that emotion to o'erwhelm her. Now she felt nothing but the duty a wife owed to a husband. She would now never know love. Her chance was gone, and it saddened her more than she could have expected.

Yet men were able to go from wife to other women. Philip could come to her bed and then hie to Lady Rich, ever hoping to gain her love by sheer, dogged devotion.

"Are your nether parts warming?" he asked, looking down on her with a hopeful expression that made her feel like one of his brood mares.

"Yes, husband," she lied, crossing her fingers for a third time in one day.

He unlaced his codpiece and lifted her dress, quickly dispensing with endearments. His ready manhood had little to do with his heart. He would do his duty, plant his seed, and be gone.

Frances knew her wifely task. She moved and groaned to speed him, trying to give every appearance of wifely pleasure, which was his due, which was the due of any soldier going to war for queen and country. *Oh, Philip, you are so blind. Don't you know that there is so much more you could have of me? So much more . . .*

He would not take the most she could give, but from his Stella he would take less and be grateful. She was the woman he longed to gaze upon ere he sailed for Holland . . . *the heav'n of Stella's face.*

He pushed and pushed until he emptied his seed into her, then fell to one side, panting until gradually quieting. "Wife, I did mean to tell you privily that I was leaving for Holland, but I waited long, not wanting to concern you overmuch. . . . You are too young to understand."

Frances said none of the many things she could have said, only what she must. "Of course, Philip. You are ever careful to hide any hurt coming my way."

She felt his head turn to her, but she did not satisfy the puzzlement that must be on his face. "I hope I gave you pleasure, husband," she said, dutifully enough to please even Jennet.

"Of course, Frances. You need not ask. If you will only surrender these wild thoughts of yours and leave off plaguing your father about becoming"—he groaned, unable to say the word *intelligencer*—"you will please me greatly."

"As you wish."

"Good," he said, sounding satisfied with his powers of persuasion.

She watched him relace his codpiece and, with a bow to her, take up his doublet, Stella's letter crinkling in it like musket fire aimed at her heart. "I must oversee the rest of my packing. We will say good-bye in the morn." He left, shutting her chamber door behind him.

Frances, her heart aching anew with the question of what could have been, felt aflame with unsatisfied desire for something . . . someone. She had not said the bitter words to Philip that she could have; nor would she ever act the hard-used shrew. Her heart would shrivel and become a parched and withered thing, good only for beating against her breast but not ever used for love. Let it be! She was numb to all emotion. In its place, she would live on within her head, where she found her pride.

Turning away from the door where he had left her, closing her away, she shut her eyes and, not to be denied, slipped her hand to the burning place and pleasured herself.

CHAPTER TWO

✑

"'Fool!' said my Muse to me
'Look in thy heart, and write.'"

—Astrophel and Stella, *Sir Philip Sidney*

---- ✑ ----

*F*rances knew that she was acting the fool. Still, she refused to listen to her own caution.

She was determined to approach her father one last time to show him a sealed letter that she had opened and closed. She had broken a short practice cipher from one of her father's books. It was not a simple one, and she had solved it alone. There was something logical about ciphers that revealed themselves to her as a painting made an image where the colors connected. With practice, she would advance to even more difficult ciphers, perhaps even double substitution. She was convinced she could, if only she had an opportunity.

And that opportunity would soon be hers. The queen had summoned her to Whitehall! She had not been meant to overhear the news, but like any good intelligencer she had her senses alert to all she was not supposed to know, especially to a lathered horse whose rider wore the royal livery and was then closeted with her father.

Frances looked again at the letter she'd prepared just this morn. There was no trace of tampering on the signet seal, the Walsingham family device of a cinquefoil five-leaf clover. By the seal he would know that she had done the work, or was it so undetectable that he would think her a liar, a sin that he hated above all things? Still, she must take this chance—nay, take every chance! Perhaps he would see her determination, and surely recognize it as an essential part of a good spy's character.

Hurrying around the formal knot garden in front of the manor entrance, she walked along a wide avenue of yew to the rose gardens that fronted the dock on the Thames. Her father's barge was anchored there, oars up in salute, ready to take him on the flood tide to London. The queen's urgent summons of her spymaster to Whitehall Palace could not be delayed for even a half day. Her Majesty was upset with the demands that far-flung spying on the continent made on her treasury. Her spymaster would need new evidence-filled reports from his agents to allay the queen's ever-present suspicion of waste.

And, Frances reasoned, a good daughter should wish her lord father a safe trip, even if she had secret knowledge that she would follow him to London soon.

She accepted some roses from a gardener, the thorns having been removed in readiness for her bedchamber, and sat on a stone bench to wait in the heavy, spreading shade of the old elm trees.

Frances lifted a blossom to inhale its spicy scent. This had been a day for farewells. Just after sunup, she had seen Philip off to London with his servants and baggage wagon. He could not wait to be gone, though she knew that he would need to busy himself with his uncle the Earl of Leicester at Leicester House on the Strand until the third hour after noontide, Lady Rich's appointed time for their tryst.

Yet it was Frances Walsingham who was Lady Sidney, and not Penelope Rich. She remembered the thrill of first writing that name . . . Lady Sidney. How young she had been, her head brimming with Philip's love poetry. Would he write such words for her as he had written for Stella? *That She, dear She, might take some pleasure* . . . When had she begun to doubt that she would ever be Philip's "dear She"? When had her innocence begun to fade? Within a year? Perhaps less? She had fiercely resisted losing her girlish dreams, though now she was happy they were dead and gone. Love dreams were a burden, and she would have none of them ever again.

It had been a more mature Lady Sidney who had received Philip's kiss this morning near the stables. He had not murmured in Frances's ear, "Eternal love, maintain thy life in me," as he had written for Stella, lines copied by half the young gentlemen of England. He had leaned down from his saddle and spoken of another life, the son he hoped he had planted in her womb.

She had managed a blushing smile, as would any goodwife, and she did not say that she hoped with all her heart *not* to be found with child in London. She would be sent back to Barn Elms immediately and eventually be shut into a dark, hot chamber to wait for the birth, kept from her books and her hopes, from any life that she would freely choose.

Philip had taken her hand gently. "Wife, I will send for you when it is safe in Holland."

"That is my dearest wish, husband," she murmured, not able to say the words with more force, having little more than a sigh in her heart.

Philip rode away, and she watched him grow smaller before crying out, "Stay safe, husband."

She watched, but he didn't turn for a last wave of farewell. He urged on his horse beyond hearing until his little company rounded a bend in the road and was out of sight, leaving a dusty, echoing space. She took a small pleasure in the thought that her kiss would still be on his lips before another's could be. It was a small sin of pride that she deliberately allowed herself.

Servants began to pass her carrying her father's chests, which contained his many unadorned black suits and hats proclaiming his Puritan leanings to all, even to Queen Elizabeth, who disliked strict religion. She preferred the middle way of her father, Henry VIII's English church, far from the dangerous shoals of religious extremes that were troublesome to the peace of her realm.

Frances ducked her head as a laugh escaped her lips. The queen's spymaster, the same one who urged Frances to follow a daughter's assigned path, could not travel Her Majesty's own middle way. Still, she thought it best to keep that thought to herself or forget it altogether. Her father had not the slightest appreciation of drollery.

His papers and books paraded past her, yet he did not appear.

She dug in her basket for a book to fill her time. Today she had been careful in the one she had chosen from her father's library, knowing he would not need to take this particular volume, since Dr. John Dee, a mathematician and one of the queen's closest councilors, had copied it more than once for the lord secretary. Pushing aside the roses, she opened a handwritten copy of Trithemius's *Steganographia, Book Three*. She had studied the German abbot's great cipher work many times, and each time its secrets became clearer to her, though she desired a teacher like Dr. Dee to help her understand even better.

Frances had not long to read before she heard her father's cane as he walked rapidly toward her on the packed-earth path. It was amazing that he could move so quickly despite his aching joints, but he had discovered that walking fast helped him to keep a better balance. She covered the forbidden book with roses and looked up, smiling.

"Good morrow, daughter," he greeted her, and sat down heavily beside her, a little out of breath.

"Lord father," she answered softly, looking on his lined, dark face, and seeing that he was ailing again.

"How grow the gardens?" he asked in a preoccupied tone that told her he was not interested in their symmetry, scent, or beauty, but in their maintenance for the queen's infrequent visits. For him, they were a symbol of his station as one of the queen's chief councilors.

"The gardens grow well, Father, although the roses will soon fade, and I will direct the pruning and mulching of the beds, which must begin in a month or so."

He shook his head hastily. "The chief gardener will attend to such."

She pretended an affront. "Surely you trust that I can order—"

"I bid you, daughter, do not look for ill, because you will surely find it." His slight smile took away the censure. "Her gracious Majesty has sent word that you are not to languish for a day longer than necessary at Barn Elms with Sir Philip gone. She commands you to court as a lady of the presence chamber."

Frances showed all the surprise he expected. "To court!"

This was where she wanted to be, but not as one of the ladies who provided a pleasing background for Her Majesty's audiences. Nevertheless, at court she would be near her father and his work, near Dr. Dee and Thomas Phelippes.

"A great honor, Father. This is a court position to bring credit to our family. Any woman would long for such favor."

Any woman but me, she thought, though she knew better than to speak the words. Her father was used to seeing beyond words.

"Alas, there is no joyfulness in your face, Frances. You are too glum with no reason, since your husband is also about the queen's business. I bid you to keep a cheerful face at court, or Her Majesty will not seek your company."

Frances changed the subject. "I will have many hours when I can care for you, if you have need."

It was true; he would need her camphor poultices to draw heat from his joints and cool his aches, which kept him abed sometimes for days. Physicians with all their bloodlettings and vile diets had never done better for him. When she cured his pain he would listen to her, hear her dreams, and grant her a place in his work. Her spirits lifted with the hope that she saw the future truly.

He took her hand. "I am happy to hear that being a pleasing background is agreeable to you, daughter." The deep worry lines on his face relaxed. "You have the fair coloring and large gray eyes of your mother . . . her sweet beauty." His face sagged for a moment with painful memory.

"Father, I am sorry to remind you of your loss."

"You do not," he said firmly, his jaw tightening. "I but remember her much softer nature. You, Frances, are unrelenting in your wants."

"In that I am like you, Father. Surely it is not only sons who inherit strength and courage from their fathers."

He dropped her hand, studying her closely, as if just now seeing her clearly. "As I said, unrelenting."

"Perhaps, Father, you see me truer than I see myself," she said, careful to keep her tone from being quarrelsome.

"You have my black hair," he said softly, as if he were just noticing. "I will order red wigs for you. Everyone at court is wearing them, as the queen does."

Frances knew she would look dreadful in a red wig, but she did not want to stand out from the other ladies and draw unwanted attention with her dark hair flowing free. It was unbecoming of a married woman. Although she expected no good outcome, she could not stop herself from one last appeal, and she held her breath as if leaping into a fast-running stream.

"I will be of very good cheer and please the queen, but I will have many hours to fill my days with other work, Father . . . work with you." She pulled the letter from her basket and held it out to him. "This I have done, teaching myself to remove the signet seal of this letter and return it so that its opening cannot be detected. See here; the seal's edges are not even raised. . . ."

His face tightened with her every word until her voice trailed off into silence.

"Daughter, have a care that you do not become shrewish. I have a good man for such work in Arthur Gregory. You do not make me . . . proud with these fanciful and unwomanly ideas."

She had no breath left to argue. He didn't disbelieve her, as she had feared. He simply did not care whether she could remove a signet seal. Her skill was a burdensome embarrassment.

"Let me hear no more, unless you deliberately wish to add to my cares." He stood too suddenly and winced with pain, his dark gaze on her. "Such disobedience brings shame to you, Frances, to your dear husband, and to me. Remember, resignation and submission are the greatest womanly virtues, and not to be ignored because you fancy your learning and brain. I made a mistake in allowing you to read and study beyond your sex."

Of course, she knew that many people thought thus, but it hurt her more when it came from him, who had heard her lessons with such pride, a pride that disappeared once she reached womanhood.

He swayed and she put out a hand to steady him, but he waved it off, his proud face adamant. "I'll send my man Robert Pauley to escort you to Whitehall. Be ready to leave in three days . . . and be ready for Robert Pauley."

Frances was puzzled. "Father, what should I be ready for?"

"He has great pride for a commoner, but is a good man for all that, and a trustworthy one."

This information barely reached her before her father, scowling, was walking swiftly toward his waiting barge, his back straight despite the cost to him in aching joints.

She had to clutch tight to the bench to stop herself from running after him, begging his forgiveness, trying to make him understand. No, that would need more time than he had. She would convince him at court.

Patience . . . she must learn patience. If she would be an intelligencer, patience was a prime skill to have, and she must own it in plenty. Somehow she would convince her father that she was worth more than he thought, and through him perhaps she could convince Philip. Staring after her father, she lifted an already wilting rose to her nose, the petals drifting across her breasts. Perhaps convincing Philip would take even more than her father's great skills. She surprised herself with how quickly her girlish dream was revived. And it was too late . . . altogether too late. It had been too late for her the first day Philip saw Penelope as a just-blossoming girl at Chartley.

Lifting her gown from the dusty path, Frances ran to the dock to wave her father off. She watched the oarsmen take the barge to midstream and pick up the tide, its flags flapping in the wind, a drum in the bow thumping as the oars kept time. She waved her kerchief, and once her father lifted his hand in farewell, as if half forgiving her.

Frances raced back to the manor house. She was going to court!

The next three days were a happy frenzy of airing her gowns, making them more fashionable with the addition of cutwork lace and the black and gold silk embroidery of Jennet and the maids. Several seamstresses were called in from nearby Mortlake to sew new gowns, bodices, oversleeves, and cloaks. Panels and taffeta lining were added to good country gowns so that they would be full and outstanding enough for court, although Her Majesty had declared they must be no wider at the hem than four feet. Two of her favorite places, Nonsuch Palace and her hunting lodge, Oatlands, were small. Moreover, no other gowns could be as wide as the queen's.

Cobblers were called, and the sound of hammers echoed through the great hall from early morn until dark. In a few days many pairs of pinked leather slippers in a rainbow of colors, some with fashionable wooden heels, all lined with satin or tufted velvet to match her gowns, were quickly made. Frances tried on every pair, testing the best of them for the hop and leap of the lavolte, the queen's favorite dance, knowing that she often asked her ladies to dance for her.

Frances smiled at the story her father had told her of Queen Elizabeth dancing the lavolte alone every morning for exercise.

At almost the last hour, Frances remembered the queen rode out on many a fine day, and she ordered buskins with heels for riding. Perhaps she would be among the ladies of the queen's party, especially once Her Majesty saw how well her new lady sat a horse.

Frances oversaw the packing of lace-edged gloves and upstanding neck ruffs, heavily starched and pleated in their wooden forms. When they were finished, she added close-knit hosen with ribbon knee ties. Lastly, her coffer of books and writing materials was included, and all carried to the great hall below.

Frances was unable to sleep the night before she was to leave for court. She lay awake, sensing that her life was about to change in ways she dared not allow herself to imagine. Watching clouds pass before the moon, she wondered what the next weeks and months would bring to justify the excitement she was beginning to feel for a court position she did not truly want.

Though she had been to court several times, she had gone as Sir Walsingham's young daughter, and not as a lady in the queen's own entourage. Was that why she felt such anticipation and yet some unease, as if she were entering an unknown and dark forest track, unable to clearly see the road out and into sunlight? Finally she was wearied from her own thoughts. It was always so much easier to read other people's. She smiled at that, thinking how unladylike her father would consider it.

She turned from her window and sank into her soft bolster, eventually easing into slumber.

*A*fter eating a bowl of thick pottage, barely warm when it reached her from the distant kitchen, Frances made her way with Jennet to the carriage and drivers her father had sent from London. Her washerwoman and maid of the chamber climbed into a wagon that would follow.

Her father's man, called Pauley, was tall, with a thin mustache tracing his upper lip and leading to a strong, beardless chin. His clothing was well cut of very good cloth and drape on his wide shoulders and well-proportioned body, all worn with an ease of manner that separated him from other servants.

He held the carriage door open and lowered the step for her.

"You must be Robert Pauley," she said.

"I am, and have no doubt from your father's description that you are Frances."

Jennet quickly stepped forward and in a guardian's voice said, "Lady Frances to you."

The man bowed low. "I beg pardon, my lady. I am used to hearing your father speak of you as Frances."

She was surprised to hear a learned man's speech, and more surprised that her father had spoken of her to his intelligencers. "He speaks of me?"

Pauley bowed again, and Frances remembered that her father

had called him overconfident for a commoner . . . nay, proud. She would be on the watch for any self-importance that might lead to disobedience. Her face might betray her youth, but not the steel behind it. She would never be one of those poor creatures who was ruled by her servants.

"He is very proud of his daughter, the wife of England's foremost poet . . . of love."

A smile tugged at the corners of Pauley's mouth. Was he mocking her? She was ready to be furious if the man was sly or arrogant, both insufferable in a servant. He held an obvious good opinion of himself, clearly much above his station.

"Well, Pauley, please make certain that all my chests are securely tied," she said dismissively, treating him as the servant he was supposed to be. She was able to recognize in his proud manner that he was ill at ease with his position, since she, too, was never quite at ease herself, always pretending to be someone she was not.

He moved quickly toward the wagon to verify the stowing of all her belongings. Without appearing to watch, she saw him check the tie ropes, cinch one, and say something to her maid that made the girl giggle and blush. This Pauley merited her close attention if he sought to jolly every serving maid in sight. A mistress must set the rules early and keep to them.

When he returned to the carriage, Frances noticed that he moved with a slight stiffness, different from the one caused by her father's swollen joints. Pauley swung his right leg so that it bent but little at the knee. He stopped at the manor entrance and picked up a bundle. The object was wrapped in an old doublet, which fell away to reveal an ivory-inlaid Italian-style guitar with a slightly curved head. Pauley hesitated outside the carriage.

Surely the man did not presume to ride inside with her.

With a flourish, Pauley bowed to Frances, assisting her into the carriage first, and with similar courtesy handing Jennet inside and waiting as she took the far seat beside her niece. "Lady Sidney, if it please you, may I leave my instrument in the carriage, since I think a westerly rain is coming on?"

He carried his bundle as if it were a newborn babe. Truly, it would be ungracious to refuse him so small a request. She nodded.

He laid the guitar flat on the unoccupied seat facing her, his doublet fastened around the instrument. For a moment he kept a loving, protective hand on the fretboard before bowing to Frances and climbing up on the wheel to sit above. The driver called to the horses, the whip cracked, and the carriage lurched forward toward the London Road.

For a moment, Frances wondered how a commoner had come to own an instrument of such quality. So, who was he? Intelligencers had secrets to sell, but if Pauley could not be trusted, surely her father would not keep him. She would discover Pauley's secret by careful questioning.

They were scarcely out of sight of Barn Elms when the rain began, not an on-and-off misty summer shower, but a downpour that quickly turned the dusty road into a bog.

Pauley's guitar bounced toward the edge of the seat, and she reached for it.

"What are you doing?" Aunt Jennet asked.

"I would not have such a beautiful instrument damaged."

"Then the man should take it with him."

"In this rain? Jennet, I could not countenance such destruction."

Frances pounded on the ceiling and the coach stopped. "Master Pauley, please come inside." At Jennet's look of disapproval, Frances added, "You'll be of little use to me if you contract consumption."

"I thank you, my lady," Pauley said, opening the door and bowing, rain running from his large-brimmed hat and sealskin cloak. He grasped the top of the door and swung inside.

She handed him his guitar.

"Thank you for your care of it, my lady. It was my father's." He began to shiver, but clenched his shoulders to control it.

She could see the resolve in his eyes and on his unyielding face. Where did a servant get such strength and assurance, and how did he have a father who could give such a rare gift? Her curiosity was aroused. Pauley's fine features, his educated speech, and now this show of family pride marked him as from a good family of some consequence. He could be the by-blow of a shire knight or even of some higher lineage. But that stiff leg? She hardly realized that she was staring at him.

He answered her unspoken curiosity with no timidity. "Lady Frances, my leg was broken and badly set. When I was an apprenticed lad a loaded ale wagon rolled over me and a barber-surgeon was not called. I set it myself." He smiled. "And discovered I had no skill for the work."

She flushed at being caught out in her impolite and personal curiosity. *He set it himself!* She could not imagine it. "I am sorry for your pain, sir."

Jennet pinched her, and Frances realized that she had given him a courtesy his station did not merit. But his bearing, his temperate, correct speech did. They no longer seemed bold, as she had first thought. . . . She must remember to be less hasty in her judgment.

"You are kind, Lady Sidney," Pauley said. "I am limited in no way. Better you know, since I am to be in your service . . . except for special duties for your father."

Aunt Jennet now sat in rigid, disapproving silence, often casting warning looks at Frances for being in such personal conversation with a male servant.

Frances ignored the warning. She was a married woman going to court. It was past time to escape her nurse's constant scolding. "Can you play your guitar in this jouncing carriage? I have never heard such a fine instrument as you have."

Pauley nodded so eagerly that his hat slipped to his lap, exposing hair as black and curling as her own. He smiled and unwrapped the instrument, and she saw it had five double strings in the Italian style. Holding it gently, he began to play and sing in a baritone soft and rich enough to lull Jennet into sleep.

> *Under the greenwood tree*
> *Who loves to lie with me,*
> *And turn her merry note*
> *Unto the sweet bird's throat . . .*

"Under the Greenwood Tree" was a tender song Frances had always loved, and today, of all days, it brought tears to her eyes. Mothers sang it to their babes, and young lovers sang it to each other. She could barely remember her mother, and Philip had never walked with her under the greenwood trees. She didn't even know whether he could sing.

Frances blinked and turned her head toward the passing fields glimpsed between the curtains hung to keep out the dust billowing up from the wheels, or as today, the rain. She must have a care and refuse to sink into self-pity, which could age a woman faster than years.

Pauley stopped playing, concern showing on his face. "I did not mean to sadden you, my lady. Forgive my poor playing. I have been in France and admit to being unpracticed of late."

Now she saw something comforting in his manner, though by no means was it the fawning way of some servants. It was a positive attitude that invited confidence. She smiled, yet kept her mouth firmly shut on all her thoughts.

She waved her hand, dismissing his apology. "Not so, Master Pauley. You are very skilled at the instrument."

"Is there something I can play to improve your sad humor?"

"I am not in a sad humor; I am merely thoughtful of my new

position with the queen," she said, determined to crowd out the heartache that she was surprised to feel, and even more surprised to hear he understood. She would not mourn a husband who did not love her, or long for more than she had.

Jennet, awake again, had heard more than enough. "Frances, let us have silence, I beg you," she said; yet as they complied, she almost instantly nodded off into a slack-mouthed, snore-filled slumber.

Frances looked at Pauley and they shared muffled amusement, then sat silent for a time as the carriage slowed for a stream crossing, the downpour having ceased. But she could manage only so long in her own thoughts without conversation to distract her, especially since this Robert Pauley intrigued her. He had the carved features of noble descent to go with his speech. There was a story there, and any good spy would want to discover it.

She did not sleep easily, as Jennet did, or close her mind against the crack of the driver's whip and the snorting of horses dragging the heavy carriage along a road never free of ruts even in high summer.

He didn't break the silence again until he smiled at a particularly loud, rumbling snore from the older woman. "Is there any place where your good nurse cannot find deep sleep?"

"I have never found such a place," Frances said softly, smiling as his sense of the comical met hers.

"Yet it seems your aunt can sleep in a jouncing carriage and you cannot, so the talent is not in the blood." He grinned, showing white, even teeth that suggested he must use the best tooth cloths from France. "I truly wish I could do more for your comfort, my lady."

"You could tell me about the special duties you perform for my father."

His gaze became cautious and his voice dropped to little more than a murmur she strained to hear. "What do you wish to know?"

"Are you an intelligencer? What did you do in France? Do you know Thomas Phelippes, the cipherer?" She pulled the *Steganographia* from the pocket under her kirtle. "I study this at every opportunity, and I long to talk with Dr. Dee about his grille ciphers. Do you know them? Do you know him?" She ran out of breath before she ran out of questions.

"My lady, you have a great curiosity."

He did not smile, but answered her seriously. She liked him the better for that.

"Yes, I have read Trithemius," he said. "I know Dr. Dee and Thomas Phelippes. As to my work, I cannot discuss that, as you must know, but I have your father's trust or he would not have made me courier to our Paris embassy . . . or have placed me in your service."

She held up the *Steganographia*. "You've read this book?"

"Aye. In the Latin, my lady."

She was startled.

"I see that surprises you."

"A little," she admitted, rather than tell an obvious untruth. But his knowledge of Latin was unusual. A servant who was educated above even some with noble titles was . . . well, unheard-of. There was no way to question him without prying, and he was already looking at her with some amazement.

"Lady Frances, please you, allow me . . . if your father had a son with such a questioning mind, I would have little employment."

He was trying to be kind, but she would not have it. "Master Pauley, as you see, my father has a daughter with such a mind and a longing for knowledge and occupation." Her voice was too loud, so she softened it, not wishing to awaken Jennet to certain reproof. "That is, if he would but recognize that I can reason and would put my gift to good use."

"I see that you, like every man, want your talent to be recognized."

She sensed that he had left something unsaid. *And a lack over-looked.* His leg and his low birth had hindered him, as being a woman had limited her life. She did not speak the thought, or need to. She saw in his steady gaze that Robert Pauley could see and understood.

*R*obert tried to keep his gaze on the passing countryside, but he could think of nothing but the young woman who sat across from him. How could her husband seek the reluctant and overused favors of Lady Rich, when he had this astonishingly beautiful and intelligent woman to wife? He wanted to touch her to satisfy his curiosity about her skin. Was it as soft as it looked, or was there steel there, the same steel that flashed from her eyes when she spoke of ciphering?

Her mouth, even when set in anger, had a touch of amusement showing in the way it turned up above a pointed chin. Her high forehead was partly covered with very dark curls blown about into a most becoming tangle above large, pale, clear gray eyes with dreams locked inside. She did not wear the white Mask of Youth or the red wig that were so fashionable, but she was all the more beautiful for being herself. He realized that he was staring fully at her now, and abruptly ruled his face into that of a polite servant, although he had never properly managed that downcast gaze.

"My lady, the court will be very lively in the next months. The Earl of Essex is attending upon the queen." He hesitated, wondering whether he should tell her that her husband's lover would come to court at Christmastide, and decided the lady Frances should not be taken by surprise. It was in his power to keep her from the humiliation that the court would anticipate seeing in her face. "And I understand the Baroness Rich will be appearing before Her Majesty with the Earl of Leicester's players."

"Women are not players," she said.

"If Her Majesty requests, they are players, my lady."

Her face showed no emotion at his answer, and he wondered at her resolve, at her composure beyond her years. Or was it indifference? Why did he think it, or wish it?

As the curtains bounced about in the rocking coach, sunlight slanted in, lighting the hollows of her cheeks and throat. To his mind she was far lovelier than Lady Rich, whose life of being adored had left her face somewhat used and empty, a hollow beauty. This lady was alive with a curious intelligence and, he thought, quiet courage.

He did not wonder that Sir Walsingham had kept his daughter from court, the lascivious court that Queen Elizabeth swore brought credit to her name because she chose to think so. The truth was always difficult for Her Majesty, if it wasn't her truth. He could see at a glance that Lady Frances was a rather cheerless young woman, despite being married to the man every woman in the realm thought the greatest lover. If that were true, Lady Sidney's face would not be so searching, looking for a thing she did not have, perhaps did not know.

He would keep her in close sight during her time at court, where the titled hounds were certain to sniff out such delicious prey, especially the Earl of Essex, the leader of the pack. And if Robert had it in his power, he would bring a smile to her face when he could. But he would have to be clever. Lady Frances was a Walsingham born and would accept no pity. He didn't know how he knew it, but he did.

The spymaster had not ordered him to guard her past this day, but he would take that future task upon himself. He did not question this desire. He did not dare plumb why he cared. She was little more to him than a beautiful face, enough for most men. Still, she had luminous eyes that looked on him with understanding, and a voice that enveloped him even in this rattling carriage.

He sensed that she was a woman who needed his caring. Later, he might question the wisdom of this decision, but he could not when she was turned to the window, the curve of her cheek showing a lonely melancholy that he understood as if it were his own.

*F*rances knew Robert Pauley was watching her. That was his current mission. How wonderful to have a servant, a companion in truth, who played music and sang to her. It would lighten her heart. She must remember to thank her father.

They rode on toward London and Whitehall, smelling the too-human scent of a crowded London and the river Thames long before they reached the city's gate, plunging deep into the throngs of merchants, women with their maids and shopping baskets watched closely by thieves and doxies. Many houses along the way sported the greenery of a tavern serving the double ale allowed by the queen, although the more popular double-double had been banned, a prohibition that Frances doubted was strictly observed.

Both Lady Frances and her servant were sunk profoundly deep into their own thoughts, avoiding any exchange that might reveal more than they already had. Once again they assumed the roles of mistress and servant only.

CHAPTER THREE

"He loves my heart, for once it was his own;
I cherish his, because in me it bides. . . ."

—Astrophel and Stella, *Sir Philip Sidney*

Late August

WHITEHALL PALACE, LONDON

Frances awoke with lines from one of Philip's sonnets in her head. What had put them there?

Last evening she had been busy settling into her new rooms, which were small but adequate, until she had gone to her new bedchamber and immediately slept, still with the sense of jouncing about in the carriage. Today she would face the queen for the first time as a woman. Taking a deep breath and with a final smoothing of her pale green satin gown and a tug of her brocade bodice, Frances walked into the anteroom of the royal apartments. She carried her head high, though she was somewhat angry that Robert Pauley had been nowhere in evidence when she had needed him that morning. He had left flowers for her rooms, but no explanation for his absence, no by-your-leave. She did not know what to make of such behavior in a servant who obviously did not think or act like

36

one. Perhaps she had been too friendly in the carriage, as Aunt Jennet had warned. She determined not to make that mistake again.

Frances took a deep breath and composed her face, knowing it would not do to scowl at Queen Elizabeth.

The royal antechamber with its gilt ceiling was hung high with rich arras tapestries portraying unicorn hunting scenes. On one end wall hung a huge portrait of the queen's father, Henry VIII, displaying his monstrous codpiece and powerful thighs. On another wall hung a scene of the queen's ancestors, fading into dim history all the way back to Adam and Eve. That would mean that she, Frances Walsingham Sidney, was a quite distant cousin of the queen, since her father's historians had paid for a similar pedigree, as had many English gentlemen.

The overwarm antechamber was full of the queen's gentleman pensioners and hopeful petitioners, sweating perfume. No wonder it was said the queen held a pomander to her nose and rarely set it aside.

In some near chamber the boys of the Chapel Royal choir sang in their high, clear voices, casting the net of God's approval over the queen's morning activities.

Frances paused to listen at the huge double doors leading to the inner royal chamber, and gathered her breath to think through her next steps.

The doors swung open and the guard announced, "Lady Sidney, Your Majesty."

Elizabeth, crowned and wearing a magnificent white satin gown laden with pearls of every size and luminous hue, sat at a large writing table facing Frances. The Earl of Leicester and Mr. Secretary Walsingham stood by the queen with armfuls of dispatches and warrants for her to sign with the goose quill she had in hand.

Though Frances kept her eyes half cast down, she could see that the great Gloriana was no longer young. Her skin was lightened with egg white, vinegar, and white lead, the application she called her Mask of Youth. She had outlived many who had started her reign with her, yet her eyes were as bright as the diamonds she wore, her legs strong and her wit stronger.

Frances knew she was in a *presence*, and the others who sought the queen's favor knew the same; even Frances's father looked subdued.

By his worried glance, it was obvious to Frances that he feared his daughter might trip on her new wooden heels and sprawl before the queen in a quite undignified heap, to his shame.

That made Frances even more determined to show herself graceful.

The queen looked up with interest and waved Frances forward.

"Ah, yes . . . 'My true love hath my heart, and I have his,'" said the queen, quoting from Philip's verses. Her Majesty's gaze was turned to Leicester, still her favorite, though gray showed in his dark beard and his doublet stretched tight across a thickening waist. Still, in the earl Frances could see the remnants of the splendid youth whom the queen must have known and must yet see.

Frances took a deep breath and quoted the next line of Philip's poem, which he'd probably last whispered into Lady Rich's pink ear. "'By just exchange one for the other given . . .' Your gracious Majesty," she said in a voice to carry across the inner chamber. If there was gossip about Phillip and Lady Rich in the court, Frances would step out in front of it, though that might be difficult. Lady Rich was the Earl of Essex's sister and he was Elizabeth's new favorite.

Waved forward by the squinting queen, who everyone knew was shortsighted, Frances flawlessly performed three deep curtsies as ordained by court protocol, to her father's obvious relief. She saw the lines of care briefly fall from his face, as he watched her with what she thought might have been pride were it not so carefully controlled.

All the queen's ladies looked on to see how well this new lady accomplished her introduction, ready to jest all about the court if she showed clumsiness.

After a morning of practice, Frances knew her curtsies were the very best she had ever done, and the slight smile on her face allowed them all to see her satisfaction.

The queen motioned her still closer and proved with her next words what everyone knew: She had not forgotten Philip's unsolicited opinion regarding her plans to marry her French duke. "Lady Frances, I like Sir Philip's poetry far better than his marital instructions."

Frances nodded, her lips puffed into a thoughtful moue. "Majesty, as his wife, I have good cause to agree."

The queen smiled up at her spymaster. "Ah, your daughter has wit, Walsingham. I like wit above all things . . . when rightly directed. Though I see she wears a gown of color, and I allow only white on my ladies of the presence."

"Most gracious queen," her father said, bowing and, having no wit himself, relying on the etiquette of introduction, "this is my only child, Frances, the lady Sidney. I will call the seamstresses to her so that she can be properly fitted. Should she retire today?"

"No, she is untutored in court etiquette and therefore forgiven . . . this once." Elizabeth stared at her, squinting a bit as if to bring Frances's face into better focus. Her gold spectacles lay, unused, to hand. "Marriage has suited you, Lady Frances," the queen said. "You were yet a child when last at court, and now I see a woman grown . . . though some wives are with child thrice over at two years into the married state."

"I have not been so fortunate," Frances murmured, feeling hot warmth creep up her cheeks, despite her best effort to prevent it.

"My queen," the Earl of Leicester said, interceding on behalf of his nephew, "our young poet, Sir Philip, is now gone ahead to the Low Countries to prepare the way for your Holland army."

The queen's mouth tightened. "That same army that will ruin my treasury . . . and take you from my court."

Leicester bowed. "An army must be well armed and provisioned."

Frances's father shifted to his better leg. "'Before all else, be armed.'"

The queen waved her quill. "I have read my Machiavelli, Mr. Secretary."

Walsingham nodded but was not deterred. "The Italian has written many times on this subject, Majesty. If you allow me: 'For among other evils caused by being disarmed, it renders you contemptible; which is one of those disgraceful things which a prince must guard against.'"

The queen's dark eyes narrowed. "Walsingham, it is all well and good to think a purse bottomless when it is not your purse. Now cease all talk of war and my treasury. I would meet privily with my new-come lady of the presence."

Frances noted that her father and some others in the chamber immediately bowed and left the room, but not the earl or the queen's ladies of the bedchamber, who were always near to answer Elizabeth's every need. They quietly withdrew to stools and chairs, taking up books or embroidery hoops, although Frances had no doubt they listened as hard as ever they could for anything worth tittle-tattling about the court.

"Sweet Bess," Leicester said, bending close to the queen's ear, "I beg you to grant me leave to depart the palace so that I may gather a troop of horse for the war. As your lieutenant general of the army, I should—"

"I will decide the matter later after more thought," the queen said, her lips tightening.

A queen did as it pleased her, and Frances was full of envy. She had already heard that Her Majesty was ever reluctant to allow her longtime favorite to depart, or, once letting him go, sent fast couriers to recall him within hours. Frances now saw the tension between them that she had heard whispered of all during her life. No matter their advanced age or the many years they had known each other, they were always on the edge of a clash, the earl wanting to break free of the royal reins and Elizabeth determined he should not, though she made favorites of every handsome, witty, and young courtier.

And Frances thought she saw something more. There was sorrow, a look of loss in their faces that was so veiled it could not be easily detected. Yet she saw it; she had seen it before. In her own mirror.

"Be comfortable, my lady," the queen said, motioning to a chair alongside the table.

"Thank you, Majesty."

The chair was not cushioned, and Frances tried to look at ease as she sat upon its unyielding surface. She had no doubt these chairs were reserved for the queen's councilors to keep them from staying overlong while presenting their demands on her purse.

The queen spoke in a commanding voice. After she'd spent nearly three decades as England's ruler, whatever softer voice Elizabeth might once have had was now long departed. "Your good father tells me that you read in the Latin. Do you know your Greek?"

"No, Majesty, I did not have a Greek tutor, although I did learn French and some Italian." Frances took a deep breath and plunged ahead before she could think better of it. She even decided to plead her youth and inexperience at court if the queen was displeased. "It is ciphering that intrigues me most."

"Ciphering is no language, but the opposite of language, since it is not meant to be understood by many."

"Your grace, it is my father's duty to see that you can read ciphering by your enemies . . . for your benefit and safety."

The queen looked close into Frances's face. "A cipher has always been work for grown men."

It took all of Jennet's long training in the benefits of silence to keep Frances from responding, *It usually takes a man to rule a kingdom.*

She was thankful the queen spoke before such a self-destructive thought could find expression even in Frances's face, and she had the sense to be glad of it.

"Lady Frances, you seem young for such an interest. Your father made no mention of it."

Frances forced a ready grimace into a smile. "Alas, Majesty, he does not approve of such curiosity in a woman."

Elizabeth nodded, her painted mouth twisting with amusement. "No, my dark Moor would not."

Could the queen be an ally? Frances dared not even think so, and arranged her face into a pleasant repose that showed nothing of her swirling thoughts. Would a great queen, a scholar herself, be a friend to another woman's hope? Frances had never heard so; the queen was reputed to be severe about her ladies' conduct, lest it bring shame to her. But how could a scholarly pursuit be shameful to Elizabeth Tudor, who was rightly noted for her translations of difficult passages and study of the classics?

Frances was closer to the queen than ever before, and allowed herself to look into the ruler's face to see what hope she could find there. She saw none under the red wig that imitated youthful hair the queen had inherited from her father, or in the dark blue eyes that had come from her mother, Anne Boleyn.

Elizabeth showed no emotion, only the radiating lines that betrayed age under the white ceruse face paint and red cochineal lips and cheeks, and in her almost invisible eyebrows, not darkened by kohl, to give her a perpetually alert look that she put to good use as she squinted about the chamber. Though the queen was soon to be fifty-two, her back was erect, her eyes clear, and her movements quick. It was said she could walk and ride faster than men half her age. Unfortunately, there was no exercise to keep her face as young as her heart and body.

Frances lowered her eyes, lest she appear to stare.

The queen stood and her ladies rose as one. The drums began

to beat outside in the hallway for the royal procession to the presence chamber. Trumpets sounded. She motioned for Frances to walk behind her, a distinct honor usually reserved for Anne, Countess of Warwick, the queen's great friend and chief lady.

"Thank you, Majesty," Frances murmured as they moved ahead, through the corridors of kneeling and curtsying courtiers.

"I show you favor, Lady Frances, to properly introduce you to my court. There are those who would use this kindness for their own benefit. Have a care. Rogues would seek to gain from your innocence."

"I will have a great care, Majesty," she whispered, the queen already moving slowly ahead.

Along the way Elizabeth motioned for some in her favor to rise, but left others on their knees in the herbs and rushes strewn to sweeten a palace of two thousand bodies and too few common jakes.

Gradually, the ladies of the bedchamber moved up into their rightful places until Frances was in the hindmost, with the pillow bearer and rear guards. Nevertheless, she kept her head up and her shoulders back, as if she were a countess.

As she passed the last corridor before the entrance to the presence chamber, she saw Robert Pauley in the shadows near a lamp. He placed a hand on his heart and bowed to her. What knavery was this? Had he come to explain himself, to wish her well, or had he just happened by on some errand for her father and stopped to spy on her? She was suddenly angry, now sure of his mission, though she knew her anger was as wrong as was his absence this morn without her permission.

Before Frances could puzzle out more of an answer as to why Pauley would be watching for her, she composed her face as the doors to the presence chamber were opened by two helmed guards with upright needle-sharp pikes. A trumpet fanfare blared and Frances, her excitement building, found herself inside the huge presence chamber lit by large windows overlooking palace orchards and the Thames beyond. Many branched candelabra, illuminating rows of glittering courtiers in their finest clothes and best jewels, lined the way. Pillars decorated with fresh flowers and twining columbine yet to flower soared up to the paint-and-gilt ceiling. As the queen's entourage passed between courtiers, foreign ambassadors, and lesser gentlemen, all knelt to the queen, some looking up, hoping for recognition or a moment to advance a petition.

Elizabeth, avoiding their pleas, strode straight to her canopied throne and sat down, her ladies adjusting her skirts so that they swirled about her shining silver-slippered feet.

Frances took her place to the side of the gold throne at the very end of the line of ladies and saw her father and Lord Burghley, the queen's treasurer, both with their inevitable sheaf of documents, ready to come forward if summoned to answer the queen's questions. Today Elizabeth seemed to look elsewhere, not wanting to hear the usually bad news her councilors brought her.

Frances had been in the presence chamber before, but never on the dais, where she could look out on so many glittering nobles.

Catherine, Lady Stanley, stood next to her and whispered breathlessly from behind her fan, "You have an admirer."

Frances looked at her. "What?"

"Shhh . . . there . . . the Earl of Essex by the center pillar in front of the queen."

Frances did not turn her head. "As you must know, I am married, my lady Catherine, and have no interest in young courtiers."

The lady smiled . . . more than smiled; she scoffed. "Don't be such a ninnyhammer, Lady Frances. The earl is a coming man, the queen being much taken with his youth, form, and face, as we all are and you soon will be. Look on him; he is an Adonis."

Frances tried to move away, but there was no more room on the end of the dais, so she stared straight ahead with what she thought was disinterest.

That did not stop Lady Stanley's amused insistence. "You are in a court where fortunes are made on receiving admiration from the right people, especially a noble and most handsome earl." She caught her breath. "One who has vowed to bed all the queen's ladies and is some way on toward that end." She stifled a giggle with her hand.

"Not this lady, madam," Frances whispered. She heard another slight giggle from behind the fan.

Still, she had to look so that she would stay well away from this earl, who wanted to despoil a lady's reputation to increase his own manhood. He was easy to identify as she scanned the crowd. There in the front, leaning against a vine-entwined pillar, one very long leg crossed in front of the other, stood a tall young man scarce beyond her own years, and exceptionally handsome. He was glorious in satin, with velvet ribbons at his elbows and knees, the very model of a young courtier who was aware that his every move was watched. And yet there was something of innocence in his swagger, something in his eyes that struck Frances as curious. Though it was well hidden, he was very watchful. For what? she wondered. He wore no giant codpiece like some of the young cockerels parading about the presence chamber, although his tight hosen left little doubt that his manly gifts were abundant indeed.

He was descended from Mary Boleyn, Henry VIII's mistress, and carried a suggestion of Tudor red in his autumn-brown hair haloed about his beardless face. He had Henry's height and swagger, which made his appearance even more a memory of the old king. It was no wonder to Frances that this youth had intrigued the queen, as had his well-favored appearance and knowing style.

"They say," Lady Catherine continued, near breathless with information and rumor, "that he looks much like Robert Dudley in his youth."

Well-done, Frances thought; how better to attract an aging queen than with memories of her legendary father and Dudley, now Earl of Leicester, the man she had loved as a young queen new-come to the throne? No wonder the queen treated his rutting disobedience as she would a spoiled child's. As Frances watched, he raised a finger and smoothed his ruff, which only brought all eyes to its many starched pleats, each one toiled over by some washer-woman in the bowels of the palace.

She bit her lower lip to keep from smiling at the man's knowl-edge of his own appeal. What arrogance! Yet she couldn't help but notice that he was looking at her in a hot way Philip never had, and he seemed to have no care that others saw, even the queen. It was beyond arrogance, to a dangerous degree of self-confidence. For a moment, fear for the young fool grabbed at Frances's throat. Would his youth and looks keep him safe forever? She continued to guard against any awareness on her face, though he was looking full at her and smiling, clearly inviting recognition.

She stared past him, but she doubted he was fooled. His obvi-ous self-regard would not allow it.

Frances heard little of the shire petitions, or the ambassadors from foreign lands with gifts and appeals from their rulers for aid against the Spanish, or more favorable trading terms for their coun-try's wares . . . a reduction of port taxes was desired by all. The crowded chamber grew hot and the air heavy with perfume. She was relieved when the queen stood suddenly and waved her ladies into line, motioning for the young earl to escort her to the royal apartments.

"My lord Essex, you have busy eyes this morn. We can put them to better use."

"To my joy, Majesty," he replied, his face as innocent as a babe's.

Elizabeth looked somewhat appeased and was soon laughing at his murmured jests spoken near her ear.

As they reached the royal apartments, Frances could not wait to be dismissed and was happy to hear the queen say that she would play on her virginals for the earl before her private audiences. Essex looked delighted.

Frances curtsied and left the chamber, only to have the Earl of Essex call to her.

"Lady Frances," he said, coming up quickly behind her. "I am sorry not to have welcomed you to court sooner."

"Are you not called to attend the queen, my lord?"

"Ah, I am in great need of a serious woman to remind me of my duty, yet the queen often has a sudden change of mind, and has just had another on receipt of a letter from the Scots king, James. And, as I said—"

Frances curtsied. As she rose he yet towered over her, even though she, like the queen, was above middle height for a woman. "It would have been difficult to welcome me sooner, my lord Essex, since I arrived only late yesterday, and you surely do not meet every incoming lady's carriage, though you might wish it." She meant for him to see that she was not a fool, and to know her lack of interest in a handsome courtier from the beginning.

He laughed. "Her Majesty remarked that her new lady had wit. Now I see the queen's finding was not idle, though she did not say the wit had a sharp, cutting edge."

Frances tried to keep any pleasure at his civil recognition from her face; nonetheless, she was pleased not to be thought another empty head. "That is lavish praise, my lord, for so small a humor, and I do assure you, it was my best."

"Ah, modesty, too, and I suspect a superior intelligence behind those intimidating gray eyes."

Although Essex's blue eyes were wide and his face guileless, Frances could not rid herself of the thought that he was cleverly waiting to pounce, like a ravenous dog at a bear baiting. Yet Lady Stanley could have been a gossip with evil intent, and the young earl not as she described him. Besides, he was dangerously good to look at, and Frances was not unmindful of male beauty.

Courtiers with curious eyes were brushing past them. Essex held out his arm to her, and she was forced to take it or seem lacking decent manners, or worse, frightened, which would be catnip to such a man. He led her to a windowed alcove overlooking a walled garden and bowed her into a seat.

"Her Majesty tells me that you are interested in your father's work. Does Mr. Secretary know what a rare daughter he has? Tell me more, my lady. I am beyond fascinated."

Frances's gaze went quickly to his face, but she detected nothing of ridicule, only interest. Yet she was wary. Robert Pauley had seemed astonished and delighted with her curiosity, but it came naturally out of their conversation. Essex might be taking advantage of any gossip he could use to gain her friendship. For what end? "I wouldn't know where to begin, my lord."

He sat and leaned closer, arm bent on his knee, chin cupped in his hand, altogether attractive . . . and knowing. "Begin anywhere, Lady Frances, anywhere at all."

She heard herself telling him of her study of cipher and her ability to lift and reseal a letter so that it remained undetectable.

Essex laughed aloud with delight and took her hand from her lap before Frances could snatch it away. Once it rested in his, she would have seemed unfriendly to withdraw it abruptly.

"Such a great skill for so small a hand."

He turned her hand over and pressed his fingers into the palm as if he intended to leave his mark. "Ah, how clever you are, Lady Frances! I do adore intelligence, especially when it is attached to such beauty. By the great Harry, a woman who wants to know secrets is not unique, but a woman who breaks a cipher . . . now, that is beyond unusual. You must show me this talent you have with wax seals, and show me soon. Perhaps I could come to your rooms to watch you work."

Frances could not tell whether he spoke true. A young and too handsome face was harder to read than a cipher. "Perhaps, my lord.

As yet I do not know what hours the queen will need me." She gently removed her hand from his grasp. "I must go now."

"Soon, lady, but I beg you, let us talk on for yet a time. I greatly admire your husband. I write some poor poetry of my own; of course, nothing to qualify me as his equal, though I will say the queen does me the honor of reading it." He tried to look humbled by the tribute, but he succeeded only in trying.

Here was a man who was clever, Frances thought, and believed everyone must love him. But she, being demure, kept her body straight and drew away from him as much as the cushioned alcove seat would allow. He was probably right about the feminine interest he aroused, except in this instance. She had not come to court to play romantic chess games with handsome young lords, though she doubted that any such argument would sway this earl.

She stood. "I must take my leave, my lord. My servants are unsupervised, and I would see to the further unpacking of my chests and caskets."

He stood, again towering above her. "Your servants are idle, if that fellow is any indication."

Frances followed his gaze and saw Robert Pauley standing at the head of the corridor leading to her rooms. He was not staring in her direction, but she suspected he was watching every move. Was he spying on her for her father as a duty, or for himself? And why would she even think the question?

"I will soon put him to his tasks. Excuse me, my lord."

Essex held out his hand. "Lady Frances, I would escort you to your rooms."

Her answer was sharper than she meant it to be. "I have a servant for that!"

He knew how to look the hurt boy, and no doubt the talent had served him well in the past, and might have served again had she not been forewarned.

She softened her tone. "How kind, my lord Essex. Another time . . . perhaps."

Frances walked away, sensing his gaze burning into her back. What would she do if he followed and insisted on being her escort?

"Remember me to your husband when next you write," he called softly after her.

Robert Pauley saw her frown as she approached. "Where have you been the morning long?" she demanded.

So her ladyship would have him waiting inside her apartment door, jumping to her every waking command . . . *bring this, take that* . . . early and late. He was in her service, yes, but for quite another reason. The court could be cruel, and, though she had a ready spirit, she would need a champion. Why he had named himself, he refused to consider, though he knew he would think on it when he took to his pallet for sleep.

"I see you have made a new *friend*, my lady, but have a care."

"I can ensure my own safety, Master Pauley."

"Of that I have no doubt, my lady. I was more concerned for the earl."

His response was so droll and unexpected that she had to smother an urge to laugh. Robert Pauley did not need her encouragement. Besides, she had heard quite enough from clever men for one day. "You have sharp eyes for everything but your duties, Master Pauley."

He bowed. "My humble thanks to you, my lady. Every now and then I must be reminded of my place by even the most gracious of mistresses."

She was shamed. He had waited for her when she could have been trapped in the earl's doubtful company. Her tongue was not usually so sharp. Why couldn't she just be grateful?

CHAPTER FOUR

❧

"O Moon . . .
Are beauties there as proud as here they be?"

—Astrophel and Stella, *Sir Philip Sidney*

September 15

The scrap of vellum slipped under her door had been written with a fine hand, and she had no doubt who had held the quill. What youth, other than Essex, would be so arrogant as to use her own husband's poetry to try to capture her attention?

Yet Frances knew that had she been really annoyed, she would not have laughed at the boyishly clumsy effort to draw her attention. True, she hadn't laughed as she first read the lines, but a sense of Essex's inability to know the ridiculous finally overcame her, and she sat at her writing table, laughing until the tears came. What had happened to the sure-footed courtier? Had he been overcome by eagerness or by a desire to win a wager?

Frances's first month at Whitehall had kept her busy with a daily round of serving the queen, trying to walk into her father's well-guarded offices as if she belonged, and, hardest of all, escaping the Earl of Essex's attentions. His behavior, though seemingly friendly, was bothersome—nay, worrisome. He was too much the affectionate youth to dismiss cruelly, and she really didn't want to hurt or anger him by rebuffing him too sharply. Though he looked and acted a man grown, suited to an earl's estate, he as often became a hurt, sulking boy even with the queen, who was more charmed by this behavior than Frances was.

For thirty pounds annual and two hot meals a day, a lady of the presence spent mornings in the presence chamber, except when the queen took to her bed and physic with an aching head or ailing belly . . . usually from too many sweetmeats or the many demands on her treasury.

When Frances bent her efforts to gaining admission to her father's offices, his guards—on strict orders, as they explained most politely—turned her away. Her father would not allow her to broach the subject.

Pauley was no help, being gone from her service more than he was with her, although he seemed to appear whenever the Earl of Essex waylaid her in one of the many dark corridors of the rambling old palace.

Just this day, the earl stood in her way as she turned into the Long Gallery. He was wearing blue satin, vastly embroidered, very much the court gallant.

He stepped closer, and though his manner was easy and friendly toward her, she felt an instant unease, as she almost always did with him.

"My lord, please allow me to pass."

"If I do, you will disappear again without saying yea." There was more than annoyance in his voice, although he was trying to hide it behind a smile.

"What would you know from me, my lord?" She must yield one day to his many offers of diversion, or seem discourteous, and he knew it. Still, the thought of being alone with him troubled her.

If she allowed it, his attentions might become almost agreeable. There was no denying the charm he dangled in front of her.

"When will you show me your skill with lifting seals, or come out riding with me one fine morning, or walk in the orchard to pick ripe apples, or go to the French dance master's classes?"

She smiled with as much graciousness as she could bring to her face. "Your offers sound exhausting, my lord Essex."

He grinned, then looked over her head, the grin vanishing. "There is your lapdog, my lady. Is he always so faithful?"

He obviously tried hard to hide his dislike. To even notice Pauley, let alone be upset by him, was beneath an earl.

"He but follows my father's orders." Frances curtsied and moved on rapidly down the corridor, grateful to Robert Pauley for dogging her footsteps. This one time. Although she hoped she was capable of taming an unruly young lord, truth be told, she had not had much practice at Barn Elms.

"You have the most astounding gray eyes, my lady. Know you that?"

She heard Essex's steps close behind her and walked faster. "You are too kind, my lord, but I must be on my way."

The earl seemed capable of hearing only agreement to his requests for her company, no matter how plainspoken her refusals. Then again, perhaps she was being unfair to this shockingly handsome young man who sought her company as no one ever had. She should never hold court gossip, no matter how alarming, against a man. Alarm was the nature of court gossip.

And he was sweet to want her company. Maybe she should learn to accept determined male attention as a compliment. Yet why did he seek her out? Did she have some needful look about her that would draw a young man to a possible new conquest, especially when he was said to have swived four of the queen's waiting ladies already? She must watch her face and eyes, lest she be seen as too forward and encouraging, or did he see what he wanted to see no matter what her face revealed? She suspected the latter from so accomplished a romancer.

Still, it was not wise to ignore the queen's new favorite. At the turning of the corridor, she looked back with a smile and lifted her hand in farewell. There, that was just friendly enough, without being forward.

She made her way for a second day to sit by her father's bed, nearly covered with vellum sheets, letters from everywhere in France, the Low Countries, Rome, and Spain. She bent to exchange the cloth on his fevered brow for a cooler one from a basin of rose-petal-filled water. Pain had marked him with deep lines, and his dark face bore a yellow tinge, as it did when his malady fell upon him.

His doctors had bled, purged, and dosed him with a decoction of campion herb to help him expel urine, and, judging from the rank odor in the chamber, had also extracted many stools. He was too weak to feed himself, though the doctors had insisted he drink ass's milk, a universal curative. Although she knew from past attacks that he was in great pain, the only indication he made was a sudden intake of breath, or a hand making a fist on the coverlet.

She walked to the brazier to reheat the bull's broth that his doctors had also ordered to strengthen him. She tried to spoon some into his mouth.

He turned his head away. "No, daughter, I cannot."

"Lord father, you must have nourishment to cure your weakness." She leaned close to his ear and whispered, "My mother, Anne, would want it so." The plea had worked on him before.

His eyes remained closed tight, but he opened his mouth and swallowed two spoonfuls.

"How does Robert Pauley in your service?" he asked suddenly.

"Well enough . . . when he is with me."

"His service is not to your liking?"

"It is well enough, Father," she repeated, and then realized that was unfair. "Nay, Father, he is diligent as my guard, remarkably so, though I do not understand him." The words were out of her mouth before she could think how strange they must sound. What understanding was needed between mistress and servant? She quickly added to explain herself, "He does seem a man of great confidence for his rank."

"Do not judge him too harshly. You do not know his origin, daughter."

"He is your man, and that recommends him to me." She had said the dutiful words before she thought to question him about Pauley's beginning, though she would when her father was stronger.

"Then call him to me, daughter."

Her father would dictate more letters, or notes to himself for later action. There was no keeping him from his work, and from long experience she did not try.

She stepped to the door to summon Pauley and found him waiting there. His eyes were half closed from lack of sleep. "My father calls you."

"Is he stronger?" Pauley asked. His expression was concerned as he brushed past her into the darkened room, and that heartened Frances. Most men feared her father, yet this man seemed to have a fondness for him.

Pauley stopped to hear her answer, but did not turn to her.

"In one way, he is the same as ever, needing to work."

Pauley went to sit beside Walsingham's bed. "Mr. Secretary, what would you have of me?"

The spymaster did not open his eyes. "Is there word from my intelligencer David Cobrett in Dieppe?"

"No word, sir."

"Write to him in his personal cipher and ask him for news of the English college at Douai. How many priests and Catholic Bibles are they spewing out, and how many are on their way across the channel to do mischief to Her Majesty's rule and to our true

Protestant faith? I must have names and descriptions so that my agents at Dover and Plymouth can arrest them before they disappear into their priest holes in the west country, or north to Lancaster, or here in London itself."

The many words exhausted him, and his arm, which had been waving in the air as if he were ciphering himself, dropped back to his side.

"At once, sir. Do you wish to sign it?"

"No. Use my cinquefoil seal and get it off by means of swift courier. I must have news of their traitorous plans. There has been quiet from Cobrett for too long."

"Aye, Mr. Secretary, at once, as you wish."

"Bring my agent's answer to me as soon as it arrives, if I am yet in this devil-cursed bed."

Pauley nodded, bowed, and turned to leave, nearly running into Frances. "My pardon, Lady Sidney."

She saw that her father had fallen into sleep, his fever seeming somewhat abated. Leaving the bedchamber door ajar to overhear if he stirred, she followed Pauley into the corridor, where the air, though chilly, was almost sweet. "You promised to take me to my father's offices. I would come with you later. . . ."

"My lady, I do not remember such a promise."

"You did not deny me."

"Sometimes we can think our dearest wish has been granted when it has not."

"I do not imagine . . ."

At that moment some roisterers stumbled into the corridor, led by the Earl of Essex dressed as a harlequin. Seeing her, he bowed and waved his peaked hat in greeting. "Hey-ho, Lady Sidney, I am gladdened to find you . . . yet so beautiful this late of day." He swayed, the worse for wine, and caught his balance against the wall. "Forgive me; I am very tired. Her Majesty has kept me from my bed playing at Maw for three nights running."

"Did you win, my lord?" Frances asked for something conversational, especially since she had heard he had allowed the queen to beat him.

He shrugged. "Not often," he said, grinning. "The queen hates to lose a trick and adores to win the pots, even the small ones. A few groats from my purse makes her happy, and she counts it a good month to take forty pounds from me." He laughed and bent forward, whispering, enveloping Frances in sweet Madeira wine fumes: "And she changes the rules if she is not winning." His eyes softened and sobered as his handsome face came closer to hers. "Ah, your faithful dog is near."

Pauley stepped forward and bowed. Frances thought, without considering his rank, that he had more natural dignity than the earl.

For a moment, Essex looked like a petulant boy. "Lady Frances, I have tried in every way to be your friend . . . for your husband's sake."

"My lord, forgive me; my father is very ill, and my worry burdens me and makes the delights you offer . . ."

He regained his bright smile. "All the more reason that you should have sun and fresh air. It is not good for the complexion to spend many hours in a darkened sickroom. Her gracious Majesty agrees, and commands that you come riding tomorrow morning. Your servant there can help the doctors care for Mr. Secretary. We ride out at first light." He bowed and walked away, as if all would be done as he wished.

Pauley spoke behind her. "The queen's command cannot be ignored, my lady. I think you should ride to the hunt in the morn. I will sit with Mr. Secretary. He will have work for me and all of his intelligencers."

His assured voice startled her, though for a man's low voice it was not heavy. It was comforting, in truth.

For a moment Essex had so o'erwhelmed the space that she had forgotten Pauley was behind her. "You advise it, then," she said, turning toward him with a half smile.

"If you will forgive me an opinion, my lady."

She swallowed a laugh. "Why ever not? It is only one of many, and I daresay not the last. But I thought you would warn me away from riding with the earl."

"The queen will see to it that he does not pay you too close attention . . . welcome or unwelcome."

She was half-intrigued and half-annoyed in turn, as she always seemed to be with Pauley. "You will allow the queen to see to my safety?"

"I trust her next to myself, Lady Frances."

He had to be jesting, and she rewarded him with a smile. "You do have very decided views on many things."

"An undecided view is of no use to anyone."

He bowed low, but she saw no mockery, although it could be well hidden in such a clever man. "My thanks to you, then, sir."

"Anything to be of good service, Lady Frances. And now, I must to business." With another and hastier bow, he turned and left her for the intelligencer offices on a lower level. She knew he would work through the night to cipher her father's message to the intelligencer Cobrett in France. And she knew another thing: Pauley did have her safety at heart. His presumption might once have angered her. She wondered why it no longer did.

The next morning it was yet dark when she rose from bed to dress for riding in a green velvet habit with a peacock-feathered cap on which was mounted some modest blue sapphires.

Her aunt Jennet brought out her new buskins. "You do look fine enough to ride with the queen, Frances," she said wistfully. "You have grown in good qualities in the past month. The excellent ladies of the court have had more influence than I ever could. You will soon have no use for me."

"Aunt," Frances said, embracing Jennet, fearing tears were about to start, "I will need you all my life. You have been mother and teacher to me. What little sense I have, you thrust upon me . . . and I bless you for it."

Jennet blinked back tears that had been ready to flow, and her face brightened. "Frances, you are a sweet liar."

"I speak only truth, Aunt." And she did. Jennet had always been near, and though at her time of life she had become a little quarrelsome, Frances believed her aunt had only her good at heart. Although her aunt's idea of good and her own were not always the same.

Jennet pushed her playfully to the polished-steel mirror on the wall of the outer chamber. "See how fine a lady you look! Sir Philip should see his fair wife now; he would take the fastest ship home."

But not to me, Frances thought, though she realized with bitter comfort that whatever wound had once been in her heart was now healed, leaving only a scar that was growing fainter.

Jennet fussed with Frances's sleeves until she was satisfied with her image in the mirror and bent to brush her new-made buskins.

"Thank you, sweet aunt," Frances said, leaving a kiss on Jennet's cheek before rushing next door to see her father.

"I am better, daughter," he announced, his voice slurred by a tincture of Paracelsus's pain potion the doctors must have given him to bring healing sleep. "Your bull's broth did strengthen me. I will be out of this intolerable bed tomorrow."

"Do your doctors agree?"

"Never. They are loath to lose a patient! Still, I must be at my work." A rare smile played upon his lips. "The queen sent me a bottle of her special herb physic, and she expects that it will work to my good . . . and quickly."

This was as close as her father came to a jest, and so Frances almost believed that he was indeed feeling less pain. Tomorrow, she

knew, he would be in his offices until late at night, but it was his
way and he would not be changed. Just as she would not be swayed
from her purpose to make his work her own, by 'ods blood! She
stopped short of blaspheming aloud. "I am riding to the hunt with
the queen, her other ladies, and my lord Essex this morning. I will
be with you as soon as the queen's audience in the presence chamber is finished."

"Good, daughter. You need to take the air. Your fair skin is
losing its bloom."

She put her hand to her face, vowing to get more exercise.

"Now, Pauley, let us to my letters."

She hadn't noticed the man sitting out of the candlelight across
the room. Had he been there all night?

He stood, walked forward, and bowed to her. "My lady, I will
help you with your mount."

"There will be many groor . in the stable yard."

"True, Lady Frances, but I would make certain they have
cinched your saddle and that you are properly seated."

Her father spoke approvingly. "Yes, see to my daughter, Pauley,
and then we will to our work."

So it was decided for her by others, as everything seemed to be.
For a moment she was truly envious of Pauley walking behind her
toward the palace mews. Although he was in her service, he seemed
to have a strange kind of independence. It was in his quiet manner
and obvious self-regard. She realized at that moment that he was a
man in no doubt of his qualities, in spite of his lower station and
bad leg. She longed for that self-regard. Her father had it. The
queen had it. Was such self-contentment not for the likes of her?
She lifted her head, vowing that she would know more of such ease,
and soon.

They walked into the crisp morning air washed by an early
shower and through the orchard, past Henry VIII's tennis court,
arriving at a mews crowded with snorting horses being led back

and forth by grooms to exercise them. A stable hand came toward her with a sleek black mare. "My lord Essex ordered this mount for you, Lady Sidney."

Frances ran her hand over the neck of the fine horse. "A good choice, don't you think, Pauley?"

He was checking the cinch and the reins, even opening the horse's mouth, as if searching for some hidden thing.

"What do you think to find?"

"A snaffle bit in a sore mouth might unseat you. The earl is fond of a jest, my lady."

This angered her. "I guide my mount with knees and seat, not by sawing on the reins. Surely you go too far in your protection of me. The earl would never wish me hurt." Frances hoped she was correct.

She barely heard his mumbled remark. "But he does like to rescue ladies in distress"—he stepped around to the other stirrup, shortening it with a grunt—"who would then show him their gratitude in ways to delight him."

"Pauley, you are always on the edge of forgetting your place. It is not for you to challenge an earl, or my judgment."

He didn't answer her admonition. She remembered that he had given his opinion of Essex when first she met with the earl. Yet did he think her such a fool that she could not resist a man who was already notorious for his fondness for ladies of not much resistance?

Pauley led the horse to the mounting block, and she was up and turning her mount toward the road to the west, but she heard what Pauley said.

"I dare to say, Lady Frances, that your father is wrong this one time. No palace, nor years, could take the bloom from your cheeks."

She looked back and saw him bow, then walk away, his limp for once more pronounced. What a strange man, much like a Spanish orange: sweet if ripe, but bitter if plucked too early.

As the queen and her party rode west toward the open heath

and forest beyond, Frances stayed in the rear, as befitted the newest lady. She breathed deep of the birch and elm trees already dropping their leaves in response to the suddenly cooler nights. She loved best the ancient oaks that defiantly kept their canopy if the weather did not become too cold, giving up their acorns only reluctantly to rutting pigs or scavenging squirrels.

The early morning air was cold on her face. She found herself enjoying the familiar movement of a horse's flanks beneath her and this escape from her own isolation inside the palace.

After some time and still at a fast trot, the queen threaded through the trees as her scent-seeking staghounds bounded ahead to flush roe deer from the birch stands and heavy brush. Essex carried her crossbow and a bag of quarrels. Her Majesty rode ahead, truly loving to best her younger men, as Frances had heard, delighting to hear their compliments on Gloriana's eternal youth and vigor. Smiling to herself, Frances had no doubt that Essex and the other young lords were willing actors in this play.

Lady Stanley, riding near the queen, dropped back next to Frances, eager as always to impart her superior knowledge of the occasion. "The queen's huntsmen have carted roe deer in for her pleasure."

"I thought as much," Frances said, swerving to avoid some thick brush. "The rut is long over."

"Of course." Laughing, Lady Stanley twisted in her saddle and said, "When a queen wants to hunt, deer step in front of her quarrels. . . ." Still laughing, the lady put spurs to her horse and leaped ahead.

Frances yelled, "Look to your path!" But she was too late.

A giant wild tusker had lumbered from the brush. It immediately charged Lady Stanley's horse, which reared, screamed with fright, and tossed her from the saddle into the boar's path before galloping away, back to the safety of the mews.

Frances saw the lady struggle to rise. She was trapped in brambles, her eyes wide with fear, her mouth frozen open in a soundless shriek. Blood ran from deep scratches on her face and shoulders. Her torn gown exposed ample breasts.

Frances's own horse shied abruptly, stiff legged, trembling, gathering its muscles to flee as the prey animal it was. She tightened her grip on the reins so that the mare would not get the bit between her teeth, then kicked the flanks to reach Lady Stanley before she was gored and dead.

The queen's men turning toward the sounds of struggle were too far ahead to arrive in time.

Without thinking, Frances jumped from her saddle into the crackling leaves, stirring an earthy, decaying odor that rose to envelop her. At once her horse, nostrils flaring, scented the animal and fled.

She snatched off her cloak, waved it at the boar, and shouted at the top of her voice. The tusker turned aside, confused by this strange new animal in its way. Seconds later it shook its head from side to side and focused its cruel, red-rimmed eyes on Frances. The boar resumed its charge.

At sight of the animal thundering toward her, Frances tried to sidestep and tripped on a tree root under the leafy ground cover. She fell to her knees, the beast so close she could smell its hot, gamy breath. Its glittering eyes narrowed into mean slits so near to her that its bulk blocked out the forest. Her gaze locked on the boar's eyes, her gasping breath whistling in her ears.

The beast was about to charge again.

She scrabbled frantically on the ground for a stick larger than a twig . . . only to grasp nothing.

The boar was almost upon her when abruptly it stopped, reared slightly, then dropped to its knees, not an arm's length distant. The huge beast slowly rolled over, the light of life leaving its eyes as blood streamed from a quarrel buried deep in its heart.

Thundering hooves filled Frances's ears as she gulped in a deep breath she must have been holding.

Essex jumped from the saddle and lifted her up, showing surprising strength for a man so slender. For a moment, she clung to him . . . safe . . . alive.

"Frances . . . lady . . . love . . . I am brainsick for you," he breathed into her ear, holding her hard to his chest.

She pushed against him as other gentlemen rode up, and she was embarrassed that they might hear the earl's endearments. Essex had been quick to take advantage. Had the queen observed them?

"Lady Stanley . . . injured . . ." She gasped, swallowing. "Go to her!"

He put Frances on her feet and ran to the other woman, who was on her knees pulling briars from her gown. She immediately swayed and fainted against him.

Her Majesty rode up, the huntsmen parting down the middle for her. She held her crossbow aloft in triumph and ordered men forward to lift the huge animal and take it to her flesh kitchen. "A perfect shot, my lords," she announced, looking quite pleased with herself.

*L*ate that night, Frances sat at her writing table with a double-branched candelabra lighting a single sheet of vellum. Jennet, fussing to make their rooms as homelike as possible . . . and perhaps to discourage her niece's scholarly interests . . . had decorated the table with a colorful turkey rug.

Frances splayed her fingers on the woven surface to see whether they were steady now. She had been shaken by the boar's charge and was not loath to admit to herself that it was probably the cause of her melancholy humor. What had Essex meant by saying he was brainsick for her? Were endearments his way of gaining access to her bed? Or worse, were they true? Her belly twisted at the thought. Was Essex the kind of lovelorn man who, the more he was rejected, the more he loved?

It wasn't her courses roiling in her belly. They had come and gone already. Philip had not left her with child.

Her husband's letter, just arrived with the rest of the dispatches to her father from Flushing in the Low Countries, lay on her writing table waiting for her answer. On a whim of quiet pleasure, Frances had removed with a hot knife the lump of red sealing wax imprinted with Philip's signet. She had no reason to do so, but it pleased her to use her skill.

Her husband was supervising the landing of supplies, troops, cannon, and horses. Though the English had come to save the northern Hollanders from being overrun by the prince of Parma's Spanish troops, bringing all their Inquisition horrors made ready for Protestant heretics, the Dutch were charging high prices for horse fodder and fresh food for Philip's troops. Many of the salted-fish barrels Philip had brought out of England had been made of green wood. The fish were rotten when the barrels were opened; thus he had no choice but to pay for supplies from his own purse, not daring to appeal to the queen's treasury so soon.

The letter said nothing directly to Frances until the very end.

> *I have purchased some satin cloth of eight ells*
> *and some inches in width, enough for the finest*
> *court gown, as befits my wife. I will not have it*
> *said that Lady Sidney was not richly dressed for*
> *court. Expect the package by the next ship. My*
> *honor to your father, Sir Francis, and to my lord*
> *Essex for his written remembrance. I have replied to*
> *the earl and asked him to take kindly care of you.*
>
> > *Your loving husband,*
> > *Philip*

It was a short letter to a lady who no longer needed to be courted . . . or counted. She smiled ruefully, remembering the one hundred eight seemingly endless sonnets he had written to Stella.

She picked up her quill, dipped it in the ink pot, and closed her eyes, thinking of what to tell him and what not to tell him about how diligently Essex was caring for her.

She had trouble opening her heavy eyelids again. Maybe she'd finish this letter in the morning, when she was more rested from her long, troubling day.

Frances had spent the afternoon and evening nursing her father while his secretaries were busy with his unending correspondence. He had intelligencers in every part of the continent, even inside Pope Sixtus's Vatican palace. She would never be an intelligencer there, but Frances could think of many other places where a lady intelligencer would not be suspect, while an ambassador's retinue would be close-watched.

She had not told her father of her encounter with the boar while hunting. She had not needed to inform him. News flowed to him in an endless stream of courtiers seeking his favor.

When she saw him that afternoon, to her relief he had eaten solid food for his supper, boar meat from the spit stuffed with pigeons, plums, and spices. "I understand that Her Majesty felled the beast with one quarrel to the heart," he said.

"Yes, lord father."

"And you were there, facing the beast," he added, shaking his head in wonder.

Frances nodded.

"Aye, I heard my lord Essex came for you just before the queen's shot. If he would give his life for you, daughter, I must find some way to repay him."

"Father, he did so, though the boar was stricken before he got to me."

"Aye, and so he corrected the report to me, as any honorable man would."

Essex rose in her esteem at this account of his truthfulness, though Her Majesty would surely have set to rights a story that did not credit her magnificent shot with saving her lady's life.

A throat was cleared and a strong hand shook Frances awake. She saw Robert Pauley's anxious face in the candelabra burning low and stretched her neck, shifting her weight to relieve the dull ache in her knees from her fall before the boar.

"My lady, you will have a pained neck, sleeping in a chair as you do. No doubt you are overtired from your exertions this day." He placed a goblet of warmed wine before her on her writing table. "My father used to bring me a hot drink when I had been at my books overlong."

His father? Would he speak freely of his birth? Did she dare ask?

"May I be of further service, Lady Frances?"

"Yes. I hear of your birth alluded to but never spoken aloud. My father seems to think I do you injustice not knowing your history . . . so I would know it."

He smiled slightly, though his eyebrows drew together. "I will have to beware my questions. You are ever outspoken, my lady."

"You have shown me that plain speaking is the best way."

"Have I? I am glad that even my unintended service has been useful to so kind a mistress."

Frances watched his face. Was he silently laughing at her? She could not tell; his humor was always hidden just below the surface.

Robert pulled up a chair, his boots brushing the edge of her gown. He looked down at his hands . . . and she did, too . . . his long and slender fingers, not like the calloused, sausage-fingered hands of a common toiling man.

For several moments he sat in silence.

"You are my mistress and have the right to know my birth." He took a deep breath. "I am the bastard son of Baron John Huntington of Staffordshire and Margaret, his kitchen maid. My mother died when I was ten years old, and my father, a kind man to me always, sent me off to King's College, Cambridge, to read for the church or prepare for Gray's Inn and the law. I chose the latter."

Frances watched him closely. "My father's path exactly."

He smiled. "Yes, I know." He cleared his throat. "When I was fourteen and about to take my degrees and move on to my law studies, my father died and his son and heir, now my master, forced me from my college and apprenticed me to a brewer here in London."

Frances knew that this was but a bare outline of his life, and from the slight tremor in his voice she suspected that he carried much injury behind the words.

Impulsively, she clasped his hands under hers. "How did you come to my father's service?"

He sat straighter, although he did not withdraw from her touch. "Your father bought my apprenticeship and took me into his service."

"How so?"

"I delivered ale to his house on Seething Lane and warned him of Spaniards plotting to plant Greek fire in his basement."

"Jesu, how did you come to know it?"

"I pretended to Catholic sympathies at the Elephant Inn, while strong drink from my own keg loosed their tongues."

"And—"

"I knew I had to take a warning to Mr. Secretary."

She stared at him. "You were even then an intelligencer."

"It was two years before he thought me ready for work of importance."

She could not help thinking, *He saw your worth, but none of mine.*

Robert withdrew his hand, stood, and bowed. "I am ever in his debt. You may ask of me . . . anything."

CHAPTER FIVE

"Thou blind man's mark, thou fool's self-chosen snare,
Fond Fancy's scum, and dregs of scatter'd thought . . ."

—Astrophel and Stella, *Sir Philip Sidney*

October

HAMPTON COURT

Frances hoped she could speak with Dr. Dee in the presence chamber today, and perhaps—*oh, perhaps*—he might appeal to her father to find some small place for her in his work. She dared not hope to be entrusted with a task of the highest importance, but something . . . *something* . . . to prove herself an intelligencer. Despite her tumbling thoughts, she mounted the dais, arranged her gown, and showed the pleasing face of a lady of the presence chamber. She searched for Dee, but did not see him. Perhaps he was on a mission for the queen. He was Her Majesty's own private informant.

She stared about her, dazzled once again by this large stateroom in Hampton Court. Was it not the most magnificent of the queen's palaces, sparkling with gilt and marble, bright with candlelight, the nobles and their ladies shining with jewels?

Whitehall had at last become unbearably noxious, and Queen Elizabeth, never able to bear foul odors, had spent her last days in the palace with her nose buried in a pomander. Then the court was plucked up and moved in more than four hundred carts, barges, and lighters to Hampton Court, ten miles upriver from London. Whitehall would be sweetened with fresh rushes mixed with herbs, the kitchens and jakes emptied and scrubbed and all made bearable for Christmas and Twelfth Night celebrations on their return.

A westerly storm rattled the long, elegant mullioned windows and howled around the corners of Cardinal Wolsey's great redbrick palace, which he had wisely and unhesitatingly given to King Henry when the king wondered aloud how a subject could be better housed than his king.

In this weather there could be no riding out or walking in the queen's walled garden, the charming private place that her father had made for her mother. Elizabeth loved all gardens, but this one was special, though she never mentioned its origins . . . or her mother's name aloud.

Queen Anne had been gone for fifty years, her head and body buried under the stones of St. Peter ad Vincula in the Tower precincts. King Henry had so successfully blackened her name, the common people still called her the Great Whore . . . though not where a bellman, catchpole, or other queen's officer could overhear, lest such outspoken opinion cost them their tongues.

Frances was shaken from her thinking by some hard-bitten words from Lady Stanley, standing in line next to her in the great state chamber. The lady had ignored Frances since the hunt.

"I near lost my post here because of you."

"How am I the cause?" Frances whispered in return, as a warning to the lady to lower her voice.

"You seek to charm the queen with your learning." The words, though soft in volume, were filled with malice.

"I seek nothing but to do my duty."

"None of your haughty language, Mistress Poet. Everyone knows your husband does not love you, but loves the lady Rich. You are cuckolded before the court, indeed before all of London. My lord Essex feels sorry for you. . . . Expect nothing more than pity from him."

It was plain that Lady Stanley tasted the words as if they were glazed in sugar by the confection kitchens. With a great effort, Frances kept her face calm, not looking at the woman whose deep bramble scratches were not quite healed, nor fully hidden by the white Mask of Youth.

Frustration in her manner, Lady Stanley deliberately bumped Frances as they stepped off the dais to wait for the queen's departure.

As Frances stumbled, Essex was there to grasp her arm.

Lady Stanley controlled her face. "What a gallant knight of old you are, my lord," she said. "We are so fortunate to have you to rescue us . . . first me and now this . . . gentle lady."

The earl turned his back on Lady Stanley, whose face flushed red under the mask and therefore showed bright pink.

He had a firm grip on Frances's shoulders with everyone in the presence watching. She shrugged against his hands. "I am quite steady now, my lord. Thank you."

Frances moved on, knowing she had made an enemy and now understanding why. Lady Stanley was one of Essex's conquests, and apparently unwilling to give him up, though Essex seemed eager to let her go. She felt some sorrow for Lady Stanley, knowing too well how deep the rejection of a woman's love could hurt.

On this All Hallows' Eve, Her Majesty did not sweep past the line of her ladies of the presence chamber on her way from her audiences, but stopped in front of Lady Sidney to raise her from a deep curtsy. Frances saw that this special attention from the queen was enough to attract many quick and wondering glances from the courtiers.

"Majesty?" Frances said.

"I see my lord Essex has a care for your safety, my lady, rescuing you from my tusker," she said, as if the boar hunt had taken place but hours before instead of two weeks earlier. The queen's steady dark blue, black-flecked eyes gave Frances no hint of her mood. "And now again, he has kept you from a hurt. He is very much a wandering troubadour of old, saving fair ladies from dragons and ogres . . . or in this case . . . wild boars."

At the queen's side, Leicester whispered in her ear, "Bess, my stepson is very young yet."

Frances did not wait for an argument to commence between the two, as it often did. "Your grace," she said, curtsying again, "I think your astounding crossbow shot was my Galahad. I thank you most humbly. Your great skill spared my life." Knowing the queen disliked any female rivals for a favorite's attention, Frances quickly added, "Sir Philip writes to me that he has asked my lord Essex to take special care of me at court."

"My nephew is a loving husband," the earl agreed, nodding.

"A *most* loving husband, your Sir Philip," the queen said, expressionless, leaving her meaning for a court guessing game.

"Majesty." Frances dipped another curtsy. She was unsure of the queen's intention. If Her Majesty was not plain and loud, her mood could be anything.

"I have talked with Dr. Dee about your interest in mathematics and Trithemius," the queen said. "Go to his quarters tomorrow at any time before the supper hour." She walked on with her train of ladies and courtiers, leaving Frances to hastily dip a knee.

Had Frances's mouth not been pursed in puzzlement at the queen's sly talk of Philip, it would have dropped open at Her Majesty's mention of Dr. Dee. Helping one of her ladies toward her ambition was rare in the queen. And she was not known for being a friend to women in the court.

Frances knew her father often brought Her Majesty most unpleasant news from his intelligencers and she was often vindictive. Could using his daughter to defy him be the queen's way of evening the score with Walsingham?

Whatever the truth, Frances bowed her head to hide a victorious smile: The queen's wishes must be obeyed.

Robert Pauley was waiting, as she had come to expect, just inside the hall outside the chamber. She looked forward to his being there each day, and felt a kind of anxiety if he were not, though she would never admit to such.

This morning he fell in behind her as they bowed and curtsied their way toward her rooms. She could hear his boots on the tiled floors . . . one firm step and one slower one. She wondered, not for the first time, what it cost him in strength and effort to walk with no more than a trace of stiffness. He limped only when he was very tired. Perhaps his natural dignity was why she heard no one except Essex mock him, though the Walsingham badge upon his sleeve was also protection against rude jests from the many young idlers at the court.

Frances spent hours after her noon meal writing a letter to Philip to be enclosed in the next diplomatic pouch going to Holland. She struggled to make it dutiful and interesting, mentioning the queen's attention, though not what had prompted it. If Frances knew anything of Philip, it was that he would not approve of her talking with Dr. Dee about ciphering.

Sweet Jesu, would this long day never end to allow the next one to begin, when she could go to Dee?

*F*rances was wrenched awake that night by her own terrified scream. Bolting upright in her bed, she clutched the bolster to her breasts. She tried to calm her ragged breathing before Jennet came rushing to her. She succeeded only in pressing her hands against her stomach to stop its roiling, though her stomach was not the part of her body that had been shaken by the vivid vision. Her night shift felt damp.

In the dream Essex had caught her in a dark corridor. Bright candlelight shone at both ends. There were people, music, even the queen dancing in the distance. But the earl did not care who saw him. "I cannot be denied now. I will have you. You know you want me," he said, and his white teeth were long and pointed, like tusks.

She tried to push him away, but she had no strength. Her dreaming arms seemed without bone or sinew. Was he right? Did she want him?

Then she felt him enter her, thrusting, grunting, and abruptly it was Philip above her, his eyes glazed and unseeing, as uncaring as ever he had been. The thrusts lasted forever until she screamed for him to stop, even if the queen should hear and see. But the queen had disappeared. The music had ceased. The dancers were gone. Full black descended about her, though she was aware of being carried to safety by Robert Pauley, her head tucked into his shoulder.

"My lady! Sssh, I am here."

Robert had her shoulders in a firm grip. She realized she was fighting him from fear and gulping in sobs of breath. He held tight to her. Gradually she stopped shaking, though she clutched at him. His arms folded about her and drew her into his chest, and she felt a very small tremor race through him. She knew then that she should draw away from Robert, but she could not leave such comfort.

"It was only a dream, Frances," he murmured so close to her ear his breath warmed her.

"It was so . . ." she said, unable to tell him more, having no words to explain what the dream meant even to herself.

"I know," he said gently. "It was vivid. Such night dreams are.

But it did not happen. Whatever frightened you was not real. This is real. You are in your own bed. You are safe. It is near morn." His arms tightened about her with each clipped sentence.

You are here and safe in my arms. She knew Robert had not said such words, but she heard them nonetheless. Had he wanted to say them? Had she wanted to hear them?

Other, fiercer thoughts tumbled about her head. She did not want such desire . . . not from Essex . . . Philip . . . nor any man. She had learned to live without a man's desire . . . even without her own desire. When such feelings came she pushed them away, knowing them to be as false as her marriage.

"I have my pallet in the antechamber," Robert explained softly, his arms loosening, setting her free, adrift. "There is nothing to ever cause you such fright."

Finally, she realized that she was losing his embrace, and more, that she was less comforted and safe without it. She did not want to leave such shelter, but she forced herself to withdraw, looking away, intensely aware that she wore only a thin night rail beneath his touch.

"Thank you. You may leave me now," she said, trying for her normal distance when she did not want any distance. The thought frightened her and provoked a determination to cease her cowering and be the mistress again, to keep her voice low and steady. "Pauley, call my maid without disturbing Jennet."

He nodded, stood and bowed, and withdrew.

She had never felt so alone.

When her maid came, Frances asked for her sponging bowl and sent her sleeping gown to her washerwoman before she remembered that Robert had called her by her Christian name. Then she couldn't forget the sound of it next to her ear, or what she had seen in his eyes . . . even the dim light could not hide . . . what? Only concern for a mistress. She could not go further with what his gaze could have meant, and with a will she cut off such thoughts, determined never to think them again.

"Mr. Secretary is to be with the queen this afternoon," Robert announced later when Frances once again emerged from her duties in the presence chamber. "Your hot dinner is waiting for you in your rooms, my lady."

She laughed. Hot food was a jest in Tudor palaces. "There is always more food than I can eat. You must join me." She was determined to act as if the comfort he had offered a mistress in distress was nothing out of the ordinary. Anything more would be unseemly and not to be considered.

She laughed again. "There will yet be enough left for humble pie to give the poor at the palace gate." When he did not reply, she added, "I do not ask you in duty, but for more amusing company than my own this day."

"As you wish, my lady."

There, she had assured him that she did not seek his company for any reason but her own entertainment. On second thought, she explained further. "My aunt eats in the great dining hall with the other gentlewomen, and I do not like to eat alone." Why did she need so many excuses? She could command him all day and he must obey. Yet could she command herself?

Robert did not reply for several minutes, until they turned into the corridor near her apartment. "Thank you, my lady," he said as if he had just retrieved his voice. "I will try to amuse you."

Frances breathed deeply. She had meant to set a distance between them, but now that his reserve matched her own, she was regretful. Why did she so insistently send a flawed message to Robert Pauley? And why did he consistently misunderstand her? Even if her words had been meant in a friendly guise, he was unused to friendliness from his betters. He would be naturally suspicious.

Bastards were never equals, or well treated, regardless of their merit. He had armored himself against disillusion just as she had shielded her heart against Philip's blinding love for Stella.

Did Robert suffer as she did? He was a man and would never speak of a sore heart. How strange that servant and mistress might have so much in common.

A kitchen under-cook was waiting with her supper. He bowed and left, the food now cold, but then it always was, because the huge kitchens were so prone to fires that they were banished to many levels below the royal chambers in all royal palaces and great manors.

"May I warm your dinner, my lady?"

"How?"

Robert pulled leather gloves from the pocket about his waist, donned them, and held the bowls over the candelabra. "Not hot, my lady," he said, "but not cold."

He made so many things easier for her. Of course, that was what a servant was for . . . so why did Robert seem so special? "Are you hungry?" Frances asked, snatching at some idle talk.

"Aye, my lady, though I would eat even if I were not. I learned to eat when I could or go hungry ofttimes."

"Then it is well you eat what you want of this meal. I have small appetite."

He held her chair for her, then lifted the first cover from its pewter plate, exposing a small bread coffin, the aroma making a lie of her professed small appetite.

"Soused pig, my lady, stuffed with a moor cock and with some boiled, spiced meats on the side." He lifted another cover, this time of pewter, and drew in a deep breath. "Baked capon pie," he announced.

She wrinkled her nose. "No fish? I do love fish instead of so much game."

"I will speak to the fish kitchen's master cook when next I go to the tiring room for Mr. Secretary's double ale. What would you like of this meal?"

"Capon, Robert, and thank you." She picked at the capon crust to open it for its spicy sauce and took a little more than usual. The crust was white manchet, and excellent. She relaxed, feeling quite comfortable now that Robert had not mentioned the morning . . . or what he had thought since. Nevertheless, that did not stop her from wondering.

"Thank you for coming to my aid this morning," she said, compelled for some reason to speak of it herself, but not looking directly at him, not wanting to read his face.

"You are most welcome, my lady," he answered, busy with his dinner. "My apologies for not being entertaining, Lady Frances. Would you like me to play for you?"

"No, you should eat your dinner while it is warm. I would not be so thoughtless a mistress."

He smiled. "You may ask anything of me, my lady," he said, and went to his pallet for his guitar. Returning, he said: "This is a happy country tune."

> *Heigh-ho, nobody home*
> *Meat, nor drink, nor money have I none.*
> *Still I will be merry . . .*

Robert nodded to her, and Frances joined in the refrain:

> *Still I will be merry . . .*

They both sang the next verse.

She laughed, thinking that she *was* merry, and grateful to him for lifting her mood. "Now I do insist you eat your dinner."

He took a little of each dish and placed it on his bread, wiping his knife before he cut with it. He chewed with his mouth closed and did not talk, nor take a bite before he had swallowed the last. His manners were impeccable and must have been learned at his noble father's table. She tried to imagine him as young and cared for in a fine manor. What hurt he had suffered to be turned out.

"You are quiet, Robert," she said, hating his silence after the music.

"Beg pardon, my lady. I do not wish to burden you with my talk." He took a drink of ale, wiped the rim politely, and set the glass in front of her again.

"Why would it burden me? Do you think my day so filled with interest, or riotous speech?" She realized her voice was too loud. "Now I beg *your* pardon, Robert."

"I understand perfectly, Lady Frances," he said, inclining his head toward a letter addressed to her husband but not sealed. "You must be concerned for Sir Philip's safety, now that the Earl of Leicester will soon leave for the Low Countries to take command. You called your husband's name in your sleep."

Was he watching her face for a response? "Yes, of course I am," Frances said, perhaps too quickly, glancing at his plate, from which he had eaten a little more than half. "But I am keeping you from your dinner."

"Not at all," he said, pushing his plate away and wiping his mouth on his handkerchief instead of his sleeve.

"The food is not to your liking, either?"

He shrugged, but kept his face pleasant. "While a brewer's apprentice, I learned to like pottage and workman's stews of potatoes, tomatoes, turnips, parsnips, and such in broth with a bread of rougher grain. I found myself with a quieter stomach and more vigor than when my meals were all too much of game."

"But food from under the earth is considered poor," she said, frowning.

"Perhaps by those who have not tasted it," he said. "Would you like to—"

Frances laughed. "Jennet would think you were poisoning me."

"The punishment for poisoning your mistress is the boiling death." He grinned to make the response, though true, a jest. "I like my food boiled, but that's as much heat as I desire."

"Robert, I will try your pottage . . . someday."

"When it is your wish, my lady, but now I must to your father's work."

"And I to Dr. Dee's chambers."

"I will escort you there, Lady Frances," Robert said. There were far too many rude young ne'er-do-wells with no better occupation than to trouble ladies without servants.

He would never have her waylaid, though she was no easily frightened ninny. Such duty befitted a servant, he told himself again . . . a servant who was fast becoming far more caring of her than he needed to be. He searched for a more truthful explanation, admitting that in spite of all his attempts to keep the distance demanded of his rank, he had been unable to maintain enough separation in his thoughts.

After he had held her trembling body in the night, he had felt the heat of her soft skin for hours. If she had branded him, he would have carried no more intense warmth.

Leading the way through corridors past the magnificent Chapel Royal, he stopped to look inside, as he always did, admiring again its hammer-beam roof and wonderful carvings everywhere. A quick glance revealed Frances's aunt Jennet kneeling at prayer in the transept shadows. He heard Frances catch her breath, and saw her turn and enter the chapel.

He followed and took his proper seat behind her, unable to look away from her white shoulders, slender but strong enough to carry her sadness. A beam from the high west-facing windows cast its light on her slender neck and the soft whiteness he was trying, and failing, to forget. Yet how could he ignore such loveliness when no one could see him? And why should he deny himself that small pleasure?

He waited for her to bow her head in prayer, but she did not, staring toward her aunt.

Then he saw what had turned her into the chapel and what she now must see with some horror: Jennet's fingers moving against her bodice as if she were saying the rosary of the old faith. Did she still secretly cling to the ancient ways? And in the queen's palace, where recusants were seen as traitors?

Robert knew what Mr. Secretary would do if he found a Catholic in his household. She would not be spared. His strict faith and dutiful reading of the law would not allow it, no matter how close in blood the woman was. For a moment Robert's mind was torn between duty and cruelly taking a beloved aunt from Frances. The moment passed as he realized he knew he could do no such thing. Refusing to wonder at a choice that made him equally a traitor, he tried to stop all such thoughts. Still, the sense of her so close was almost more than he could abide.

What he felt for Frances was not just the hopeless excitement of an impossible and even dangerous attachment. There were more of those in Elizabeth's court than he could count . . . even a high lady or two who would not mind a discreet tumble with him in any dark corridor. Yet he could think of no one but his mistress. *Fool!*

This madness had started in the coach on the way from Barn Elms. He had recognized something in her face, her eyes, something that he saw in his own mirror . . . betrayal.

Or could he have seen what he wanted to see?

He had to take his roving mind in hand. She was merely being kind to him. And she was a married woman, a queen's lady, and he . . . a bastard of low rank.

He clenched his fists, forbidding further runaway thoughts,

though he doubted the ban would last the day. She would come to
him again in the night.

Frances breathed deeply, inhaling incense, trying for a face
of solemn reverence, though she had long since had to
deliberately wear that mask. If the sacrament of marriage meant
nothing, then she had come to doubt all church ritual. Her rejection by Philip had ended in her rejection of the Church . . .
although she kept these feelings hidden and secret. In Elizabeth's
England, as in her father's house, it was best to follow the new
Protestant faith.

Before she moved on, Frances bowed her head as was right on
All Souls', praying for her mother's peace and hoping she was in
heaven, hoping there was a heaven, since there was no peace on this
earth. When she lifted her head, she saw she could not warn her
aunt now, but she would later.

Jennet knew that recusancy had been treason since 1570, when
Pope Gregory had excommunicated Elizabeth of England and
named her a heretic, thus allowing her assassination by any Catholic. In the pope's eyes it was no crime; nor would it prevent the
assassins' entry into eternity. The queen's life was now under daily
threat, and so were the lives of Catholics in her realm.

Frances glanced at Robert. Had he seen Jennet as she had?
When she turned to him, his head was bowed in prayer, but she
could not be certain. Would he take the tale to her father? He had
no cause to love Jennet. Yet Frances trusted him not to bring hurt
to her. It was blind faith, but she was convinced he would never
bring harm to anyone she loved.

Quickly, Frances rose and walked past the spectacular great
hall, with its high mullioned windows and walls covered with
Henry VIII's fantastical hunt tapestries, and stopped before Dr.
Dee's door. Robert knocked; a servant answered.

Frances had no more than spoken her name before Dr. Dee's

deep voice boomed from beyond the antechamber. "At last, my Lady Sidney, you honor me with a visit. I have been waiting for you."

"Good doctor, the queen gave me leave to come today."

"Yes, we have been quite busy with a new star chart that would foretell the progress of the Holland war draining Her Majesty's purse."

Nodding to acknowledge Robert, Dee strode into the room, doctor's robe billowing. He bowed and kissed her hand, his white beard sweeping across her arm. "You are most welcome, madam. My former pupil Sir Philip is indeed fortunate to have gained so beautiful a wife"—he took a quick breath and spoke on—"and, from what Her Majesty tells me, a lady of learning."

"The queen is too kind. I only *aspire* to learning."

"As do we all, madam." He paused and looked into her eyes. She thought he must have been very handsome as a youth, with his clear complexion and straight nose. His wide-set eyes yet had a sparkle, and she expected he would make very old bones.

"Doctor, I am most interested in ciphers."

He frowned. "I believe your interest is true, my lady, but as a friend of your father, I must pass a word of warning before we begin. Since I wrote the *Monas Hieroglyphica* more than twenty years ago, and more lately have delved into the world of spirits and angels, I have been suspect of trafficking in the realm of the devil. How much more would a lovely young woman like you be thought to do a witch's work?"

"Doctor, I am not afraid of the ignorant."

Dee smiled. "It is the ignorant we should most fear, my lady." Then he nodded. "But you are as I expected. The queen also said you were a woman of spirit." He pointed the way. "Come into my library. Master Pauley, you may wait here."

Robert bowed. "My pardon, Lady Frances, Dr. Dee, but I must attend on Mr. Secretary Walsingham."

"Of course," she said.

Dr. Dee nodded. "I will escort Lady Frances to her rooms," he said, and led Frances into the next chamber.

She looked back once, but Robert was quickly gone, the door closing behind him.

The room she entered was full of books and manuscripts in beautifully carved bookcases that stretched from floor to ceiling, their glass doors standing open. The doctor's library put the one at Barn Elms to shame. It was grand enough to take away her breath. "I have heard you have the best library in England, Doctor, and now I believe it."

"Many of my best volumes are at my home in Mortlake, near your manor of Barn Elms, my lady. You are most welcome there at any time." He swept his arm about him. "For now, please look as you like."

Frances began tracing her finger below the titles of the leather-bound books, astonished, thrilled, almost overcome by such treasures. Here was Dante's *Divine Comedy*; several of Erasmus's works, including *In Praise of Folly*; Sir Thomas More's *Utopia*; Boccaccio's *Decameron*; and Montaigne's *Essais*. She touched each one reverently and turned to Dee, who was smiling at her.

"By the light in your face, I see you are a true lover of books, my lady."

"Aye, good doctor, of certain books. I am not a one for"—she took in a cautious breath and looked about to see whether they were alone—"sermons or long tracts on religion, new or old."

"Sit yourself, my lady," he said, holding out a chair at a long table for her. "You will not find too many such here, unless the kabbalah is your interest."

She sat in the chair he held for her and wondered how she would broach the subject of his grille cipher she had heard so much about. She didn't have to.

"I understand from Her Majesty that you are your father's daughter and have his interests."

She smiled, relieved. "Yes, Dr. Dee, most interested. I have read Trithemius's *Steganographia*, but I wish to understand it better."

"Everyone needs a guide to Trithemius. His work is magical, though magic is simply gaining knowledge of the hidden forces that rule over nature."

"Book three is full of secret codes that I cannot divine."

"Do not despair, my lady. Many have tried to understand his ciphers, but no one has yet been able to break them, though I continue to try."

"Next, I am most interested in your grille code, if you would be so kind as to explain it."

Dr. Dee smiled. "Ah, and you could delight Sir Philip with a secret message."

Frances did not deny this idea, since it so pleased the doctor.

"I taught the grille cipher to him. It is quite simple and yet secure." He took a piece of vellum and scraped off the geometric figures of the previous drawing and turned it to the back. "This is the grille cipher I made for Philip; he will recognize it immediately."

Dipping a quill into his ink pot, Dr. Dee quickly drew a frame and then ten lines across and ten lines down, marking a number of squares. With a knife, he began to cut out the marked squares, leaving holes in the grille. "This is a very good method for short communication that cannot be read unless the other person has the same grille with identical squares cut out. If you wanted to write, 'Philip, come quickly by Twelfth Night. I must see you,' you would write your message in the random squares so that they appear as single or double letters on the sheet beneath."

Frances leaned forward, looking intently at the letters as they appeared under the open grille squares. Her heart seemed to swell inside her breast. It was simple, though secret as well, and she understood it readily.

"Then, good doctor, I would need to fill up the page beneath with a more innocent message so that my real meaning may not be read unless that person had the right grille."

"Excellent, my lady. You have a quick mind. It would, indeed, all be unremarkable to someone without the grille."

Frances smiled, thinking how surprised Philip would be to receive a grille message from her. Would he be angered? Yes, she decided, he probably would be, since she had entered a realm reserved for men.

She leaned back in her chair. "A grille message would be amusing, Doctor; I might do that, but . . . I am more interested in learning how to break ciphers of some length and seriousness." She took a deep breath. "You should know now that my father does not approve of my curiosity about ciphers." She had to be honest with him.

Dee sat back and stroked his pointed white beard. "And he is right to disapprove, my lady. Breaking ciphers is far more difficult than your interest in mathematics . . . and ofttimes more dangerous."

Frances tried hard to keep anger from her voice, though she did not hesitate to allow her disappointment to show. "I hope, good doctor, that you do not believe a woman's brain is too delicate for ciphers."

He smiled. "Once I did, but, my lady, I have been an agent for Her Majesty these too many years to think such now."

"Please tell me everything I should know." She heard the pleading in her tone, but did not care. She would sacrifice pride for knowledge.

"I cannot tell you everything, my lady."

She closed her eyes and heard her heart pounding in her ears. "You refuse to help me."

Dee smiled and raised a hand as if to wave away any misunderstanding. "No, no, not that. Ciphering is not something that can be completely told even by me . . . even by your father, Mr. Secretary." He took a deep breath, stirring his beard. "What I am saying is that *you* must do it, my lady. There are a few things I can tell you, but in the end you must have the head for it. To know that . . ."

"I do have the head for it!" Her voice was more excited than she intended. "At least, I must try, or never know for certain." She pleaded with him. "Please, Doctor, what is the knowledge I must have to begin?"

He leaned back, looking at her with an interest that had never lagged since she had first appeared at his door. He spoke in a low but clear voice. "First, you must determine in what language the message is most likely enciphered. Your father deals with English, French, Spanish, Italian, Latin, and German, and he has secretaries who know those languages. The Scots queen, even when writing in French, uses English words and Latin to confuse."

"I have no doubt my father's secretaries are most skilled, Doctor; nor do I seek to replace them . . . only to see, for myself, what I can do . . . especially with what the Scots queen is writing. She is a woman, after all. That might give me some advantage."

His face relaxed as she spoke. He understood as no one else had.

"There is nothing straightforward about ciphering, my lady. Have you heard of the bead cipher?"

"No," she answered, leaning forward.

"Different-colored beads or stones can stand for letters or numbers."

Frances was astonished. A bead cipher! How ingenious!

"But let us not complicate. We will study the most common letter-substitution ciphers. You see, in each language certain letters in the alphabet are more common."

"Yes?" she said, urging him on.

He smiled. "In English the letter e is most frequent, followed by t-a-o-n. In French, e is followed by s-a-i-t."

Frances looked about for a blank sheet. "May I write those down?"

"I will prepare charts for you to study, my lady, but it must be our secret. In the wrong hands, they could do harm. It is not meant for everyone to know these things."

Her reply was eager. "If I could not bury a secret knowledge, then I would make no good intelligencer."

"Women are not known to keep secrets, Lady Frances," he said, his mustache lifting in a tease.

Frances laughed a little, relaxing. "Good doctor, we do not tell all we know. You men would not like it." She became serious again. "But surely there must be more to ciphering than letters substituted for letters."

"Oh, there is, my lady. There are frequencies of double letters, but the way you thwart the decipherer is to not use them. Instead of double l, t, or s, use only one substituted letter to make your message less easy to decipher. That is not all. Always look for patterns, repetitions. And there are place-names and greetings that will give you clues if you know the sender, as your father usually does or has his suspicions."

"And if I were ciphering, I could disguise common names. . . ."

"Exactly, by using a number . . . or another symbol, previously agreed upon . . . which you will not know, but must guess. When you break a cipher, it is knowledge and intuition you need . . . with a blind man's luck mixed in."

Frances nodded, drinking it all in as if it slaked a great thirst. "London could be the number one . . . or wait, good doctor, that would be too obvious. Another number representing its rank in world cities."

"Agreed on by both parties, the sender and the receiver. That will make it more difficult for the decipherer . . . you, my lady."

She nodded, knowing that it would take trial and error, which made her all the more eager to begin. Now that she knew this much, she wanted most of all to try her hand—and head—to see whether she had the natural ability necessary. She thought so, felt it in her heart, but must see it on paper.

Dr. Dee talked on, so she had to restrain her impatience, wanting to begin immediately. "And, my lady, there are letters added that have no meaning at all, called 'nulls,' inserted just to confuse and make deciphering more difficult. And most difficult of all, Lady Frances, is to keep a cipher short. The longer the message, the more repetition, the more likely it can be broken."

"I will remember. I will remember everything, Doctor. But now I must leave you to your work." She had seen Dee eyeing an unfinished chart.

Following her glance, Dee nodded. "I am busy preparing the queen's chart of the planets' alignment, but I will make your ciphering chart next."

Frances nodded and pressed her lips together, excitement almost closing her throat, her mind on deciphering, on seeing random letters become a message of importance.

She wanted to start immediately, but suspected that she might have to wait longer than she wanted.

A real intelligencer would wait as long as necessary.

CHAPTER SIX

✍

"To you, to you, all song of praise is due,
Only in you my song begins and endeth."

—Astrophel and Stella, *Sir Philip Sidney*

✍

Early December

WHITEHALL PALACE, LONDON

In spite of the howling storm outside, Frances heard the door
to her rooms open and close. How was it possible that Robert had completed her father's task and returned so fast? Yet she
heard him move about near his pallet, soon followed by the soft
sounds of his guitar and his low voice singing a wishful song:

> *Now is the month of Maying*
> *When merry lads are playing,*
> *Each with his bonny lass*
> *Upon the greeny grass.*

She knew the popular madrigal and sang along in her softest
voice so that she finished the last line alone, hoping Robert had not
heard. Still, the words, the very thought of May, warmed her, as did

Robert's quick return. How had he become so indispensible to her in so short a time?

*R*obert heard her low, sweet voice, though he knew she had not meant him to hear. He understood that much, although nothing more of this madness that had come so hard upon him. Being this near to her again was worth the hard ride from the Essex coast, though it had nearly foundered two horses. He regretted never being able to tell her where he went or for how long. And it was just as well to spare her. Taking seizure orders from Walsingham to sheriffs about local Catholics was not work of which he was proud. Mr. Secretary demanded his quick return, although that was not the reason he had spurred through a night and day.

He tried not to dwell on the truth behind his haste. He did not dare, lest he betray himself and show a lover's face to his mistress. He refused to allow such thoughts to grow and be seen by many in this court who could read them only too well. If his emotions were discovered, with luck he would be dismissed from his intelligencer post. It was the least punishment he could expect. Without luck, he would be publicly flogged and openly laughed at, then sent away into his own hell, never to see her again.

He gripped the edge of his pallet. He must control his imaginings. She needed him, needed his care. He would put aside all these other feelings that he must forswear. Lady Frances Sidney was his master's daughter, married to a famous, if unworthy poet. Even now, she was probably in the next chamber writing to her faithless husband. Robert flung himself on his pallet and turned his face to the wall, hoping to sleep . . . demanding sleep of himself.

*W*hen Frances was certain that Robert had fallen into an exhausted sleep, she moved her writing table and chair nearer to the fireplace, its sparks rising into the night. She wore half gloves to keep the cold from her hands. Jennet, bless her, had placed a brazier behind her chair. Happily enveloped in warmth, Frances listened to the howling snowstorm outside the palace. No wonder Robert had returned so quickly.

This winter had grown cold enough to freeze the edges of the Thames; though watermen plied their boats midcurrent, they had to break the ice near the water steps on both the city and Southwark sides to discharge passengers. Merchants along Cheapside spoke happily of the possibility of a frost fair if the river froze solid, as it had in years past. Hopeful apprentice boys sharpened their bone skates in anticipation of the racing sport they might have.

Frances took up a quill and tried to turn her mind to writing the palace news to Philip.

The queen now suffered from a severe croup after her cold and foggy return downriver from Hampton Court to keep Christmastide at Whitehall. She longed loudly, between strangled breaths, for her well-loved and warmer palaces of Greenwich or Nonsuch, but they were too small to hold her holiday revels. Half the nobility of the realm, those not too old or infirm, had traveled with their retinues to Whitehall to deliver their Twelfth Night gifts to Elizabeth. The courtiers that Whitehall could not accommodate filled all the inns of London, Southwark, and the many noble houses along the Strand riverside.

Frances knew that Elizabeth would never forgo her Twelfth Night gifts, certainly not the jewels, nor the useful pearl-laden gowns and slippers made especially for her. If she was pleased, the giver might expect a rich wardship, or a high post in his county. Inferior gifts she would accept, but give to her faithful ladies and servants in the coming year. The queen wasted nothing.

Frances had asked Philip a month ago to send her black satin or damask or enough else for a new gown, but she had received no cloth.

The Earl of Leicester had at last made his escape to Holland with a splendid troop of horse, and even Elizabeth Tudor could not call him back from midchannel. Thus, she lay all unhappy in her privy bedchamber's huge bed, under its feathered and jeweled canopy, coughing and complaining mightily, cursing a clumsy lady who, with shaking hands, spilled Her Majesty's special sugary cough potion. When her physicians did not come to her or leave her fast enough, she threw whatever was at hand. Fortunately for them, whatever was at hand was usually an embroidered bright yellow or orange silk pillow, although once it was a bowl of lemons.

Dismissed with other ladies of the presence, Frances had sped from the stifling, overcrowded royal apartments back to her own chambers to work on her ciphering and, in truth, to wait for Robert.

Dr. Dee's packet of letter-frequency tables for English, French, and Spanish ciphers lay open on her table.

She began to draw up a cipher grille to send to Philip, but she put it aside, unfinished. It was a game but no real test for her. She longed for a true message to decipher. How else would she discover whether an intelligencer's head sat upon her shoulders?

In her outer chamber, she heard Robert Pauley leave his pallet and begin to softly strum his way through "Greensleeves," embellishing the short melodic lines of the old tune and making them his own.

Frances sighed and closed her eyes. At least Essex had stopped waylaying her to beg for walks in the gardens, which were now all bare trees, empty limbs reaching toward a cold sun. Instead he was in a long, brooding sulk, striding along with his head thrust down until every beautiful lady at court, except Frances, spent time cajoling him to dance, play at cards, or to be his old dazzlingly merry self. The queen thought him in mourning for her lost company, and no one disputed her.

But Lady Stanley had a theory about the lady he mourned, and whispered it about. She hinted that the lady in question was married to a poet and would be unable to resist the handsome earl for long.

Naturally, the news immediately attached to the lady Sidney had sped along the corridors and through the clustered, gabbling groups of courtiers down to servants and eventually to Aunt Jennet's ears.

Jennet had rushed to Frances one morning when she scarce had her eyes open from sleep. "You must do something," she demanded. "Tell your father. Find out where this calumny began. If this tittle-tattle is not stopped, your reputation will be at the mercy of every woman's mouth!"

Full of cold fury at Lady Stanley, Frances pushed words between her clenched teeth. "Aunt, I will not bother my lord father with this but will handle it myself. I know who says these things." She dressed hastily, but yet took great care with her gown and hair. In service to the queen, she wore the wig and wove in a pearl headband.

Both Robert and Jennet tried to dissuade her, or at least to accompany her, but Frances walked out alone and through the palace into the great room to find Lady Stanley amidst a group of chattering, simpering ladies.

"My lady Stanley," Frances called from a few paces away, "I would have private words with you . . . now."

All the ladies turned to see who was speaking, and some even covered smiles in anticipation of something far more interesting than their present exchanges.

With a look of expectation, Lady Stanley took one step toward Frances. "Welcome, Lady Sidney. By pure happenstance we were *not* speaking of you at this time," she said coyly. "Come join us; we have nothing to hide. Do we?" She looked about her as the other ladies smothered their nervous laughter.

Frances held her hands tight together before her, lest their shaking show her great anger and be seen as fear or guilt.

How best to answer? She must use the mind of a cipher expert to see where Lady Stanley was most vulnerable and strike where she least expected a hit.

"I come as a friend, Lady Stanley, with a caution. You have besmirched my lord Essex's name before the court. When he hears what you have said, he will not be the friend to you that you desire him to be."

Lady Stanley showed surprise at these words. They were obviously not the personal outrage she had expected. "My lord Essex? But you are . . ." She began twice, then seemed to lose her way. She no longer simpered, but looked from lady to lady for support. They were edging away, one pleading urgent business, others nodding hasty agreement, aware that they could not afford to offend the queen's favorite.

With mounting satisfaction that she kept from her face and voice, Frances delivered a second blow. "My lord Essex has been charged by my husband, Sir Philip, to have a care for me while I am at court. As well, Her Majesty knows and approves." Frances took a deep breath and, although her voice was low, she softened it yet again, since other courtiers had stopped and were looking on with interest. "Do you doubt the queen's wisdom, Lady Stanley?"

Finding herself standing alone, that lady lifted her chin in a futile gesture of defiance that few saw, since all looked on Frances with some reluctant admiration. Frances turned her back and walked away toward her rooms, though she was sorely tempted to turn for one last look at Lady Stanley standing alone amid whispering courtiers.

Robert waited just inside the corridor, his dark eyes showing approval followed by concern. "You have not heard the last from that lady. She now has a double reason to slander your name."

"I have no fear of such gossips; sooner or later they go too far and are caught up in a net of their own lies." She smiled at him to remove any sting from her words. "Would you not accept a risk for the pleasure of seeing such a lady exposed?"

"I would be sorely tempted, but, if you allow me, mistress . . .

the cornered creature is most to be feared because it acts blindly even against its own well-being."

Frances walked faster, not really wanting to hear, though she suspected he was right. "My lord Essex will surely make his wishes known to her when he is recovered," she said, insisting on the certainty she wanted to believe.

Robert did not reply.

That evening the wind swept in from the river Thames and howled around Whitehall's towers, shaking its oriel windows, making Frances's cold supper of whiting and cod from the fish kitchen feel even colder. Robert, true to his word, had talked to the master fish cook. As she held the dish over her candelabra, she thought to remember to thank him, not only for the fish but also for a way of warming cold food. Why hadn't she considered using candles that were everywhere in her chambers? In the future, she would think for herself and not depend on the way things had always been done. A cipherer's mind must be inventive.

Frances sat at her writing table, chin in hand, a much-used candle guttering low as she thought of a dozen more clever retorts for Lady Stanley. When she heard footsteps, she knew them to be Robert's without looking up.

His low voice came close to her ear. "My lady, if you will quietly follow me, I will take you to your father's offices."

She leaped to her feet, nearly colliding with him. She had been denied access to her father's offices for so long. This was her opportunity to question the cipherer Phelippes. "Do you speak true? Won't you make trouble for yourself?"

"Your father has gone to Barn Elms to see to his hounds, my lady. They have not been hunting for hares these many months and are grown fat and lazy. Mr. Secretary will not return for several days."

"But Father will surely learn of this . . . and . . . and censure you."

"That is true and his right, Lady Frances, but it could be no worse censure than hearing your sighs and seeing the deep frown making lines between your eyes."

She put a hand to the spot, but felt no lines. "You exaggerate."

"To make a lasting point one must always craft it larger."

She smiled. "Is that another of your truths?"

"It is now," he said, a wry twist to his mouth. "Follow me."

They walked past the lord treasurer William Cecil's rooms, where light burned late into every night. Next they descended a narrow stone stair to the guarded door that had been such a barrier to her since she had arrived at Whitehall these four months gone. This time, Robert Pauley's presence was her passkey, and the halberdiers opened the large oaken door, iron hinges creaking. They stood aside, their pikes raised in salute, lantern light glinting off the sharpened ax blades atop the weapons.

Frances stepped inside to a corridor of rooms marching back in succession, smelling of dust, vellum, ink pots, and a private jakes somewhere, fortunately out of sight. At least there was no sharp smell of smoke or tallow. Beeswax candles shone bright from a row of small writing tables, where the scratching quills of secretaries sounded like summer crickets calling their mates.

At a larger table in a corner of its own sat a man who held a paper sheet close to his eyes. Frances knew he must be Thomas Phelippes. Obviously shortsighted, he smiled on sight of her, rose, and bowed. He was a small man, his face pitted from the pox, his blond hair worn long, almost sweeping his shoulders. In spite of his commoner's face, his wide blue eyes shone with intelligence and curiosity.

He bowed. "My lady Sidney, welcome. I have heard from Pauley and Dr. Dee that you have an interest in my work."

Frances heard a low whispering from the other clerks until
Phelippes turned to stare them into silence. "I do, Master Phelippes, a very great interest." She took a steadying breath and told
the truth, always the best course. Even if truth startled, it was still
admired.

"I would be an intelligencer and decipher messages that
threaten the queen's peace." She saw what an effort it required for
the man not to laugh outright, and chose to ignore it. Sometimes
winning admiration took time.

She would be pleasant with Phelippes, while keeping her back
straight to remind him and all of the secretaries that she was born
a Walsingham.

*R*obert saw her body stiffen with determination that would
not be recognized by a chief cipherer, who had not
watched her every mood and move as he had. And remembered
each one, indeed was rarely free of remembering. Robert felt as if
he had watched Frances all his life. His senses were all the sharper
since he knew that he would spend the quiet times of his life with
these memories and nothing else. What strange mood had she
wrought on him? She was beautiful, but so were many women in
this court. She had humor and intelligence, but so did many courtiers. Elizabeth tolerated no mirthless dolts. Yes, Frances was trapped
in a loveless marriage, though she was far from the only such
woman. Still, what was so special about this woman—her determination, defiance even—was part of the attraction. They were alike
in yearning for their rightful place in life and in being denied it.

Robert shook off this mood that had been coming on him all
the days he had been away. He had been wary of affection since a
lad. Affection died or was betrayed. He would hold to that thought
until he could grip it no longer; then he would ask Mr. Secretary
to send him to France, Italy, Turkey . . . as far from these hopeless
thoughts as possible.

———

"*Y*ou are working on a message now," Frances said, nodding at the writing table in front of Phelippes.

"Aye, my lady. I do not think this message of great importance, but the cipher is new and must be broken. It will surely be used again."

Frances drew in a deep breath, gaining courage. "May I see it, Master Phelippes?"

"Well . . . ah . . ." He shrugged and looked about him, smiling, his eyebrows lifting in feigned helplessness. "I can see no harm in it. You are Dr. Dee's pupil; is that not so?"

She had not thought of herself in that way, but it was true, at least in part.

Phelippes spread his hand on the message. "We are flattered by your interest, my lady."

She nodded, though she knew the words were flattery without meaning.

A chair was brought to the table and a candelabra, which brightened the space and drew other cipher clerks to gather near this interesting break in their dawn-to-moonrise workday. She smiled a greeting at them and sat down, eager to see the cipher. Phelippes had neatly recopied the original on fresh vellum and begun to mark repeated combinations.

Frances quickly saw other repetitions. "These numbers could be nulls," she said, belatedly realizing that she had spoken her thought aloud. She hoped the man did not think her a know-all. "What language do you think, Master Phelippes?"

"Probably French, but it could be English. It's from the Catholic queen to the French ambassador, addressed to his secretary."

"Mary, queen of Scots," Frances whispered, amazed that she held a cipher recently from the hand of that woman . . . whore, murderess, and traitor, but once queen of both France and Scotland.

"Aye, she will never be done with her plots," Phelippes said, his lips drawn tight across his teeth, "but this time she may go too far, and even Her Majesty will no longer ignore her treason." There was grim determination in Phelippes's raised voice, as if he were tutoring her, and the secretaries moved in closer. "If not, we will—" He stopped abruptly, and Frances knew he had said more than he wished.

"The original will be resealed and sent on," he explained in a lighter tone. "It is an obvious advantage to your father that he has full understanding of the Catholic queen's plans, and that the traitors who plot with her do not know that we do."

"Why don't you arrest them before they can do actual harm?" Frances wondered aloud, although she suspected the answer.

"My lady, if the trap is sprung too soon, many will escape to plot again," Phelippes said. "That mistake was made with the Duke of Norfolk. The queen's leniency did not stop him, and he lost his head within a few years for plotting to rescue Queen Mary from the Earl of Shewsbury, who was guarding her. The duke then planned to lead an uprising to take England's throne. He put himself forward one time too often."

"Yes, of course." Frances thought she knew the answer to her next question, but she had to ask. "What will happen to these plotters?"

"Lady Frances, you know what happens to traitors who plan to kill our Protestant queen and put Catholic Mary on England's throne. They will die after we wring from them everything they know, especially who pays them for regicide and the betrayal of their country to Spain." His voice had risen and become determined, harder, pitiless.

Frances held her body tight to suppress a shiver of dread. She knew what a traitor's death meant: a racking so absolute that the man's broken body had to be dragged to Tyburn, after which he was carried to the scaffold to be hung, but cut down living and butchered like an animal while still alive, his entrails and manhood cut out and tossed on a brazier before his fading eyes. She had no desire for such entertainment, although she knew the road to Tyburn's tree was crowded with jeering Londoners seeking such bloody diversion.

"Do such thoughts trouble you, my lady?" he asked, squinting at her.

She shrugged, not trusting her voice, although hoping to reassure him. "I know the law and will follow it." An intelligencer could not be cowardly or shrink from duty.

Still, troubling questions raced through her mind. Did her own dear father and the English people have a cruel nature, brutal beyond even the Romans with their gladiators and crucifixions? Or had modern life in London formed them, where dogs baited bears in the pits and tore them to pieces while crowds cheered and chewed on hazelnuts? Death was everywhere in life. People succumbed to plague in the streets; country folk starved after bad harvest years. Half of the children born died before their fifth year. Had the English made the world, or had the world made them what they were?

And what would living the life of a spy do to Frances Walsingham?

She had been protected from such brutal truth, being a country lady. Would the knowledge gained from ciphers harden her, too? If so, she would welcome some hardening. Never to regret, never to care about what had been lost would be a blessing. Yes, that was what she wanted.

She was brought back to the present by the somewhat perplexed expression on Phelippes's face. She smiled to reassure him that she did not shrink from him or the law.

Now some of her father's overheard conversations made more sense to her. He was trying to entrap Queen Mary in a plot to kill the queen of England, and Phelippes would help him. Plotting the queen of England's death was the one thing that Elizabeth could never forgive her cousin. Proof of Mary's intent to supplant her was Walsingham's quest . . . and now his daughter's.

Frances pushed aside any further questions that might bring a fearful answer.

Phelippes lowered his voice and stared at his hands. "My lady, there is every indication that this present conspiracy is well financed with Spanish gold, and that some of the traitors have access to the court and possibly"—his voice grew even more confidential as he met her gaze—"even Queen Elizabeth's own person."

Frances felt her mouth open at that news. Traitors in Whitehall, perhaps someone she knew and saw every day? A picture of Aunt Jennet in the Chapel Royal came unbidden to her mind. She must talk with her aunt, warn her to take greater care. If she were seen by a Catholic plotter, they might try to recruit her, or at least report her to turn away suspicion from themselves. She dared not go further and think her very proper aunt could be a Catholic plotter herself! Tomorrow would not be too early to warn Jennet.

She returned once again to the ciphered message. "These must be common words," she said, looking more closely at the letter combinations, "and that would mean that these same letters could expose other common words."

"And thus break down the cipher entire," Phelippes agreed, apparently delighted with her quick understanding. "Yet, my lady, I urge you to caution. If they have made it easy for us to break, it could hide something we don't see. And remember, some symbols stand for whole words, and a few messages are doubly encrypted, though the same methods break them . . . if you are patient."

"I am patient," she said, although she was not certain whether that was as true as she wanted him to believe.

"And now, my lady," Phelippes said, leaning his chin on his hand in a familiar gesture that those who had suffered the pox used to hide their scars, "I beg pardon, but I must decipher this message and get to others even more important."

Frances leaned closer and spoke in a low, friendly voice. "Master Phelippes, I admire your skills above most men's. You need not hide the brave scars that marked you. I see them as proud symbols of your fight to survive to serve Her Majesty well, as you do."

Phelippes seemed startled, though he dropped his hand and his face relaxed its tension. "You are correct, my lady. It is not a becoming habit."

Pauley, who had been leaning against the shadowed wall, stepped forward and spoke in a low voice. "Perhaps, Master Phelippes, you could allow Lady Sidney to try her hand with this less important cipher. She is the most eager apprentice for this work that I have ever seen."

Phelippes's pale eyebrows rose in surprise, but then settled in agreement. "It looks to be one of the Scots queen's constant demands for cosmetics to hide her aging beauty," he replied, a little unkindly. He raised one shoulder briefly. "You may take it to your chambers, Lady Sidney," he said, "but you must allow no one to see it." He did not say, *especially Mr. Secretary*, but he looked behind him toward her father's empty writing table and his caution was clear.

"Of course, Master Intelligencer, I will guard it with my life."

"I doubt you need go to such lengths," he said, smiling at her.

Robert escorted her to her chambers and, without being asked, brought new candles for her candelabra. "My lady, I know you will wish to begin work immediately."

She looked up at him, the candlelight outlining his strong features, which she decided were handsomer than Essex's or even her husband's. "How do you know that?"

"It is your way."

His words pleased her. Though he had spent only a few short months in her service, he knew her better than most . . . she suspected better even than Jennet, certainly better than Philip.

Satisfied with that answer for now, Frances bent to the cipher.

CHAPTER SEVEN

~

"Doubt you to whom my Muse these notes intendeth,
Which now my breast o'ercharged to music lendeth?"

—Astrophel and Stella, *Sir Philip Sidney*

~

Christmastide

Frances stared into the three-branched candelabra on her writing table, captivated by its flickering flames. Why did lines from one of Philip's sonnets to Stella fill her mind whenever Robert softly played and hummed his music? Even when he was not present in the outer chamber, his voice sang through her mind along with Philip's words.

"Why are you frowning so, Frances?" Jennet, coming up beside her, spoke a little above a whisper so as not to startle.

"Just deep in thought, Aunt."

"You are thinking of Philip."

"Yes," Frances answered half truthfully.

"Write to him about the lady Stanley before the court gossip reaches him, as it surely will. There will be some who cannot wait to bring him such news under the guise of friendship."

"I have done so, Aunt." She did not add that she had not received Philip's reply, nor very much looked forward to one, which would probably place some blame on her for making such an unseemly spectacle of herself. And she did not tell Jennet how difficult it was to write to Philip at any time, even letters of court gossip and her work in the presence chamber. She had so little sense of him, sometimes even forgetting his features, requiring his miniature to remember his face. She would tell no one of this trick her mind played. She did not understand what so completely blocked memory of her own husband. The forgetting was no deliberate move on her part. It had just happened gradually over the last months, until now she had to think hard to remember his kindness . . . his guilty consideration.

"Please let us go and talk by the warm fire." Frances shivered involuntarily, aware of the bone-chilling cold of her chamber as she stood and took Jennet's hand. They walked to the upholstered chairs placed comfortably just far enough from the hearth to disperse the acrid odor of burning sea coal and save their slippers from flying sparks.

Frances motioned her maid to move a brazier closer behind them before dismissing her. This would be no conversation for a servant.

Pouring sweet Madeira into two glasses from an unstoppered green bottle, Frances offered the drink to Jennet and they both settled into their chairs. With a quick breath, Frances began: "There is something most urgent that I must warn you about."

"Warn me?" Aunt Jennet laughed, but shifted uneasily on her chair.

"I should have spoken earlier, but . . ."

"What is it, girl?" Jennet said, her voice testier than she probably meant, because she immediately smiled and shrugged.

"I saw you praying in the Chapel Royal."

Jennet, puzzled, started to interrupt.

"No, Aunt, hear me." She lowered her voice to little more than a whisper. "I saw your fingers moving against your breast as if . . . as if you were saying . . . rosary beads. Do you yet cling to the old faith in your heart and in Her Majesty's own palace . . . the queen who is governor of the Church of England? If so, do you not know the peril you invite?" Frances stopped for breath and for the look of anger on Jennet's white face.

Her aunt clasped her hands in her lap, her knuckles red from squeezing too hard. "Have you spoken of your suspicions to your father?" she asked, her head bowed, her chin pressing the pleats of her neck ruff flat.

"No. But I must warn you—"

"There is no need." Jennet sat rigid, staring into the fire. "I was but a young girl, but I remember the burnings at Smithfield during Queen Mary Tudor's time, and I heard of those when Henry the Eighth forsook Rome."

"Jenney, the queen would never . . ."

"Never? I take no chances. Long ago, I had a physician make some poison capsules for me to kill rats. I have them always with me."

Frances shivered. "But you would not—"

"I will tell you, niece, what I would not, and that is . . . burn. I haven't the courage of those who have done so. I would recant and lose my life and heaven altogether."

Frances put both hands high on her stomacher to press against her heart. "Aunt, think what you say! Her Majesty has not given up all Catholic ways. The Chapel Royal has many candles and fine glass windows from the old days, a preacher who wears an alb . . . and choristers. It is even whispered that she keeps a crucifix in her cabinet, but she is queen . . . and you are not." Frances took a breath, her last argument on her tongue. "She is much criticized for these practices by the Puritans."

"One of them is your father, my brother-in-law," Jennet replied, her mouth drawn into a straight line. "I cannot forget, nor forgive this queen who has replaced the Holy Virgin Mother with herself, a false virgin."

Though Jennet had kept her voice low, Frances looked about warily, nervous in a palace where so many doors and walls had spies listening. "Have a care with such speech, Aunt."

"I have had much practice in hiding my speech."

Frances forged on. "Promise me that you will outwardly practice the new faith, or . . ."

Jennet pulled herself up in the chair. "Or? Would you report me, niece? See me sent to the Tower into the tender hands of the queen's torturers?"

Though her aunt's voice was low and calm, Frances was startled. "You know I would not," Frances answered, "but others could. My father has enemies. And now I have enemies. They look for all ways to reduce Walsingham influence and raise their own."

"Through me? A spinster nobody, unwanted, unneeded!" Jennet attempted a scornful laugh, but it strangled in her throat.

"Jennet! That is untrue, and you must know it. Why do you torment yourself so? Now promise me what I ask." Frances allowed her voice to rise, more fearful than ever for Jennet, who scarce hid her defiance. "You concealed your recusant ways at Barn Elms. It is even more important to hide them at Whitehall. Don't you realize that my father knows who plots against the queen's majesty? Should any plotters approach you, turn them away at once!"

"And deny my faith." Jennet nodded sadly and stood, her eyes half-shut as she looked long at Frances. "The pupil always becomes the teacher in the end." She drew a deep, trembling breath. "I will obey as I can, of course. I have no other choice, or lose my bed and bread." She dipped a knee. "May I be excused, my lady?"

"Jenney, please don't . . ."

Aunt Jennet, head high, body unnaturally stiff, walked toward her chamber, casting a large receding shadow against the paneled wall until she passed out of the light, her wooden heels thudding against the stone-paved floor.

What more could Frances do? She could send her aunt back to Barn Elms, but her father would object and question her. As for Jennet, she would never agree to return to Surrey, where she would have no meaningful occupation, and a good reason could not be found to put her there. Frances feared a distance had opened between them, one that might never be breached.

At once, she knew she could enlist Robert's help. He heard everything spoken and guessed at the unspoken. He would know whether Jennet's name was being used by other recusants, or was under suspicion in her father's office. Robert would not betray her father, but he would find a way to warn her. She knew that as surely as she knew she could trust him in all things. She wondered briefly when such trust had come to her, but she could not remember being without it.

Frances finished her wine, so sweet on her tongue at so bitter a moment. She sighed, stood, clutched up her skirts, and went to her writing table, moving the brazier closer as she went. Her shawl lay over the back of her chair. As she sat down, she snuggled into the thick, soft material.

Phelippes's copy of the substitution cipher from Mary of Scots lay concealed under her tapestry seat cushion.

She had slit one side of the tapestry and slipped the vellum underneath the sheep's-wool padding. The cushion hid the cipher nicely. Only Robert knew where she had put it, and he had nodded his approval. On her writing table she had a quire of paper, a sheet of which she withdrew. She retrieved the cipher and sharpened her quill.

Pulling the cipher to her, she studied each letter, identifying repetitions, though they had been broken into five-letter code groups to further confuse someone trying to break it. Since Phelippes had told her the message was meant for the French ambassador, Chateauneuf, she chanced that name underneath cipher letters, as they appeared three times together in the message, though all the letters were without spaces, to confuse.

The letters began to blur, and Frances leaned back and squeezed her eyes tight to rest them, then looked again.

GRPOCPJECJI

Then she saw the same letters repeated three times. Now Frances was certain she was right and had the name, Chateauneuf. Mary had not used a symbol for the name. A mistake!

Now Frances had nine letters deciphered, including two vowels.

On a separate page of the quire paper she wrote the alphabet and the cipher letters she was sure of underneath.

In the next hour, Frances counted the times each letter appeared and put them in numerical order from most instances to least. She knew she must account for a variety of spellings. Searching for repetitions, she assigned an English letter to some of them until she came to the middle of the cipher.

She listed the five-letter code groups meant to disguise the true length of the words.

TPFST YHCBO GRPFO NWQSG RFOTP WCZCL

There were several Ps, and she put an E under them, but later decided to try As, and saw that the first word must be Mary. Such a number of As would indicate either English or French. She was certain that the language was not Italian, but she would have to determine that no word ended in I to be sure.

At first she puzzled at the placement of some of the Es, in first, second, or last place, which suggested French. But many others suggested English. Thinking, she brushed the quill feathers back and forth against her cheek. Could Mary Stuart have written in both languages, alternating? The clever Scots queen was full of tricks, having attempted many daring escapes during her near eighteen years of imprisonment in England. Once, she had even tried to slide down a rope from her tower to the ground, jumping the last several feet, only to be caught almost immediately. Mary had no lack of courage, but good fortune did not cling to her.

A piece of sea coal fell from the grate, and a spark sizzled against the stone on the hearth. A quick look reassured Frances that it had not flamed on the turkey carpet placed under the chairs to warm slippered feet.

She stared for a long time at the cipher without making progress. Perhaps she did not have an intelligencer's brain after all. The thought was painful, like a blow to her head, but it might have to be confronted. Just not yet.

Upset and disappointed, her eyes blurring, she stood and paced the room until she heard the case clock strike a new hour. She spread her hands across her bodice against her roiling stomach at the thought of returning the message to Phelippes undeciphered. They would laugh at a woman who thought she had the brain of a man. Oh, they would not laugh in her face, but as soon as she left her father's office and for a good time after. Inevitably, the tale would make its way through the gossips to the entire court, even to the queen, who would think less of her. Elizabeth Tudor did not accept failure, since she never failed herself.

Frances felt her anger rise at the idea of such failure and returned to her writing table, determined not to give up. Not yet.

Staring at the cipher page, she saw something she had passed over. Some of the odd symbols that were not letters were repeated. They could stand for countries or names of rulers. One of them could be the king of Spain . . . another, the pope of Rome. The Scots queen had sought their help for years.

Where to start? Frances stared at the message until the letters began to blur and shift again. She leaned back against her chair and closed her eyes, only to open them wide a moment later. She had heard that Cordaillot had been appointed secretary to the French ambassador Chateauneuf. Surely, if this was indeed a true message about Mary's cosmetics, it would not be addressed to the ambassador, but to the secretary. And yet the repeated name had an N, meaning an E three letters from the end, and only one repeated letter. It could be an A if she were right and Mary's messages started with her name and title, as was usual for rulers.

Thrilled, she was now completely convinced that the letter was to the ambassador, at least in part, and had some importance. Phelippes had been wrong in that.

The name Cordaillot was repeated twice, and both times the name was run together with other words to further disguise it.

She wrote the name:

CORDAILLOT

She went on to other words that could be French and deciphered most of the name by its vowels. Her head in her hand, she worked on, determining that the Scots queen had indeed combined two messages, one a cosmetic order to Cordaillot, and within the message another, shorter one in English to the French ambassador.

She clapped her hands together in excitement.

"Did you call, my lady?"

It was Robert's voice at the doorway between her reception and her privy chamber.

"I did not know you had returned."

"You were deep in thought and I did not want to disturb you. May I pour you some ale, since you have been at dry work?"

"A hot cider would be even more welcome, thank you, Robert," Frances said, pulling her shawl about her shoulders, though she felt warmth enough in Robert's comforting presence.

"At once, as is my duty, Lady Frances."

She frowned. Why did he insist on such formality when they were alone? She did not ask him, fearing to appear foolish, or worse, in need of his friendship or sympathy.

He brought her a cup of cider. "May I be of any further service, my lady?" His body leaned away from her as he spoke, showing no eagerness to do more of her bidding.

There came a pounding on her outer chamber door.

"Are you welcoming visitors at this hour?"

"See who it is and tell them to return tomorrow, unless it is Mr. Secretary returned from Barn Elms early." Frances hoped it was not her father. He would require her attendance when she wanted only to work on the cipher, just as she was beginning to triumph over its mystery.

It was not her father at the door, but the Earl of Essex, and from his haughty tone he was in no mood to wait or be delayed by a servant.

Frances quickly slipped the cipher message and her worksheet into their hiding space as Essex, unbidden, strode into her privy chamber, holding his long French sword away from his longer legs. He was wearing a padded codpiece with a jeweled pin holding it to his shirt. From his right ear hung a large pendant pearl, and on his head a tall, pleated velvet crowned hat held a trailing peacock feather. Even in the dim firelight, no adornment could be missed.

"My lord." She stood and curtsied. "I am happy to see you in health again."

He put his hand over his heart. "God has answered my prayers," he said, and grinned in his charmingly boyish way, obviously relieved of the ill humors that had nearly brought an end to court revelry for a fortnight, dashing so many female expectations. "Lady Frances," he said, bowing over her unoffered hand, which he reached to grasp. "Great good news! The queen is recovered suddenly."

"I am gladdened to hear it," Frances answered, wondering why he would deliver the news in person, trying to remove her hand from his grip without success.

"Her Majesty wishes you to attend her at the tennis court with her other ladies tomorrow morn at ten of the clock." He beamed, his face proud and confident. "I am to play against that Devon upstart Walter Raleigh. The queen has wagered for both of us. She will never completely lose." He laughed fondly. "I have promised her that I will win; thus she will win twice, my money and my apology!"

"I am indeed happy that Her Majesty's health is so renewed," Frances said, attempting again to retrieve her hand.

"And you will be there, my lady?"

"Of course. The queen commands it."

He stepped closer until she felt his warm wine-scented breath carried on his whisper. "And, Frances, what if I command your attendance?"

She laughed lightly to relieve the tension with which the Earl of Essex always seemed to surround her, hoping to discourage any further advance. "Surely there are other agreeable young—"

He smiled again, his mouth tightening, and came closer still, until she could smell his lavender-scented clothes. "Oh, my lady, there are many women quite agreeable, believe me, beautiful women in plenty in this court. And there are interesting minds. Though it is rare to find both equal qualities in one woman." He glanced at her writing table. "And," he added, nodding at Robert, who approached closer, "not nearly so well guarded by a faithful cripple-leg manservant."

Frances finally pulled her hand away, betraying her anger. "My lord, cruelty does not endear you to me."

A knowing look swept his face. "Ah," he said. "You have a woman's gentle heart and feel pity for the man."

Frances thought to say nothing, then changed her mind. "I feel gratitude to a man whom my father holds in great faith—"

"Not as great as yours, Frances. There is talk already about a lady of rank with such a faithful shadow."

"There are idle tongues talking about every lady at this court, including the queen, my lord, most of it wishful braggadocio." She was angry now and no longer hiding it. She backed away.

The earl grabbed her arm and pulled her to him. "Lovely Frances," he murmured, "so far unobtained, but not, I think, forever unattainable." He took a trembling breath. "For that I pray. I will have you in the end. I see in your face that you know it already."

Frances shivered, despite the warmth of her shawl. "Sir, you are hurting me, and I must ask you to leave!" Again she smelled the heavy scent of sweet wine under the lavender pastille.

Robert was suddenly beside her, grasping Essex's hand and removing it. "My lord, I will show you to the door. It is late and the lady Frances is obviously weary. I wish you good fortune in your match tomorrow."

Essex glared at him, then threw back his head and laughed, although it was harsh humor.

Robert loosened his grip.

"You're an impudent fellow, Pauley, more than impudent. I could have you flogged for laying hands on me."

"I do my duty to my mistress, and mean no disrespect to you, my lord."

"Do you not?" He gave a shrug, and feigned amusement left his face. "This lady shows you mercy," he said, staring down at Robert. "I will show you none in future. Depend on it!"

Frances lowered her head, not wishing to say another word to Essex, nor to look into his face.

He bent over her hand again, his russet curls falling over his forehead. She was certain that he was aware of the handsome impression he made.

"Until the morrow morn, then, my lady," he murmured, his breath warm against her hand. He whirled about to look in Robert's face. "On my honor, you will regret your actions this day, churl."

After her outer door slammed, Robert escorted her the few steps to her writing table and replaced her cold cider with a new hot cup, the cinnamon and clove spices assaulting her nose, reviving her. Surely Robert must know that she did not invite the earl's attentions, that she held him in low esteem. "I am sorry that you—"

He looked into her face, his features softening, although she saw his eyes narrow.

"I would take such scorn from no man, lord or no, but for you, Frances."

She bowed her head, not knowing what to say to him, not knowing what she wanted to say. He had called her Frances without hesitation, as if it belonged on his tongue. She ought to issue a reproof, but she couldn't. He must not guess that, through weariness, she wanted to lean toward him, against him for strength.

"Shall I leave?" he asked.

"No," she answered immediately, then thought to add an excuse: "I fear he might return."

"No man whom you do not wish to see will ever pass me again, no matter how high his rank."

"Thank you, I . . . You must believe that I never want to see my lord Essex when he is in his cups, or in my private chamber."

*R*obert's heart pounded against his jerkin. He could see that it was important to her that he believe her words. Why? Did she care so much for his good opinion?

He wanted to say, *I honor you above all women*, but he said nothing, nor allowed her to see anything of what he was feeling.

He was uncertain of her own feelings. . . . Sometimes he thought that she . . . But no, it was his own desire he saw reflected in her eyes. Of a certainty, he would show her nothing but the face of a loyal servant. If he had been recognized as his father's son, all would be different. Then he would have a right to love her.

He almost shook himself. For a moment, he had forgotten that she had a husband, a famous husband. How could he forget? He sensed that she did not love Sir Philip Sidney. Whenever his name was mentioned, her face dimmed like the sun passing behind a cloud. Yet she was no less married.

Robert took a chair and watched her caress her cheek with her quill feathers as she studied the cipher.

"See, Robert, it is a message within a message. In English, the Scots queen tells her agents at a tavern . . . the Plough Inn . . . that she is to be moved to . . . I can't distinguish the name . . . on Christmas Eve."

"Chartley," Robert breathed. "The country estate of the Earl of Essex."

"Ah, my thanks, there is the C and Y deciphered."

Robert's stomach churned. How had Mary known that? Not even her keeper, Sir Amyas Paulet, had been told that a move from Tutbury was imminent. He knew only that he was to inspect the Earl of Essex's moated manor of Chartley in Staffordshire for its strength to withstand an attack. Knowing of the move could mean only that someone close to Mr. Secretary's plans was a traitor. Or perhaps the information had come from Burghley's office.

She frowned. "I'm near finished, but can you tell me why the Scots queen is being moved, and about this inn?"

"The Plough Inn is a hive of treason, Frances, and Mr. Secretary has had men there for some time. They are gradually gaining acceptance by Mary's plotters. As for the Scots queen, Mary complains about the cold at Tutbury, Paulet's manor, and Elizabeth agrees that she should be moved to a warmer place for the sake of her aching bones."

"And it's warmer at Essex's country manor?"

"Sir Paulet will be sent to determine its suitability."

She nodded and returned eagerly to her cipher.

Frances looked up at Robert, her face triumphant. "I can fill in so many words now and read the English lines." She drew a fresh sheet of paper and wrote one letter at a time as he looked on.

Mary, queen of England, Scotland, Ireland, and France, moved to Chartley Christmas Eve. Tell Babington to arrange rescue. All his requirements will be met, including the earldom.

Robert saw her shock to see that name. Sir Anthony Babington was handsome and wealthy. He came often to court and walked with the queen as one of a throng of young men she strolled with in her garden.

She turned to him, her eyes brimming with tears of happiness, her face showing pride. "Robert, I have deciphered an important message. I am an intelligencer."

"There is none better."

She blushed. "I hope you do not think I require such praise."

"I speak truth where I see it, Frances."

He reached for her free hand and covered it with his before he thought, before he could take a warning that came quickly as she turned to him.

Standing, he stood away from her and bowed. "My lady, I will escort you to your father's offices tomorrow early, after you have made a fair copy of the English message."

Robert left before Frances could speak, leaving the warmth of the chamber behind him.

CHAPTER EIGHT

⁂

"O Make in me those civil wars to cease;
I will good tribute pay, if thou do so."

—Astrophel and Stella, *Sir Philip Sidney*

Christmastide

The hour was very late when Frances finished the cipher and went to her bed, yet sleep came with difficulty. She did not want to watch Essex on the tennis court the following morn, even though his long, lean body and russet curls would be a handsome sight to see. If she paid him too much attention, the queen would be jealous. If she paid too little, Essex would be angered.

Frances had asked for none of it, but Essex wanted to make an impression. He was truthful about his desire to bed her. With such a confession, he obviously thought that she could be aroused to desire him.

The earl did not need to brag of his prowess. It was widely known that his presence was compelling; women were drawn to him. Why wasn't she? Was her heart truly dead for all time? She had thought so just short months before, but now some days and more nights she was unsure, though it wasn't Essex who troubled her heart.

What she longed for was warmth, closeness, wooing. . . . Who would blame her if she allowed a man of the court to give her ease? The court knew her husband did not love her and thought the less of her, thinking it a pitiful fault. If she gained the attention of some lord, even Lady Stanley would no longer heap scorn, pity, and scarce-hidden amusement upon her . . . the latter the worst insult of all.

But she could not, and sighed heavily into the bolster, knowing that the queen believed that all her ladies must be pure, her court the least licentious.

Frances shook herself to be rid of this dreaming. Her mind opposed it. She had more serious concerns. Time to put aside a woman's longing. There was no time for it.

She opened the bed curtains slightly and turned to her window, searching for the moon and stars, but found only heavy fog.

One thought brightened the darkness of her fortress bed, covered on all sides with thick curtains against the cold, which nonetheless seemed to creep in beside her: When early morning came, she would return her deciphered message to Phelippes. She hugged herself with the thought of the surprise on his face when he read the traitorous words of the Scots queen that Frances had pulled from the cipher. She felt no sorrow for Sir Anthony Babington, the conspirator whom Mary had named. He was often at court, even near the queen's person, all the while a viperous traitor ready to strike when ordered.

Was her work finished now? Would Phelippes dismiss her with a smile of thanks? She prayed not. She wanted to know what became of the coded information; she wanted to be a part of stalking and capturing the traitors at the Plough Inn. Would Phelippes think she asked too much? Of course he would. It was one thing to humor the master's daughter and another to have her take on the dangerous secret work of England's men.

She heard a soft groan and knew it was Robert deep in sleep beside the antechamber door, guarding her even as the palace remained silent. A faithful servant. Always there.

Even as she thought it, she turned restlessly against the linen sheets, her fingers pulling at a loose embroidery thread on her counterpane. Servant was all he could be, should be. . . . Still, she trusted him, trusted his strength, his warmth, and his kindness in this unkind court.

Frances had poured herself an extra glass of wine before retiring to bring on fast sleep, and yet she was wakeful, wondering what dreams would make Robert moan aloud. Perhaps she should go to him. A hot trembling surged through her, and she pushed such a thought from her, allowing herself to think on the subject no longer than a few seconds, finally snuggling into her pillow. She forced her eyes tight shut, hoping for sweet oblivion.

When she opened them again, there was a hazy light in her window. The thickest fog rolled away as she watched. The day promised to be bright for a January morn, if not truly sunny.

Donning her shift, gown, stomacher, and oversleeves, she had her maid dress her dark hair, since she refused to wear a hot, heavy red periwig.

Frances drank ale and ate some bread and cheese to break her fast, then cleaned her teeth with tooth soap and rough linen. She called for Robert but found he was already dressed and gone, his pallet neatly folded with a note addressed to her lying on top.

> *With apologies, my lady. Urgent business calls me*
> *away while you yet sleep.*

She would descend to her father's offices alone and quickly, lest she be late to leave with the queen and her ladies for the tennis court. She did not wish to anger the queen, whose dreadful temper had not, as yet, fallen on her.

Lighting a fresh candle, since many hall lanterns were burned low at this early hour, Frances hurried down dark halls and stairs until she reached the landing before her father's offices. She was pleased when the sleepy halberdiers on guard allowed her through without question.

It was bright inside, the long chamber's candles and lanterns newly lit, shedding yellow light over gray stone walls and herb-strewn floors. Only Phelippes and Robert were at work. They both stood and bowed to her in welcome.

She walked to Phelippes's desk, withdrawing the cipher and her deciphered copy from her stomacher. She laid both on his table.

"The Scots queen is deep in a plot, Master Phelippes."

"Let's see what you have for me, Lady Frances. Pauley, bring a chair for my lady."

When she was seated, Robert produced a small glass of ale and placed it by her hand. The chief cipher clerk stared at her written words, his lips moving. "Excellent . . . excellent. My lady, you do have the brain of an intelligencer. Mr. Secretary would be proud."

"Master Phelippes, such knowledge might worry him and aggravate his kidneys." She wanted her father to be proud, but it satisfied her that his chief secretary admired her work. And Robert. He was smiling at her. Yes, he truly knew what this triumph meant to her; he was the one person in the world who did. She felt less alone for his regard.

"Pauley, put more men to watch the Plough. Now is the time to get a man deep inside the group—Bernard Maude is a good choice . . . and he must let it be known that he is sympathetic to Mary Stuart. Maude should be to Temple Bar, close to the Inn, within the hour."

"I saw my lady break the cipher and sent our agents an hour ago . . . Maude for the inside and another to watch Maude," Robert answered.

"Good man."

Phelippes slapped the table, his blond hair still unruly from sleep, his face grim. "Mary Stuart will not escape us this time. This cipher will convince the queen, else I will . . ." He stopped short of finishing the thought and looked up as if remembering Frances of a sudden.

Will . . . what? she wondered. "What would it take, Master Phelippes, to convince Her Majesty to . . ." She could not say the words *order a queen's death*, but that was Phelippes's intent, she was certain, and no doubt her father's as well.

He shuffled paper sheets on his table and pretended not to hear her.

Apparently, the next move was not for her to know just yet, and so she did not press him. "Do you have another cipher for me?" she asked.

"Not now, my lady, but soon. Please go about the court as if you know nothing. If we have a traitor in these offices or close, he must not be aware that we have any knowledge of him."

Or *her*, she thought, unable to remove the idea of Jennet's clinging to the old religion.

She nodded, hiding her fears for Jennet. "Knowing nothing, Master Phelippes, will take no great ability. What do I know of what you plan?" Trying not to show her true disappointment, Frances stared at Robert. His answering look said without words to press the matter no further.

Robert opened the door for her, whispering, "Well-done, Frances. Phelippes is impressed."

"Not as much as I wished."

"Have patience. I will speak for you. For now, we must find our traitor."

She looked up into his face, his strong features lit by lantern light. He was her friend, but he was a man, too, with a man's limited expectation of women. "I will earn a position here, Robert." She saw he believed her and that he was troubled by the knowledge.

Frances left him and hastened to her apartment. "Aunt," she called, and Jennet appeared, also dressed and holding Frances's cloak.

"Have you been abroad this morn, Jennet?" Frances asked.

"Why would I be abroad on a cold morn when I have no business?"

"Last night, then?"

"Do you now think me a layabout woman?"

Frances had no answer without revealing why she asked. "Jennet, I must be with the queen."

Her aunt did not question Frances further, as she once would have done. There was a new understanding between them. They were less than they had been, and Frances regretted that, though it gave her more freedom.

"You will need your warm cloak, niece. The tennis court will be cold, and the winter garden is frosty and swept with icy breezes."

Obviously Jennet had overheard all of Essex's conversation last night, and Frances wondered what more she had heard, or seen, or guessed. She huddled inside the cloak, allowing Jennet to presume nothing. "Aunt, please accompany me to the royal chambers. I will feel easier for your presence."

"Sensible," said Jennet. "It is not wise for even married women to be in public alone, lest there be risk of rude talk."

Frances smiled, not as angered by Jennet's lapse into needless instruction as she once would have been.

Jennet left her with Her Majesty's other ladies of the presence gathered in the antechamber under the arras and a huge, overbearing portrait of the queen's father amid a cloud of varying scents. In minutes the gentlemen pensioners opened the wide double doors and the queen stepped from her privy chamber, faultless in dress, every feather, fur, and jewel catching and holding the light.

Frances sank into a low curtsy as the queen moved into the corridor behind gentlemen pensioners, drummers and trumpeters making way for her. Elizabeth demanded ceremony. No subject within her sight was allowed to forget for one moment that she was queen of these isles.

Frances Sidney could not help but admire Her Majesty. She followed at the rear of the royal entourage and longed for some of the queen's power to rearrange the world. She would elevate Robert to be her chief councilor. She smiled at the idea of always having a friend by her side, one who never scolded, except with good humor.

The entourage moved slowly from the palace into the Thames-side gardens lined with paths of different-colored sands, newly raked before the queen's morning passage. She came to her gardens early most mornings in summer, bringing her shears and a copy of *The Gardener's Labyrinth* with the newly added section on grafting.

Today, some palace gardeners worked between the parterres and fountains. The peach and apricot trees espaliered against warm redbrick walls had lost their leaves, but a few leaves still hung on a row of rosebushes inside the privet hedges. A lone, withered damask rose clung to a branch. The queen snipped it off and held it to her nose.

The Earl of Essex rushed up out of the tennis court and knelt before the queen, kissing her hem. "My lord, you did not attend me this morn," she said. Her voice was mockingly angry, but her smile was not. She swatted his head with the rose, and its aging petals fell about his shoulders. He plucked a petal off his cloak and, with his handsome young face smiling up at her, ate it, smacking his lips.

The queen smiled at him and playfully swatted him again, this time with her feather fan. All the ladies laughed in their turn. Essex was amusing when he chose to be. There was nothing of the drunken bad boy about him today, nor any sign he had been deep in his cups not hours earlier.

Her Majesty was still smiling as she passed into the tennis court and took her seat. Essex removed his doublet and laid it on the queen's lap to hold for him. It was a brash move, which could have earned him an angry tongue-lashing, but the queen's humor was high, and she laughed at the impetuous earl and waved him to the tennis court like the naughty boy she liked to think him.

Wondering about the queen's feelings for Essex, whether motherly or womanly or a confusion of both, Frances took a seat on the benches behind the queen with the other ladies. They all waited for the Earl of Essex's next outrage, since he seemed to have no sense of when enough was enough. The striped wooden floor of the tennis court lay below them, well lit with many lanterns and torches.

Frances had never seen a game of tennis, although she had a vague knowledge of the complex rules. Sir Walter Raleigh stood at the far end, his pointed beard and hair immaculately groomed, himself mature and handsome, a dark contrast to his opponent. Raleigh moved within the court opposite Essex. Both the players and their people bowed low before the queen in her high-backed chair. She waved her kerchief, signaling the game to begin.

Frances was surprised to see Robert standing courtside in front of the Essex attendants. As if to mock Frances, Essex shouted, *"Tenez!"* and ordered Robert to toss the ball. Essex needed a server in imitation of the queen's father. King Henry had not tossed his own ball, and neither could this earl be expected to toss a ball for himself. Essex did nothing without calculation. Was he comparing himself to a king for Elizabeth? Or punishing the common man who thwarted an earl's desire? Frances strained forward to look at Robert's face. He showed nothing of what he felt. He was a perfect intelligencer even when away from her father's offices.

Again, Frances leaned forward, this time to see the queen's face. At times she delighted in the earl's antics, at other times not at all. This time Elizabeth's face showed her attention, but nothing of what she thought, which might be more dangerous. Or might not. The queen herself had an intelligencer's face when she wished.

Raleigh threw off his embroidered doublet, which was even more magnificent than the earl's. His fine linen shirt was open to the waist, and some of the queen's ladies gasped at so much bare male chest and dark hair.

Sir Walter was known to spend fortunes on clothes, fortunes won from his piratical voyages to the New World that few nobles could match with their estate rents. Certainly not Essex, who was deep into debt, and owed the queen; his stepfather, the Earl of Leicester; and half the lenders at the Royal Exchange.

"Toss it well, churl," Essex called to Robert, loud enough to force a frown from Frances. She quickly made a blank of her face, since several ladies turned to see the effect of the earl's behavior on her.

Body erect, head high, Robert made a perfect toss, which Essex hit with his sheep-gut-strung racket against the three-sided penthouse behind Raleigh, who hit the ball back hard in his turn, and the game was on.

Frances did not know all the rules, but she could see that they were complex and open to argument from the followers of each player.

The queen applauded at every return, choosing no favorite. "Lady Sidney," Elizabeth said without turning to her, "my father built this court and played the game well . . . never losing."

"Yes, your grace, his skill remains legend."

A triumphant shout went up from the bystanders at both ends of the court. Raleigh had hit a very hard ball that bounced against the penthouse behind Essex and bounded almost to the center line toward Essex. For any other man, the point would have been lost, but his long legs stretched to reach the ball and pound it back toward Raleigh.

Essex shouted his triumph too soon. Raleigh returned the ball with equal vigor, advancing toward the middle line, menacing the earl's return. Frances could see that Essex was troubled. She knew that his pride would not allow him to lose in front of the queen. What would he do?

The returns of the hair-stuffed leather ball became harder and harder, both men taking chances. Essex had the advantage of legs that propelled him across the court with seeming ease. Raleigh had a steady maturity and broad-shouldered strength, which allowed him to make fewer rash moves. His very steadiness angered Essex into more reckless play that slowly put him on the losing side.

Angrily, he pointed to Robert and shouted, "Cripple-leg, Raleigh has paid you to ruin my game! Your toss is too high, intending for me to lose. Down on your knees and toss the ball well this time, or suffer mightily for it."

Frances held her breath. Robert was always in control of his temper, but Essex sorely tempted him beyond what a proud man should be expected to bear. Robert said nothing; nor did he comply with the earl's demand. Instantly, he turned his back on Essex and walked slowly toward the nearest door.

The queen's ladies gasped. Essex's face turned a dark, angry red and he grabbed up his sword, unsheathing it as he ran after Robert.

Her Majesty watched intently, as if in her great hall being entertained by her favorite comic actor, Will Kempe, dancing a wild jig.

Essex reached Robert at the moment he turned to meet the onslaught. His voice rang through the tennis court. "My lord, you have the advantage of me in rank and weapon, but such behavior shames you and I will not be party to it. I acted as your server for the sake of Mr. Secretary and Lady Sidney. But I am their man, never yours to ill use."

The earl, who had taken a step back, raised his sword. His face twisted with fury, his mouth gaping. "You will pay with your life—"

The queen rose to her feet. She stalked toward Essex, her eyes darkly terrible in their anger. "Hold! Dare you to draw a weapon in the presence of your queen?"

Arm raised, the earl froze at the sound of her voice, his face flaming as he saw Frances run to stand in front of Robert, her arms spread wide, protecting him.

The queen's voice raged over all. "My lord Essex, attend me at once!"

He sank to his knees. Regaining his voice from a heaving chest, he said, "Majesty, allow me to explain—"

"Attend me, my lord, without words. *Now!*" The queen's command was not to be denied, and Essex trailed after her like a whipped dog.

Two strong hands on her shoulders moved Frances aside.

"I do not need a woman for shield," Robert said, his voice not angry, but worse, cold and without friendship.

"I—I am sorry. I could not stand by."

"Why?"

She stammered out a few words. "I—I don't know."

"Don't you?"

"Truly, Robert. I feared for your life. I did not think—"

"Always a problem, my lady," he said, leaving her with those words.

A broadly smiling Lady Stanley approached Frances as she reluctantly joined the other ladies at the end of the queen's entourage. "Lady Frances, you do appear to be the center of all excitement these days. Sweet Jesu, the court cannot allow a day to go by without another whispered tale of your exploits. This one between the earl and your servant will last a fortnight."

Frances pressed her lips together, saying nothing, her ruff

hiding her reddening neck. She nodded slightly and continued walking.

"Oh, yes, I did forget me," Lady Stanley said over her shoulder as she passed Frances, amusement apparent in her every word and movement. "Her Majesty commands your attendance at three of the clock for a private audience." She laughed. "Say your prayers well, my lady."

*T*he hands on her case clock seemed to stand still until three in the afternoon. Frances saw no one but Jennet, who said nothing. Frances tried to eat dinner, but her throat closed on the first bite and she gagged on the second. It was useless. There was nothing to do but wait, imagining the worst: packing, calling for her carriage, arriving at Barn Elms in disgrace, the long winter ahead, years of winters stretching endlessly before her. And what would Philip hear? What would she say to him? Would she ever be an intelligencer . . . or see Robert Pauley again in this life?

Perhaps in this life, but not this day, or this week, as it happened. Word came from Phelippes that Robert had been sent on a mission for the queen to the south coast, his date of return unknown.

Frances did not try to divine what that could mean; rather, she did try, but could not be happy with any of the obvious answers.

She made her way to the royal apartment, leaving Jennet in the corridor before announcing herself. The doors to the queen's privy chamber opened minutes later, and Lady Sidney was ordered to attend upon the queen. She entered the huge room as the queen's ladies of the bedchamber exited through a side door with curious backward glances. Elizabeth sat on her throne chair and said no word of greeting.

Frances made a formal entry with three deep curtsies. She tried not to hold her breath lest she grow faint. Then she tried not to breathe too fast, lest her bosom rise and fall too quickly. A short prayer seemed to work best. For good luck, she chose one of the queen's own:

O Lord, make thy servant Elizabeth our queen to rejoice in thy strength; give her her heart's desire, and deny not the request of her lips, but prevent her with thine everlasting blessing . . . from sending me away, Frances finished with her own words.

"What say you, mistress?" Her Majesty said.

From her tone, it was not an invitation to speak, so Frances held her tongue against her teeth. Elizabeth did not like excuses, and what excuse was there? And for what?

"I have sent your servant away for a time to think upon his duty and upon his station, which I also urge upon you to preserve you from dishonor."

"Majesty, as you will."

"Aye, as I will. You do not ask after my lord Essex."

"No, Majesty, I do not."

Elizabeth's face relaxed some. "I have sent the young gamecock from the palace. He has fallen into a lapse of judgment, but then, you have full knowledge."

"And no liking for his behavior, Majesty." The words had escaped her before she could stop them. Frances then put on a blank face, since relief at the earl's going would not be any more appropriate than agreement with his actions.

"It is his earnest desire to join his stepfather, the Earl of Leicester, in the Low Countries. He wants to be a soldier, as do most young men as soon as they can grow their beards." The queen sighed and covered her face with her feather fan, the handle sparkling with pearls as white as her face.

Frances noticed that Her Majesty's eyes were sunken and dark ringed this day. This queen felt loss deeply, perhaps the more deeply because she could not speak of it. The Earl of Leicester was her lifelong confidant, and he was in Holland, and now her young favorite Essex was gone as well. Frances thought the queen suffered their absence intensely.

"My lady, do you have any behavior you wish to confess?"

Frances frowned. "I have behaved in no way to shame this court, myself, or my name, your grace."

"Knowing the ways of rash young men as I do," Elizabeth said with a slight lift of an eyebrow, "I have good reason to believe you . . . in the Essex matter."

Frances felt her body relax. Perhaps too soon.

"But," the queen continued, "knowing the hearts of young women as I also do, I have reason to warn you of an even more dangerous association . . . with your servant, Robert Pauley. There are those who have come to me with tales that make me not rejoice, but worry for your shame."

As never before, Frances felt the bone chill of the winter cold invading the stone walls of Whitehall Palace. What shame? What tales? She knew a bold move was important now. "Majesty, upon my oath as a Christian woman, I have given no reason for your worry. I do not know what others have said, only that my behavior is without stain. But if it please your grace to give me any and all instruction, I will listen as I would to a caring mother."

"You are bold today, Lady Frances, but clever, as I first thought. Of myself, I will say this for your ears alone: I have known unsuitable yearnings of the heart for men lesser than I. Although queen, I am a woman."

Frances bowed her head to hide her flaming face. Was the queen confessing something to her, which in itself was dangerous? Confessors always regretted their honesty. What was the queen intending with this?

Elizabeth rested her nervous fan in her lap. "I have heard of your work on the latest cipher from the Scots queen. Dr. Dee tells me your mind is quick and your desire strong. I do not tell secrets to those whose faith and silence I have not already tested. I would test yours, Frances Sidney."

Frances held her breath, not knowing what would come next.

"My lady, you have lost me my partner at cards. You shall take his place tonight for Primera. Come to me with a full purse, ready to fill mine."

"I am but a poor player at cards."

"Good!"

"I will come to you with pleasure, Majesty," Frances replied, forcing a smile. She curtsied, backed to the outer chamber, and made haste to her own.

Robert Pauley stepped from the shadows of her anteroom.

"Robert!" She was suddenly breathless.

"I am not here, but gone to Plymouth these two hours past."

"The queen said . . ."

"Aye, she could not punish an earl without placing a harsher sentence on me. Bless Jesu, I am too valuable to send to the Tower, so I am for Plymouth, but I will haste to return for Twelfth Night. You will not suffer that alone."

"Suffer?"

"Lady Rich will be playing a part with you."

Stella! "Lady Rich . . . with me?"

"The queen is not truly cruel, but she was persuaded to this by Essex as a great jest on the baroness. You must keep your wits about you."

"But I will need you."

"No, mistress, you will not. You are brave and quick-witted. You do not need me. But I will ride hard to return in time." He took her by the arms and held them tight for a moment, his face unreadable; then he was gone, quickly, into the shadows of the corridor.

Frances knew instantly that Robert was wrong this time. She did need him, more than she had ever realized.

CHAPTER NINE

❦

"He cannot love; No no, let him alone. . . .
They love indeed who quake to say they love."

—Astrophel and Stella, *Sir Philip Sidney*

Twelfth Night, January 6

N̄o no, let him alone. That line from her husband's sonnet could have been meant for her.

Yet she knew that she could not and did not truly desire to let Robert alone.

He had promised to return from the south coast by this day. Where was he? She felt her anger rise and her heels strike the stone floors a little too hard.

Wouldn't a good servant do as he had promised?

She straightened her shoulders and almost laughed aloud at her own counterfeit reasoning, her own clinging to that obsolete mistress/servant bond that had long ceased to be. Exactly when it had gone she could not remember; nor did she want to remember.

When had it happened that she, a married woman, Queen Elizabeth's lady of the presence chamber, and the daughter of one of the queen's most trusted and powerful advisors, had become dependent on a serving man? And more than dependent, she admitted, her breath quickening, wondering whether every courtier she passed could guess why her eyes shone so bright. She herself could scarce understand how such feeling had grown and why Robert so rarely was absent from her thoughts, though of late he seemed to stay more often from her presence.

Was she a fool? Did Robert dare harbor such emotions for her? Sometimes she thought there was more in his eyes than duty and admiration, but was this just a lonely woman's wishful fantasy?

Yea, he was kind and cared for her comfort and safety, but weren't those also the acts of a good serving man? What else could she want from him? She dared to answer that question only in the silence of her most secret self, and then to immediately lower her gaze lest it be read and understood.

She tightened her lips and clenched her fists, her nails pressing through her gloves, railing against this constant self-questioning. She knew she was drawing curious stares, even as a group of courtiers bowed and she curtsied in return. "I am on my way to practice for the Twelfth Night masque," she said in a light voice to explain her agitation, smiling for the curious.

Was the Baroness Rich forced to wait for her? Good! Let her wait, as once Frances had waited for Philip's return, carrying the woman's scent on his doublet and shirt.

The queen had kept her ladies about her long past the usual hour, though there was no formal audience this day. Her Majesty called for endless distractions to ease her mind, playing the lute, reading aloud, dancing a country jig, singing in six-part harmony as she played upon her glass virginals, a wonder of the age.

Lord Burghley had brought the queen distressing news of the war in the Low Countries. Leicester's army was ill fed and unpaid, many deserting because the Dutch refused to contribute their promised taxes or grant the agreed-upon supplies.

"As I knew it!" Elizabeth fumed. "They will beggar my treasury to save their own wealth." She stomped up and down her privy chamber, herbs and lavender crushed and scattered beneath her furious feet, her ladies staying well out of the way.

The queen sent a secretary to Burghley's quarters repeatedly to see whether a letter to her from Leicester had been mislaid, then stomped about some more, waiting for Burghley's answers that were never to her liking.

Frances had been gladdened to escape the queen's whirling fury, though she found no ease of mind in any place. Now, as she hurried to the entrance of the great hall, Dr. Dee stood in her path, his face troubled, both hands clutching a chart.

"My lady," he said, somewhat breathless, "I was making my way to your chambers."

"Good doctor, may we talk tomorrow? I am late now to practice for the masque at tonight's revels."

He reached for her hand and she gave it to him, allowing him to draw her aside.

"I must get immediate word to Philip, and your father will forward a letter from you faster than I can send it. I hear Walter Williams, Mr. Secretary's diplomatic messenger, is to leave for the coast of Holland later this very day."

The doctor's voice was urgent.

"Of a certainty, I will assist you as I can, but what troubles you so, Doctor?" As if she needed a cartload of other troubles.

His voice grew softer. "I have drawn up a star chart for Philip—"

"Aye, Doctor," Frances interrupted, a bit impatient. "Philip showed me the chart you drew for him in his student years."

Dr. Dee put a hand on her arm, his voice low and urgent. "Yes, yes, my lady, but this is a new chart, made just last night. He must know that he faces mortal danger at age thirty-one."

"But that—"

"—is his age now, aye. And the very reason he must be warned to take all care in battle. Like most soldiers, he is too eager for glory."

Frances could see that Dee was distressed, unusually so. "You mean the stars were wrong before?"

"The stars are never wrong," he answered, his white pointed beard lifting and falling with each urgent word, "but mortal man does not read the stars clearly at an early age." He looked about and lowered his voice even more. "I have talked to my angel, Oriel, and received this warning." Dee pressed the chart into her hands.

Frances nodded, knowing Dr. Dee could speak no more in public about the angel he called through an incantation with a candle before a scrying mirror. Many called it witchcraft, and he had faced harsh questioning once before, barely escaping death in Mary Tudor's reign for the burning offense. Still, Elizabeth often consulted the doctor with worrisome problems and when she wished to know the outcome of a difficult decision. No one dared accuse Her Majesty's astrologer outright, though some muttered against his ways.

"Promise you will get word to Philip in today's dispatches. With a good ship and an easterly gale, he could have it in short days."

Dee was so obviously distressed and in earnest that Frances could not ignore his request. "I promise you, good doctor, your new chart will be in the dispatches before the Twelfth Night feast hour. Worry no longer. Philip is not foolhardy." Perhaps in love, she thought, but surely not in battle.

"Pray it is so, since I can do no more," Dee said, bowing, then walking quickly away, his long tattered-edged robe swirling about his legs, dragging rushes along with it.

Moving into the great hall where tables were being set for the Twelfth Night feast, Frances saw a raised dais upon which the actors in Robert Greene's *Pandosto, or, The History of Dorastus and Fawnia* were milling about.

The play was about jealousy. Essex had obviously thought it a great joke and, just perhaps, a proper lesson for a lady who was unwilling to yield to his charms. The queen must have been easily persuaded, since she, too, loved to watch a pot boil as long as its heat did not reach her. Even a little vulgarity, as long as it was witty, was tolerated in this most perfect of courts.

Looking without appearing to look, Frances saw that the lady Rich was not yet on the stage. Was she ill? Or . . . more like, did she intend to make an entrance suitable for a baroness and the love idol of Sir Philip Sidney, the captivating Stella?

Frances took a deep breath and advanced on the stage, composing her face into a proud mask as she went, aware that all in the room were awaiting some interesting reaction. She would tolerate neither sympathy nor derision, nor give them more to gossip about. Nor would she have it reported to Essex that his scheme had succeeded. He would get no satisfaction from Frances Sidney this Twelfth Night.

The Baroness Rich was to play Bellaria, the chaste wife of Pandosto, the king of Bohemia, falsely accused by her jealous husband of unfaithfulness with his best friend, Egistus, the king of Sicilia.

Frances, knowing how Essex had delighted in casting these roles, was assigned the part of Pandosto's faithful handmaiden, Helen, who was ordered by the king to poison Egistus and Bellaria. It was a sympathetic part, because Helen could not bring herself to do the deed, a miscalculation on Essex's part, surely.

The playwright welcomed Frances onstage and gave her a copy of the handmaiden's part writ large, a smaller role, and that sure to please the lady Rich.

They began the rehearsal without her.

"Lady Sidney," Robert Greene told her, "you have a low, projecting, and yet agreeable voice, and it pleases me for you to read the introduction and scene changes, enhancing your small part." He held out a half quire of paper inked with words.

"Exactly so! Give the charming Lady Sidney more speeches, or she is ill used by this play," exclaimed a loud female voice.

Baroness Rich paused at the double carved doors, twitching at her jewels so that no one would miss them. At last she entered between bowing servants, her silver gown gold edged and hanging full about her, the gold exactly matching the shining blond of her hair. Her glowing eyes swept the great hall with slight interest until they rested on Frances. Her small smiling mouth, red against pale and perfect skin, opened in recognition. "Ah," she said, her smile widening to show straight white teeth.

The lady's beauty was all of England's ideal of perfection. Half the women in court used every known cosmetic pigment and ass's milk to approach Stella's flawless perfection, without touching it.

Frances determined anew to stubbornly keep her black hair, even if she stood out as a crow amongst a flock of doves. If she were not herself, she was everybody and nobody.

Although Frances had seen Philip's Stella at court in earlier times, Penelope Rich's radiant face and form seemed enhanced by the babes she had birthed almost every year since then. Was she charmed, beloved of the ancient gods as well as of men?

Frances was sore-tempted to believe the woman a witch, especially since the baroness approached her deliberately, softly smiling, ignoring everyone but Frances.

"My lady Sidney, how agreeable that we meet this Twelfth Night and entertain the court together."

Without so far uttering a word of our parts, Frances thought. Yet it would be unthinkable to turn away from the baroness. Frances dipped a curtsy and took her outstretched hand, no doubt disappointing the onlookers, who were leaning forward eagerly, expecting delightful female combat. Frances would never give them that satisfaction.

The rehearsal was over by two of the clock, and Frances escaped, claiming urgent business with her father.

"We will meet again for the masque," the Baroness Rich called after her.

"We will, Baroness," Frances replied, making a hasty curtsy. She was determined to keep her mind closed to everything but her part in the play. If Lady Rich would do the same all could be well. If not . . .

Frances hurried away to deliver Dr. Dee's chart to her father's office before his courier departed for the coast.

Her father, finally returned from attending his hounds at Barn Elms, denied Frances entry to his office. She dared not ask for Phelippes lest she raise her father's curiosity. With Robert gone, she knew nothing of what the intelligencers were finding at the Plough Inn. She passed Dee's chart to a halberdier with instructions that it was to be included in the next diplomatic pouch.

Once back at her chambers, she opened the door, hoping to see Robert returned. Her hope proved empty. Aunt Jennet sat by the fireplace, her body rocking to and fro, her head in her hands.

"Jenney," Frances called, and rushed to her side. "What is wrong? Are you ill? Come lie down with a cold compress."

"A compress will not cure this ache," Jennet said without looking up.

"Come, Aunt, what can be wrong?"

"I am accused!"

"Accused? How? Of what?"

"I do not know. Your father will not speak to me, but commands that I keep to these chambers."

"What have you—"

"Nothing! I have done nothing against my conscience."

That answered none of Frances's questions. It raised another. "But have you stood against the queen's law?"

Jennet stubbornly kept her silence. "Jesu help you!" Frances murmured, realizing the prayer was earnest, her first in months.

Jennet took a deep, trembling breath. "I have sent a note to a man who will help me to leave Whitehall and flee to France."

Frances dropped to the settle beside the hearth as if an unexpected blow had deprived her lungs of breath. Her eyes closed tight in pain. Pieces of her life seemed to be crumbling away.

Jennet searched for Frances's hand and lifted it to her lap. "My child, I have loved you like a mother for all these years, but I cannot forswear the true faith. Don't ask it of me. I fear the devils in the Tower may tempt me beyond my body's endurance soon enough."

"It cannot come to that, Aunt." The words were almost another prayer. "Who is this man who will help you?"

"I have never met him. A gentleman gave me the name if I was ever in danger of being accused."

Frances pulled at Jennet's oversleeve. "A gentleman . . . by the name of Sir Anthony Babington?"

Jennet's body jerked upright, her eyes wide and staring into Frances's face. "How do you know that name? Is he suspected?"

"A guess only. His family is known Catholic, though they pay the fine for not attending the English church." Frances rose quickly and went to Jennet's bedchamber, lifting a small chest from under the bedstead and throwing in gowns and cloaks and night shifts. "You must leave for Barn Elms at once. I will speak with the queen, beg her—"

"Never! It must not be known that you helped me . . . or know anything of this." When they heard a faint knock, Jennet turned her face toward the outer door. Fiercely, she clasped Frances to her, then grabbed up the small chest and disappeared into the darkened corridor, where a man in Babington livery waited to take her to safety before Frances could object further.

She sat down upon the bed, clutching at the bolster, her body shaking with sobs.

Robert found her thus short minutes later.

"What has happened, Frances?" he asked, kneeling before her.

"Jennet . . . is accused."

He looked about him. "Did she run?"

"Yes," Frances said as if with her last breath, "but where?"

"To a safe house, but running is an admission of guilt," Robert said, his face tired and dirt stained from hard riding.

She began to shake and clutch at Robert's sealskin cloak, which had shed much of the rain that was falling hard outside. "What can be done? What will my father do?"

He bit down on his lower lip. "There will be a hue and cry." He took a deep breath. "I must report what news I have from Plymouth and the south coast. We must keep a closer eye on Spain. Word comes from Cádiz that the harbor is full of shipping and provisioning. They will attack us when they have finished with Holland." His voice softened. "When I speak to Mr. Secretary, I will try to discover what I can about this sad business with your aunt."

"You came to me first?" She dared not make it a statement.

"I promised you to return this day."

"Did you? I had forgotten."

He laughed. "For an intelligencer, you are not a great pretender, my lady."

She smiled at being discovered . . . and changed the subject before she revealed how happy she was to have him close again. "I must play in the masque within a few hours and be at my best. Essex's sister . . ."

"Yes, Lady Rich will be there, but you will play your part well, as difficult as I know it to be."

His hands were warm on hers, and she believed him, lifting her chin.

———

*R*obert had never seen a more fearless woman. She was full of worry for her aunt and yet was forced to face the woman who had her husband's heart in front of the entire mocking court. Still, she went on with the tasks before her. When other women would have fallen in a faint, Frances remained strong.

For a single moment, he did not cast blame on Essex. What man could not love her . . . beautiful, stubborn, and resourceful? And married, he forced his mind to add another truth to the silent tribute. Yet he didn't blame himself for this hopeless love. He was a man and no saint. And she would never know from him how deep she had burrowed into his heart. He wouldn't heap his torment on her slender shoulders. He did not want her pity. Or would it be dismay?

He knew one thing: All the world's women, and he expected there would be many in his future, would never remove her from his heart. Robert acknowledged that he would search for one more woman to love and accepted that he would not find her.

He had ridden hard to return to Whitehall to keep his promise. The wintry roads from Plymouth were like Irish bogs, but with each labored, sucking hoofbeat, he had leaned forward, urging himself and his horse on past exhaustion toward the spire of St. Paul's rising above London in the distance. Toward Frances Sidney.

"My lady, I must report to your father," he said, standing and stepping back from her when he found his will weakening. "I will see you at the masque."

*S*he nodded, her eyes following him to the door of her outer chamber. Yes, the masque!

Mere hours later, the great hall was full of revelers. As Frances and her changing maid entered the door to the tiring room behind the raised dais, she could hear the musicians playing a lively galliard and dancers stomping, already full of ale and wine.

The music stopped, and with a scramble of feet the dancers returned to their benches.

Behind the scenes, Frances donned her flowing white gown of clinging silk, waited for her cue, then stepped onto the stage. Her eyes searched for the reassuring sight of Robert, but she could not find him.

Queen Elizabeth, magnificent in a jeweled gown under her royal canopy, turned toward Frances and lifted her hand in the royal signal to begin. Frances curtsied low, took a deep breath, and spoke the play's prologue.

> *Majesty, lords and gentles all, we present* Pandosto, *wherein is discovered that by means of sinister fortune, truth may be concealed yet by time is most manifestly revealed.*

Frances turned toward the queen seated alone at her high table, almost surrounded by servers from her kitchens. She took watered wine and waved them away.

> *Majesty, our play is pleasant for age to annoy drowsy thoughts, profitable for youth to eschew wanton pastimes, and bringing to both at last a desired content.*

She curtsied, and when the queen nodded, Frances exited stage right.

Immediately, Lady Rich, costumed as Pandosto's queen, Bellaria, in a flowing white gossamer gown covering only one shoulder, entered stage left followed by her dancing handmaidens. Everyone in the tiring room heard the audience gasp as one. Essex had chosen well for the chaste queen of Bohemia. Lady Rich could have been a golden, wingless angel come down to the Twelfth Night masque to teach the court the beauties of chastity. No one laughed, though Frances heard a traveling whisper of "Stella!"

How they must have anticipated watching the public performance of wife and mistress.

Frances ignored the whisper, controlling her face and body, outwardly tranquil.

The queen imagined her court virtuous, and her stern demeanor stopped the crowd's most outrageous comments.

The playwright, playing Pandosto, king of Bohemia, entered with Bellaria and announced all that must be done to make his dear friend Egistus, king of Sicilia, welcome to his court.

Endless servers and carvers from the flesh kitchens walked upon the stage bearing huge platters of turkeys, a boar, and the queen's swan still adorned in its feathers before they exited and delivered all to the Twelfth Night revelers' tables.

Egistus entered with his retinue. Pandosto embraced his dear friend and Bellaria did as well, smiling angelically over the handsome Egistus's shoulder, though the smile was made sly on her lips by an uplifted eyebrow. The audience erupted in laughter, expecting what was to come.

Soon, Pandosto, with many fearsome frowns, grew jealous of his friend and suspicious of his wife's easy friendship. His suspicions quickly turned to anger, then to hate with many evil looks. Both his wife and friend sought to determine what had angered the king so, but he refused to say, to their dismay.

Pandosto called Helen, his cup bearer, to him. "'My wife has proved unchaste, and my false friend, the king of Sicilia, would put a cuckold's horns on me.'"

Frances was able to act credibly distressed, since she knew how he felt, although she had never confronted Philip in like manner.

"'My king, Queen Bellaria is most honorable and chaste,'"

Helen insisted. Frances was able to put honesty into the words, although she thought it was probably the best acting of her life.

There was a thin trickle of laughter from the audience.

The king marched around the stage, his face bloated with anger. "'They must both pay for dishonoring me.'" He handed his cup bearer a flask. "'Administer this poison to them so that their lives be forfeit for their crimes.'"

Helen fell to her knees. "'Please, sire, by heavenly Apollo, ask anything of me but murder.'"

But Pandosto, gripped by jealousy, threatened Helen with painful death unless she obeyed.

All unknowing, Queen Bellaria was sitting with Egistus by a pond, watching her favorite swan, when Helen came upon them, white as death, thanks to an ample application of cerise from one of the queen's ladies behind the curtain.

"'Here comes your husband's faithful cup bearer,'" the Sicilian king announced, turning to Frances. "'What distresses you, Helen? My great friend the king of Bohemia has not been taken ill, has he?'"

With many moans and wringing of hands, as if unable to bear the burden of the crime she was to commit, Helen fell to her knees and confessed.

Egistus leaped to his feet.

Bellaria fell to the ground, then struggled to her feet and, with an anguished cry of innocence—a too-anguished cry that rang through the great hall—she leaped into the pool that was inches deep. The king of Sicilia pulled her out, searching for some dialogue, since Bellaria's attempt to drown herself was not in the script. The playwright as Pandosto, standing forward of this action, looked lost, turning first one way and then another.

The great hall was quiet, everyone leaning forward, not wanting to miss what Lady Rich would do next. But Frances was angry now. Not about to allow the woman to take over the play, Frances as Helen threw herself to her knees again, sobbing loudly over Bellaria's soggy body.

Lady Rich moved a shoulder slightly and deliberately exposed an ample breast, wet with a dripping, red nipple. She opened one eye. "No man is watching you now, Frances. They are watching me," she murmured out the side of her mouth.

"Aye, my lady, there is much of you to see."

"'I do not want to live if my dearest husband thinks me a wanton,'" shouted Bellaria, back on script, snatching up the goblet of poison from Helen's hand and downing it with a smack of her lips, about which she circled her pink tongue slowly.

The audience laughed until Queen Elizabeth held up a hand and stilled them.

Bellaria collapsed slowly and elegantly into a heap, one breast still peeping from her Grecian gown.

Egistus, obviously angered at the way he had been upstaged and forgetting most of his speech, declared Pandosto, king of Bohemia, his enemy and fled with his retinue back to Sicilia, vowing his innocence. He took Helen with him. Frances cast a triumphant glance back at Bellaria, now fortunately without dialogue, though her heaving breasts belied her pose as corpse.

When Pandosto heard that his wife, Bellaria, had knowingly drunk from the poison goblet, he rushed to her body and wailed out his woe with a few whispered complaints for Lady Rich's ear. Stella was making this tragedy of jealousy into a farce.

A large grave monument was wheeled onto the stage, its giant gilt letters pronounced by the grieving husband, sobbing on his knees:

> *Here lies entombed Bellaria fair,*
> *Falsely accused to be unchaste,*
> *Who ere thou be that passes by,*
> *Curse him that caused this queen to die.*

Frances entered and stopped by the king's grieving body, pointing with one hand:

> *Oh miserable Pandosto, what surer witness than*
> *conscience? What plague worse than jealousy?*
> *You have committed such a bloody thing, as repent*
> *you may, but recall you cannot.*

The players came upon the stage, including Lady Rich in a dry gown, her breasts enclosed on orders of Her Majesty. Many shouts of "Stella!" greeted her, as did thunderous applause when she curtsied to the audience. Frances also was appreciated, if not quite as enthusiastically. She cared less about the loudness of her applause than she loved the sight of Robert standing to do her honor.

The playwright was escorted to the queen's table and given a thin purse of coins, and the queen called for her musicians to strike a merry tune as the writer began to tell her about the second part of his play, where Pandosto and Egistus were reunited as friends.

Relieved to have her part performed and done, Frances was escorted to her father's table, where she took a seat next to him.

"Although I never see women players in the theaters, you did well, daughter. Was the queen pleased?"

"I think not, but I thank you for thinking well of me, Father. The Earl of Essex chose the play and players."

The spymaster seemed moved by this information. "The earl's attention honors you."

Frances's gaze swept the benches until she found Robert Pauley well below the giant silver salt shaped like a ship on wheels. That he was at her father's table indicated Mr. Secretary's high regard for the intelligencer.

The servers began bringing in the feast, which was no longer steaming hot. A boar's head covered in herbs and yew, a souse of pickled pig's feet and ears, and finally a huge turkey stuffed with a goose, stuffed with a chicken, stuffed with a partridge, and served in a bread coffin half the width of the table.

Frances had little appetite, and even the giant sugar plates and elaborate baskets filled with apricot comfits from the subtleties kitchen did not much tempt her.

"You have little appetite for a feast night, Frances," her father said. "Are you missing Philip this Twelfth Night?"

"Yes," she said, though she had not thought of him except for Stella's tomfoolery. Then she could not stop the truth from her lips. "But it is Jennet who concerns me most."

Her father's face became set in hard lines. "She is no longer your concern, daughter."

"But, Father, she—"

"—is now lodged in the Tower, after we raided that Catholic den of traitors. I will do—"

At this terrible news, Frances knew a sudden blackness sweep her eyes and she felt her body slipping away from the bench.

She knew nothing more until she awoke in her own bed, her arm in a bowl with the queen's doctor preparing to bleed her.

CHAPTER TEN

❧

"Absence will sure help, if I can learn how myself
To sunder, from what in my heart doth lie."

—Astrophel and Stella, *Sir Philip Sidney*

Candlemas, February 2

GREENWICH PALACE

Frances lay in her bed with newly warmed bricks heating her feet. Though she yet shivered, her heart was cold with doubt concerning Robert and worry for Jennet. Was her father sending Robert away? Was her aunt suffering tortures Frances dared not imagine? Could she hear agonized shrieks?

Though her father swore Jennet was yet untouched, Frances knew that the Tower touched every prisoner, driving some mad before they reached the hands of the torturers. Frances had heard enough about royal prisoners to imagine too well what agony it must be for Jennet, waiting in a dungeon cell for the guards to come and drag her to hell.

Would Jennet swallow her poison pill as she had planned, or lose the desperate courage she would need to follow her plan and give up any knowledge she had of other Catholics?

And, as too often for Frances, one trouble followed close on another. Robert's image near swamped her thoughts, leaving her every day without an essential support.

Yet a certain presence could hurt almost as much as a bitter absence. Essex had returned to England from the Low Countries with dispatches for Burghley and private letters for the queen from his stepfather, the Earl of Leicester. He was full of soldierly bravado, though he had not yet seen battle. From his swagger and the behavior of the swooning ladies in the court, including the queen's own ladies of the bedchamber, he might have returned thrice wounded and ten times decorated.

Frances did not think him a coward, but he was certainly a man who would snatch any benefit where he could, especially if it brought one of Elizabeth's pretty young ladies sliding into his bed at night. He complained loudly to his admirers that he got no sleep.

Frances opened the curtains and left the warmth of her bed for the hearth settle, where her slippers, shift, bodice, and gown were hanging to remove the chill. Noting that the time was near for her to join the queen's procession to the presence chamber, she hastily dressed and rushed to the royal apartments.

"My lady Sidney, I bring you good news from your husband, Sir Philip," Essex said, bowing to her in the presence chamber after the queen's audience and under her always watchful eye. He had put muscle on his long-limbed form and was beginning a beard, which did not please the queen. Frances thought Her Majesty preferred he remain a young boy . . . her boy.

And to Frances's mind, the beard was scraggly compared to Sir Walter Raleigh's very short curly beard with turned-down mustache to frame his sensuous lips. He had quickly taken Essex's place in the hearts of some ladies and was always near the throne, which did not please the earl at all. It contented the queen to have handsome young men vying for her attention.

Essex handed Frances a packet of letters, bowed, remarked on her apparent good health and on the first signs of spring, and walked away. He made no entreaties to visit her apartment or walk with her. Perhaps he was over his immature desire to swive every new court lady, or at least this one. He was affecting a reserve that Frances had no doubt he thought quite mature . . . and intriguing.

With relief, she took her letters and would return to her chamber to read them after seeing her father once more.

She had pleaded with him to show mercy to Jennet several times, without success. She must try again, now that he was almost recovered from his latest attack of the flux, the same that had troubled him for years.

Mr. Secretary was resting in his chambers, letters and documents spread before him on the counterpane, alone except for a doctor preparing an enema. He lectured as he mixed. "If a man have a flux then obviously his black bile humor is at fault and must be completely cleared from his body, even if it weakens him further."

Frances had heard this opinion many times, but still wondered at its sense, since purging always weakened and never strengthened. "Father, may we be alone?"

The doctor scowled. "Mr. Secretary, I have here a heavy decoction of privet, which is sovereign for all fluxes."

"Give it." Impatient, Mr. Secretary took the flask and, with his other hand, waved the doctor into an outer chamber. He turned to Frances, nodding at her packet of letters. "What news of Philip, daughter?"

"I have not read my letters as yet." She spread her shawl and covered the packet in her lap. His eyes narrowed into the black look that she had seen before and knew as a warning sign. "Father, I will give you all the news of Philip's comings and goings as soon as I read them, but I must—"

Censure was plain on his rigid mouth. "You should be reading your husband's letters now, as any good and loving wife would. If you have come to plead for your aunt, do not trouble me again with that unhappy matter."

Frances tried not to wring her hands, but she could project no calm. "Jennet was very wrong, Father, I agree most heartily, but she did no more than half the court and half of England."

His face became set into even harder lines. "Then we must build more and larger jails and hire new and better torturers, daughter. Rome shall never rule England or assassinate her queen while I live."

Frances thought, not for the first time, that her father might be a little at a loss for wits. Yet he was not finished and stared at her.

"The recusants are traitors all, many wishing to enthrone the Scots queen and give England up to Spain and the Inquisition. Frances, would you see an auto-da-fé in St. Paul's churchyard?" His face was set in a way that was meant to cease all her womanly chatter and concern. She knew she should leave off pleading, but she could not.

"Why, Father? Could you not send her to Barn—"

"Never again to my manor!" He closed his eyes and drank the privet draft, which soured his face further. "I am the queen's high servant and spymaster, and I cannot be seen to harbor a traitor . . . even if I desired to, which I do *not*. Jennet has forfeited my goodwill and her place in my household. If I am not seen to stand fast for the true Protestant faith and the saving of this realm, even in my own family, how can I do my work for God and queen?"

"But, Father—"

"Leave me at once, Frances, and speak no more on this matter. Jennet must be dead to you, as she is to me. Put her from your thoughts and trouble me no more. My work is pressing and such needless distraction—and from you, daughter, while I am ailing—

I would not have believed. . . ." His head fell back on the bolster and he closed his eyes. The doctor approached with his tubing, stopping any further censure.

Yet another question preyed upon Frances's mind. She leaned in to kiss her father's cheek. "Pauley, Father. Why is he gone from court more than he is here?" She had not meant to ask about Robert, but the words were out before she could stop them.

Mr. Secretary's chest heaved, expelling the last of his patience. "He asks for every difficult task and quite suddenly wants to be away from court."

She kept her face free of any emotion. Was Robert wearied of court life? Or of her?

"The man works like a fiend from hell. He does not displease me and has returned with most valuable information." Her father paused, smiling suddenly, and lowered his voice to a whisper. "Mary Stuart has been foolish enough to send her complete and new cipher to a recusant, and Pauley has intercepted and copied it, then sent it on. We will be able to read every treasonous word the woman writes. Yea, Robert Pauley is my most valuable intelligencer. Why do you ask, Frances?"

"No reason, Father." Though his words were like hammer blows to her ambition, she kissed him again and left, her head dutifully bowed. Yet her mind was full of sorrow. Phelippes would not need her now. Was her brief career as an intelligencer over? She determined to find a way to continue what she had started.

Her heart was full of reproof for Robert. For a moment, or perhaps more, she had wondered whether he had left court to escape any feelings he might have for her, but that was too much like one of Philip's sonnets. More likely he found being her servant too burdensome for him. Was she so demanding a mistress that he would run from her and make every opportunity to do so?

In the crowded corridor, she stumbled on an uneven stone,

drawing unwanted attention and concern from passersby. The court was always wary of sudden weakness, which could signal illness. Although the weather was still not warm enough for the plague or sweat, one could never be too cautious when living with two thousand people, though the fresh air sweeping from the channel was sweeter here in Greenwich than in London. And the fiery torches in every corridor kept disease at bay.

Frances waited until she was in her chambers before she allowed tears to form and fall. Had she failed in every way? Jennet was lost to her, and Robert had left and taken his friendship with him. Her father was immovable when he saw his duty so clearly. Frances doubted that even she, his only child, would escape his sense of justice if she should be tempted by the idols and saints of the popish Church.

As for Robert, she was at a loss to understand his behavior, or her own anger and distress, which were equal to or greater than the anguish she felt for Jennet.

Was she ready for Bedlam?

Frances sat near the hearth to read Philip's letters, though they would require writing to him when she had less and less to say. She broke the wax seal on the first one and read as the firelight flickered over the page. He asked about the Twelfth Night masque in several casual ways. She had written to him just the bare outlines of the play and that it had been well received. If he expected news of Stella, he would not receive such word from her. That would extend a good wife's duties beyond her limit.

But was she a good wife? Didn't a good wife need a good husband? She had tried to be what Philip and her father wanted her to be, but she felt less and less like a married woman now. And—she caught her breath at such a thought—she felt more and more like the young girl at Barn Elms who had yearned for her next meeting with a handsome poet, expecting so much from a man's love. Still, what she'd felt then was nothing compared to the ache she felt now, the one she dared not name.

Frances shook her head to rid it of such thoughts before they led to a place in her heart where she did not wish to go, to a door she could not open without releasing danger. If Robert could stay away, then she would have a similar strength.

From a green glass decanter, she poured a cup of Madeira and allowed the sweet, heavy liquid to fill her with warmth that the fire before her could not reach no matter how hot it burned.

Calmly, she suspected that Philip had heard from Lady Rich and wrote to her many times for each letter he received. He needed no further word on the lady from his wife, and she would dispatch none. She thought such things without rancor. She simply had no desire to play the stylish games that courtiers enjoyed, or ever again to play the naive wife.

Surprised, Frances heard Robert at the outer door and her new maid's greeting, the former one having taken ill and been sent to Barn Elms with the groom. The air in her chamber, no matter how befouled by the odor of sea coal, now carried the persistent scent of woods and earth and fresh air, Robert's scent. "Attend me when you will," she called softly, hoping he would hear her.

He appeared immediately, wearing a fresh shirt and doublet with the ties not completely done up. His hosen remained spattered from riding roads sodden from spring rains.

"Yes, my lady."

She half turned from him, hiding her eyes, fearful that he might see the joy no mistress should show. "Pleasant trip?"

"Your father was pleased."

"That's all that ever matters. . . ." The bitter words quavered and caught in her throat and she could not push out better ones, being now without breath or strength. Shaking, she leaned forward, and, to her shame, tears began to flow and her body to tremble.

———

*R*obert feared she would slip to the stone floor. He knelt to her before he could think better of it. His arms went about her, holding her up against his chest, her head buried in his shoulder.

The warmth of her slender body beset him with the hunger he had tried to escape, creating a stir in his trunk hose, and he did not dare to move his head for fear his lips would reach her cheek. The combined scent of Castilian olive oil soap and rosewater rinse in her hair tantalized his nose and was near to undoing him. "Do not weep, my lady. Your tears will break my heart."

"Ro-bert . . ." She sobbed now.

He held her limp body tighter. "What can I do? Tell me and it is done."

"Jennet. Can you help her? Help me? Take me to her, as you regard me."

"To the Tower? No, Frances. No, I cannot. But ask of me any other thing and—"

She took a deep, shuddering breath, and cried out, "You . . . you could not leave me alone . . . quite so often."

"Alone? But . . ." He could not go on pretending he did not understand her meaning. "I promise I will leave you . . . your service . . . no more than your father absolutely demands." His face was in her hair and he smelled the deep, infused rose fragrance in her long curls.

Do not leave me. These were words he had waited to hear from her sweet mouth, had dreamed of hearing. But still he forced himself to draw back. His heart was overbeating and he feared losing control, the tight curb that he had worked so hard to maintain all these months. When he felt himself losing the battle, he left the court for a stiff ride on deep-rutted roads, preferring the discomfort of a horse's back in mud and rain to the constant dull pain and cold, sleepless nights with Frances Sidney in the next chamber . . .

far above him in rank and another man's wife . . . forever beyond his reach, though not his thoughts and never his dreams.

Gently, he released her to sit back in her chair. Caution had begun to make its way to her face and into her great, gray eyes. She swallowed hard, pressing her lips together.

Robert stood. "My lady, forgive me. My concern overcame . . ." He could not go on trying to explain with words he could never make believable.

Frances smoothed her gown and searched for some escape from the danger of Robert's closeness. She found the safest subject of all. "Has the weather warmed?"

He coughed. "I was about to suggest a walk in the gardens. Freshened air and exercise will improve your—" He broke off what sounded like a physician's prescription and went on in a lighter, more companionable tone. "My lady, on my return to London today, I saw plows in the fields, though it be long past January plow day, and early lambs on unsteady legs. It is warming and green buds are sprouting at the ends of branches, tiny, green leaves emerging on rose stems. A warm cloak and pattens to protect your slippers will—"

"Yes," she said, too quickly. "The very thing to lift my spirit."

"I will follow you at the usual distance, my lady," he said, bowing.

Frances nodded without looking at him. He would see far too much and know too much. His gentleness had calmed her, but frightened her as well. She was drawn to the warmth of his tenderness like a newborn lamb to its mother.

He held the door open, then fell behind her as any good servant would when she set foot on the gravel garden path, teetering some in her high pattens. With a groan of impatience, she soon slipped out of them and set them beside the path to gather up on her return. "Better ruined slippers than a fall," she said, not looking back to where he had stopped well behind her. She walked on to the walled garden, breathing deep of air and earth freshened by a recent rain, sensing the heat of the pale sun, which warmed her anew as each cloud moved on.

Essex appeared from behind the wall, startling her. She shuddered a little inside at sight of the too-handsome face that was uncomfortably close to hers. How could one man create two such unlike feelings at once? He'd had this effect on her before: delight at his handsome face and dismay at what she saw there, repulsion and attraction. Yet despite his face and form and his undeniable appeal, she did not admire or trust him.

"Ah, my dear Frances, we both need an escape from the fetid bodies of servants and overbreathed air." He offered his arm, but she pretended not to notice. With a frown, he dropped it. His following words were those of a frustrated boy used to getting his way in all things. "Perhaps you prefer your cripple-leg as escort."

She faced him. "My lord, you speak such ill to no purpose."

"Oh, no, my lady Sidney, you are quite wrong. I have a purpose. I will loose the vile hold your servant has on you."

Robert stepped forward between them.

"My lord, you do offend Lady Frances."

"Who are you to teach me conduct! I give the lady a warning, which is my duty as lord in this court. There is no offense in duty." The earl put one hand on his sword, one of the new long French rapiers that were all the rage in fencing schools, his other hand coming to rest on a poniard.

Oh, dear God, no! Frances shuddered. Robert was armed with only a knife used for cutting his meat. And if he tried to fight a noble as a commoner, he would be taken in irons to the filthy and plague-ridden Fleet Prison next to the river Fleet, London's open sewer, running toward the Thames. There he would be thrown down into a deep cell where no light could penetrate.

Robert held his ground, facing the earl. "I am without a sword, as you see, my lord Essex."

"By Jesu, you play the hero for your mistress, and I will have none of it." In a swift move, Essex grabbed at his sword, sliding it out as if it were recently greased. "What you require in great measure, churl, is a lesson in humility before your betters!"

Robert's voice was low and strong, his body erect. "My lord, I *am* humble when before my betters."

Frances caught her breath, hoping Essex missed Robert's heavy meaning, or could not believe it. The latter proved to be true.

"Return to your work, you baseborn bastard! I will escort this lady as she deserves."

Robert bowed. "Beg pardon, my lord, but I cannot leave until dismissed by Lady Sidney."

Essex looked to Frances and saw no dismissal there. His face flushed an angry red and he raised the blade. The sun, full out now, glinted on its point. He advanced, the sword circling in front of Robert's face. "I'll leave you with a scar that will make your fine face fit for only a kitchen maid like your whore mother."

Though he did not cringe away, Frances saw Robert's face redden and a tremor shake him. A confrontation could no longer be avoided.

"My lord, you have spoken against my honor."

"Cripple-leg bastards have no honor!"

Heedless of the danger, Robert Pauley stepped forward.

Frances cried out. "No! Stop this at once!"

But both men were beyond hearing her.

A pile of pruned branches lay nearby, and she moved quickly to grab up a fair-size limb as big around as her wrist, and almost simultaneously jumped between the two men. She brandished her weapon at Essex. She had watched Philip and her father practice often enough. She knew the stance, the nine parries, and the lunge.

With her tree branch extended and her left arm gracefully positioned over her head, she smiled. "The queen has forbidden it, but if you seek a duel, my lord, then test *my* arm!"

Essex leaned his long frame backward, amazement fighting amusement on his attractive face. "That is a very threatening position, my dear Frances." His mouth was tight to control his smile. But caution was beyond him, and he finally erupted into laughter. "If you insist on calling me out, perhaps our engagement would be more fairly fought in a less public space, on satin sheets rather than on gravel." Now he smirked. "I'd like nothing more than to give you a lesson on how I could best you . . . and with what weapon." He so amused himself that he laughed aloud.

Robert, his face a study in control, said, "Lady Frances, I thank you for your kindness, but I have always fought my own battles." He slipped the branch from her hand. "Begging pardon, my lady, for laying on my hands, but I would place you out of danger, as is the duty of any good servant in your father's service." He lifted her with ease to safety beside the gravel path.

A silent prayer filled her heart. What had she brought about?

He turned to meet Essex. "My lord, I am ready for your rebuke." He threw the stick aside, his jaw set in firm lines.

Frances saw more courage in his face and form than she had ever witnessed in Essex, who, though taller and richly dressed in black velvet and beribboned trunk hose, was suddenly the much smaller and poorer man. She made sure her thoughts were written plain on her face.

With a grunt of disgust, Essex sheathed his rapier. "What gain for me in fighting a crippled groom of no consequence? I will have the queen dismiss you as a servant who does not know his place!" He turned to Frances and leaned down very close to her face, almost as if he might touch her with his lips.

She stood very still, unafraid.

"And, Lady Sidney, you will see more of my *swordplay* very

soon, I promise you." With those parting words, he walked away toward the palace, laughing most heartily.

Frances, so relieved that Robert had not taken a sword thrust for her, sagged toward the ground.

Robert caught her about the waist. "Again, I must beg your pardon for touching you, my lady," he said softly.

She bowed her head and with a full heart said, "You have not acted as other than a great gentleman. It is over, Robert. Let it be."

But the matter was not over, as Frances had hoped. Later that day, the queen sent for her.

In great haste, Frances penned a note for her father, briefly telling him what had happened in the garden, careful not to chastise Essex or praise Robert overmuch.

> *Lord Father, surely Robert is too necessary to your work to be sent from your service. Please beg the queen to be forgiving.*

Frances thought she was almost certain to be banished from court for creating such an unseemly scene. She walked none too swiftly to the royal apartment, its windows overlooking the river Thames and the gardens where she had lately been. Had the queen watched the tableau? The courage Frances had so recently felt rise in her heart was now absent as she approached the royal apartments. She would rather face Essex's sharp rapier than the queen's sharper tongue.

She found her father kneeling before the queen and curtsied deeply as the ladies-in-waiting left to avoid the anticipated explosion. Frances did not dare look in Her Majesty's face.

"Perhaps, my lady Sidney, you should cease your lessons with the French dancing masters and repair to the city fencing academies in Blackfriars."

Frances raised her eyes to see the quizzical look on the queen's face, which matched the tone of her voice. Yet there was more there. Elizabeth of England was amused—perhaps more than amused.

Her voice was tinged with mockery. "Perchance my lord Essex should return to Holland, where he can satisfy his appetite for warfare, although the Spanish will give him more swordplay than you, even more than he may desire." She raised her fan now to cover her mouth, which was twisting into a grin. "Perhaps I should even make you my official sword bearer, Lady Sidney."

A burst of laughter came from the adjoining room; her ladies were unable to stifle their amusement.

Frances's head sank lower into her chest. She wished to be in any other place and time but this one. Elizabeth, shaking with mirth and not ready to surrender her jest just yet, added, "I wonder if Sir Walter could use another good arm in my personal guard." Her fan came up to her face again. "I think a silver cuirass would suit that gown very well."

"Majesty, I—" Of all responses, laughter was the one that Frances had not anticipated. This Tudor queen could ever surprise. "Majesty," Frances began again, "I am always happy to serve you in any way you desire." It was all she could think to say.

Elizabeth did laugh aloud now, bringing some of her women sidling back into the chamber to witness this rare event. "Oh, I think I have enough men poseurs with their swords for one palace. What I lack are ladies with courage. You will stand closer in the presence chamber, Lady Sidney, since I find qualities in you that I quite like . . . though they are not what I demand of my ladies. Henceforth, you will confine your exercise to dancing and riding."

But Elizabeth had not finished. "And, Mr. Secretary, I take heed of your pleas for your man Pauley. He is indeed an intelligencer of spirit and worth. Yet it would be a good thing to have him restricted to his singular occupation in your service instead of also serving as your daughter's protector . . . when, indeed, she seems well able to protect herself." A low laugh rumbled in her throat, which she again covered with her fan. "I will place a guard at her door, since she seems to be honey to men." Her voice turned stern. "I will have a decorous court."

"Yes, Majesty, I will make it to be," Walsingham said, and bowed his way out of the royal apartments with Frances on his rigid arm. "Say nothing more, daughter."

They walked swiftly into the whispering crowd waiting in the outer chamber. When her father was momentarily detained by Baron Burghley, Frances was confronted by a furious Lady Stanley, who spoke low in half-bitten words.

"You gain attention in any way you can, Frances Sidney!"

Before Frances could respond, Lady Stanley spoke again. "I am widowed, my husband dying when he was cut for the kidney stone. I have come into my dower money and estates." She lifted her proud head. "My lord Essex will soon turn his attention to me."

Frances stopped, curtsied, and murmured, "I hope he does, Lady Stanley. I am most sorry to hear of your recent bereavement."

Her father retook her arm, bowed to Lady Stanley, and they left.

Frances wondered how long it would take Lady Stanley to write to Philip about this most recent adventure. As fast, she suspected, as the swiftest courier could reach the fastest ship crossing the channel to the northern ports of Holland.

Casting furtive glances at her father, she walked with him to her apartment. They stopped and she bowed her head, hoping for his blessing but expecting far worse. "Father, I—"

"Daughter," he said, his voice surprisingly soft, "there is no blame attached to you in this matter."

What? She thought she must have heard him wrongly.

He almost smiled. "I was once young, daughter, and remember that young men are ever led by their jealous cods."

"But Philip will hear."

"I will write and explain that there is no fault in you. In one way, I am proud, Frances, that you protected your servant as any good mistress should, especially one so valuable to my service. You have the Walsingham courage." He said the words somewhat reluctantly, and walked two steps toward his own chambers before turning back to her. "But don't make it a habit, daughter, or I will have to send you to train at Blackfriars fencing schools, as the queen commands." He did laugh then, a sound she rarely heard, and was still laughing as she entered her own apartment.

Her mind whirled. The queen's response was always unexpected, but not her father's. He never changed. She realized that she had seldom seen her father amused since her mother's death. Her mind filled with possible explanations, but she quickly came to an answer for his strange behavior. Yes, that must be it: He was proud that an earl was attracted to his daughter. Her father longed for a baronetcy, wishing to be ennobled for his work. She wished with all her heart that his advancement had not cost her the high price of losing Robert's service.

She opened her door onto a bower of spring blooms set in vases and pots and hanging from the walls.

Robert stood in the middle of her receiving chamber. He had turned late winter into spring for her. She was important to him, as she had not been to any other man. Her heart, which had been so empty for so long, was filled with his caring.

He had gathered his belongings to move from his corner pallet. His arms were full, his guitar slung over his shoulder; he was ready to quit her service. He bowed and gestured toward the flowers, his hand on his heart. "My lady, my hope is that you accept this poor offering for the trouble I caused . . . a better garden than the one you found earlier."

She was overwhelmed by his gift. "I am grateful. . . ."

"'Tis a trifle, my lady. I know the master of the hothouses and he gave them to me."

She feared tears might come, but blinked them away. "You are leaving as the queen ordered. Perhaps this is the best outcome." She did not mean the words, but she thought it best to say them with some sincerity.

He nodded and she walked past him and the bower he had made of her receiving chamber, her heart near to shattering.

As she passed him, his whisper was low, but went straight to her heart. "Since I cannot possibly be in more trouble than I already am, I would give you a last service. Be ready at nine of the clock and I will take you to the Tower."

She turned to him, her gaze questioning. "Robert, how can I allow you to risk all?"

He moved swiftly toward the door. "Until the ninth hour, my dearest lady . . . nine of the clock after full dark."

CHAPTER ELEVEN

❧

"Bliss, I will my bliss forbear,
Fearing, sweet, you to endanger."

—Astrophel and Stella, *Sir Philip Sidney*

❧

rances waited nervously, pacing in front of her windows
and watching the moon rise in the rain-washed sky over
the Thames running at ebb in front of Greenwich Palace. She waited
and watched, knowing that she was putting Robert at risk for his
livelihood, his freedom, perhaps even his life.

She longed to save Jennet, but at what price? Robert was no
longer her servant; both the queen and her lord father had commanded that he work only as an intelligencer. And still she relied
on his courage and friendship. She could not stop thinking about
the warmth and comfort of his arms about her as he left her in her
bower. Strange that in a few months she had come to think of him
as a good, even . . . yes, her *dearest* friend.

Not more. Nevermore. That would be impossible. The corner
that had once held him in her outer chamber seemed so dark now.

No sweet songs would ever be heard from there again, and she knew her life would be the lesser for it. Yet in the night, she would remember his guitar and his low, clear voice as if both were yet there.

Still, she must close her mind to all such imaginings.

Frances swathed herself in a black, hooded cloak, silently counting as her case clock struck the ninth hour.

Her sleepy maid, Meg by name, appeared at the bedchamber door carrying a candle and rubbing her eyes. "It is late, my lady. Should you not wait until the morrow?"

"Back to your bed, Meg. I will return anon from my business."

"Aye, my lady," she said, bobbing a curtsy, gladly seeking her warm pallet once again, for she would be up before dawn, setting the fire, replacing candles, freshening bed linen, brushing gowns, and hoping to break her fast in the servants' hall before all the food was eaten.

Not for the first time, Frances thought the girl too forward. Had she been sent by Mr. Secretary to report to him? Or by the queen? Or Essex?

Frances turned quickly away from thoughts that seemed to run wildly in every direction from good judgment. She doused the candelabra on her writing table, throwing the room into deep gloom, then opened her door a crack. Thanks be to God that the guard promised by the queen had not taken up his post as yet. While she crossed her fingers against such calamity, thinking what to pray next, Robert came quickly around the corner. He wore a large cloak and a rain-battered, wide-brimmed hat that shadowed his face, though she would know that strong jaw and wide, expressive mouth under his dark mustache anywhere.

"Are you still for this adventure, my lady?" he asked quietly, looking down at her.

"Yes," she whispered. "I trust you to guide me."

He nodded, and she thought she saw a slight smile as he took her hand, leading her quickly to back steps used by servants coming up from the kitchens below. His hand tightened on hers and they moved swiftly through the flesh kitchen, past a spit boy asleep on his crank at the fireplace.

They moved through an arch into another kitchen, where a baker preparing dough for tomorrow's bread looked up and grinned at Robert.

"Ho, Master Pauley! A good tumble ahead this night, hey."

Frances stiffened, then thought the man must be used to seeing gentlemen and ladies in search of dark spaces to hide their passions, perhaps even used to seeing Robert on other nights. How often and with what ladies? Some low maid, surely. She shrugged her uncaring, but her lungs felt too full and she realized she was holding her breath. Better the cook think whatever he pleased than that he know the true purpose of their night roaming.

"Are you known to this man?" Frances asked lightly when they reached the courtyard, as if she were hardly interested.

"Yes."

"But you are unconcerned. You have come this way at night before, I vow." She was prying into his life when she should not. And she did not even want to hear his true answer.

He denied nothing, and she took his silence as a confirmation. He was a man like any other, after all. Had she thought he was a monk? Or hoped? Why would she want to believe in his purity? The thought was ridiculous, and she pinched her arm hard to encourage remembrance of her rank.

Robert's hand tightened on hers as she tried to pull it away. "Do not forget our task, Lady Frances."

She said nothing until they approached the water gate. "I forget nothing, Robert." She had meant her tone to be uncaring, but it wavered. Since the Christmastide masque, her acting ability had declined, and this was no play about jealousy. It felt like truth. Yet why should she care what Robert did with his life?

"Stay here until I call you," he said, his breath touching her cheek with warmth.

He approached the two guards. "Ho, John. I'm for a night in London. A silver shilling for a boat and a promise of bad memory." He lowered his voice, but spoke with a bit of bravado. "The lady has a husband . . . unfortunately."

The guards laughed and one said, "Have a care, sir, but for another silver shilling you could buy my sister." He slapped Robert on the back. "Don't you know you could hire a Bankside whore for a month with such coin, begging your lady's pardon."

The guards tried to look under Frances's hood to determine her identity. Though her hand trembled, she held her hood tight about her head, half shielding her face.

Robert stepped in front of her. "Alas, no second shilling for your sweet sister, John." He winked and lowered his voice. "Perhaps another night, eh?" Firmly holding Frances's arm, he quickly helped her down slippery stone steps grown green with river slime to a boat tied to an iron ring. He handed her in and agreed on the waterman's price, though it was exorbitant.

The man whined in a high voice, "'Tis full night, sir, and I be rowin' against the tide." His whine rose. "And there be danger in the river."

"I'll pay your price, man; just dig in your oars."

Quickly, they moved into midstream, where the tide ran swift and cold air swept up from the channel.

Robert settled Frances, and when she shivered, he placed his arm and cloak tight about her shoulders. "To the Tower, waterman," he told the oarsman, who sat midway between them and the prow.

"Good sir, know ye not that the gates be locked at this hour?"

"We have business, waterman, which is none of yours."

"Beg pardon, sir." The boatman dug his oars deeper into the murky Thames, and the small boat struggled ahead.

Frances shivered as gulls shrieked overhead and the cold, wind-blown spray hit her face. Robert tightened his hold.

"Don't look out on the water, my lady. The river is a burial ground for those avoiding the cost of a churchyard, or to murderers hiding their crime to save them from a trip to Tyburn's dreadful tree."

Though his arm warmed her, she shivered violently again at the thought of ghastly dead bodies floating around her.

"You can yet change your mind," he murmured, close to her cheek.

She dared not turn to look at him, lest her lips graze his mouth. "You know I cannot."

"Yes, I do know that," he said.

The tide was beginning to turn now as the moon rose, allowing the waterman to let the current take him. "Which water stairs do ye seek, sir?"

"To Galley Key below the Tower, and wait for us."

"Aye, sir, but the waiting be costing ye another shilling."

Frances was outraged. "Thames watermen's prices are fixed by the lord mayor," she protested.

Robert held a finger to his mouth for quiet. "We need him to be here when we come out. That is more important now than a poor man taking advantage where he can."

"I will repay you all the coin you spend," she whispered fiercely.

Now she was glad of the chill wind that swirled about her, since it blew away the stench of the river so that it did not linger in her nose or on her clothes. She felt Robert's arm about her and knew she leaned too much into his yielding shoulder.

The Thames ran swift and they soon came to Galley Key. Frances heard the watchman's chant near the pier. She saw him approach holding his poled lantern: "Look well to your locks, fire, and your light, to the bane of thieves, and all will be well!"

From a nearby tavern, Frances heard the haunting notes of a hautbois, the city never sleeping.

The waterman tied his boat to the steps, and Robert helped Frances up and onto the constricted, muddy, and refuse-strewn street next to the Tower moat.

"Walk in the center channel, my lady. The rain has washed it clear and into the river."

They came upon a narrow bridge leading to the Bulwark gate. Robert rang the bell.

"Who rings?"

"Robert Pauley from Mr. Secretary Walsingham's office."

The iron gate swung open, leaving room enough for them to pass inside.

"I expected you sooner, Master Pauley, and alone."

Though Frances had trouble calming the tremors that raced through her, she stood straight, or hoped she did. She yet had reason enough to wonder why Robert had been expected. Perhaps he made regular trips here for her father, returning with whatever information had been gained by examination. At times, she knew, just the sight of the rack and pincers was enough to break down a prisoner's resistance. She thought Jennet was made of more resolve, though almost everyone babbled in the end. Some recusants and most of the Catholic priests resisted, some until their bodies were so broken they had to be dragged on sleds to a traitor's death at Tyburn.

Frances shook her head to rid it of such images. She would never watch the spectacle. No man deserved such a death.

Robert showed the guard, resplendent in the queen's red livery, a parchment with Mr. Secretary's red wax seal.

Frances held her breath until her throat ached. Had Robert used her father's seal to gain unlawful entry into the Tower? It was a capital offense, and she was the cause of it. She pulled on his cloak. "We must turn back at once," she whispered.

"Too late for regrets, my lady."

They followed the guard into an underground corridor as cold as frost.

Frances held back a few steps. "Robert, what were you think-ing? Do you not know what risk you take?"

"Did you think there was no peril when you asked me to save your aunt Jennet?"

His words, though not an accusation, hit her like so many stinging blows. She had not completely considered just how dan-gerous her request had been. Or had she, and ignored her own warnings? Was she so used to getting everything she wanted from servants that she thought of nothing but her own wishes? She could not be so selfish.

"Can we turn back?" She was willing to leave Jennet to her fate rather than risk Robert, who had no fault in this except trying to please a mistress.

"It is too late. I beg you, Frances, not to worry. All will be well."

"How can you say that? Do you mean to take Jennet from this place?"

"Yes."

"You will be caught and it will be my doing."

"Calm yourself, my lady," he said. "I will soon explain every-thing. You ask too many questions and will raise the guard's suspi-cion. You must trust me. Lower your voice, I beg you."

"I can lower it," she said, showing that she could, "but nothing will save you when they learn you have counterfeited my father's signature and seal to rescue a Catholic recusant. Hanging will be the best death you can hope for. I do not care about myself, or that I will be locked up in Barn Elms until my husband returns from Holland." She lost breath before she could finish the lie. She cared very much about being locked up in a distant house with bitter memories.

She dared not even think the words that were really on her mind. *And I will never see you again.* But there was no beginning or finishing of that thought.

"Yet," he said, glancing sideways, "you care about Jennet."

"Of course, but . . ."

"Are you trying to say that you care more for me?"

She squared her shoulders, fearing the direction his words were taking.

"Robert, it is a mistress's duty to care for her servants . . . all her servants."

"But I am no longer your servant."

"A former servant." Would he never cease his endless probing?

They walked through a maze of stone-walled corridors embedded with centuries of chill, up and down stairs worn by ancient boots, until they came to a long corridor with small iron-gated doorways on both sides, scarce wide enough to pass through into tiny cells.

Though she blamed herself for this muddle, she thought Robert mad. Then she knew herself to be just as mad, or close to it. Screams and groans and the odors of indescribable agony reached her before she could cover her ears, or clamp a hand over her mouth as bitter bile rose.

Robert's hand clasped her arm tighter still as he murmured, "If I did not know you to be brave, I would never have brought you here."

She straightened, stepping as erect as she could, and her hand fell away. Frances wanted him to hold tight to her arm, for warmth and to comfort her, but she could not ask. If he were daring so much as his life, she would have to find her own courage. She knew she had valor bred into her. Her mother had suffered greatly in three stillbirths and had died without a groan. Her father ailed and yet kept to his work. She had to take hold of her own daring, if not for her own sake, then for Robert's.

The guard stopped and turned to them, holding his lantern high. He pointed to a cell. "The prisoner you seek is in there."

"Thank you, yeoman. I will commend you to Mr. Secretary," Robert said, clapping him on the back and handing him a silver shilling.

Frances moved quickly to the barred cell door. "Jennet . . . Aunt . . ." she called, seeing no shape in the deep gloom.

A shadow moved in the dark. Rising from the straw, a filthy, bony woman, her gown in rags, crawled forward. "Frances?" she questioned. "Child . . . dear child, I thought never to see you again in this life."

"Dearest Jenney, what have they done to you? Are you hurt? Tortured?"

Holding to the bars with grimy hands and broken nails, Jennet pulled herself erect. "Starved and questioned," she said, stopping to wipe a trickle of blood from her dry, cracked lips, "but not put to the hot irons yet, although they have been shown to me . . . and more. . . ." She bent her forehead to rest it near Frances. "I cannot use my poison. My life is God's to take." She looked up at her niece. "Mayhap I will die first." Her voice carried a hopeful note that broke Frances's heart.

"No, Jennet, you will not die. We have come to take you from this place. Robert has arranged all." Frances pulled her cloak aside and, from the pocket tied about her waist, drew a cloth-wrapped piece of cheese and a small bread loaf. She pushed them through the bars.

For a moment, Aunt Jennet seemed as if she did not recognize what she held. "Food," she croaked, and fell on it, forgetting all the fine manners she had taught her young charge, and breaking anew her niece's heart.

"Robert," Frances whispered, aware the yeoman guard had moved too close for normal speech.

"Yes," he said. "It is time for us to leave."

Frances's voice shook. "Not without Jennet."

"No, not without her." He walked toward the guard and spoke quietly.

The man took out a ring of large keys and with one opened Jennet's cell door, motioning her forward. "Come out, woman. Mr. Secretary has decided to show you mercy."

For what seemed like hours to Frances, but could have been minutes, her aunt stared, unmoving, crumbs of bread and cheese scattered about her mouth. "Your father will take me back? I am leaving this hellish place?"

Frances looked to Robert, her joy mixed with a question. "Why didn't you tell me my father intended Jennet's release before we left Greenwich?"

"We had to look like a man and woman out for a lark. How could I trust that you would not—"

"You thought me so weak and silly that . . ."

"No, Frances." He took hard hold of her arm. "I thought you so loving that you would not be able to still your weeping. Leave off now. You may chastise me later if you still wish it."

"But my father . . . ?"

"Your father has come to realize that this is a stain on his family honor that it is better he remove in a happier way."

"Did you help him to realize the stain?"

"We both did. Now, enough talk. We must get to the boat before the cost drains my purse. The waterman will not expect another passenger and will see it as an opportunity."

Frances said no more, but took Jennet's bone-thin arm and helped her stumble through the corridors and down well-worn steps to the water gate and out to Galley Key. The boat waited there, swinging on its mooring rope.

As Robert had foretold, the waterman eyed the new passenger and held out his hand, which Robert filled with the last shilling in his possession and added sixpence to hasten the trip.

"Waterman, take us to the south side of the river below London Bridge to a ship, the *Rendsborg*, flying the Danish flag." He shook his head at Frances as soon as her mouth opened to question him.

He wrapped his own cloak about Jennet as she sat shivering, trying to tame her wild hair.

The sun was rising downriver, and the tide was running hard toward the channel. The waterman was skilled and steered confidently as they shot between the pillars of London Bridge.

They reached the ship as the anchor was being winched snug to the windward side, a lug sail unfurling to gain steerage, a loud voice shouting orders.

"Ho, the captain!" Robert shouted.

A bearded man leaned over the aft castle. "Aye!"

"Passenger for Calais."

"Who be ye?"

"The man and passenger you are expecting."

"Ye almost missed the tide."

"But I didn't. Toss a ladder over the side."

As the heavy rope ladder fell down amidships, Robert grasped it and held it steady. "Say your good-byes quickly."

Frances kissed Jennet, who seemed not to know as yet what was happening to her. "I will miss you, Aunt. Someday, perhaps . . ."

"Not in my life, niece, but I will pray for you each day I live."

"And I for you, to the same God."

Jennet looked hard at Robert, the blowing river mist already cleansing her face and bringing some color back to her cheeks. "Take my thanks, too, Robert Pauley," she said, relinquishing his cloak. "You are a better man than I knew."

"That is my lot, madam." Robert smiled slightly and handed her a sealed letter. "Money and the name and address of a recusant English family in Calais who have need of a governess." He hoisted her up to meet the hands of two seamen hanging easily over the side. Jennet was soon over the polished wood railing and standing on the deck of the already moving ship.

Frances waved while her aunt stared back at her, still unbelieving, until the lug sail filled and the ship moved down toward the channel.

Jennet, standing amidst the spars and rigging, her hair unpinned and whipping about her face, was no longer the prim lady she had been and insisted Frances should be. Aunt Jennet lifted her hand once and then was quickly gone, around a bend, out of sight.

"*B*ack to Greenwich quickly now," Robert ordered the waterman.

They moved along in silence for a time, except for the splash of oars to keep them centered in the river's tidal flow. He could no longer see the topsail of the *Rendsborg*, though he could see Frances straining for a last sight of the ship.

They faced the morning sun now slanting over the horizon.

"I regret the loss you suffer," he told Frances, hoping she would believe him.

"If not for you, I would have much more to regret." He heard the words, though her face was muffled in his cloak. Later, he hoped, he could find the exact place her lips had touched, and at the same time he damned himself for a brainless fool.

Although he said nothing, she spoke again. "You are the kindest, most valiant man I know, and I have not been so myself. I did not always appreciate Jennet, or know her worth. She was loyal to her faith and to me. I shall miss her always." The last words quavered on her tongue.

He smiled at her, hoping she would not cry. He did not trust himself not to embrace her if she did. "My lady, if you find need for guidance or lessons in behavior, you may seek me out. . . ."

She laughed, the tears disappearing in the river breeze. "You look like no nurse I ever saw, Master Pauley."

"Frances, intelligencers come in all disguises."

They sat in silence, cloaked in their own thoughts, until they bumped into the Greenwich water stairs.

They continued without speech, retracing their steps past curious guards, through kitchens, upstairs, until they reached her apartment. She took hold of his arm, not knowing how to thank him, or how to say good-bye. There would now be few opportunities to see him.

"Remember, if you ever need a friend, I—" Robert breathed in as if he were almost out of air. "Fare you well, my lady," he said, making a quick, respectful bow and walking away, at first slowly, then faster.

CHAPTER TWELVE

❧

"O unjust Fortune's sway,
Which can make me thus to leave you,
And from louts to run away!"

—Astrophel and Stella, *Sir Philip Sidney*

May Day, May 1

HAMPTON COURT

Mr. Secretary Walsingham kept Robert busy and generally far away from court, and from Frances, and had for months. She heard of him only through her father's chance remarks, or saw Robert for no more than fleeting moments in her father's bedchamber or crowded palace corridors, when amidst a throng. She could in no way speak to him as she desired. He did not appear to look her way. It was as well. What could he possibly say? In truth, how would she answer?

In private, she railed against what she tried not to acknowledge in public. She could not accept the reality of her feelings for her father's man, yet she could not deny them without becoming the most dreadful liar to herself.

She wanted him in her sight. At least she wanted to know where he was and when he'd return.

Countess Warwick, the queen's first lady of the bedchamber, had remarked how loose Frances's gown had become, though Frances had attempted to conceal it with a lacy shawl. She had no appetite for food, often drinking a simple of thistle in some wine for melancholia.

Frances, a married woman bound by the Church and all decent and polite custom, had to be faithful and true in thought and deed to a husband who did not love her. And worse, she was forced to turn her back on Robert Pauley, who did love her. Or did he? Though she could not forget his arms about her, the comfort of them, the thrill, no words of love had passed between them. Could she be merely a silly woman, no better than the kitchen maids yearning after stable boys?

And yet there had been more in those embraces, she was certain . . . most of the time.

She would never know Robert's thoughts now, and that was the heart's ache of it. They could be extreme sympathy, which she mistook for more out of some battered womanish hope for affection not yet quite dead under her breast. She tried to stanch her rampant wishes, but they flowed through her like the Thames at high tide, unstoppable by her will alone. She must find strength to thrust her own emotions deep down lest they show on her face, and the very observant Countess Warwick next to her in the presence chamber be made too aware of them.

She sighed. She had long practice in pushing feelings away, no matter how often they slipped back into her head. Perhaps every woman did, since a woman's emotions must first conform to her father's or husband's, or even her brother's. She had no right to own them for herself.

This day Frances had made her way through tapestry-hung halls to join Her Majesty's entourage to the presence chamber. She held herself upright, having little choice, encased as she was in a farthingale and many shifts.

Bright morning sun cast diamond outlines on the shining marble floor of Cardinal Wolsey's old palace. She liked her new place, away from Lady Stanley, closer to the queen's throne and next to the kind Countess of Warwick.

Fortunately, Her Majesty had nevermore mentioned Frances wearing a sword. Today, she had adorned herself with the string of matched pearls that Philip had sent for the third anniversary of their nuptials. At the last moment this morn, she had removed a small bunch of dried flowers from under her bolster. Like a young girl she had rescued them from the bower Robert had made of her receiving chamber that last day of his service, and had tucked them into her kirtle. She realized with a slight smile that her ornaments were as conflicted as her heart.

Leave off! she commanded, silently stopping her rambling thoughts. She must take care not to become a self-pitying creature, a pain to live with and a bore to befriend.

Anne Warwick put her hand on Frances's arm. Did her distress show so plainly?

Always the lady closest to the queen wherever she was, Anne was also the wife of the Earl of Leicester's brother, thus doubly tied to Elizabeth. The queen had been without Leicester's close comfort while he was in Holland these last many months. She would have him there as general of her army, but she would have him also by her side. Thus, Elizabeth was ever unhappy, often angered by what she herself had commanded.

Even a queen could not always have the man she wanted.

Elizabeth had not married the earl when young, but had never been quite able to let him go, despite the ugly suspicion by many that he had murdered his wife, Amy Robsart, or hired a stealthy murderer to break her neck. The scandal had ruined any hopes Leicester or the queen might have had of a closer union. Even after his later marriage to Lettice Knollys, Her Majesty's beautiful but detested cousin, Elizabeth would never allow the wife to come to court. Essex was Lettice's son by her first husband, Walter Devereux, although it was said in close whispers that he looked the image of Leicester as a youth.

The old scandal made Frances look upon the queen as a woman with a history that was easily understood. The court was full of such intrigues and tangled possibilities for endless tittle-tattle. Frances would not be made such a target.

Determined to bring her thoughts under control so as not to be a subject for such gossip, which would probably have her mourning Essex, Frances paid close attention while Chateauneuf, the French ambassador, droned on about imagined and real insults to his person and embassy in London's Salisbury Square. Londoners hated the French and Spanish, and unruly apprentices often threw street offal at their carriages.

After what the queen considered enough time spent listening to a recitation of wrongs, though the ambassador obviously had not concluded, Elizabeth grew impatient with Chateauneuf. This was made plain by the tapping of her long white fingers on the arm of her gilded throne chair. If she found a petitioner too rambling, she would lose her tolerance and dismiss him until he was better organized, or brought her a more pleasing proposition in the form of a gift.

Today, Her Majesty seemed distracted, as was almost every lady in the chamber. Frances knew the cause. Walter Raleigh, recently knighted by the queen, who had first sought to groom him for higher position, stood near the dais. His striking good looks made all the ladies present forget the Earl of Essex's absence. The two jealous courtiers had almost fought a duel, for which the stated punishment, never practiced, was the loss of a hand. With a giggle, muffled by a cough, Frances imagined that Her Majesty would never tolerate a court half-full of one-handed handsome men.

Raleigh was almost too well favored, his dark brown, curling beard snipped close to his jaw, his perfect features lit by bright blue eyes. A large white lace-trimmed and pointed ruff, just an inch smaller than Elizabeth's own, sat on his neck, surely held there by wire, since no Dutch starch could keep such rigidity. Raleigh's magnificence was crowned by a velvet cap the color of his eyes and adorned with large jewels.

Every gaze, including the queen's, lingered long on him, though he had his eye on one of her ladies.

Anne leaned in to whisper, "Mistress Throckmorton has caught Sir Walter's attention. He needs be careful. The queen does not share her favorites . . . or her ladies."

Frances smiled. These were well-known truths. Raleigh knew them, but he was an adventurer and naturally reckless. He was also after a position on the Privy Council. Perhaps he would trade love for a seat at that table? Or perhaps he thought to have both.

Though the queen toyed with the idea of elevating Raleigh, Frances doubted he would ever move up to the first rank of advisors. He was too uncontrolled and Elizabeth too good a judge of a man's worth to her and her kingdom. She would keep him dangling, with just enough favor, to decorate her court and write poetry for her—what woman did not want to be a Stella?—but she would never trust his self-serving advice.

"Sir Walter!" the queen said, talking over the French ambassador, who flushed pink from the slight.

"Majesty," Raleigh said, sweeping his cap from his head, his curls falling in a most becoming fashion about his head.

"You have recently had your portrait painted by Nicholas Hilliard. When will you present it to your queen and the court?" Her tone was droll, leading Raleigh willingly into one of his rhyming jests.

"Your grace," Raleigh said, advancing to kneel on the dais.

> *The Artist uses honest paint*
> *To represent things as they ain't,*

He then asks money for the time
It took to perpetrate the crime.

Laughter rippled through the courtiers.

Elizabeth covered her smile with her feather fan, since her teeth increasingly suffered from her love of sweets. Raleigh was well pleased with himself, and he bowed first to the queen and then to the court.

The Danish ambassador now stepped forward, but the queen rose, signaling an end to her patience and the morning audience. Frances gathered her skirts to join the entourage to the royal apartments, where Elizabeth would take a lone meal. She disliked dining with others unless it was with her ladies or a state affair.

Frances did not blame the queen. Whenever she sat down, someone approached to whisper a request for her favor.

Lady Stanley, her face carrying an unusual high color, her lips in a slack sneer, stumbled into Frances as both stepped from the dais.

Frances's patience quickly went the way of the queen's. "Have a care! My lady, if that was deliberate and Her Majesty saw your behavior, you could be sent from court." Lady Stanley's face was twisted in pain at the rebuke. Frances knew she should hold her tongue, but she could not. "Your suitors would grieve the loss of your fortune, if not your person." The words were hurtful, and for the moment she meant them to be. She was tired of the woman's childish tricks.

Frances began to regret her harsh words as she marched away, and she determined to beg the lady's pardon before the day was done. She heard a commotion behind her, but the queen's entourage was formed, and she fell into place behind the Countess of Warwick and the leading trumpeters, drummers, and halberdiers.

Later, she passed into the corridor, making a swift way toward her chambers. For the past several months, she had always looked to the shadowy place Robert had stood when he waited for her as her servant. Today, to her surprise, he was there. He bowed. She hoped he had not seen her display of temper toward Lady Stanley. Should she stop and speak to him of the lovely weather or the excellent hunting in the deer park, or continue with a nod of recognition? Her cautious heart forced her to the latter, giving her another action to regret. She was no more than ten paces on when she turned swiftly back to ease her mind of the last fault.

Robert watched as she passed. She was angry. He could not blame her. She could count on no one. Her father would care for her as he saw fit, but he would never give her the recognition that she wanted and needed. Frances required accomplishments and friends who recognized her need. She was richly adorned in her person by God and had no requirement for what most women of the court sought: clothing and jewels, a higher position and title. She needed the love he could give her, though such love could never be. Even as he thought it, his body warmed to her.

As he had hoped, he saw Frances walk swiftly back into the corridor, toward him. "Master Pauley, I beg your pardon for not speaking. I was too hurried," she added.

She curtsied completely, an excessive courtesy she had seldom shown him. "Were you . . . waiting for me?" Though she spoke with stumbling words, she seemed to be trying hard to keep the customary tone of a mistress.

Dare he betray how much he had missed her?

He bowed again. "There is no need to explain, Lady Sidney. Indeed, I waited here for you on orders of Thomas Phelippes, though I would happily have waited to greet you of my own accord."

Frances knew it was best not to respond to the latter, to ask what he meant, or whether he had missed her as she had missed him. She leaped to the other conclusion she desired. "Have you a new message for me to decipher?"

"Aye, my lady, perhaps two messages, one within the other, as with the first you deciphered," he added, and looked up and down the emptying corridor. Most people were in the great dining room for their dinner at this hour. He had to take care not to be seen passing anything to her. The news would speed throughout the court. "May we walk along together?"

"Of course." She did not care what people thought. She might later, but not now. She had missed his tall figure and stiff-legged stride, his deep, temperate voice.

As they moved on toward her chambers, they heard voices ahead, and he stepped into an empty alcove. She saw him slip his hand into a slash in his doublet sleeve and extract a small packet wrapped in green ribbon. "Phelippes and his clerks are near overwhelmed with messages from the Scots queen. Something is about, but we know not what."

She took the packet and turned it over.

They heard voices receding, and she made a move toward her door.

"I may not enter your apartment, my lady. The guard . . ."

"You did not always follow orders, as I recall."

"I seek to mend my reckless ways, Lady Frances," he remarked drily.

"Always a good thing," she said, suppressing a smile. He could forever bring her to amusement even when he only half tried. She sobered. "How is this message to be delivered, and to whom?"

"I will come for it at midnight in this alcove when the palace is asleep." A nerve jumped under his eye. He turned his head so that she would not see how uneasy he was to be so near her again. He knew that he could not call on his strength of resistance any further. He had caught rare glimpses of her over the past few months, but never dared approach. What would he say? What business could he invent? Until today . . .

Were these his only words to her? He could keep his response to business as well as she, though he ached to think that these months apart might have ravaged their friendship. Or had she found another to dote on her?

She frowned, her prideful face obvious. "If we have captured Mary's new cipher, what occupation is there for me? Is this some make-work you have invented out of an old kindness?"

He took her arm and pulled her into shadows away from the window, shaking with frustration. "What have I ever done that makes you eternally suspicious? I have not earned such distrust. Indeed, I have done everything to receive and hold your confidence." His hand tightened on her arm. His voice dropped lower until she could barely hear him. "My lady, I speak the truth, and I believe you know it."

He heard how tired he sounded, and how offended. He fought to control his tone. "There are too many messages from the Scots queen and many of them are meaningless . . . too many. Phelippes thinks there is a hidden cipher in this one that is the real message . . . a code within a code, and just the work for you. That is the truth. If you do not believe me, I will return the message to Phelippes with your regrets."

He knew she was sorry and upset, now trembling, too.

"Forgive me, Robert. Since you left . . . my service . . . I am not used to kindness, or truth. This is a court of games and deceit."

He swallowed and tightened his mouth, leaning toward her as if he would step into her arms. With an obvious effort, he straightened himself.

She spoke some stumbling words quickly to stop from happening that which neither could ever undo. "Phelippes trusts me . . . to find a hidden cipher?"

Robert took a cautious step away from her. "He trusts your intelligence, my lady, as do I." With a further half bow, rigid and still hurried, he left her.

Frances stared after him until she heard the laughter of people returning to their chambers from the great dining hall. She fled into her apartment and leaned back against the closed door, her hand trembling on the latch. She refused to think on what had happened or hadn't happened with Robert, although she knew that this night in the dark of her bed she would think of nothing else, wondering what he had seen and what she could have done in a different way . . . and what it all meant.

Quickly throwing off her full-cut oversleeves, which impeded any but the daintiest of movements, she sat down at her writing table and pulled the candles closer, past her dinner dishes, the food cold now, the gravy congealed.

Her quill was dull. She needed well-pointed ones. "Meg," she called to her maid. There was no answer.

Walking through her sleeping chamber to the closet where the girl slept, Frances found her washingwoman laying out clean shifts and hose to be put in their proper chests. "Where is Meg?"

"She be gone, my lady."

"Gone? Where?"

"I know not. She did not say. I must return below, m'lady. I left a tub of linen sheets a-boilin' that must be wrung and spread on bushes to dry."

"Go, then," Frances said.

When Meg returned, she would be dismissed. There had been all too many unexplained absences.

The washerwoman scuttled out with her empty basket, and Frances returned to her writing table to nibble at the cold fish and stuffed and spice-sauced pigeons. She did not take the time to heat the meal, but made it more palatable by swallowing it with pieces of fine white bread.

She found her penknife and sharpened what was left of the quill nib, then pulled Phelippes's message close, cut the ribbon on a new quire of paper, and extracted a sheet. The message as broken by intelligencers using Mary's new cipher seemed straightforward enough. It was full of complaints about her lodgings at Tutbury Castle not being fit for a queen, though she saved her major grumbles for her keeper, Sir Amyus Paulet. That strict Puritan seemed to delight in finding new ways to restrict Mary Stuart's demanded privileges. After complaints about Paulet, the Scots queen added a long list of instructions for books, gowns, and new underlinen. It was said that she did not wear undershifts more than once, complaining of their rough texture when not washed in her scented French soap.

This message was certainly one that could have been sent in clear text, English or French, as the queen desired. Frances did not wonder that Phelippes was suspicious. It was all a bit too neatly construed to be as innocent as it first appeared.

First, Frances scanned the beginning letters of each word, looking for repetitions. She could find nothing unusual, and she suspected that Phelippes had already tried this and the next letters as well. Copying backward from the last letter of each word led down another false trail. She leaned against the cushioned back of her chair to think and drink some thistle-infused wine from a nearby decanter.

The door to her receiving chamber burst open and her maid ran in.

"My lady . . ." the girl said, her chest heaving.

"Where have you been, Meg?" Frances kept her tone from anger.

The girl hung her head, still trying to catch her breath.

Frances repeated in measured words, "Where have you been?"

"My lady . . . the lady Stanley wishes to speak with you . . . most urgently."

"Are you in her pay?"

The girl looked up, flushed, but showed courage and did not retreat. "My lady, my mother has twelve children, many little ones. My father is a pikeman with the queen's army in the Low Countries and there be no pay for months. He threatens to desert, but if caught he'll hang for sure."

"Why did you not come to me instead of spying? Honesty is worth a shilling of good charity from me."

Meg lowered her head, working her mouth before finding words. "I was afraid. Your father—"

"I will attend the lady Stanley later."

"Mistress, she ails most miserably." The girl twisted her gown, unable to keep her hands still.

"Are you saying she is in danger for her life?" How could Frances believe the girl? A spy could well be a liar.

"She has lost her power to speak!"

Frances remembered the lady's stumble from the presence room dais, the twisted face, and could not help but believe the maid. "Wait for me in my receiving room and take me to her."

Frances quickly hid Phelippes's message and her worksheet in the cushion. With a quick look in her steel mirror, she tucked a stray curl under her silver-netted caul, smoothed her green satin gown, and joined the maid. Why had she been summoned? There were physicians aplenty in the court.

Meg led her down a series of corridors lit by torches and lanterns to a door with several women standing outside staring in. They stepped aside for Frances.

Someone whispered as she passed, "Lady Sidney has been struck with an apoplexy. Please, my lady, do what you can to ease her troubled mind before she goes to God."

The room was shuttered and dark, hot from a blazing fire. Frances warily advanced to the woman's bedside, half expecting an elaborate trick for some devious purpose.

A woman bent toward the bed, pushing between two physicians applying leeches to the lady's neck. "Lady Frances is here, Catherine."

A limp hand moved toward Frances and she came to the bed-side. The physicians stepped away as she came closer. Lady Stanley's face, which had always carried such high color, was pale now and without a trace of ceruse applied. Bolsters were propped under her neck; her mouth was twisted and slack, drooling.

Trying hard, Frances kept the horror from her face. What had struck the woman down? "Catherine," she said, leaning close, "it's Frances Sidney and I've come to—"

The lady's eyes opened, one lid drooping. Her mouth worked in a ghastly way, trying desperately to push out words that were locked inside.

Lady Stanley's hand groped toward her and Frances put out her hand to meet it. "Do not trouble yourself," Frances began.

With a terrible effort, the woman croaked, "Must . . . must . . . no time . . . terrible wrongs." Her gaze was pleading.

"All is forgiven and forgotten, my lady. Court rivalries mean nothing. Nothing. I most humbly beg your pardon for ever think-ing they did. You must rest now."

She raised herself a few inches and then fell back. "No . . . must confess."

What was Lady Stanley saying? Did she want a popish priest?

"I . . . I inform . . . your aunt."

Frances drew in a deep breath of surprise, as if she were breath-ing for them both. Lady Stanley had been so vindictive as to inform on Jennet to punish Frances? She almost pulled her hand away, but the woman's nails dug in.

"More . . ." The woman was gulping air as if what she took in did not reach her lungs. "The queen . . . I told of fight . . . in gar-den. My Essex . . ."

Her breath was coming in weaker gasps. Frances looked at the physicians, one of whom put his ear to her chest. He stepped back and shook his head.

Frances could not hold on to a useless anger against the dying woman. . . . Everything was trivial now in the dark face of eternal death. Even Jennet would not want it; nor would Robert.

"All forgiven, Catherine, and forgotten," she said, whispering into the woman's ear.

"All?" was the slightest response.

"All, Catherine, I vow. I will pray for you."

Her eyes closed and the barest sigh escaped her lips.

Frances, shaken at this quick turn of events, placed Lady Stanley's hand on her quiet heart and stepped back.

"What could have happened, master physicians? Just hours ago, this lady was in the presence chamber serving the queen. Now she is cruelly struck down."

While one bent to remove the leeches and replace them in his jar, the other tugged on his beard. "When God calls, man—and woman—must answer." He pulled on his beard again. "Galen taught us that a sudden attack on the brain results from an accumulation of dense humors blocking the animal spirit."

His leeches swollen with blood and safely returned to their jar, the other doctor nodded, apprehension on his face. "Humoral imbalance is to be avoided at all costs, my lady."

"How do you avoid it?" Frances asked, a little alarmed that death could come so swiftly inside a palace guarded strongly against outside evil. To think she could carry death about in her head, all unknowing, was frightening.

"Do you wish to consult with me, Lady Sidney?"

She was not ready to pay large sums for foul-tasting potions with ingredients she feared to know. "Perhaps some other time, master doctor."

The doctor bowed, but murmured, "At all costs, my lady."

She left the room swiftly, Meg following close behind, and they headed for the Chapel Royal, which was empty at this time of day except for the most devout.

Frances's faith was not strong, but she walked toward the altar and knelt to pray, as she had promised Lady Stanley. They had not been friends in life, but Frances was determined to befriend her in death. Had her angry words caused Lady Stanley's death, or was it God's punishment for her treachery? Frances understood that she would never know, but she did know that she had learned to forever watch her tongue, however difficult that would prove to be.

Another troubling prayer reached her quietly moving lips: *Lord, help me to end hiding that I am an intelligencer born.* God knew that she was deceitful and she must end such cunning, no matter the cost to her.

When she finally stood, her knees aching, her faith was stronger than it had been.

Meg was waiting at the door, holding her hands in a somewhat unsuccessful attempt to still their shaking.

The maid did not speak until they had returned to Frances's chamber and been admitted by the halberdier on duty. When would the queen tire of her jest and remove the guards, which were unnecessary now for her safety?

Meg hesitated at the threshold, but Frances motioned her to come in and close the door.

"Such disloyalty—"

"Beggin' your pardon, m'lady. I deserve no mercy at your hands. Beat me if you will. But have pity on the little 'uns. . . ." Tears began to flow, and Meg threw her apron over her face.

When Frances heard herself speak, there was no rancor in her voice. Instead she sounded like Jennet teaching right from wrong. "Once trust is lost, Meg, it can be recovered only with great difficulty . . . and diligence. Dismissal would be the least punishment."

The girl sagged noticeably.

"Yet, Meg, I am strongly inclined to give you a chance to redeem yourself. I cannot have a dozen hungry children and an old mother who must be well along in her thirties pressing on my conscience." *My crowded conscience*, she thought.

The girl began to weep again with relief.

"Dry your tears, Meg, and send this to your mother. . . ." Frances pulled two silver shillings from the pocket she carried inside her kirtle.

"My lady, you be an angel come down from . . . How can I . . ."

Meg tried to kiss her hand, but Frances stopped her. "There are clothes to store, Meg."

The girl whirled about and almost ran to her duty.

Frances poured a glass of wine and went to her writing table. One good act a day would not make her saintly.

She removed the ciphered message from the cushion and sat down. She was tired almost to sleeping, anything to escape from the burden of this day's events.

She drew the ciphered message close and began methodically to use Mary Stuart's code, going through the message backward, letter by letter, and line by line. The scratching nib of her quill, the only sound in the room, echoed loud in her ears as she labored on through the ticking of the big case clock. At last, the third letter from the end yielded results. The same code twice in the same message! The Scots queen was growing lazy, or worse, overconfident.

> *Ambassador de Chateauneuf, my dear friend in the*
> *faith King Philip of Spain sends an armada this*
> *summer to free me from the pretender Elizabeth*
> *and help me to my rightful place on the throne of*
> *England. Prepare your plans to liberate me from*
> *my long prison. As to my cousin Queen Elizabeth,*
> *follow your conscience and the pope's bull of 1570.*

Frances quickly folded the deciphered message and retied it and the original cipher with the green ribbon. She must hasten to

Robert waiting in the shadowy alcove. The pope had as much as ordered Elizabeth's assassination with his bull when he absolved Catholics from hell for her murder. Although Mary was too clever to directly order Her Majesty's assassination, these words were close enough to incriminate . . . and they demanded death for the Scots queen.

Snatching her shawl, Frances was out the door, pretending to the guard that she needed a stroll to hasten sleep. When she turned the corner, she raced for the alcove and Robert.

CHAPTER THIRTEEN

"I might—unhappy word—O me, I might,
And then would not, or could not, see my bliss,
Till now, wrapt in a most infernal night. . . ."

—Astrophel and Stella, *Sir Philip Sidney*

May Day, May 1

Robert had spent some time staring into the dark corridor when he saw Frances's cloaked figure slipping toward him. He knew her tall, slender form as he knew his own in a mirror. He had not meant to be so early. Yet he could not stay in his chamber, so eager was he to see her again, unable to delay the pleasure of deciphering her gaze as it settled on him. Were those eyes saying what he wanted, or was he acting the fool?

The situation was almost amusing, he thought, his lips pursed in irony. The court would laugh. Like the Greek gods on Olympus, the God of England played great jests on his creations, offering beauty and then snatching it away.

He looked out again into the corridor. Frances was moving slowly toward him, sideslipping the pools of lantern light to stay in shadow, pausing every minute or so to determine whether she was being followed. By Jesu, she was a natural spy! He felt some pride, as if he had been the teacher of her skills, though he had not. She was a born intelligencer, and he wondered that Mr. Secretary had not seen it long ago. His sharp eyes usually saw everything, but his own daughter was too close, and he too farsighted where she was concerned. He had one idea for her and one alone: as wife to a famous man to bring honor to his name.

Robert had avoided the alcove farther down the corridor where he had told Frances to find him. Alcoves were too often used by midnight lovers. Tonight he had chosen to stand in a little-used exit from the kitchens below.

Cooks and their helpers had by now fallen exhausted onto their pallets. Robert knew he and Frances would be safer in this place than in any open alcove. As she passed him, he reached for her and pulled her into his arms, one hand across her mouth to stifle a scream that might bring guards running.

"Frances, have no fear," he whispered into her ear.

He knew he should loose her immediately, but as he turned her about and against his body, by all the saints, he could not in an instant give up her warm flesh under his hands. Could a parched man push his ale away?

For an instant, perhaps more, she seemed to move into him, become a part of him. He felt himself losing what control he possessed. How quickly good intention fled. He pulled back from the brink of folly at the last possible moment.

"My lady," he whispered, his voice hoarse, "this is a safer meeting place at this hour." He stepped back and made a half bow to reestablish their natural distance and save himself from an act that could well end her regard and friendship.

Frances leaned against the rough stone wall, shaken by the sudden physical contact for which she had been completely unprepared. Her hand on her breast, she struggled for breath. "Don't ever do that again!" Her whispered words sounded of anger, lest he think her response was more than fright, although, in truth, it was.

"Be still," he urged. "I beg pardon for taking hold of you. You might have cried out."

"I might have fainted."

"A hundred apologies, my lady. Now let us to our purpose." He pointed to the stone stairs leading to the kitchens below and sat down on the top step, motioning for her to sit beside him. "If anyone looks in, we will look like lovers. . . ."

She complied without response to the words' provocation, her hands held tight in front of her.

"Did you have success?" he asked.

"Aye," she answered, lifting her gaze to his face, knowing they were too close, their shoulders touching. She had but to make a quarter turn. . . . "Both messages," she whispered.

Robert took a deep breath and held it a moment, wrenching himself back to duty. "So, Phelippes was right."

"As he thought it might be, the message was a double encryption, but she used the same cipher for both."

"Mary is not usually so hurried."

Frances shivered. "This time that could prove fatal for her," she whispered.

Putting his hand on hers, hard clasped in her lap, Robert said softly, "Frances, this is Mary Stuart's doing, not your own. Remember in past years, Queen Elizabeth's inquiry found that a casket of Mary's own letters proved she schemed to murder her husband, Lord Darnley."

"I know all that, yet to behead a queen . . ."

"Then she married her accomplice Lord Bothwell after she accused him of rape, raised an army against her people, left her throne behind, and has since plotted with Spain and France to murder and replace our queen. She would return this realm to the old faith and more Smithfield burnings. And she is probably many times a whore. I beg you to remember all that."

Frances's answer was a bit puffed-up. "What I do, I do for England and my sovereign."

"Commendable."

Her words had been meant to cover her unease at the weight of his warm hand, but they had been the wrong words, because she could not say the right ones; she could not ever think them. She nodded, inches from his face, wanting him to see through the dim light that she acknowledged the truth of what he said. "I will try to remember that the Scots queen is a scheming enemy, a friend of Catholic Europe, and not just an aging woman locked away with Sir Amyas, a bad-tempered keeper." She did not pull back her hands, though his remained on hers.

Robert sensed that she might allow him a liberty. A man knew this when a woman trembled so slightly that she hoped it was not felt. Though in the end it was nothing she did; it was what she did not do: pull away quickly, show outrage at the advantage he'd taken.

He needed only reach out and embrace her. Would she allow it? And if she did . . .

Silently, he begged his wisdom to prevail. They had merely grown close with their common interest. Surely she did not return his deeper feelings. She was married to the poet all England loved. She was his master's daughter. He stood abruptly.

Frances looked up at him and took sudden command of her face. Hastily, she stood, flushed, shaking out her skirt and shifts to cover her chagrin. "Our business is now complete, Master Pauley."

"Yes," he said, fearing to say more words that might break through his pretense completely and allow her a clear view of his heart.

"One more kindness," she whispered. The words she spoke

next had lately been growing in her mind, even confessed in prayer, and now she would have them out. "Robert Pauley," she said, once again the mistress, "I alone must convey the Scots queen's message to Thomas Phelippes. I will admit to my father that I deciphered it, and the first one, as well. It is far past time he knew the daughter he sired."

Robert was worried for her, but he knew that he was also thinking of himself. Her confession would implicate him and Phelippes. Mr. Secretary's temper was terrible when roused. Still, he would not beg her on his own account. "My lady, is this wise? Your father is unused to having his authority challenged. The message may be welcome, but the messenger may not."

"We will see, Master Pauley, but I am finished with deceit." She left him and walked with purpose toward her father's office, descending stairs intermittently lit by lanterns and torches. Her father would be working late into the night, as would Phelippes.

She would not allow herself to turn back to ease Robert's worry. Not even for him would she continue pretending to be nothing but a lady of the presence chamber, an unloved and childless wife, a nothing. Yet she knew she must protect Robert and Phelippes as well as she could.

The halberdiers crossed their pikes as she reached them, barring her way.

She held up the Scots queen's message. "I have an urgent letter for my father," she said in a commanding tone. "He will want to see this at once."

They hesitated, looking perplexed.

"At once!" she repeated in a harsher voice that she realized sounded quite like her father's not-to-be-denied tone.

The halberdiers hastily lifted their pikes and allowed Frances through the door. Lanterns and candles threw small pools of light on the stone floors and walls in the long room peopled with a few secretaries bent to their work.

She knew not what would happen. Her father's anger she expected, but moreover, she could be banished from court by the queen. Her Majesty might be intrigued by a lady of the presence who deciphered messages. Yet if Elizabeth discovered that lady also wanted to be a spy outside the court, conduct far beyond the bounds of expected behavior, Her Majesty might find such spying activities entirely unamusing.

Another deep worry nagged at her, but she refused to allow it to deter her determination. Taking a deep breath to quiet her nerves, she walked straight to Thomas Phelippes, who was busy at a table scattered with quills, an ink pot, and papers, a pewter plate of cold goose resting in its own grease pushed to one side. He stood and bowed, while taking a quick look over his shoulder to Mr. Secretary's room in the back.

"You were right, Master Phelippes," Frances said before the man could whisk her aside. She did not lower her voice, determined to force recognition. She walked around his writing table and spread Queen Mary's letter in front of him, placing her deciphered message beside it. "There is indeed a second message within." She traced her decipher with a finger. "You should read this at once. It will require action."

Phelippes raised her decipher to the candlelight.

"What goes here, Thomas? As well you know, my daughter is forbidden these offices."

She jerked about, as did Phelippes. She had thought herself ready to confront her father. Now she trembled. Had she been witless?

It took not a tick of the clock for an answer. Yes, witless and uncaring of what trouble she brought to Phelippes . . . oh, Jesu, and to Robert, too.

She took a deep breath. "May I speak, Father?"

"Speak, then, though I doubt you have words to explain your disobedience."

Thomas Phelippes spoke first. "The blame is mine, Mr. Secretary. You are well aware, sir, that Queen Mary—"

Her father's eyes narrowed, his dark skin flushing, which turned it darker still. "That devilish woman again!"

Phelippes continued. "—has sent message after message lately to her contacts in London at the French embassy, near overwhelming your secretaries here."

"I am aware of the increase. . . ."

"Mr. Secretary, to my mind she may suspect we are intercepting them and so seeks to—"

"Yes, yes, I know all that. It's a favorite trick, hoping we will miss one or tire of womanly nonsense." He glowered at Phelippes. "What has that to do with my daughter, the queen's lady, who is forbidden this office?"

Phelippes drew himself to his full insubstantial height, the pocks on his cheeks whiter against his skin. "Beg pardon, sir, but the lady Sidney has an intelligencer's mind."

Mr. Secretary's mouth opened to speak, but Phelippes held up the cipher and the pages of Frances's careful work. "The Scots queen double-ciphered this message, but Lady Frances was quick to see and decipher it."

Walsingham took hold of the message and scanned it. "Nonsense. You did *not* break this cipher, Frances." His dark eyes on her held hope that she would admit a lie.

"Yes, lord father, I did," she answered, her tone proud.

"Against my wishes?" he said, unbelieving.

She stood as tall as she could, but did not fail to notice that Robert had entered and moved to stand nearby. Did he mean to give her support? By all the saints, had her desire to confront her father's narrow mind entrapped Robert?

"Against my wishes?" he said again, louder, which caused a nearby secretary to hunch lower on his stool.

"Lord father," she said, her tone placating, "I am but what you gave me of yourself. I can be no other than what I am. Would you have me not serve the queen's good, when she needs all her loyal subjects? I could not so betray her . . . and you."

Her father breathed heavily, looking almost defeated, but his next words proved he was far from it. "You are one of Her Majesty's ladies, and I must have her permission to send you home to Barn Elms. I will seek that permission at once. Come along with me, daughter. Now!"

Frances grasped at some delay. "Won't the queen be abed?"

"No, she sleeps ill and often calls me to her at an even later hour." He picked up her decipher and scanned it quickly. "She'll want to see this at once. We may have that *devilish woman* this time."

"Thank you, lord father."

He set his mouth to ignore her words, his dark eyebrows drawn together before he continued. "The queen cannot discount a direct threat to her person." He looked toward Phelippes, who gripped the table. "What other meaning could Mary have sent with this last sentence? This means assassination!"

"I am pleased to have helped, Father," Frances said, and with these words she could not keep some triumph from her voice, though Robert lifted a warning hand.

"Come along, Frances, but I advise you to leave behind your willfulness." Her father headed for the door, treading heavily. "I will deal with Phelippes when I return—Pauley, too, since I can see his part in this deception."

She looked to Robert, but his face showed nothing except concern for her. She would have that much to remember and regret. Yet what could he do? What could anyone do against her father?

"Mr. Secretary," Robert said as Walsingham passed him and paused, "the fault is mine. I, too, saw Lady Sidney's ability and desired to aid—"

"You greatly exceeded my orders. As I said, I will deal with you later." His tone allowed for no further response.

Robert bowed, and as Frances looked back at him, he smiled a troubled encouragement. *I am sorry,* she mouthed. She had been dutiful all her life; now her first misstep caused harm to those least deserving of it.

The stone corridors to the royal apartments echoed under their feet until they reached the doors guarded by Raleigh's royal sentries in their shining silver cuirasses. They were announced, and Mr. Secretary bowed while Frances curtsied the required three times as they approached the long refectory table where the queen sat working.

"Walsingham . . . my Moor," the queen said, turning from Dr. Dee's star chart, "what of such great import brings you to me at this hour?"

"Majesty, the same Scots queen that brings me to you at all hours."

She shifted in her high-backed chair, looking uneasy.

He bowed again to take any sting from his voice. "And a further request concerning my daughter, the lady Frances."

Elizabeth sighed with a closed-lipped smile for Dee, seated across from her, and reached to receive the message her spymaster held out. She read it quickly, her face showing nothing through the white Mask of Youth. "So, Mary thinks the pope rules here."

"She thinks the pope rules everywhere, madam. This is evidence enough of her treason."

"Yes, yes, I know you want my cousin's head, but the whole of Europe would condemn me for it. . . ."

Walsingham shifted on his feet, though his face showed nothing.

"I do not see the words 'assassinate Elizabeth in her bed' here, and until I do . . ." She picked up Dee's star chart again as if to dismiss them, then looked up. "Nonetheless, a fine piece of work. Take Thomas Phelippes the gratitude of his sovereign. Ah, you had another request." She looked at Frances with interest. "What of my lady of the presence?"

"Phelippes does excellent work, Majesty, but not this time. . . ." Walsingham's face reddened, and he seemed reluctant to expose his daughter's shame.

Frances curtsied, having no such shame or hesitation. There was no retreat possible. "I deciphered the message, Your Majesty," Frances said in a voice she carefully controlled lest it quaver.

Dee looked up and chuckled, holding his finger on a planet's arc. "Majesty, I knew this lady would make an intelligencer when she first came to me begging to learn the secrets of the grille."

Walsingham looked more astonished.

The queen was guarded. "A secret intelligencer amongst my ladies?" She seemed to savor the words, then turned to Dee. "First my philosopher signs himself 'Zero Zero Seven' and now you, Lady Sidney. Should I name you Intelligencer Zero Zero Eight?"

She slapped one hand against the table, whether in disgust or delight Frances could not tell, because she dared not look into the queen's face. She glanced at her father, but he was expressionless, as he could easily be, giving away little of what he was thinking, yet she could guess well enough.

Frances felt her heart would leap from her breast. She could already smell the rank Thames as it flowed in ebb past her rose garden at Barn Elms.

"Walsingham, do I never know what is happening in the shadows of my own court?"

Her Majesty's expression was most strange. Her eyes were narrowed, but her mouth was in better spirits, leaving Frances unsure whether the queen was jesting or ready to explode in one of her famous palace-stunning tirades.

"And, Lady Frances, you again, I vow. First, you challenge Lord Essex and now your father, who looks to be very angry with you. For so slender a figure, you do choose most worthy opponents."

Having sat at cards with the queen, Frances was not unaware that there was one trump card to play in this game. If rightly played, it might not save her, but it would lessen the punishment she would suffer. She quietly thanked the Lord that the queen's father, Henry VIII, had closed all the nunneries where disobedient daughters had once ended their lives. She drew herself even more erect. "Majesty, my worthy lord father does not believe women have the mind for intelligencer work. I sought to show him that we do."

Her father was quick to explain himself. "It is well-known, Majesty. Women have flighty minds and cannot sustain mental work for long periods."

"Oh, such is well-known, Sir Walsingham." The "sir" had teeth in it, though all the queen's words were precisely measured, as they often were in the presence chamber . . . the tone of absolute command.

Walsingham shifted his feet as the queen's eyebrows rose and her black-flecked, dark blue gaze settled on him.

Dee hid his face behind the star chart, but that did not save him.

"What say you, Doctor?"

"Majesty, I have been so privileged in my life to learn that a woman's mind is capable of almost anything."

"Almost, Dr. Dee?"

"Beg pardon, your grace . . . any work of the mind, if she has even one small part of your abilities." He struggled to lift his bulk to his feet and bowed.

Elizabeth nodded, somewhat mollified, then looked up at her spymaster. "Mr. Secretary Walsingham, you place great demands on your queen's purse for your intelligencers, always wanting more."

Knowing her father also spent great sums of his own money for the queen's work, Frances felt sorrow to have brought Elizabeth's indignation down upon him. "Majesty, if I may . . ."

"You may not," the queen said.

From high hope, Frances's heart slipped down to utter despair.

The queen was not finished. "And now, Mr. Secretary, I see you do not accept the skills of a lady who is already rewarded from my own treasury and would cost me not a penny more. What is more, Sir Walsingham, I do not place great demands on her time, but I pay her very well." Elizabeth, drumming her fingers, appeared to wait for Walsingham's submission. It was not forthcoming, and red began to creep up her royal neck.

Frances noted that at this very late hour, the Mask of Youth had cracked and begun to fall away to expose some mask-defying wrinkles, but she kept any sympathy from her face. Elizabeth read expressions as easily as she read Latin and Greek.

"Come now, my good sir Moor, I must to my bed before sunrise. What say you to a new intelligencer who costs me not even one more groat?"

Walsingham bowed low. "As you wish, Your Majesty. As you always wish."

"Good. That was decided faster than any action by my Privy Council."

Frances curtsied three times, backing to the door, which was now being opened by liveried guards behind her. She dared not look up, lest whatever her face revealed change her sovereign's mind. Unless her intelligencer instincts had deserted her, there had been an undertone in the queen's words. She did not usually take a lady's disobedience so lightly. A father, after all, was a king in his family; any disobedience, any disruption in the Great Chain of Being, was a threat to her realm. Could it mean that the queen, so often brought costly bad news by her spymaster, relished the chance to score a point and win the game? Frances felt a twinge of conscience, which she successfully managed to overcome by the time she reached her father's office. Did she have an ally in Queen Elizabeth? Perhaps. Perhaps not. She suspected that the queen's amusement might not last through another adventure. In future, she resolved to take greater care.

CHAPTER FOURTEEN

∽

"I wish you so much bliss,
Hundreds of years you Stella's feet may kiss!"

Astrophel and Stella, *Sir Philip Sidney*

――――――――――――――― ∽ ―――――――――――――――

St. Swithin's Day, Mid-July

GREENWICH PALACE

ometimes, or truthfully many times, Frances admitted to herself that she achieved what she wanted only to find it wanting. It had happened with her marriage; it was happening again. She sat behind a writing table in her father's offices like every other intelligencer, though in a corner out of his sight. But now almost every reason for wishing to be there was gone.

Had she won a battle only to lose everything she treasured? Had she lost her father's love? Had she lost Robert? She closed her eyes to thrust away such painful thoughts, but they crept back upon her nonetheless.

Had she ever been loved? Oh, aye, she'd been needed by her father and by Philip, but her father wanted her to be a replica of her mother—soft, yielding, pale Anne Barnes—and Philip had given his heart to Stella.

No, Frances Walsingham had never been loved for herself, not in the way she dreamed of being loved, and she felt great regret, for in gaining her desire to be an intelligencer she had harmed others.

Her father, in a temper when they had returned from the royal apartments and the queen's startling decision, had not forgotten to deal with Phelippes. Now the man who hoped to be awarded estates and honors for his work was so cowed, he scarce looked her way, and gave her only deciphers that swallowed her time while producing nothing of real importance.

And Robert was gone, where she did not know. She longed to talk with him, to explain herself if she could, and to ask his pardon for the trouble she seemed always to bring him. As a lady of the presence chamber, she thought of witty things to recount about the court and the queen, but the time for telling them passed, and she quaked to meet him suddenly without preparation. She could not tell him the truth, since she resisted knowing it herself, no matter how many times that truth waylaid her. She could not say that she missed him, wanted to hear his voice. And she could never tell him that she felt happier when he was near, when she could look up and see his head bent to his own work, his hair falling forward so that she wondered what was hidden in his eyes.

He'd been sent on some mission by her father, which no one would speak of—she knew neither for how long nor the nature of his errand. He could be in France, even in London, though that sweltering city was to be avoided in high July, since the three great and deadly scourges of hot weather, plague, and the sweat summered there.

Robert could be anywhere. Perhaps she would never see him again, and if she did, he might avoid her like trouble, or hate her for the many problems she'd caused him. Why wouldn't he be angry? If he pleased her, he displeased her father . . . caught in the middle as no man would want to be. If he had ever felt tender thoughts of friendship, they must be extinguished by now.

Restless and heartsick, she twisted a quill in her hands until it broke. She put the pieces aside with several other broken quills.

Frances had not been able to see Robert alone before he left. She had wanted to, rising those first days as he walked by her writing table, knowing not what to say to him but wanting some exchange with him and hoping her words would be welcome. He had acknowledged her by inclining his head with a small smile as he would any lady, but he did not speak or pause to allow any words from her.

Her Majesty and the entire court had left Hampton Court for Greenwich, and soon after, with a huge train of wagons and coaches, she was off for her summer progress to show herself to her people.

Frances had not been invited to accompany the queen, but told to keep to her ciphers, thus saving Elizabeth the feeding and care of one lady of the presence. The queen also relieved her purse of the cost of feeding her entire entourage by visiting her country lords and gentlemen, those who had not fled from the thousand courtiers and servants that trailed Her Majesty. The queen's great favor had been known to bankrupt entire families.

Frances knew that some, on hearing that they had been chosen for a royal visitation, locked their doors and left their estates behind them until word reached them that the royal train had moved on to another lord.

Disappointing the monarch would not come without cost. The absent lord would need to ensure that his Twelfth Night gifts for the queen were very grand, indeed. Elizabeth always won. At the thought, Frances covered an admiring smile and felt somewhat less dejected.

She smoothed her new blue satin gown with its lace ruff and cuffs and a silver-embroidered brocade kirtle and partlet. She loved the lush color after the endless white gowns Elizabeth demanded of her ladies of the presence.

Phelippes approached. "A message for you came this very morning from Holland."

"Thank you, Master Phelippes. Is that where Robert has been sent?"

"I cannot say, my lady, or risk Mr. Secretary's great anger." He returned to his table.

Frances drew the message across the table. The letter was sealed with Philip's signet. It was a grille of only a few lines, though he said nothing of her grille to him. And so short, unlike Philip, who often had instructions for her about the care of his estates that required two close-written pages. What few words had needed to be ciphered?

> *Wife, I will be going into battle soon.*
> *If I return to you, I will be a loving husband.*

> *Philip*

Her hand trembled as she put the letter aside. *If I return . . .* Was it a forewarning or a soldier's natural caution? Or was she being a foolish and remorseful woman? The words Philip had written would once have thrilled her, but this day they left her full of guilt.

She longed for clarity, yet nothing was clear. As though seen in an unpolished steel mirror, Philip's image was blurred to her. He had been gone for near a year, and now even his miniature brought him no closer. When she tried to recall her early love for him, nothing moved in her heart. Too much hurt had come between them, too much betrayal. She bit her lip in remorse.

Perhaps her father had been right long ago when he had remonstrated with his child: "Frances, you always want what you cannot have. Why can you not be satisfied with what God has given you, what He has made of you?"

Because then I would be nothing.

The outer door opened with a burst of talk, and her father and Robert strode in, bringing with them the scent of clean channel wind from the river Thames.

Frances stood and approached her father for his blessing, which he gave somewhat hurriedly. He was heavy-lidded, his eyes sunken; he looked inexpressibly tired. His sickness could come upon him again at any time.

She did not look at Robert. If she saw coldness in his face, she could not bear it.

"Attend me," Mr. Secretary commanded, and every intelligencer crowded about him and the table upon which he'd spread a crudely drawn map. "What I am about to speak, let no one breathe outside this office on pain of most wrathful death." He paused and looked into every startled face before continuing. "We have recently had great intelligence from our people at the Plough Inn, especially my man Bernard Maude, who has gained the confidence of the plotters. He reports that they plan to free the Scots queen and assassinate Her Majesty Elizabeth. The exact dates are closely held by a very few men. Assassination is what they have always wanted, but now they plan to do it soon, perhaps in the next weeks . . . or days. You see the import of this news."

Phelippes shifted his feet and Frances saw others swallow hard. But each bowed, indicating that they knew very well.

"Pauley, here," continued Walsingham, laying a hand on Robert's shoulder in fatherly pride, "has developed a plan to prevent Mary Stuart from escaping Chartley and save us from popery, while we keep the treasonous young cockerels checked at the inn. The plan is a dangerous one . . . most perilous."

Frances felt her heart beat faster. Had Robert agreed to put himself in danger to regain her father's confidence?

Robert's face showed nothing.

Walsingham took a deep breath and continued. "We knew

that the Scots queen was planning something, but she has grown ever more cautious. What we are intercepting are messages meant to calm us into believing that she has abandoned any thought of escape or raising a rebellion. There has been no word to Sir Anthony Babington, who is the prime conspirator. Yet the Catholic plotters remain at the inn day and night awaiting her messages. Why? They are certainly not there to faithfully fill her orders for new night shifts. . . ." His face turned a deeper red and he added the familiar "That devilish woman!"

The intelligencers shifted their feet and nodded politely.

"She has obviously found a second and better way to get her messages out to Chateauneuf in London and to Mendoza, the Spanish ambassador in Paris. Pauley will tell you the rest, as much as he can. Remember you are sworn to strictest silence."

Robert stepped to Walsingham's side and pointed to the map. "The Scots queen is here at Chartley, the Earl of Essex's manor in Staffordshire. She is in need of a different cipher she can feel secure in using for her new escape plans. She will fear to use the one she has been using now for too long. This new cipher will be delivered to her from the nearby town of Burton by a Catholic sympathizer, who is willing to risk all for her . . . and for a hefty purse. She would never trust him unless he was bought with her gold. This brewer and real traitor is currently residing in luxury at the Tower of London."

Every man laughed.

Not laughing, Frances briefly felt again the cold, wet stone corridors and slimy steps that led to the cells below, where all hope died slowly and painfully. Unable to keep an urgent question to herself, Frances interrupted, "But won't Mary's supporters know you are not the real brewer and . . ."

Robert's urgent voice broke into her warning. "I will pose as this brewer's brother. I can be convincing, since I was once a brewer's apprentice. I will deliver a cask of ale to Mary that contains a new cipher from her London conspirators; then I will take away an empty cask with her reply . . . in the bunghole. Even her strict keeper, Sir Amyas Paulet, the man Queen Elizabeth has assigned to be her jailer, must not suspect this deception. He will want to deliver the cask, and Mary will never trust anything that comes from his hand." Robert paused to take breath. "She will trust me . . . I pray."

"Aye," Phelippes said, slapping one palm against the other, "the trap has its bait. The plot is just venal and complex enough to intrigue that queen."

Walsingham nodded, his eyes gleaming. "We will put the plan into play immediately. She has other means of getting messages out. We must divert her to ours as the safest. In that way, we can have complete knowledge of her plans and *in her own hand*." His voice grew husky as if the words caught in his throat. "We must have such direct proof before our queen will order Mary's death. Pauley, when can you leave for the north?"

"Tonight, Mr. Secretary."

"Good! I must depart for the queen's progress to advise her of this plan and other state matters."

After hearty congratulations and manly shoulder slapping and punching, Robert received a purse of gold for expenses and left quickly.

As he reached the door, he turned for one last look and saw fear for him writ clearly on Frances's face.

An hour later, Robert heard an insistent knock on the door of his lower-floor rooms, and knew who would be on the other side. "Come."

The latch was raised and Frances stepped inside. He had stoked the sea-coal fire in the grate, hoping the warmth was a sign of his welcome.

"Robert."

"Yes, Frances."

"Take me with you."

He was not terribly surprised by her words. They, too, were half anticipated, along with the strength he would need to deny her this desire . . . or anything.

When she spoke, the word was not a command, but a humble request in her most courteous and pleasing voice. "Please."

What could he say? Not that it was his earnest desire to take her away forever. Never the truth between them. Instead, he said, "The danger is far too great."

"Hear me, Robert." When he did not object, she explained what he had already guessed. "The queen is gone on her progress, leaving me behind to do the intelligencer work I begged for. My father is joining her with dispatches from the Earl of Leicester in Holland. No one will miss me."

Robert continued to speak not a word, his face set.

She stumbled on: "I will give out that I have taken to my bed with a woman's complaint." She closed the distance between them to an arm's length. "I broke the cipher. I have earned the right to be a part of this important plan."

Robert shook his head hard, so near was he to being drawn into her wishes. "Such is unthinkable, my lady! Your father would never allow it."

"But you could."

His face softened as did his voice, deep and calm. "I could never in this life put you in the path of such danger."

She had first seen such tenderness when he held his guitar on their trip from Barn Elms, and next seen when he had knelt to hold her after Jennet's imprisonment in the Tower. Still, his reason had not dissuaded her.

"How could you alone make the deliveries to the Scots queen? No outside men are allowed to see her. Paulet is very firm about that rule."

Robert turned his back on her. He knew, in frustration, she could have pounded on him with her fists. Instead she used logic, which he admired.

"If you go alone, I have great concern that something could go wrong for this important mission," she said, hoping a reasonable response would move him. "I am greatly vexed . . . full of worry."

His shoulders shook. "My lady, you are happiest when you have something to worry about."

She could not see his face, but she knew his dark eyes flashed with amusement. Yet she was in no mood to be jollied. She would not beg. Nor would she surrender. If he did not know that, he knew nothing of her.

He was putting himself on the path of danger, yet he meant to protect her when she could help the mission succeed. . . . She knew she could. And she owed him for the trouble she had caused.

Still, argument was useless. How could any man, even Robert, believe that he needed a woman on a risky undertaking? "Good fortune, Robert," she said. With no further word, Frances walked to his door, opened it, and shut it softly behind her before rushing to her chambers. She entered, calling for her maid. "Meg!"

The girl ran into her bedchamber.

"Help me, Meg, and quickly."

"What would you have of me, mistress?"

"A lad's clothes. You must know some boy in the kitchens who is about my size."

"Aye, mistress, but not well enough to take off his clothes."

Frances held her temper. Everyone wanted to play the fool today. "Buy them for twice what new would cost, cap, boots, and all." She handed Meg a gold noble. "This should buy his silence, and mind you they are clean and not lice ridden."

Meg looked at the coin in her palm and gasped. "So much, my lady."

"Quickly, Meg! You must be back within the half hour."

"Faster, mistress."

And indeed she was. "The boy's best," she said, near out of breath. "Never worn, not even on Sundays or holidays. I told him it was for me to act as page. He thinks we are escaping the palace in disguise to meet your lover."

Frances scarce listened, removing her own gown, kirtle, and undershifts, stepping quickly to the steel mirror. She had always thought her breasts too small, but now, donning the breeches, hose, shirt, and doublet, she was glad of their size. The doublet was large, and that hid her paps all the better. She wound her pocket about her waist, making the breeches fit well enough. She looked again into her steel mirror at her reflection. She scrubbed at her face. "I must remove all traces of the Mask of Youth and cochineal color from my lips and cheeks if I wish to be a proper servant boy. But my hair is too long; it will never remain under this cap. Meg, get the scissors, quickly."

"Oh, nay, my lady, not your beautiful hair."

"Quickly, Meg."

When Frances had the scissors to hand, she held her breath, closed her eyes, and cut off one side of her hair that fell far below her shoulders, almost elbow length. "Meg," she said, her eyes yet closed against what she must do, and to avoid the strange-appearing boy in her mirror, "you cut the rest, and do not be timid."

"The same all round, mistress?"

"Aye, Meg. Do it."

The scissors made cutting sounds, and hair fell against Frances's hands as they were clasped tight in her lap. When Meg ceased, Frances opened her eyes. She was transformed indeed. Before her sat a boy, not full-grown to man size, but tall and long limbed, with one hose falling down to wrinkles, as with most boys. She reached for her hair, curling up now with the weight of it reduced. She donned the cap and stared into the mirror, scarce recognizing the smooth-faced boy staring back at her. Without her gown and shifts, she looked taller and much thinner, perhaps not strong enough to be a brewer's boy.

Meg eyed her. "My lady, do not walk so confidently, or someone will notice that your face is not bearded, though your height declares you to be nigh to a man."

Frances nodded. "Thank you, Meg. Now, take you to a wig maker in London and have a wig made of this hair, a wig like the queen's, with ringlet curls placed in a large bun on either side."

"Yes, my lady."

"If there is inquiry made while I am gone, give out that I am abed with my monthly flux."

"How long will you be away?"

"It could be a fortnight."

"I'd better add another flux."

Frances smiled at her quick wit. "As you will, but do not allow anyone to come in to see me."

"Measles, then."

"Aye, but doing well enough. I don't want alarm to spread among the servants of the palace."

"I will take great care, mistress."

Frances reached into her pocket and retrieved a coin. "Give this to your mother for her babes."

Meg looked her thanks, then showed it: "Let me go with you to the stables so that we look a very maid and her lover."

Frances smiled her gratitude. "You are experienced, Meg?"

The girl shrugged. "Perhaps, mistress."

The maid and boy left Frances's chambers arm in arm, moving along the hall quickly to the kitchen stairs. Everyone glanced up at them, but quickly back to their supper dishes without lingering interest.

They made their way to the stables, where Frances saw a heavy brewer's cart drawn up in the yard, four great black sturdy and dependable Percheron horses dozing with their heads down, twitching away flies. Meg went on to distract the stablemen while Frances climbed across the tailgate and slid her slender body between the barrels. It was too late to change her mind; nor did she want to, though, to her surprise, her hands shook. She gripped the boards tighter. She had not long to wait.

"I'm off, lads." It was Robert's voice. "Did you give these horses feed? Water?"

"Aye," came the answer from the stables.

"What are their names?" Robert asked the stableman.

"The lead horses are Quint and Claudius. The wheel horses are Marcus and Colby. But your barrels are empty, Master Pauley. Why do you need four dray horses for so light a load?"

Robert raised his whip. "The barrels won't remain empty."

"So you'll have drink on that dry road."

"Aye, but first I'll stop at every inn along the way," Robert said cheerfully, to the stablemen's laughter.

"Quint! Claudius!"

Frances heard the slap of reins and the wagon jerked forward, bouncing her between two rows of barrels, though she had little room to move. She clung to the loosely fitted bottom boards of the dray, which allowed her fingers just enough purchase, and wondered how many bruises, if not broken bones, she would collect through her thin boy clothes, though the wool was woven thick enough to make her itch. Fortune must be with her. God's grace, the ale barrels were well lashed and did not roll atop her.

Questions raced through her mind, and she damned herself for not thinking of them before. What if the Scots queen's men had a spy in Walsingham's office? It was possible, though her father was careful, very careful of new men. If Robert's mission was known, there could be an attack anywhere along the road.

She shivered a little and prayed that they had only brigands to fear, and not desperate men trying to save themselves from the rack in the Tower.

After what seemed hours, she could sense in the dryer, warmer air that they had moved away from the Thames and into the woods on the road north. Clamping her teeth together, she hung on to the swaying, lurching wagon, hitting every bump and hump in the road. Surely she was being pulled by the most cloddish, ill-gaited horses in the realm. She would complain to Robert Pauley about his taste in horseflesh, if she were still able to speak when they stopped. She grimaced to herself. Perhaps complaints were not called for from an unwanted passenger.

She shivered a little, knowing she could not pretend even to herself that this was a jest on Robert. The road ahead was too full of danger. All the local sheriff's men could not protect the roads from bands of thieves that would as soon take lives as a wagon and horses with empty ale casks.

Still, she understood why he had chosen the big Percherons. They could pull heavy loads and make seven miles an hour, day after day.

She shifted here and there, but still could not get herself comfortable. Endurance was called for, a quality every intelligencer must have. In this ale wagon, that important skill found her.

Frances guessed it was near three hours, with the sun beginning to sink down to the western treetops, before Robert stopped in an inn yard to water the horses and his throat. She welcomed the opportunity to assess her bruises, though she wondered at her ill planning—a flask of ale, some bread, and cheese had been forgotten in her haste.

Robert had not been so negligent. She heard the sound of ale leaving a flask and making its way down his throat. Next the scent of the sun-warmed bread and ripe cheese reached her, and her stomach rumbled so that she thought sure to be found out. Another hour, she promised herself, her lips pressed tight, and it would be too late to return her to Greenwich . . . just until the sun was truly gone. She hung on.

Last light was still shining through the wooded verge some time later, when Robert hauled on the reins and the wagon stopped so suddenly that Frances was thrown against the barrels. At her outcry she was discovered.

Robert jumped down from the seat and climbed onto the wagon. "What folly is this?" His hand grabbed hold of her leg and pulled. "Come out of there, boy!"

"Stop!" she shouted, as if he still followed her orders.

He began to shake her hard and her cap flew off. "Frances?" He stared at her, dropped his arms, then reached to touch her hair. "Your lovely hair . . ."

"Off to the wig maker's, in anticipation of my return," she answered, brushing the dust from her breeches, trying to show a casual manner she did not feel. "I asked you to take me," she reminded him.

"Ah, I see. This deception is a fault of mine."

She nodded vigorously, trying to hide her fear and rubbing her arms contritely, hoping that the sight of her bruises would elicit some forgiveness.

"I could put you on the next cart going toward the river."

"Aye, you could, but I pray you won't."

He frowned. "Prayer is indeed called for, my lad."

"I pray that I will be an intelligencer in all ways once in my life." Her voice trailed away, though he heard her next words, which were scarce more than a breath: "Until Philip returns and I am shut away forever."

He took hold of the lead horses' lines and pulled the wagon farther onto the verge, where all four began to crop the grass.

Robert turned his stern face to her. His words were harshly spoken. "Now, lad, we need wood for our supper fire."

She lifted her head, hope in her voice. "So you will allow me to be an intelligencer in truth and be part of this deception?"

"Since you act deception so well . . ." He bit down on his angry words, but continued firmly. "I will allow you to get the firewood, boy, and mind you it be dry."

Frances walked about, gathering twigs as large as she could, piling them in the crook of one arm, almost wishing she had an apron to fill. A little proud, she raced back and dropped them in front of Robert.

"Two times as much," he said without looking up at her.

He was testing her, and she knew it. However, she was determined not to fail, and this time took off her doublet, filling it with all the dry wood she could find, though it grew darker as she bent to her work, aware with every low bow that she was aching in almost every joint.

"There!" she said, triumphantly emptying her doublet on the ground in front of him, expecting his praise.

"Did you see a stream?"

"Aye."

"Fill this pot," he said, pointing to a small black iron pot hanging on a hook from the side of the dray. He rested his back against a tree trunk, a contented smile on his face.

"What are *you* doing?" she said, tired of being used like a . . . well, like a servant.

"I am resting, my lad, since I'm the brewer and you my apprentice. It is a position you sought, is it not?"

In ill temper, she snatched the pot from its hook, washed it in the stream, and filled it with water. If he thought to show her a servant's way, then she would be a good one. An intelligencer, like an actor, must learn many parts.

When she returned with the pot full, he motioned to the buckets hanging alongside the dray. "Fill them several times for each horse. These big horses need thirty gallons a day."

She held their pails while they drank, lest they turn them over, Claudius nudging her shoulder for more. "You big clod," she whispered, as he flicked an ear closer. She liked him. He was warm and friendly, and she needed both.

It was full dark when Frances finished, having damned herself a dozen times for this fool's errand and having no kind thought of Robert. She shivered a little.

"Come to the fire if you need to warm yourself," Robert said, compassion in his voice. "When the sun goes down it can be cold nights."

"I am *very* warm," she said, watching him throw some grain into the boiling pot hanging from a wood tripod. "I've worked like a horse; now will I eat like one?"

"They have been kind enough to allow us some of their grain and dine only on grass."

"Grain and water?" Her stomach spoke its hunger.

"Perhaps some bread and cheese, as well." He grinned. "Then I'll send you packing back to Greenwich on the next decent coach. By this time, I think you are eager to go."

His words erased her aches. She knelt near him, prayerfully. "Please, Robert, please give me this one chance to show what I can do."

"I would think you have shown that by now." He knelt to stir the pot, the grain beginning to thicken. "If I allow you your desire, Sir Philip—your husband—will see I never come out of Fleet Prison."

She sat suddenly. "He will not care so long as I do not make him a cuckold."

He did not look at her, continuing to stir the pot. "I cannot promise that."

Frances stared at him, her heart beating so wildly that he must see it, her lips trembling, all the while searching for something to say and finding only the ridiculous. "Then you make no mind of my short hair."

Robert handed her a spoonful of hot oats, which she was hungry enough to eat. And another after that. "Can you perform apprentice work with a better will?"

"Yes."

"And cease to talk when I ask it of you?"

Her answer came more reluctantly this time. "Yes."

"A lad may be needed. I do not know, but sending you back could make gossip that could reach the Plough Inn and alert the plotters when now they are sure of their success." He looked into her face. "You make a right handsome boy, Frances, but a far prettier maid." He knew to turn his back at the look on her face and roll up in his cloak. "We'll start again as soon as the horses rest," he muttered.

"Where will I sleep?"

For answer she heard his steady breathing and crawled under one edge of his cloak, her back to his, his warmth her mantle. The earthy green scent of trees and grass cooling after a warm day filled her lungs, reminding her of the woodland at Barn Elms. Behind her an owl hooted.

With difficulty, Robert breathed steadily as if asleep, until sleep came truly.

CHAPTER FIFTEEN

*"Love . . . which breaks the clouds and opens forth the light
That doth both shine and give us sight to see . . ."*

—Astrophel and Stella, *Sir Philip Sidney*

Lammastide, August 1

ON THE ROAD TO CHARTLEY

The brewer and his apprentice had filled their ale barrels and loaded the dray at the Burton Brewery, where some of Walsingham's Staffordshire men had taken charge. Frances's shoulders ached from carrying the smaller kegs, including one with the cipher for Queen Mary, from the brewery to the dray, as any good apprentice would. A deeper ache came from sleeping on the cold stone floor.

For half the night she had wondered why she had ever thought a man's life was easier in this world. In the morning, she had waked to find Robert's doublet tucked about her shoulders and the man scent of him in her nostrils. When had he placed his doublet there? Had he watched her sleeping? She smiled at such a thought and knew the wondering would stay with her far longer than her aching shoulders.

She averted her eyes from the man beside her driving the dray, yet saw all of him, his image engraved on her mind, his strong hands grasping the reins in front of her. He began to sing as he had that first day on their way from Barn Elms to London.

Under the greenwood tree
Who loves to lie with me,
And turn her merry note
Unto the sweet bird's throat . . .

He was teasing her. A man who was on a mission to fool the Scots queen, and almost surely to save the queen of England's life and her realm from papist conquest, could yet sing a joyous song. She could sing one as well. So she did, lifting her voice to blend with his.

He turned his face to her, smiling, and despite the woodland's shade, she saw that his eyes were bright with good humor.

"By my faith, lad, you are a daring woman," he said, laughing at the absurdity of his words.

"Some would call me foolish, mad even."

"Aye, that, too," he said, opening his shirt to allow the cooler air under the trees to reach his skin. "And you should never wear the white mask again over your . . . lovely face. Why pretend youth when you own it?"

Frances turned her head from his sweet words, but not before she had allowed herself to look upon his broad, muscled chest with a swatch of dark hair disappearing lower under the linen.

Her life was not over, she thought, hugging the idea to her heart, not over before it began, as she had feared. Then with one special insight came another: She could not turn aside from him, from what she now saw so clearly as a great and deeply felt love for Robert, a love she had felt for no other man, nor ever thought she could. Aye, Lady Frances Sidney, the wife of the realm's most admired poet of love, a lady of the queen's presence, yearned for the arms of a bastard and landless commoner, a servant. She ached with a love that ravaged through her like a sweet plague.

She had not been able to accept her forbidden feelings at court, but here in the countryside atop this dray in disguise there were no distinctions of rank. In truth she had new sight to see what had ere now been so poorly lit.

Once, she had thought that being an intelligencer was all she wanted in this world, having given up hope of more.

Yet the hope had returned with Robert. She wanted more. It was not greed, but need that had grown in her since first she had looked on him. She had not known it at once, indeed had mis-named such shadowed feelings, and pushed them away when they first began to clear. How blind she had been. What months she had wasted.

She glanced beyond the dray horses as the sun broke through the clouds and rising dust on the road to Chartley Manor, wondering what this day would bring that no day before had brought. That was the part of being an intelligencer that she loved: No day was ever the same.

They had crossed the river Blythe and were surrounded by the green, rolling countryside of Staffordshire. Sunlight glinting through leafy old horse chestnut trees cast spun gold patterns across the road. She thought of Aunt Jennet's beloved embroidery and was warmed by the memory. As a girl, she had not prized her stern aunt, though now she did. No letter had come from her old nurse in France. Letters were dangerous. Still, there had been word that she did well and was content in her exile. She had children to teach and her Catholic faith to live openly, a faith that condemned her to death in England, just as Frances's own Protestant beliefs would condemn her in France. Where would these enmities end . . . with the death of queens? Not Elizabeth, pray God, not Her Majesty. Frances could not picture the realm without the last Tudor.

A line of carters passed them, taking their animals back toward Burton for market day, their milk goats tied to the tailboard, wooden cages full of squawking chickens and green cabbages. She pulled her cap down and looked straight ahead as Robert responded to hearty greetings and salutes, leaving the brim low to shade her face, lest she return to Greenwich berry-brown. How to explain, after rising from her sickbed, the complexion of a husbandman's wife?

This trip had been unlike any she had known or, no doubt, would know again. She had never been seated in a brewer's dray, nor dreamed of adventuring with a much-loved man. She was aware of Robert's every move beside her, his voice urging on the horses, his shadow moving down the road as if leading her forward. She felt his shoulder and arm pressed against hers on the narrow seat, heating her almost to a sickness.

"'Which breaks the clouds and opens forth . . .'"

After hearing herself speak Philip's words, she took a deep and dusty breath, looking off to the side, away from Robert's sight, tears starting suddenly for no reason. She tried to stop them, to hide them, but she could not.

Robert pulled to the side in the deep shade and turned to her. "Tell me what word I have spoken that brings you to tears, or . . ." He took a deep breath. "Or is it a memory of your husband's words?"

Choking on the dust of the road, she said, "Neither." She could manage just that one word.

He reached for her hand. "All will be well, Frances. Trust me in this. If this venture should become known, I will explain to your father that I thought a boy necessary and there was no other one to trust on such a charge. I will take the blame on myself and you will not be—"

She covered her face with her hands. "You would protect me

from my own folly? Sweet Jesu, Robert, you have not an understanding of what is . . . and I cannot explain without betraying . . ."

He jerked toward her. "Betrayal? Who? What have you done?"

"I am a married woman. . . ."

*R*obert was confused by her words, though his heart leaped
against his shirt with what they might mean, what he
wanted them to mean. There were words she was trying to say—or
was she trying not to say them? Could she love him, or was she a
lonely young wife left at court, seeking adventure while her husband was away? He could not believe it of her, but where was this
leading? To the Tower for him? To adultery and hell for them both?

"Frances, I have known . . . since first I saw you . . . your deep
unhappiness," he said, his words broken. He was uncertain how
far to go with them. "Is there naught I can do?" He paused again
as she turned toward him, open to his words. Was she also open to
his arms? How could he allow himself to think that she wanted
him? He had lost his good judgment, his ability to know what
secrets faces did not reveal. He forced his mind to stop all such
imaginings.

He was aware that she was trying to form words, and sought
to end her confusion. "Frances, sweet lady, do not say what you will
regret and I will ne'er forget."

She lifted her chin, as if determined not to make of herself fool
enough to set him laughing.

Robert took his handkercher from his sleeve, poured out some
ale from his flask, and, lifting her chin with one finger, wiped away
the dusty tear streaks. "Apprentice boys do not allow their masters
to see tears, Frances."

"Did you never cry for what you lost when you became a brewer's apprentice?"

Robert snapped the reins. "Ho, Quint! Claudius!" He turned

the dray back onto the road. "I have no memory of boyhood tears, Frances. Bastard apprentices cannot wash away their station, though they cry tears enough to fill the river Thames."

While he was apprenticed to the brewer, she had been the cosseted only child of the queen's spymaster, living in the manor of Barn Elms with servants and all the luxuries allowed in a Puritan household. He understood little of her life, except her loneliness. That he understood full well. Sometimes, as now, his body ached for her, almost betraying him. Each time it was more difficult to calm himself to softness. He demanded much of his manhood for her sake.

They moved on at a good pace, though they now had a wagon heavier for the full casks and barrels.

"'And give us sight to see,'" Robert said quite suddenly, finishing the couplet she'd begun at least two furlongs earlier, but his words came so softly she scarce knew whether she imagined them or heard him speak softly over the sounds of horses' hooves and rumbling dray. Finally, she was unsure that he had actually spoken. And, if he had, how could she respond?

She cast a quick sidelong glance at him, trying again to read what he could be thinking. He looked ahead, though she saw his jaw tighten, as if he dared speak no further in an intimate manner. She was sore-tempted to ask him, but dared not. She wanted to know and was afraid to know. She was all mad confusion.

Robert had been a polite but silent partner on this trip after the first night. He had allowed her to cling to the seat beside him rather than amongst the barrels of the dray. She had thanked him politely, though he assured her that he was giving her only her apprentice's due, since she had proved to be so willing.

He seemed to know Philip's poems to Stella as well as any young man at court—better, perhaps. But she sensed that he was not thinking of Stella when he spoke Philip's words. Not for the first time Frances wondered whether there was another woman he thought of, longed for. Her heart shrank from the possibility, but her mind would not give it up. A young and pretty lady's maid, perhaps, or a lonely widow in a cottage by the road he visited on his travels? Or both a lady within and one without the court?

Hold! she ordered her runaway mind. She did not really want to know about Robert's women. It never helped a woman's heart to know a man's secrets. She looked at his profile, hoping he would turn her way, but he did not. In spite of her better cautions, she yet wanted to know his mind. When would they ever be like this again? "What do you think of Philip's sonnets? You have never said."

"You have never asked." He blinked rapidly but did not turn to her, keeping his eyes on the road. "Now that you do ask, I will tell you. I think Philip Sidney's sonnets speak the heart of every man who cannot have the woman he loves."

She took a deep, shuddering breath, knowing the truth of what he said for herself. "Is there a woman you love and cannot have, Robert?"

His jaw tightened and he lifted his strong chin. "God's grace, Frances, I have loved women."

"You do not take my meaning."

"I take it, Lady Frances, but I choose not to answer. Even a servant can have his own privy thoughts, his privy heart." So saying, he pulled his wide hat down to shield his eyes from the sun, and perhaps from her, and tugged on the reins as the road turned toward Chartley Manor.

She had angered Robert. He had a dignity that she should recognize by now, since it matched so closely the conduct she tried to make her own. Yet she had to say what was true. "A servant is not allowed to choose his life. Neither can a wife."

He nodded thoughtfully. "Then we are much the same." Robert grinned, though he shook his head in disagreement. "Yet we are far from the same in many things. But maybe in one thing . . ."

Again, he slapped the reins sharply over the horses' backs to stop his thoughts from becoming words that he would very likely repent.

They rode ahead with speed and in silence.

A torrent of wondering thoughts filled her now. She had admitted far too much without really saying unfaithful words. What would Robert have thought of her?

They mounted a hillock, the manor of Chartley and the castle ruins beside it coming slowly into view on the rise. Abandoned since the Battle of Bosworth a hundred years ago, the castle keep, towers, and crenellated battlements still stood guard beside the newly built, impressive timbered manor. "The castle and manor belong to the Earl of Essex," she said, somewhat surprised that she voiced the thought aloud.

"Say nothing more, Frances. Apprentice boys do not comment."

She nodded. "Aye, master brewer."

They passed over the moat and into the outer bailey, the place strangely quiet for the hour after dinner. Were all the household out in the deer park hunting, or were they resting out of the heat inside the thick timber walls?

Robert hailed a passing groom. "Here be good Burton ale for Sir Amyas Paulet."

"You are not the old brewer."

"Nay, he went for the easy life with a sister in London."

The groom laughed. "Aye, he was e'er complaining of his back."

"While he rests his back, I have good ale here for the manor, and a special keg of double ale to deliver to the papist queen."

"Hold there, brewer. No one passes but with Sir Paulet's orders, and he allows no man to go to the Scots queen's chambers. She has charmed better than you."

Frances whispered to Robert, "Will they allow a boy?"

"I will hold here in the bailey," Robert said. As soon as the groom left, Robert warned, "Frances, do not move or speak."

Robert wrapped the reins about one of the stakes on the side of the dray that held the kegs in place. He jumped from the wagon and led the horses to a trough for water. "A groom here to brush the dust of Staffordshire from coats and manes," he shouted, holding a silver penny aloft.

A boy ran from the stables, brush and cloth in hand, and soon the dust was flying and the horses' gray coats began to shine again. The boy looked up at Frances: "Boy, ye be blessed in yer master. He pays others to do yer work."

Frances held her breath at the stable boy's puzzled look until he shrugged and walked back to the stables, clutching his penny between his teeth.

Robert busied himself beside the dray, his hands testing the ropes holding the larger barrels.

"When will Sir Paulet come?" she asked softly, looking toward the multistoried timbered manor. "He has seen me in the presence chamber alongside Her Majesty."

"Do not fear. He will not expect a lady of the presence to be on a dray in his bailey. It is the unusual man who does not see what he expects."

"Paulet is not the usual man," Frances said, still worried.

"Then deny and grovel. All men of his rank believe a cringing lad."

"I have learned how to shrink myself to nothing."

He looked at her and nodded thoughtfully.

She could see a large formal garden stretching beside and behind the manor. Essex's mother, the Countess of Leicester, Lettice Knollys, was said to be fond of gardening when she was not at Leicester House in London. She had gardening in common with her cousin the queen, though Elizabeth hated her Knollys cousin for marrying the Earl of Leicester. Lettice's eldest son, Essex, had spent his boyhood at Chartley with his sisters and returned as often as his court duties allowed.

Paulet suddenly came from around the stables. "Hold there, brewer!" The words came from a deep, rumbling voice in a chest too small to hold it.

Frances watched with some foreboding as Sir Amyas took manful steps forward on his short legs. She remembered him from the presence as a small man who made much of his bearing. A pack of hounds bounded and frolicked about him.

Frances coughed, preparing to speak as a boy if addressed, though she hoped a dusty-faced apprentice would not even gain Sir Amyas's notice. She could not hear Robert's words, though from Paulet's face, he was questioning the new brewer with mistrust. Somehow Robert must gain entrance to the Scots queen's quarters, or their mission would fail, and with it their chance to put an end to Mary's scheming.

A pup broke loose and ran toward the horses, nipping at Marcus's legs, barking furiously. The team shied, rearing in their traces, and jerked the dray forward into the trough.

"Whoa!" Frances yelled, and quickly grabbed the lines, hanging on.

Sir Amyas walked toward the cart, picked up a pebble, and threw it at the pup. It yelped and ran away, tail between its hinders.

"Brewer, control your team. Your boy is too lean to hold them."

Robert reached the team as Sir Amyas gave the order. "Come down, lad."

Frances quickly complied, remembering not to extend her hand to Robert for support.

Sir Amyas strode to the wagon with his big man's style that had brought giggles from the ladies beside the queen. Frowning, he poked amongst the barrels and kegs. "Which one is for Her papist Majesty?"

Robert pointed to the small keg under the seat. "That be it, good sir."

"Bring it down," Sir Amyas ordered.

Frances held her breath as Queen Mary's keeper inspected the keg, turning it this way and that, knocking on it in several places. "It has not a hollow sound," he said, opening the bung and letting ale spill to the ground. He nodded, satisfied.

Robert reached to lift the keg to his shoulder.

"Nay, brewer, no man but me may see the Scots whore alone. Her wiles are well-known. The keg is not heavy," he said, nudging Robert aside and hefting it. "You there, boy, take it upon your shoulder. I have other urgent duties."

Robert's face did not change, though his eyes held caution and more than a little fear.

Frances touched her forelock in salute to Sir Amyas before taking up the keg as she was bidden, though the weight sat hard on her shoulder. She dared not look to Robert, though he moved closer to gentle the horses. His whisper just reached her ears: "You know what to do?"

"Aye," she breathed, grasping the keg tighter.

Sir Amyas called a liveried servant, who was wearing a helmet, plate-armor cuirass, buckler, and broadsword. "Take this brewer's boy to the queen's apartment; then return to me and guard this dray. I want no messages passed or words spoken."

Frances followed the servant through the great hall, noticing the luxury of the graceful Flemish furnishings. A heavily carved refectory table, which must have come from the old castle, was set before a huge fireplace. Arras hangings hung on the walls in front of her. One she swore depicted a young Essex riding with hounds toward a stag. A second hanging on the far wall showed him dancing with a circle of pretty, graceful village maids. She stopped a smile before it reached her face; how like him to want to look at himself as he feasted.

They wound up a wide staircase to a balcony and to the very last door, where two heavily armed guards barred the way.

"This lad here delivers the Scots queen's double ale."

The guard scowled. "This ale should be for our throats, eh, and not the old whore inside."

"Cease such poor talk," commanded her escort. "You know Sir Amyas's orders. Respect but do not trust. Now unlock the door and stand aside."

Frances breathed easier.

"Can you find your way back to the bailey, lad?"

"Aye, sir," Frances said, the words trembling.

"Do not be afrighted, boy," her guard said, slapping her across the back. "She is a kindly woman, though her Catholic soul be damned to hell."

"Not soon enough," another guard at the door grumbled, removing a large key from his belt and unlocking the door.

Frances stepped inside to a large chamber and hesitated, her knees weakened with uncertainty. Should she go on or wait until she was ordered forward? Several ladies-in-waiting were at their occupations, folding clothes into chests, mixing kohl and cochineal, one reading aloud in Latin and another plucking softly at lute strings. At the far end nearest the windows high in the wall was a dais. Queen Mary sat in a large chair under a cloth of estate, neither gilt nor so fine as Elizabeth's, but a clear reminder of her status as former queen of France and then of Scotland. Frances knew Mary would dispute the idea of her rule being past and done.

As her eyes became accustomed to the dim light, she saw the words embroidered on the cloth of estate: *En ma Fin gît mon Commencement.* Frances translated: "In the end is my beginning." *She knows*, Frances thought. *She has always known.*

A lady approached Frances. "Her Majesty wishes to greet you, boy. She sees few enough from the outside and has little news."

Frances knew that Mary received much news from London and France, but this was no time to dispute the lady's words. She followed the lady forward toward the throne, trying to control her fear of discovery.

With downcast eyes, she reached the dais, and found it impossible to kneel with the keg on her shoulder. She placed it in front of her, removed her cap, bowed her head, and knelt.

A soft voice spoke before her with both a Scottish burr and a French inflection, a combination she doubted she would e'er hear again or soon forget. "You may stand, young English lad, or sit if your sagging shoulders are a sign of your weariness."

Frances stood. Though the queen's damask gown was beautifully embroidered, the hem and sleeves were frayed, showing age and wear. She wore a triple pearl necklace of great worth, a crown centered with a large table diamond. Stroking a little dog in her lap, Mary smiled at her, a kindly smile that crinkled her hazel eyes. She had the perfect oval face so prized by Florentine painters, though her face had now grown old, with fine wrinkles despoiling its beauty. Atop that royal head, she wore a golden-red wig, very close in color to Elizabeth's. Though Queen Mary was nearing her mid-forties and had grown fleshy over the nineteen years of her captivity, she had the distinct remains of the startling physical beauty that had been remarked of her since she was a girl even by her many enemies. She had attracted the Duke of Norfolk to offer her marriage, at the cost of his head. Frances thought Mary's rumored attractiveness was one reason why Elizabeth had ever refused to meet with her. Her Majesty could tolerate no beauty contest.

Mary, though seated, was obviously tall, some said taller by much than her cousin, which had once provoked Elizabeth's angry rejoinder: "If she is taller than me, she is too tall!"

Frances believed the tale and could see Elizabeth saying such words with great relish. The thought brought a smile to her face.

Mary motioned for her to sit. "Boy, are you so eager to serve me that you smile, or are you smiling to be relieved of your burden?"

"Both, Majesty."

The queen looked amused. "We have here a truth-speaking lad."

Frances held her cap against her doublet to hide any evidence of her breasts and sat at Mary's feet, grateful for the relief, though yet wary of what would come next.

Mary looked down at her with kindly eyes. "We must all carry heavy burdens, if God so orders." She crossed herself at her breast and her ladies followed suit.

Frances did the same, glad that her father would never know. She looked up at the high windows for somewhere to direct her gaze. Sunlight flooded across the ceiling, but did not reach so far below, leaving the lower chamber in dim light. Though the windows were high in the timbered wall, they were yet barred.

The Scots queen's gaze followed hers. She smiled. "Sir Amyas is determined I will not escape him."

A nearby lady laughed. "Her Majesty once let herself down the side of Hardwick Manor, almost escaping the Earl of Shrewsbury. She was close held after . . . though never so close as now with Sir Amyas."

"The rope was too short," Mary said wryly, "or I was."

All Mary's ladies smiled sadly at the memory, though the queen turned her attention back to Frances.

"You have traveled from Burton?"

Frances thought to keep her answers short. "Aye, Majesty."

"Since the early hours?"

"Aye, Majesty."

"You have not heard matins? I am sorry. They have taken away my priest."

Frances did not look up.

"Then you will join us in our devotions." It was not a question.

And be damned forever, Frances knew her father would think, if he ever heard of it.

She bent her head forward, for a confidence. "Majesty, I dare not stay so long as will arouse Sir Amyas's interest." Frances lowered her voice even further. "There is a new cipher for you in the keg. The men at Plough Inn fear . . ." Her voice trailed away; she was aware that she could say too much and expose herself as knowing more than an apprentice lad should.

Mary's eyes opened wide, a torrent of hope filling her face before it disappeared. "But the keg is full of ale." Mary tapped the keg with her foot.

"Inside the bung, Majesty," Frances murmured. "It has a hidey-hole."

The queen looked about, alarmed. "Quietly, lad, these walls could hide spies' ears." She motioned to her ladies. "Empty the ale into our stone jars."

When the keg was returned, Frances leaned in to hold it up to the queen, who eagerly removed the bung and with a long finger reached in and up to retrieve the tiny roll of tightly wound paper wrapped in sealskin.

"Boy, how often will my ale be replenished?"

"Twice weekly, Majesty."

One of Mary's women brought a candle. Before she read, Mary stopped to look at Frances. "Here we have a lad pretty as any lass and we do not see to his thirst." She ordered another lady to pour Frances a cup.

"Many thanks, Your Majesty." Mary had recognized in Frances a thirst that she herself had forgotten. Gratefully, she accepted the pewter cup.

It would be difficult for Frances to hate this queen, no matter her papist practice. She had been warned against the queen's wiles, but she saw none, only kindness to a dirty-faced apprentice. Not for the first time, she had some regret for her part in this entrapment; nor would she ever forgive herself, at least never completely. Torn between two queens—perhaps the Plough Inn men had similar feelings.

Mary called for pen and paper and had no sooner secreted a response into the secret bunghole than the outer door banged open and Sir Amyas rushed in, through the chamber and to the dais. He did not kneel, or even bow.

"Boy, are you being kept here against your will?"

"Nay, Sir Am—"

"For shame. A lad seduced to popery by . . ."

Mary stood. "Sir Amyas, the boy was tired and thirsty. In Christian duty, I could not turn him back to the road with no rest or drink."

"Madam, you have offended propriety!"

"Not a whit, Sir Amyas," Mary said. "As a sinner I am truly conscious of having often offended my Creator, and I beg him to forgive me, but as a queen and sovereign, I am aware of no fault or offense for which I have to render account to *anyone* here below."

"Madam, you twist words to suit your purpose. Make peace with your God. You will soon needs make peace with our Queen Elizabeth."

Mary's face lit with hope. "Will she see me? Is she coming? If only we sister queens could meet . . ."

Her keeper made a growling sound deep in his throat and yanked Frances toward the door. "Listen no more to the Scots witch, boy, lest you find yourself amidst the fires of hell."

Just able to get out an agreement, she said, "Aye, sir."

"Hold, Sir Amyas!" A lady came up fast with the keg. "Her Majesty will need this to be refilled."

Sir Amyas scowled but took the keg and looked it over carefully, shaking, then smelling it. Satisfied that it was hollow, he handed it to Frances.

She tried to look back, offer with her eyes some small thanks to the proud woman on the dais who had touched her heart, but Sir Amyas pushed her through the open door and the guards slammed it shut on Mary's lonely imprisonment.

"Boy, tell your master that I am off to Greenwich tomorrow with the tally for the Scots queen's care. He will get his payment when I get mine."

"Aye, Sir Paulet."

In the great hall below, Frances followed the waiting guard out to the bailey. Her first sight was of Robert pacing beside the dray, his pronounced limp indicating his tiredness. He kept his face expressionless, but she could see the relief in his shoulders as they relaxed.

"Boy, is all accomplished?"

"Aye."

"Let us away. We have long hours back to Burton." He took the keg and placed it under the seat.

"Come, lad," he said, loudly for other ears.

They drove through the gate and turned onto the main road before he removed the sealskin-wrapped message from the keg and put it safely in the pocket tied about his waist.

Frances looked ahead through the swirling dust. "The queen of Scots is well betrayed."

He slapped the reins to speed the lead horses. "I sense your sympathy, but the fault is hers, not yours. Many before you have said she weaved a spell on them." He slapped the reins again. "It is a hard business to be an intelligencer, Frances, and now you know it. I would have spared you, but you would not be spared."

"Will she be spared?" Frances asked, looking up at him.

"No, she will not. There can be only one queen for England. Which would you have?"

She did not hesitate to name her, though speaking at all was difficult. "Elizabeth."

CHAPTER SIXTEEN

✺

"Oh make in me those civil wars to cease;
I will good tribute pay, if thou do so."

—Astrophel and Stella, *Sir Philip Sidney*

———————— ✺ ————————

August

On the Road to Greenwich Palace

While her husband was away in the Low Countries, Frances had hoped to draw this year over her like a large feather blanket that would warm her for the rest of her life. She wanted to remember it as a time in her youth when she was herself. Her plan had succeeded and more. But now she had a bigger problem: Robert Pauley.

She stole a glance at Robert, who was hunched over the reins beside her, sometimes calling encouragement to the horses plodding furlong upon furlong back toward Greenwich. He no longer sang cheerful tunes. They spoke little, each deep in their own exhausted thoughts.

Slowly Frances threw off the spell that the Scots queen had cast on her, for spell it was to feel such compassion for one who meant to take the English throne from Elizabeth, send her father and

Frances herself to the Tower to rot or to lose their heads. Powerful enemies gone, Mary would quickly turn the realm back to the days of the Protestant burnings at Smithfield. At first, it was difficult to think that the lady with such kind eyes could bring such terror, but Frances knew that the Scots queen would believe she was saving souls and that the fires on earth were no hotter than those in hell.

As a young girl, Frances had read John Foxe's *Book of Martyrs* and knew what horrors had been visited upon Protestants by Elizabeth's Catholic sister, Mary Tudor. Her father had also read the book aloud for the education of all his household. Every evening, the tales of tortures and hideous deaths at the stake of all who questioned Catholic doctrine had left low and high alike terrified at Barn Elms. For many a night, a sudden scream would speak of nightmares in the servants' quarters.

As they drove on, darkness came slowly, and when the night settled it was complete. A quarter moon gave little light, less when clouds drifted across it.

"We will stop for the night . . . when we reach the Falcon and Dove," Robert said, breaking his silence. "These horses need a good rest, water, and feed. And we could use a hot meat pie with turnips and gravy in our bellies."

"And cheese? And good bread of the last baking?"

"Aye"—he nodded, a smile starting—"as much as you can hold, if the innkeeper has a meat pie that has not gone bad and any fresh bread beyond crumbs remaining." He looked full into her face. "You must be hungry, Frances."

"Never as much as when you speak of such a supper."

His smile widened. "I had not noticed my words had effect ere now."

In the dark, under the shadowy trees, this was dangerous speech, and she did not answer, though she thought of another hunger of which she dared not speak.

He turned his face back to the road. "Tomorrow we'll drive on until we reach Greenwich, or this adventure will count for naught."

"Aye, we must get this message from Queen Mary to Phelippes. I do not know what she wrote, but she was smiling as her pen scratched the words."

"She sees the end of her imprisonment, Spanish or French troops landing on our coast, and perhaps a seat upon the throne of England. She pictures herself riding down Cheapside in Elizabeth's open carriage and being hailed by all the Catholics she thinks still yearn for the old faith . . . and her. That would make her smile." Robert turned once again to Frances. "You have thrown off the effects of her charm at last?"

Frances nodded. "I felt great sorrow for her as a woman locked away from all she was, but no sadness for her as an enemy of our queen."

"You are good, Frances."

She stole a sideways glance at him, but he was not looking at her. "I am an intelligencer and an Englishwoman," she said, pride in her voice.

"The most beautiful," Robert muttered.

She knew not how to respond to such an extravagant compliment. A thank-you seemed lacking, but more might invite what she both feared and desired now with all her body's force. She was walking the way of betrayal of her family and of her husband. Was this the path to all forbidden love, yearning and fear until the heart was exhausted and flesh won out? For love had taken root in her heart and spread throughout her body, feeding on her until she had no thought, no emotion except that which began and ended with Robert. So thinking, she said nothing, and dared not look at him with her thoughts so clear on her face.

They drove on, slowing for the next sharp bend in the road.

From a wide bush, several nesting quail rose up, wings flapping, feathers flying.

Robert looked hard at the place and grabbed his whip, ready to lash the horses into a gallop.

Too late.

From both sides, shouting, leaping men rushed from behind trees covered in darkness. One grabbed the horses' lines and hauled on them. The big beasts tossed their heads, flared their nostrils, and snorted.

By Frances's hasty count, there were eight or nine ragged men. She gripped Robert's arm.

"Still yourself. Show no fear," he ordered in a low voice.

The nearest man, obviously the leader, burly and dressed in a stained yellow satin shirt meant for covering a more full-bodied man, pointed a pistol at Robert's head. "Give up your ale, brewer. We men of the road be of great thirst, and ye have too much for one man and his pretty boy."

Frances felt Robert's muscles tense under her hand.

"You and your men would be welcome, sir, but the barrels are empty of all my ale, just today delivered to Chartley." He looked about quickly for some advantage, one arm now extended in front of Frances.

The man turned his leering face to his men. "Aye, the lords suck up all the ale in the land, don't they, lads . . . while taking our few acres and cots for their sheep runs?"

Their faces twisted with anger, the men shouted their encouragement. "Take the pisspot's purse!"

The leader grinned, his teeth black where they were not missing. "All the better if yer barrels be empty," the leader of the footpads said. "Yer purse be thet full, eh, lads?" He came up alongside, a cocked and primed pistol pointed at Robert's heart. "That keg there 'neath yer seat be yet full, I wager. It be slakin' our thirst for now. Yer purse of Sir Paulet's coin will buy us all the ale we can pour down our gullets for a fortnight."

The men, a ragged, dirty, starved lot, grumbled agreement, looking unhappy, thirsty, and tired.

Frances gulped air until she grew dizzy. A bend of the road, and everything had changed.

The leader brandished his pistol, a flintlock of fine make, the moonlight glinting off its brass fittings and striker plate. "I be takin' that keg under yer legs, brewer. Ye're trying to hide it, and that be good sign it be the best."

Robert did not move.

"Quickly now, ere I put a ball through your pretty lad there, or use his arse to ease my prick!"

Robert grasped the reins tighter. "Frances, jump into the back . . . now," he muttered.

The man jammed the pistol into Frances's side. "Do not think to jest with me, good sir," the man growled. "I took this fine pistola from a gentleman who told me it was of the best Flemish make, though that did not save him when he tried to cheat us of an emerald ring hidden in his boot, eh, lads?"

The men crowding around the dray growled their response, each laughing and jabbing his mate with an elbow. It was a game they had played before, and perhaps was their only pleasure. They were like a pack of dogs at a bear garden, baiting, taunting, growling, and circling their prey.

"Now, sirs, ye have only to trade some ale and yer purses for yer lives. I warrant they be worth all ye have, come to it."

Tiring of talk, he waved the pistol first at Robert, then at Frances. "The keg!" he yelled, impatient.

Several men swarmed the dray, dragging Robert and Frances down to the ground. The leader snatched up the keg and shook it. "Swine turds! It be empty. Where be the gold ye were paid for yer ale? By the great Harry, search them, lads. They be hiding something precious. I can see it in their faces."

As hands seized Robert, Frances saw his pocket of coins ripped from about his waist and his doublet searched for other valuables. "Run!" he yelled to Frances, while two men now held his arms fast.

A man with foul breath and rank body pushed Frances to the road and pressed against her, hands searching under her doublet for a purse. He grunted, slavering over his find. "Ah, Rowley," he called to the leader, his hand cupping one breast, "'tis not a lad I have, but a lass, a right nice, clean one by the smell on her. No poxy two-a-penny whore from the Southwark stews, that be certain. If the barrels be empty, then we will have good sport without drink."

"Hold!" Rowley shouted. "Ye used my name, pig turd!"

Frances felt the arms of the man above her become rigid. "Ye'll hang before me. Twice piss on ye!"

Rowley walked to the man sitting on Frances and shouted, "Thrice turds on ye!" The big man lifted his fellow off Frances by his tattered jerkin and threw him into the ditch at the roadside. "I have first right," he growled. "Any of you horse farts deny me?" He stood spread-legged, holding the pistola, menacing them.

The horses, already nervous, tossed their heads and strained against the lines, almost breaking free.

The man who'd discovered Frances's sex stood and slunk back into the dark, growling, "Draw lots; that be the rule we all put our marks to."

Frances scrambled to her feet.

Rowley started for her.

The hands holding Robert had loosened as the men watched the merriment. Robert broke free and leaped on Rowley's back. "Frances . . . run to the woods!" he yelled.

Rowley twisted about like a wolf in a trap, weakening Robert's hold. The thief raised the pistola and fired.

In that instant, Robert staggered back, a red stain blossoming on his shoulder, spreading down his doublet. He slowly collapsed to his knees onto the road. "Frances . . ."

She saw blood run down his fingers and drop into the dirt. Full of fear for Robert and fury that she was treated so, she yelled, "No, Rowley! Leave be and I will see you well paid . . . !"

Rowley swung round on her once again, lusting for more than gold. He grabbed her, pushed her into the dirt. Climbing on her, he seized her breast. Laying down his pistol near her head, he grabbed her other breast and she screamed, pushing against him with all her strength as he sought to rip away her trunk hose.

She could not scream again; his weight was too much for her. She could not draw breath; his reeking body brought bile to her mouth.

Jesu, help me! She must not be defiled before Robert. She must not be the cause of his death. He was trying to crawl toward her, pulling himself along with one arm, his face twisted with agony and fear, his open mouth groaning words that she could not understand.

The footpads stood like groundlings at the theater, their eyes bright with what they would see, mouths gaping at the scene in front of them.

"Help me!" she pleaded.

But not one of them expressed anything but envy and lust as they looked on, grinning.

Frances pushed at Rowley with all her strength. "Stop!" she ordered, but he was beyond stopping. Satan could not have ordered him.

His club of a fist hit the side of her head. Pain ripped through her, and sparks exploded behind her eyes. She battled for consciousness, knowing what she would wake to if she did not fight him.

Rowley sat back on his heels, his hand tugging out his erect prick, his eyes glassy with excitement, far beyond seeing. She kicked and twisted without moving him. She pushed once more with all her strength. This time her hand slid to a bone handle sheathed at Rowley's side.

A meat knife!

She twisted her arm from under him. Pain shot through her. Still, she grabbed at the knife. Raising it as high as she could, she brought it down on his back, feeling the flesh give way and the knife scrape along bone, lodging there.

He grunted, his eyes wide with shock, and toppled to her side, his hands desperately clawing at his back.

Frances grabbed the pistol and waved it at the rest of the band as she scrambled to her feet. She rushed to Robert, menacing the man who had his foot planted on Robert's back. The man moved away from her.

"Robert, you must get up," she said, never taking her gaze from the men who moved to surround her. She waved the pistol in an arc.

Holding to her arm, Robert stood. Blood had pooled beneath him.

"Stay with me, sweet Robert," she whispered, hoping he heard her.

She held the pistol on the footpads, but they advanced through the deep shadows until they heard the hammer click into place.

"Did Rowley load with new powder and ball?" one asked.

"I know not," replied another. "He be fast, but . . ."

The man who had discovered her womanhood looked about, standing tall. "I be leader now," he said, kicking at Rowley, who was fast becoming a corpse.

"Nay, we must draw lots, arse!" a man yelled. "Ye said it yersel'." He raised his fists.

Frances and Robert backed away. "Climb up quickly," Robert whispered hoarsely, his mouth scarce moving. "We must be off before they decide what to do."

"The keg," she said, and, reaching down with his good arm to where Rowley had dropped it, he tossed it back under the seat. Then, with her pushing, he climbed into the dray.

In doing so, he used his last energy. His face paled and his teeth began to chatter as if he'd been caught out in a winter storm. He slumped against her, managing a few words: "Frances, get you away. Leave me. . . ." He slumped across her lap. She held him with one arm, grabbed the harness leads, wrapped them about her fist, and found the whip Robert had dropped. She grasped it, every part of her body bruised and aching.

Frances saw three men advancing stealthily on the dray. She lashed out at them and they jumped back, though from their curses she knew that her whip had found the flesh of one of them. At the crack of the whip, the horses, pawing the dirt nervously, lunged ahead down the dark road.

A scream followed her. The dray had crippled a footpad who'd fallen from its sideboard under the wheels. Frances felt no remorse. She did not slow the team to a walk for several furlongs.

Robert made no sound. She felt his face and found it warm. He was alive, but the rough shaking of the dray kept the blood flowing anew from his wound. "Don't die," she whispered. "Don't leave me."

"Never . . . of my will," he murmured.

The moon was high when she saw the lanterns of the Falcon and Dove yet lit, the innkeeper hoping for late business. She pulled into the inn yard, her strength at its end.

"Robert, you must sit up. If the innkeeper espies your wound, he will call the sheriff or local beadle." She pulled his cloak up from the floorboards and wrapped it loosely about his shoulders. "Can you walk?"

"Aye. See to the horses; there's good coin in my hat. They did not find that pocket."

"Clever, Robert."

"I know their ways," he said, but produced no smile.

A sleepy-eyed innkeeper stepped from the door.

"Ho, innkeeper. I stopped here on my way to Burton."

"A fast trip, sir, and a profitable one, I pray."

Robert nodded, his mouth tight.

Frances spoke up in her croaking boy's voice. "My master and I will have a room with clean bed linen."

"Aye," the innkeeper said, "my best linen sheets just come from the washerwomen in the village." He looked at Robert, smiling. "And ale, too, lest yer master has a'ready had his fill."

Frances realized that the innkeeper thought Robert was in his cups and seized on the idea. "A groat if your potboy helps my master to his bed. His head already aches."

"'Tis done," the man said, barking loudly for the stable boy. "Hay and water for these horses, Will, yet first help the brewer's 'prentice with his master, who be his own best customer this night."

Robert found strength enough to climb the steep stairs to the room above, leaning on Frances and the stable boy.

The room was small, the ceiling low and slanted under the eaves, with one small window to allow air and light, though not much of either. The room was stifling, yet Frances dared not open the pane to the noxious night air. Even in the country, physicians warned that night air must be avoided lest pestilence or evil spirits enter.

Robert staggered to the sagging rope bed and fell on the straw mattress, his cloak parting to reveal a bloody shirt.

The stable boy stared and backed to the door.

Frances, carrying Robert's hat after it had fallen on the stairs, fished in a small inside pocket and pulled out a coin. "You earned your groat, but I've a silver shilling for you, Will, if you say nothing of what you see here to the innkeeper."

The boy held out his hand.

"Nay," said Frances, making her face stern, "no coin until we leave and you have kept your silence."

The boy frowned.

"Yet, lad, if you tell me where I may find a doctor in the nearest village, you will have a silver penny this instant."

"Now?"

"Aye, and the shilling later if you have kept the secret. Not a groat more, if you do not."

"I be showing you where to find the doctor, but it be late and he may a'ready have taken to his bed."

"I need him brought quickly."

"My master'll have my hide if I leave, so come silently."

"A moment of time."

Frances went quickly to Robert and opened his shirt to see the wound yet seeping blood. At least his life essence was not flowing so fast. She took a deep breath and tore some sheeting, which still smelled of lye soap, to pad the wound. Her trembling had ceased and a calm had o'ertaken her . . . an intelligencer's calm. Robert had no one but her, and she would not let him die or spend his strength in worry for her. She bent to his ear. "I must go for a doctor to take out that ball."

He groaned. "Go quickly, then."

She turned to the stable boy. "Is there a back stairs?" He nodded, and she prodded him out the door, closing it softly. They moved along the short corridor to the stairs and quickly down.

"Which way to the village?" Frances asked, her hasty words just understandable.

"The cart trail there behind the stables."

"Far?" she asked, eager to start, to run as she hadn't since her girlhood.

"Nay, not long, two furlongs or so only."

She clinked the coins transferred from Robert's hat to her

pocket. "Remember, a silver shilling is yours if you are faithful to your word."

The boy looked at her, his eyes bright. "Ye must love yer master."

She swallowed hard. "Aye," she said. "I do love him well for the man he is and his goodness to me." There, she had said the words that had hidden themselves so deep inside her for so long. They were free now and yet also captive in her heart.

Will sighed and his shoulders slumped. "Ye are fortunate. That is not my lot," he said, and headed for the stables, his day's work not yet done.

Though she was bruised and aching, she walked swiftly behind him, grabbed up a lantern with a goodly candle, and began to run for the cart trail. The lantern swayed wildly, light dancing up and down huge old trees, showing her feet a safe way down the rutted trail, scarce much wider than a footpath. A turned ankle was a danger even in full day, but she could not worry about that with Robert's life ebbing into the sheets back at the inn.

Breathing rapidly, she soon saw the lights of village candles and lanterns ahead. A larger, two-story house loomed above her at the turn of a small green containing a horse trough. A sign bearing the mortar and pestle of an apothecary hung in front, and on the door was the chevron and three silver lancets identifying the owner as a member of the Worshipful Company of Barber-Surgeons.

Relieved, though yet near breathless from her swift passage, Frances pounded on the door. There was no light in the windows and no sound from inside. She pounded again, this time with both fists. "Awake!" she shouted, over and over.

Stepping back, she saw the faintest, flickering yellow light in an upstairs window, and to this she shouted again, "Doctor, come quickly! You are called to the inn! A wealthy merchant!"

The light disappeared to reappear at the door in front of her.

It opened.

An unshaven little man in his nightshirt and bare feet, wig askew, held a candle up to see her features. He swayed, catching himself on the door post. "It is late, young sir"—he hiccuped—"and I am abed. Your business . . . your business . . . must wait until . . . the morrow."

Frances stared at him. The man was obviously far gone with wine, some of it spilled down his nightshirt. A walk down the cart track would sober him. "Doctor, you must come with me. My master and I were attacked on the road, and he has taken a pistol ball in his shoulder."

The doctor weaved back and forth, the lantern light moving with him, his eyes unfocused, his mouth open in an idiot's pose.

She was close to shrieking at him, striking him. He was drunk, too drunk to stand up, too drunk to be a surgeon. "Do you have a 'prentice, sir, anyone, who can come . . . *now!*"

Close to choking on her own fears, she grabbed the man, who was about to fall on her. She pushed him back into a chair, finding herself with more strength than she'd ever used before, not knowing she had so much.

"'Prentice left me for the armies on the continent. Rotten pisspot. Wife died. Alone now," he mumbled, tears starting as his head lolled onto the back of the chair.

Frances swallowed hard, her heart aching from this news and pounding as if she were still running. "Tell me what I must do," she said, shaking the doctor by his nightshirt.

"Get the ball out. Cauterize . . . stop . . . bleeding." He was gulping the words.

Frances's voice was now low and her words spaced far apart so that the man would hear her well. With each word, she shook him to keep him from sleeping. "How do I get the ball out?"

"You will kill him."

"I have to try. Now, how do I remove the ball in his shoulder!" She kept shaking him.

"A probe . . ." He looked about, his head lolling back. He jerked a thumb toward a back room. ". . . surgery there. Take it and . . . leave me . . . peace."

"Laudanum for the pain?" She had seen her father lanced for deep boils. Her strong father had screamed so loud as to be heard all over Barn Elms.

The doctor did not answer. He had fallen asleep from drink, and all her shaking would not wake him.

Frances ran back to the room the doctor had named his surgery. The barber-surgeon had but recently worked at his trade.

She saw a blood-spattered oaken table and floor, a bloody leg floating in a barrel of water. Her empty stomach roiling, she looked away quickly to the long table filled with beakers. On a nearby shelf stood jars of specimens that did not bear close scrutiny.

Rolled in a sealskin on the table, she found the barber-surgeon's bloody instruments and examined them for probe, lancet, and knives. Small jars of yellow unguents and balms were in a folded section, and a modern surgery text by the famed French surgeon Ambroise Paré lay nearby. By the smell of it, a stoppered flask contained laudanum. She snatched up all and, taking off her doublet, rolled them securely inside and tied them with the sleeves.

Grabbing her lantern, still glowing though the candle was more than half-gone, she retreated back to the entrance. The doctor had fallen out of his chair and lay on the floor amidst his own vomit. The stench was unbearable. Yet she bent and retrieved a leathern wine flask by the door. Philip had once told her that soldiers carried wine with them into battle for the washing of wounds. Though the doctor could not hear her, she spoke a promise. "I will return all when you are better able to use them without killing your patients."

Out the door and across the green she went, stopping at a rain barrel to splash water on her face and drink deep. Frances then ran for the cart path as the sliver of moon was setting, but before there was a glow in the eastern sky. She knew the ruts and trail this time,

and her passage back to the inn was swifter than before, though
with every breath she was whispering over and over, "Praise Jesu if
Robert be allowed longer life." She looked to heaven, praying that
God would answer her prayer.

The inn was dark and quiet, but the stable boy was sitting,
half-asleep, on the stairs. The lantern light woke him.

"Where be the doctor?" he asked, rubbing sleep from his eyes.

"On the floor by his door."

The boy nodded. "The drink be killin' him."

"Why are you here?" she asked, hurrying past him.

"To help."

"And to keep an eye on your shilling?"

He nodded. "And to keep an eye on me shilling. I been cheated
before."

"Not by me. Now get to your bed. I may have need of you
later."

She left him and went quickly to the room, opening the door
and holding her breath against what she might see. What she did
see was not what she expected.

"Should you be sitting upright, Robert? Look, you have lost
more blood."

"Where were you? Don't you know I—"

She opened her doublet and spread the doctor's instruments
and unguents out for his inspection.

"Where is the doctor?"

"You see the doctor before you."

His mouth twitched, either in pain or amusement. "Is there
nothing you think you cannot do?"

"Many things, but standing by to see you die is not one of
them."

Going to the window, she removed the leather-wrapped stopper and cleaned the instruments in the wine from the leathern
flask, a picture of the floating leg before her eyes.

Opening his shirt, she was gladdened that her belly was empty. Dried blood covered his left shoulder.

In an effort to sit straighter, he groaned between his teeth. "The ball . . . may have gone through clean. Look." He breathed a shallow breath to keep from moving again.

Relief weakened her limbs and she sat down on the bed. "How do you know?"

"I feel blood on my back."

"Can you bend forward?"

"Give me leather to chew on, lest I cry out and wake the whole shire."

Frances pulled out the leather wine stopper and held it to his mouth, which opened enough for her to push the stopper between his teeth as they clamped down.

A small hole somewhat jagged and red revealed itself in his left shoulder. She bent to see his back and sighed with relief. This was the exit wound, smaller than the first.

"Christ's nails," she said softly, taking a deep breath, and, without thinking, kissed his cheek. "I will not have to probe."

"Doctor," he said, his mouth twisted in pain and pleasure, "I find your balms exceeding all other curatives."

"Hush, Robert," she said, kissing his other cheek, caring nothing that it was wrong to do such, thinking only of him and not of her married state.

". . . all other curatives," he repeated. "But your surgery is not done."

"What say you?"

"If the ball carried some piece of my shirt in with it, the wound will suppurate and I will not last the fortnight."

Frances sat down quickly and whispered softly again, "What say you?"

"You must probe, darling doctor. Frances, you must probe. . . ."

CHAPTER SEVENTEEN

"From so ungrateful fancy,
From such a female frenzy,
From them that use men thus,
Good Lord, deliver us."

—Astrophel and Stella, *Sir Philip Sidney*

"Good Lord, Frances, a lady cannot do such work," Robert said, his head lolling back on the cushion she had placed behind him, though his mouth turned up in grim humor. "Women are midwives, not surgeons." He knew his words would never discourage her, but he wanted what she did to be done in defiance of custom, in disobedience of him. That was always Frances at her best.

"Hush!" she said, her tone impatient to cover her fright and uncertainty. "The wound must be probed. You said so yourself." She was tired and hungry, troubled to her heart that she would fail in this, the most important task of her young life. Aye, even more important than becoming an intelligencer. Was her hand steady? Was her courage sufficient? She shivered, silently praying that God bless her hand so that she would not kill him, though hurt him she must.

Through the window she heard the near, sweet *coo-coo* of a woods dove calling for a mate. Robert's gaze moved to the window and he smiled. He had heard the same call, and that shared moment steadied her.

Taking a deep breath, Frances realized that she could not show her fears—not to Robert, not to herself—for once shown, once acknowledged, they would have power.

"Think you that I would allow you to die, brewer?" Her tone was light but firm, steadying her hand, convincing even to herself.

"Would my death not solve . . . solve a problem?"

She looked into his eyes so that he would see that she knew exactly what problem he meant. "No, never solved for me." She had not intended to respond with the whole truth, but she no longer followed her best intent. What came from her heart was more real than what she had been taught, or even what she had vowed.

He spoke the next words quickly. "Frances, wait . . . wait until the barber-surgeon is sober. This is no work for a lady of the presence chamber."

She would not allow him to spare her at the cost of his life. "The surgeon I saw may never be sober." She drew a sharp breath and held it. "Robert, you know that once the wound begins to suppurate, it will defy the best Oxford doctors." She frowned, her face a handbreadth from his. "And what work is not for me? Have you forgotten so soon that I fought the footpads of the road?" She swallowed hard. "Mayhap killed one!" She filled her lungs again to steady her trembling hands. "It is my fault you are wounded. If I had not defiantly stowed myself on the dray—"

"Those men would have left me for dead in the dust. You saved my life with your courage . . . my dearest Frances . . . and I will owe my next years to you, all my years." For a moment his eyes shone most bright through the pain. "Yet I would not have you do this bloody thing."

"Phelippes must answer the Scots queen's message, Robert, and set the plan in motion. We cannot fail in our prime duty as intelligencers."

"Aye," he said, his mouth relaxing, "you have the right of it. Hire a horse and go on without me."

"How could I explain bringing a message from the Scots queen?"

He sighed, his chest heaving, his mouth abruptly tight from the hurt of his wound. He lifted a dark brow. "I see you are seldom wrong, a troubling skill in a woman."

Impulsively, she bent to Robert and kissed his beardy cheek, scratching her lips most pleasantly. "Not for you, dearest." She pulled back and whispered, "Hush, now."

"I find your particular potions very healing, Doctor," he said, a smile emerging from the grimace of pain as he shifted his shoulder more upright.

"If you are an obliging patient, you may have another dose later."

"I would bear the tortures of Hades for one more . . . or two," he said, his gaze never leaving her face. "And next time, dearest doctor, I will help, if that suit."

He knew that even in death he would bless her. He would see her lovely face glowing before him as the dark o'erwhelmed him. Many times he had faced deadly danger and thought it unworthy of his life. Not this time. If he must die, he would die content, having given his love and received hers. He was certain at last that she loved him and meant him to know it.

Frances cut away the shirt from his shoulder and put the leathern wine bottle to his mouth. He drank deeply, and she poured the rest on the wound. She shuddered slightly, knowing how the wine must sting him, and how much more she would hurt him with the probe. "Are you ready?"

He nodded, teeth clenched.

Propping Ambroise Paré's book against the other bolster, she extracted the probe from its sealskin nest, then, with a blurred etching on the well-thumbed page to guide her, bent to the task she could not avoid if Robert was to live. Her hand trembled violently, and she prayed earnestly for God to steady her. How soon her abandoned faith returned when she was troubled. She smiled slightly at the thought that she was faithless to faithlessness, and found the strength to steady the probe.

With his good arm, Robert reached for her hand and looked into her gray eyes, shining with tears. "We will do this thing together, Frances, as we have done so many things. . . ." In a softer voice, he added, "As I would do all things."

She half smiled her gratitude, wondering at his open emotion. Did he think to die? "You will live . . . and live long, Robert," she said urgently. With his hand on hers, she guided the probe to the raw, red wound in his shoulder.

His hand tightened slightly on hers. "Frances"—he breathed her name like a soft spring breeze against her cheek—"whatever comes, you must know that you have all my heart for what you do and who you are . . . before, after, and forever."

She met his gaze. "I think I loved you from that first day," she murmured, "but it was so impossible."

"It is yet impossible, sweet Frances." He took a deep breath. "Though such an obstacle does not stop love . . . ever." He nodded slightly. "Begin, dearest surgeon."

Her hand moved the probe, steady now with his hand as blessing. It disappeared inside the wound.

His hand did not tighten, though his breath caught and quivered in his chest. "Push it through, Frances."

The second, deeper probing caught on something, and,

holding herself steady, she pulled it out and laid the small piece of once white, now bloody cloth on the flap of the sealskin surgery kit.

Robert's hand had gone limp and fallen away as the probe went deep. From all the time spent in her father's sickroom with his doctors, she remembered one important thing: If you worked with a knife or probe, work fast. Though tears like stones caught in her throat, she was gladdened to see him now insensible to pain.

Paré's guide open in front of her, she searched in the surgeon's kit for the golden vial of unguent, part yellow wax, olive oil, and turpentine, for closing the wound. Thanks be, Paré's unguent had resolved the need to burn a wound to cauterize and close it. With the greatest care, she applied the salve. It was more difficult to treat the exit wound on his back, but she pulled him forward just enough, despite his groans, and succeeded. Reading again the instruction for bandaging, she looked for linen bandages soaked in colophony and, after cutting the roll into squares, applied them. There was not enough bandage roll remaining to pass around his broad chest and body.

Drawing in a sharp breath, Robert opened his eyes, trying to focus them on her face. He swallowed hard.

With some triumph she held up the bloody piece of shirting.

"Well-done. You have talents . . . to amaze."

She pushed the bed curtains aside and stood, and with only a slight hesitation she stripped off her shirt and tore the sleeves into long pieces.

He looked at her, naked to the waist, his eyes wide and alert.

"Aye, my breasts are small. I know it well," she said, braving the truth to take the sting away before he spoke his mind. Philip had not liked her breasts and had avoided looking at them.

"They are perfect," he said, shifting forward with less pain to receive the wrap she had made from her sleeves that would hold the two colophony bandages in place close against his wounds. And as she tightened the strips of her shirt about his chest, he kissed one breast. "I love this one well." And then his lips reached for the other. "I love this one even better."

"Hold yourself still," she said, after shivering slightly, fighting distraction by sudden pleasure. Breathing deep, her breasts lifting, she knew she would never think of herself again as being a woman whose body could not please a man.

"Blessings on you, Robert."

His dark mustache twitched with his smile. "I have just been twice blessed by your bosom, Frances."

She looked deep into his black eyes, hoping to see truth there. Could any woman once betrayed have full faith in a man's words?

And yet she did. It was a small miracle. She had thought—nay, determined—never to love again, thought her heart closed to such girlish emotion, yet here it was, love full and strong as if quite the first love she had ever felt.

"You are delirious, fevered," she said, making an excuse once again to delay complete belief, not yet ready to accept that which had so long been denied. Would she always love best the love she could not have? Was that her imperfection? Heaven's great continuing jest!

He saw her uncertainty. "You must know that you have owned my heart for some time, Frances, and I have hoped for yours."

"Yea," she said, though yet fearful of showing her whole heart. "It is the fever talking; otherwise you would know that one day I must leave you behind, keeping only this memory."

"Do you think, sweet Frances, that I do not know there is no hope for this to end well . . . as I would wish it . . . with you as my wife, the mother of our children?"

She kissed him lightly on the lips. The kiss was tentative at first, but she gathered courage from desire and her mouth found his once again, with more certainty. He held her with his good arm close and then closer, until she began to heat. "We cannot, Robert. . . . We cannot. Your wound."

"God's grace, Frances, can any man lie abed with your beauty and be unmanned?"

"I doubt such matters concern God."

"If He made me in His image . . . ?"

The question hung between them, forcing a smile from her as the sun, moving across the sky, came full into the room. His sweet wit would follow her forever.

Yet she needs must force her attention back to the work at hand. She surveyed the bandaged wounds. "Not the best, but not the worst for a first-time barber-surgeon apprentice. Praise God, the unguent did its work. No fresh bleeding shows through."

But he had some pain. She could see it in the set of his mouth and the tight muscle in his cheek. She held the laudanum to his lips and whispered, "Take a sip or two, Robert. No more."

He did as she asked. "Let me sleep now and I will be a'right. . . . Sleep quickly mends."

Quietly, Frances backed off the bed, though the lumpy straw pricked her knees through the hosen she wore. As she stood, she felt the chamber spin and knew she must eat. It was late morn and the smell of pottage from the outer kitchen wafted in the window with the breeze. Retrieving her doublet from under the surgeon's kit, she dressed to go down the stairs to the inn's main room, hoping no patron noticed that her sleeves did not appear above her hands.

Will, the stable boy, crouched in the hall outside the door. "Why are you here?" she asked. "For another penny?"

"Nay, I would help ye, lass."

Was her disguise so easily breached? "What say you?"

He shrugged and stepped closer, his voice low. "I be seein' the boy players in the inn yard in their lady gowns, but I ne'er saw the turnaround. Though a stable boy, I be no dullard." He drew himself up with some dignity. "I will not tell my master yer secret, if ye take me from this place into a better. . . . Please, I beg you."

She decided to answer the harsh way. Begging would put her

in his power. "You threaten me at your peril, boy. 'Tis a hanging offense to deal so with your betters."

"It be a church offense to dress as a man if ye have no prick!"

She pulled him inside and shut the door. "Hush, boy!" She spoke no more threats, as the boy was near to tearful despair.

"I beg pardon, mistress, but I must away from this place. My master has me for"—he hung his head, searching for words—"for unnatural acts each night in the stables . . . which will send me into hellfire. Either hanging on earth for sodomy or burning later in hell!" His hand went to his heart. "Ye must help me! I be seein' yer kindness to him," he said, a thumb jerking toward the bed, "and ye give me hope."

It was clear the boy was desperate, but so was she. "How can I help you?" She made a gesture toward the bed. "I must give him all my strength."

"I be strong. We be helpin' each other. Yer secret be safe with me."

Had she a choice, trapped in this tangle? Removing several pennies from her pocket, she handed them over. "Take these and bring some pottage, bread, and broth . . . and ale in about one hour of the clock. He will awake then. Hot broth, boy."

"I have horses to feed and groom or get a beating. Then I be here with yer wants." He took the coins and was away, but turned to her after a few steps with a begging face. "My name be not boy. My name be Will."

She almost laughed at his impudence, though she admired his courage. She could trust him.

Frances went to the bed, where Robert slept deeply, and felt his forehead and cheeks for fever. Finding none, she rolled the barber-surgeon's sealskin kit back into a tied bundle, of a sudden weary in her bones. She curled herself beside Robert, settled a hand to his chest to feel it rise and fall; then, satisfied, she closed her eyes and slept.

———

*F*rances woke to a knock on the door. The sun had moved down the slanting ceiling. It was well into the late afternoon. Going to the door she questioned, "Will?"

"Aye."

The knock had awakened Robert and he struggled up, flinching with pain, yet not crying out.

Frances opened the door and motioned the boy inside.

"I be sorry to take so long, but my master told me to sweep the inn yard and bring in water from the well. He suspects nothing but that yer master be havin' a bad head and sick belly."

The aroma of good, brawn broth made her stomach rumble. She took the bowl to Robert and without a spoon held it to his lips. "Take small sips."

He accepted small sips, then took the bowl when his stomach called out for more. "Some bread, Frances, please," he said, balancing the bowl on his chest.

She tore off a piece, dipped it into the broth, and fed him.

He opened his mouth obediently, his eyes on her until Will came near and parted the bed curtains. "What is the boy doing here?"

"He knows I am not who I seem."

Robert stared at the stable boy, his eyes hard.

"Name be Will, sir. I be tellin' no secret to my master."

Her hand tightened on Robert's arm. "We need him and he has need of us. I will explain later." She bent close to whisper in his ear, "Do you think to travel tomorrow?"

"Aye, early, before dawn. I am stronger with the salty broth."

She looked skeptical.

"Truly," he said, reaching for the ale bottle and taking a long draft, healthy color flooding his pale face.

Frances stood and went to Will with the barber-surgeon's kit.

"Take this to the village and pay for the loan of it," she said, handing him a silver shilling.

He looked at the coin for a moment. No doubt it was more money than he'd had in his pocket at one time in a year. She could see the calculation in his gaze. Then he shrugged, and she knew that he had decided to be true. She did not begrudge him the thought; she blessed him for his choice.

"I be takin' the kit to the village this night and then hidin' until we leave."

"Have the team in harness and the dray in back before dawn. Can you put a heavy harness on?"

"Aye." He flexed his thin boy arms. "I be strong. Ye be havin' no regret helpin' me, lady."

She heard him slip down the back way, while behind her Robert's feet hit the floor. He hung by one arm to the bed curtains as she ran to him. "Back to bed with you," she ordered.

"Nay, dear surgeon, I must walk about. A man rapidly loses his strength in bed. Lend me your shoulder," he said, his good arm reaching for her.

She drew him up and, bracing herself, steadied him, standing close, body touching body. A great heat rose in her, as if the sun reaching now to the uneven floorboards had slipped under her skin and was trapped. She tried to hide what she felt, but he must sense her warmth, for his arm tightened about her.

For a moment Robert was alert to her anxiety and silently cursed his weakness. Then, holding her close, careful of his balance, he walked in a halting shuffle about the room, each step surer and firmer than the last.

He allowed himself to think a moment only of holding her like this for all his days. Too much of her young life had been stolen. He could give it back to her.

Stopping his wilder thoughts before they became too real to him, he looked to his next step and growing energy. If it would not pain his shoulder, he would have laughed to think that he was alone with her in a bedchamber, and less a man than he needed to be. Indeed, than she needed.

Though her voice trembled as his body moved next to hers, she had to admit the truth of what he had said. "You were right, Robert. You do seem to gain in strength."

He smiled down on her. "Aye, my lady. I am right. Yet you have never said such a pleasing thing to me ere now. I would hear it more often." His teasing gaze searched her face. "Henceforward, I doubt you will ever mistake me." He turned slowly toward the bed and, after she pulled back the bed curtains, he sat, looking up at her, seeing her hesitate. He took her arm and lowered himself slowly to the pillow, half sitting.

"Frances, I want to say so many things."

"I want to hear you say them." His need was clear, as was hers. She felt her heated blood rush to her veins. Now that his body was not pressed against hers, Frances missed the warmth and firmness of him. Slowly she walked around the bed and climbed in on the other side, blood rushing to her woman's part.

Robert made no move to touch her.

"As your surgeon," she murmured, "I caution you against sudden . . . movement—"

"Frances, there is nothing sudden in what I would have of you." He stared at her, his dark eyes glowing within the dim light of the curtained bed. "I have wanted to give love to you since that first day in your carriage, when your deep sadness mirrored my own."

Her heart pulsing in her ears, she moved closer, the dry straw jabbing her knees. "Robert, I would have truth between us at last."

"Truth has always been my dearest wish."

Taking a deep breath, she knew nothing now except the certainty so long buried under her cautious, untrusting heart. "Robert Pauley, I have longed for you and called it other names. Now I would be truthful with myself, whatever it costs me."

His gaze never left her face, looking up and down, side to side, devouring her beauty. Yet he made no move to her. She must come to him completely, even across so small a space.

She must ever know that this loving was something she freely gave and was not cruelly taken. Something had happened with Sir Philip to make her think herself less the lovely creature that she was.

Robert knew that must have changed her from what she could have been. He would give it back to her if he could. But only if she came to him freely. Could she?

Frances was waiting for him to reach out to her first, but still he did not take hold of any part of her. And he suspected she had always been taken. Would she know how to offer herself as he wanted? As she wanted? Dreaming it was one thing, but to embrace him, forsaking her vows . . . Could she do such without regret? If not, could she live with her regret? Could he? God's grace, his mind was awhirl!

He heard her gasped words. "I cannot live without . . . at least once knowing what it is to freely give myself to a man who loves me for myself."

Robert could not bring himself to do more than wait. Custom, rank, and privilege separated them. Though his manhood spoke its urgency, if the chasm of their separate stations was to be bridged, it must be Frances who came to him, or he would forever heap blame upon himself.

"Robert," she murmured, "I love you. Only you." She caught her breath. "What must you think of me? A wanton? I have tried—"

He reached for her with his good arm, and she moved the rest of the way to him.

"My love . . . Robert . . . do not injure yourself."

He pulled her face down to his, their lips almost touching. "I will not need two arms, sweetest."

Her breathing was shallow, but quick. "What must I do? How can I help?"

He laughed without sound. "Frances, I need no help."

"I want to say so many things to you."

"What o'clock is it?" His mouth curled in jest, though his breathing was heavier now that she was so close.

Half laughing, she moved her lips to his, lightly at first and then, as the flame burned hotter, his lips took command. As Robert's mouth pressed against hers, taking her very breath into himself, she knew she would never rue this night as long as she had life.

His arm was indeed strong enough to hold her close until he began parting her clothes and once again exposed her breasts. "They are so white," he said, and she shifted so that he could kiss them again, and again. "Have you been revealing them to the moon at night, as so many fine ladies do?"

She laughed, albeit with a catch in her throat. "I have never believed that old wives' tale. If the sun browns, that does not mean the moon whitens."

"You think for yourself, sweet, and in you and on this night I find it a good thing."

Frances yet found the clothes she wore hindering the closeness she wanted. She stripped off her doublet, sleeveless shirt, breeches, and hose. A deep sigh rose from her chest: She was happy she had so few boy clothes to remove.

She spread her garments over the mattress to ease the scratching of the straw on her bare body.

"Help me off with my breeches," he said, tugging them down as far as he could.

She did as he asked, and since he wore no codpiece he was completely exposed to her gaze.

For a moment they just stared at each other as the gloom within the bed curtains deepened.

"Frances, you are beautiful in my eyes . . . womanly perfection." He caressed her neck and her dark hair that shone as bright as the best-grade sea coal, with an inner light that looked as if it could burst into bright, warming flame at any moment. What light shone through the window was trapped in her short locks.

As his hands stroked her tenderly, she could not hear her own breath. "What shall we do, Robert?"

"I think you know."

And she did. His manhood was fully erect. She slid her leg over him and looked down into his face. "This may be too much for you, dearest."

He laughed; his gathering strength deepened his voice. "Frances, I will not have you do all the work of bedding." He sat upright, pushing the bolster in tight against his back until they were face-to-face. His hands covered her breasts. "Oh, mistress mine, forever after I will call my love Frances, sweetest Frances."

She knew that other women would someday look at him as she did now. "Even if Frances is not her name?"

"Frances will always be her name."

With a deep breath, he pushed himself into her and she moaned with excitement, bending, kissing his mouth, his cheek, his eyelids, smoothing his hair from his forehead.

She was drowning in the dark depth of his eyes as he filled her, touching her deepest self, which had remained truly untouched until this moment. "I love you, Robert, only you." She gasped. "No one but you will ever share it." There was such a fire building inside her that she could not stop such words, wanton though they seemed.

She had never known a woman's body could soar so. Then any thought left her; the past left her. All she knew was the pleasure of Robert's body, then of Robert himself, all of him.

They moved together in common ecstasy, his hand hard clasping her buttocks, drawing her closer and closer to him, so heated he felt no pain, a great strength flowing through him and into her.

She threw back her head and opened her mouth, his hand suddenly covering it to hold the pleasure scream inside, the first she had ever felt with a man.

Emptied, Robert fell back, his eyes still feasting on her.

Frances, breathing rapidly, looked down at him as he slowly left her; then she toppled over to the side, looking up at him.

Through the small windowpanes, she saw the stars come out one by one.

They slept and woke; they kissed and held each other's bodies, time passing, time not passing. They caressed until the hour before dawn, when they dressed reluctantly and made their silent way down the back stairs.

Will waited, the horses' hooves muffled in straw-packed cloth bags, the wheels greased. They moved slowly and quietly from the inn yard and turned onto the Greenwich Road as the first faint light of dawn appeared in the east, Will riding the lead horse so Robert need not drive.

They moved steadily toward Greenwich Palace, and her old life threatened to envelop Frances. With one last look back at the inn, she clung to Robert's good arm and whispered, "How I am to live without you?"

"We are in love's hands, sweetest."

"Love's hands . . ." she repeated.

"Aye, Frances, and love is never conquered."

They drove on, the morning sun rising to their right, and held the keg between them with the queen of Scots' cipher secure once again in the bunghole.

CHAPTER EIGHTEEN

∽

"What if you new beauties see?
Will they not stir new affection?"

—Astrophel and Stella, *Sir Philip Sidney*

GREENWICH PALACE

The moonlit ribbon of road led south to the riverside castle of Greenwich, clouds gusting across the moon, the wind moaning like spirits escaping hell. At last, they were through a rear delivery gate into the sheltered stable yard. Usually quiet at such a late hour, the yard was full of carts, horses, and hostlers running from wagon to castle doors, carrying into the palace masses of gown and jewelry chests, chairs, tables, and parts of Elizabeth's huge bed, her arras tapestries, her big case clock, the picture of her father, Henry VIII, and every other thing a queen must have to travel on her progress comfortably.

Frances jumped down and went to Will, who held the lead horses, Claudius and Marcus. Standing on her tiptoes, she gave the gentle giants hugs. "If ever I have my own carriage, I will have you to pull it, with fine hay, apples, and pears every day in your stalls."

"They will remember your promise," Robert said, then drew Frances into the overhanging shadows. "Her Majesty has returned early, perhaps at your father's request, since he hopes to bring the Scots queen to her end . . . and soon. Now haste to your chambers before we are discovered. We cannot lose all now." He held her tight against his chest, his one good arm as strong as two. "I must take the keg with Mary's cipher to your father at once. Come to his office later"—he grinned—"fully recovered from your measles."

She nodded, dreading that they must part, hoping to stay a moment in the strength of his embrace, though she was careful not to touch his wound, seeking his stubbled face with her lips. "How can I live without you near?" she whispered.

"I ask myself that same question and receive no satisfactory answer."

"'What if you new beauties see?'" It was the question that had been worrying her heart for all the trip from the inn.

His gaze was intense. "They will not stir my affection, sweetheart. There will never be another to me as you are now, Frances. You are the queen of my heart—forever." He knew her. Kind, determined, courageous, daring, an intelligencer to her boots! "No other woman has your eyes, your beautiful face, your mind. If I had been born my father's rightful son, I . . ."

She drew in a breath to calm her pulsing heart. "What? What would you do?"

"I would come to your father and beg for you."

Surely this was a game. "And what dowry would you ask?"

"None but you," he said softly.

"That is not done . . . no dowry."

"Then I would be the first. Only in my dreams . . ."

"You have dreamed of me?"

"More than I've slept since that first day."

His voice was solemn. This was no game to him, nor to her, though there were no winners, just pawns.

He whispered, "Remember . . . forever."

"The queen of England will be filled with jealousy," she whispered, trying to jest. They moved into deep shadow, and she stood against his body to keep him close for one last moment, until she heard the clock tower begin to chime. She tilted her lips to his and he met them with his own, exploring her mouth.

"I must away, Frances . . . your father."

"And I must speed to my chambers and quickly recover," she said, smiling. "Her Majesty may call me at her pleasure."

"Speak not of pleasure, lest I cannot leave you." His arm about her shoulder, he took her a few steps to a small, darkened staircase.

"Robert, you must see a doctor about your shoulder."

"Aye, I will, but I think I have had the best surgeon in all England."

"Apprentice," she corrected. "When will I see you?" She had to have some assurance.

His chest heaved with a deep breath, though he winced. "Soon . . . soon, but we must be cautious. My ruin would be great but yours much greater." His hand slid down her arm, prolonging the stroke until at last their fingers touched and parted.

He called to Will, pulled a flare from its sconce on the castle wall, and handed it to the boy. "With good care, light your mistress's way. She will direct you when you reach the upper corridor."

After their close days and nights, she was lost without the near heat of him, the sound of his breathing in her ear, the security of his love close to her heart. With one last, long gaze, she tore herself away and stumbled up the stairs, back to the life of Lady Frances Sidney. Although she knew she should not, she looked behind and glimpsed him walking away. Her heart aching, she knew this must be her life to the end of it . . . leaving Robert.

As she must needs, she turned herself to what came next. "Will, go before and make fair certain that the corridor is empty. I would not be seen dressed in this way. I sense my disguise is at its end."

Cautiously, they made their way, clinging to deep shadows, stopping without a breath when palace guards marched by, then slipped at last into her chambers and heard the lock click shut. What had made her think she could do what she had done these last days? And yet she had done her work and done it well. A thrill of triumph filled her. It seemed an entire lifetime since she had last left Greenwich. "Wait here in my receiving chamber, Will." He sank into a chair, exhausted, his eyes closing. "Meg! Meg!" she called, throwing off her doublet.

The girl appeared, her night shift deeply wrinkled, scrubbing sleep from her eyes. She stared beyond her mistress at the ragged boy behind her. "Mistress, ye be home and yet whole . . . though yer shirt has lost its sleeves and ye bring a stable boy, from the smell on him."

Frances managed a weary smile. "Aye, Meg, all in good time. Now I must needs recover quickly from my measles. The morn will come soon enough. Have any inquired of me?"

"Several, mistress, but only one said he be returning today, wishing to see you." The girl grinned. "My lord Essex come back from the war in the Low Countries, but yesterday . . . and from his horse straight to your door."

"God's grace! What did you say to him?"

"As ye instructed, that ye could accept no visitor, lest ye infect the castle."

"As you see, I am recovered, praise be," Frances said wryly. "Now, Meg, I must bathe and ready myself for the day. Did you get the new wig?"

"Aye, though quickly done."

"Let me see it," Frances said, staring down in exhaustion. "It will be a new day soon enough."

Dressed in her bathing chemise, she sank deep into the tub dragged into her inner chamber before the fireplace by sleepy-eyed servants called from their pallets in her father's apartment. The water was yet warm despite its long trip from the laundries below the castle. She sank into it, her knees resting on her chest while a disapproving Meg stood nearby.

"Ye have already had one bath this summer, mistress, and many washings. Me mam says ye tempt Satan for vanity with two baths of a summer."

"I tempt the queen's nose to rebel without a bath and clean hair," Frances said, leaning back and sluicing the water over her breasts and stomach. "And when I am finished, put the boy Will in and see he scours the stables away . . . the straw from his hair, as well."

"He will defy me, mistress."

"It is my command, and he must learn obedience no matter how I send my orders. If he is to be of my servants, he must know that I do not ask for more than he can do, nor for more than is my right as mistress." She slumped in the tub. The tutoring of servants had been Aunt Jennet's business, but now must fall to her. She wished her old nurse with her once again. Then, trailing the cooling water one last time over her shoulders, Frances motioned Meg to add more lavender petals. "I charge you to go to my father's chambers and ask his steward for a suit of livery to fit Will. Then inform him of his duties as a groom of my chamber."

Meg looked confused. "What be his duties? He looks good for nothing as a lady's groom."

"He will learn to bring my meals hot from the flesh kitchen, accompany me about the castle and to the garden unless I am with the queen, guard my door, empty the close stool, bring in coal for the fireplace, carry messages—"

At that, Meg's eyes sparkled, and her mouth turned up knowingly.

Frances made her face disapproving. The girl was too quick to think herself clever, and that was always dangerous in a servant who knew as much as she did. She must speak sharply. "Meg, you did good work for me while I was gone, but now that I have returned, you become my chambermaid once again and not my protector."

The girl hung her head, though her mouth yet simpered. "Aye, my lady."

It was amazing to Frances how quickly a maid could think above herself. Holding amusement inside, Frances thought how like herself the girl was. Were all women ready to leap their bounds, given the chance?

"When Will is dressed in livery, show him the kitchens. I will break my fast early with some small pullet eggs, bread, and cheese . . . and a tasty Spanish orange would not go amiss. I am close to starved. After which, you may take him to the servants' hall and see the boy fed."

"Boy? Mistress, he be near to a man, if I see a'right."

Frances stood. "Man, then." Meg wrapped her in a blanket. "Now I will dress and don my new wig."

After days in a youth's loose clothes and a night without any, Frances thought her gowns a fine embroidered prison, tight and burdensome, though she approved of her reflection in the big steel mirror. Standing straight, she saw a new confidence in her appearance.

The wig was spectacular with a few more curls pulled out to the sides . . . and it was black, not red, thanks be. Fortunately Meg had found the wig maker short of red dye, the bear garden having called for it all to dye Harry Hunks, its popular old fighting bear who had lost too much fur to the attacking dogs.

As dawn reached through her windows to better light her chambers, she reluctantly applied the white Mask of Youth and cochineal red for her lips and cheeks. The mask dried rapidly and felt tight. How effortless it had been to be without anything at all covering her face, open to breezes and sky.

Working rapidly, Meg had her ready when the queen's call came.

"You are a fine lady's maid, Meg. None better. When you leave me, you will make your way very well."

"I thank you, mistress, but I hope never to leave you."

Frances bowed her head. "None know what the future brings." It was a hard truth spoken aloud, echoing about the chamber and back to her.

Will, clean and smelling suspiciously of lavender, strutting a bit in his green livery, followed Frances toward the presence chamber, his gaze darting everywhere. "I never seen halls so grand, my lady, or roofs so high . . . with gold and jewels set as stars. By the rood, be they no thieves about?"

"With the queen's guard around every corner and in every doorway . . . do not play the bumpkin, Will, or the other grooms will have you for their toy."

She smiled. "I be watchin' for them," Will said, and the way his chin went up caused Frances to cease her worry for him. The boy had learned to battle in the hardest way.

"Will, do not speak so readily unless spoken to," Frances warned.

"That be harder still, my lady . . . who was yesterday a boy." He grinned.

She shushed him. "Never speak of my disguise, and lower your voice, or even better, do not express your opinion." Will had too quickly found his wit. Still, she was happy that he would make his way.

Everywhere, Frances looked eagerly for Robert's face, but he was nowhere to be seen, not around any corner, nor in any alcove. Disappointed, she took her place in Elizabeth's entourage, motioning Will to join the other grooms waiting in the corridor. Her feet fairly itched to rush to her father's office, but the queen must come first.

"My lady Frances," Elizabeth said, a pale, thin eyebrow arching.

Frances curtsied, bringing her knee almost to the floor, despite the bruises still smarting from her encounter with the brigands of the road. "Majesty."

The queen looked hard at her. "You are little marked with spots."

"A mild attack, your grace."

"Good. I myself had no spots from the small pocks, when I was young . . . er."

No lady dared mention that Elizabeth had first worn the Mask of Youth to cover her pock scars, though she had not been horribly disfigured, as many were. And her hint of scars took nothing from her fascination. "Aye, Majesty, your recovery was miraculous."

"Just so." The queen leaned forward to whisper, ropes of huge pearls swinging from her shoulders, "And I must hear something of your adventures."

Of course, Elizabeth would know everything. She had numerous spies, including Dr. Dee. With another close, curious look at Frances, the queen swept into the presence chamber and past her lords kneeling with bowed heads. When she came to one bent head Elizabeth ruffled the russet curls, now sun-streaked from a soldier's life, and the Earl of Essex lifted his handsome, young, adoring face to her. She motioned him to stand and he did, resplendent in a silver-embroidered velvet suit of foreign cut, the doublet padded and puffed to twice its size.

He sent a quick smile toward Frances, but offered Elizabeth his arm. He was thinner and peasant brown, though even more strikingly handsome compared to the pale courtiers nearby. He led the queen to her throne, and she took her lone place under the gold cloth of estate, motioning the court to rise.

"Sir Amyas," she called, and the short jailer from Chartley approached, sweeping away his tall hat as he knelt.

Holding her breath, Frances saw the man's gaze pass over her face with admiration, but leave it without recognition. She had to hide a smile of triumph that her disguise had been such a good one.

"We are happy indeed to see you at court, Sir Amyas. How go matters at Chartley?" The words were said while the queen's eyes searched the chamber. She did not truly wish to hear more of Mary.

"They go very well, Majesty . . . except for these bills . . . and that woman's continued demands to be treated as a queen. . . ."

"Fingle-fangle," Elizabeth said dismissively. "Do I look like an accountant? Take them up with my treasurer, Lord Burghley." She motioned Burghley forward. He came, leaning on his cane. Sir Amyas Paulet, bowing, handed him a sheaf of foolscap filled with numbers. The queen waved Paulet away. "Later we will hear your reports, but no complaints, Sir Amyas, in our private chambers."

"Aye, Majesty," Paulet said, his shoulders slumping, making him shorter still. He probably knew he would never get full payment, though perhaps an attainted traitor's estate or two. He brightened and backed away, bowing. Pleasing Elizabeth was all the payment any Englishman could hope for.

"Cod's head," the queen murmured, though Frances, suppressing a smile, heard the insult.

"Walsingham, what have you for me that does not make demands on my poor purse?"

Frances's father, perpetually sober faced, stepped forward and bowed. "Majesty, I crave private audience on grave matters of urgent state business."

"You have come, as do they all, to raid my treasury for the Holland war," the queen insisted, her hand rising and falling, sensing too much trouble to forestall, probably knowing something of his business, or suspecting it would also concern her longtime guest, Mary, queen of Scots.

The public audience went quickly, Elizabeth accepting as many petitions as her impatient temper would allow, passing them on to Burghley, who would present them later with his recommendations. Finally her patience frayed and came to an abrupt end. She stood and the court knelt. "Come, walk with me, my lady Sidney."

Frances fortified herself with a quick prayer as the trumpets blared and the drums pounded, the guards marching off in unison.

They swept from the presence and down the short corridor to Her Majesty's apartments. She motioned Frances inside her reception chamber, ordering the doors closed behind them, leaving several anxious petitioners outside.

"Ale," she called, pointing Frances toward a chair at her big writing table.

"My thanks, Majesty," Frances said, drinking deeply.

An attendant watered the queen's ale, as she never touched strong drink. Then all in the chamber were waved into a side room, and Frances prepared herself for an inquisition.

Elizabeth arranged her long white fingers in her lap. "You have good spirit, my lady, as I first observed. I have heard something of your adventure, but tell me all. Did you leave the castle in disguise only to find measles?"

The question confirmed to Frances's relief that the queen suspected much, but knew very little. "Aye, Majesty, disguised, as any good intelligencer would be." Frances had seen others caught in the queen's curiosity say too much and have Her Majesty happily snap shut the trap.

The queen's head lifted and her deep blue eyes looked into the distance. "Many times, I slipped away in disguise as a maid, once to see my lord Leicester win at archery . . . though he lost . . . to a pigeon." She smiled slyly.

There was a clamor in the outer chamber.

"The Earl of Essex is an eager boy. Soldiering has not taught him patience," the queen said, her face unreadable, motioning the guard to open her outer doors. "And I must see my spymaster."

"Majesty," Frances said, and backed from the room, happy to escape more questions.

Essex bowed as Frances walked past him into the outer chamber. "Lady Sidney, may I call upon you later? Sir Philip has sent gifts and letters to you, not three days gone."

Essex seemed changed. He no longer swaggered even when not moving. His face, though leaner, held a man's calm assurance. His eyes held sadness, as if he had stared at death on too many battlefields. War had been his maturity. She wondered how Philip might be altered, though a brief pale image of her husband was blurred by Robert's face.

"I must to my father now, my lord," Frances said. "Most gladly will I welcome you at three of the clock."

"Shall we walk in the garden?"

She hesitated, remembering their last meeting there.

"If you will."

He smiled and bowed again. Gathering her skirts, she moved to her father near the huge portrait of Henry VIII. There would be no escaping Essex without insult, but she would take her servants.

"Lord father," she said, bowing her head for his blessing.

He smiled, or at least his mouth turned up on one side. "Frances, it is good to see you so in the queen's favor and in health."

"And you, Father," she said sweetly. He knew nothing. The great spymaster had been deceived by a daughter he thought no intelligencer. Or had he?

"Aye, I am in health," he answered. "I was able to persuade Her Majesty to return from her progress as our great business proceeds to its finish." Something near to full satisfaction touched his face briefly and was gone.

When her father was called to the queen, Frances found Will

waiting in the corridor admiring the guards, gleaming silver breast-plates and their red liveries with the Tudor rose on their sleeves.

"Come, I must to my father's office, and you to my chambers, where Meg will have duties for you."

She fair ran to her chambers, scrubbing her face until it was clear of the white mask and glowed pink; then she raced down the stairs. The guards, uncrossing their pikes, bowed her inside. The long room was as gloomy as ever, with clerks bending to their tasks, candlelight wreathing their earnest faces. Her gaze swept past lanterns that created shadows to dance on the gray stone walls, until she found Robert.

The queen had not listened long to Mr. Secretary, who was already at his big writing table bending over a large map roll, Robert beside him. Her heart told her that it couldn't be a map of France. Surely the continent was not the place to send the best intelligencer in all England.

Phelippes called to her. "Lady Frances," he said, and lowered his voice. "I have heard of all you did to bring the business at Chartley to success, and I must tell you—"

She waved him to silence, dreading that her father would hear. "I beg you, do not speak of it further. What about the Scots queen's cipher?"

"Not enough, my lady."

"Not enough? But the message goes to the traitors at the Plough Inn in her own hand!"

"Aye, but Her Majesty will believe only Mary's evil intent, when she calls for Elizabeth's death in plain words."

"Must she draw a dagger? And yet she doesn't."

"Nay, she is too clever, but we are close . . . very close, breathing down her regal papist neck. Your father will not stop now." He looked back to Walsingham's office again. "Sir Amyas just left, but it is a good thing you weren't here. He would not recognize you as a lady of the presence, but here he might give you a closer look."

"Why was he here?"

"Sir Amyas longs to be quit of Mary. Having another mission for Pauley, your father entrusted Sir Amyas with the keg for the next message"

"A message? Babington has responded already?"

"Aye, within hours. Since we have her new cipher, it took little time to read it and make a copy for Her Majesty."

"Is that what my father and Master Pauley now discuss? Is something amiss?"

"I am not privy to their talk, my lady. We will know in good time, but the matter moves swiftly."

Frances looked on his table and saw he had been drawing a hanged woman over and over. He saw where she looked and gathered the papers into a pile, dismissing her.

She must yet learn not to ask questions, to have an intelligencer's patience, though it went against her nature to be docile and left wondering.

Her heart was sore as she went to her writing table. There was one purpose here and one only: to bring the queen of Scots to her end, to rid England of the threat of Catholic rule, uprisings in England, and Spanish or French soldiers parading through London. Yet Frances sore ached to think of that aging beauty at Chartley, a ruler without a realm, a queen with no crown who was gradually being maneuvered toward a waiting headsman.

There were no messages or work on her desk for her, and thus she did nothing, the hardest job for her. At last her father left his office with the rolled parchment held against his chest, Robert walking behind, his eyes meeting hers with a loving message. Though his intent may not have been there for others to see, it was there for her.

Walsingham, his face grown darker with anger, gathered all his men about him, and though not specifically invited, Frances stood and joined the others.

"We *will* have that devilish woman soon," he said, gripping the parchment roll so hard his fingers turned white. "She grows eager to escape, and impatience is the mother of mistakes. We must give her encouragement." His mouth widened, and for him it was the broadest of smiles.

"Aye, Sir Walsingham," Robert said, taking up the narrative. "The fastest way is to get inside the confidence of the young traitors under Sir Anthony Babington, deeper inside than ever before. They have become cautious with our man Bernard Maude at the Plough Inn, but Babington, in his letters to the queen of Scots, seems eager to put his head in a noose." Robert stopped, and everyone except Frances moved in closer.

"We must get a new man inside that group of traitors who is so trusted he can push them to act. They think themselves clever. It is easy to work with men who parade their quickness for Mary's approval. Babington is Catholic, overeager but careful, though not as cunning as he thinks. We read his every word. He expects an earldom from Mary, and that has made him lose some natural caution. An imprudent man is apt to play the fool."

Walsingham advanced the narrative. "Maude, at the Plough Inn, has pushed too hard. Babington thinks Maude may want to take his place and gain all that Mary has promised her young lord. Pauley will be introduced amongst the traitors in the usual way . . . from prison."

Frances opened her mouth to cry out, but Robert had anticipated her distress and his face warned her to silence. Holding her breath, she heard his next words as in a nightmare.

"I am to the Fleet this night and to the Tower tomorrow, chained to a priest who was captured on a recent ship from France. There can be no better companion to bring acceptance amongst the traitors."

Walsingham advanced again, a warning hand in the air. "No word of this plan must leave this room." As if to underscore his words, a torch flared on the wall behind him and went out, leaving his face in darkness.

Frances, unable to hold fast to her desire to shout against putting Robert in such danger, went to her writing table as if only routinely interested. Quickly, she grasped her shawl from the chair and walked out of the room, fighting a lump in her chest that near stopped her breath and a desire to shriek her objection: *Robert. Always Robert is sent to danger. He has done enough. Send another.* Of a sudden, the excitement of being an intelligencer drained from her.

She had reached the top of the stone stairs when Robert caught her arm. "Frances, I must speak with you."

Two courtiers strolled by at the end of the corridor, arguing about the lord admiral's players.

"They hold no candle to the Earl of Leicester's players," one man announced. Espying Robert, the man shouted, "What say you, sir?"

"Will Kempe is the greatest actor!" Robert yelled, giving the name of the queen's favorite.

They took the bone, laughing, and went on arguing even when out of sight.

"Frances," Robert whispered, and turned her into the first alcove, where he sat beside her, stretching his stiff leg in front of him, his shoulder resting against the cushioned window seat. "You must see that this is the only way to gain the traitors' confidence."

"I see that you are chosen for danger time and again. You are trusted and known to be brave." Her voice would not lift to a pleasant pitch even on her command. "But . . . the Tower," she said, the words shivering from her memory of that place of pain, "and you are not healed. You must not do this thing!"

He shook his head, denying her words, his fingers lacing through hers. "We must move fast. . . . I know you see that. We have no time for another man to slowly rise in their confidence."

She, too, shook her head, but not so forcefully, knowing that what he said was true.

He tightened his grip on her. "The traitors are ready to act, ready to attack the queen, thinking that Catholics will rise and Spanish soldiers will land. Babington is young enough to believe what he wants." When Frances did not agree, Robert spoke more urgently. "We cannot wait, sweetest. We must know when they mean to attack the queen *before* and not after. Babington must be pushed."

She knew he spoke truth. "But why you? Always you."

"The queen is in danger every day we do not stop them. You know that. They will try to kill her as soon as Mary gives clear orders, mayhap sooner to show their loyalty to her." He scanned up and down the corridor. No one was coming, and he clasped her to him, wincing a little. "Don't you see that I might get some preferment, and that would put me more rightly in your company?"

What? Was he saying that he was doing this for her? "Robert, Sir Walter Raleigh is begging the queen for advancement; he is most handsome and writes her verse. Yet Elizabeth refuses even him."

"Am I not handsome?" he whispered, his eyebrows lifting in jest. "And would I not grow in splendor if I saved her life?"

She closed her eyes and shook her head, making herself light-headed, since she had not slept. "Robert, you'll be doing this for naught." Her heart ached to say it, but truth was truth. Not even love could change certainty. "Philip will be home soon, and that will mark the end of what we are to each other."

"Never the end."

Her heart could hear no more. "Good-bye," she whispered, and slipped from his arms.

As she moved down the corridor to her chambers, exhaustion was sweeping over her like western clouds bringing in a storm. She must sleep. Then she could think what to do.

Meg put her to bed with lavender sprinkled over her pillow

and a glass of wine. Frances refused the touch of laudanum Meg spooned for her and lay with her eyes wide, imagining the sound of Robert's guitar and his low voice singing in the anteroom. Would she hear him all the days and nights of her life? And would it be her only happiness?

She slept nightmarishly, dreaming of the Tower, descending endless stairs that never reached the stone-piercing screams below. When she woke, she parted the bed curtains to see that it was almost dark. Meg had laced her wine with laudanum despite her protest, and for that she should be whipped, but Frances could not order it, since Meg had acted from kindness.

The girl was curled at the foot of the bed watching her. "My lady, shall I send Will to the kitchens for your supper?"

Frances stretched, and her stomach rumbled. She was hungry. "Aye, Meg, I will have some pottage left from the dining hall. What o'clock?"

The case clock chimed eight, and Frances knew that Robert was gone. Even now he could be entering a filthy, straw-strewn cell in the Fleet, chained to the priest.

Meg smiled as Frances closed her eyes. "Mistress, he left this note for ye."

Eagerly, Frances reached for it before seeing Essex's crest on the red wax seal.

> *Your maid tells me you needs must rest further from*
> *your illness. I would not hinder your complete*
> *return to health. Tomorrow I have a duty for the*
> *queen, but we will walk together come the day*
> *after.*
>
> > *Essex*

The word *will* was large and splotched, as if the quill were held to the paper hard and the point splayed out.

Now Frances felt the hours drag by to the next day like a chain and heavy weight about her. She joined the queen's entourage the next morning. She went through the activities of her day, little better than a puppet, speaking seldom, craving news, but there was none. As the hours passed, several times she haunted her father's office, where every secretary was quiet and waiting.

Phelippes whispered to her, "Another cipher has gone to Mary from Sir Anthony about the priest sent to the Tower with a man known to be of your household." He grinned. "They are breathless with the possibility of making Pauley a double agent to know exactly what your father knows of them and what he plans." He grinned, then sobered. "But—" He clamped his mouth together on the rest of his thought.

"What?" Frances questioned, taking hold of his doublet.

Phelippes flushed and looked away.

"Tell me!"

"I should not worry you, my lady. I know Pauley is your . . . special friend."

She straightened, erasing the anxiety from her face. "He is my servant, and his welfare is my concern and duty."

Phelippes shrugged. "To convince Babington, the priest must see Robert tortured, refusing to speak or renounce the old faith."

Her hand flew to her mouth to stop its outcry.

"My lady, Robert knew this. It was his plan to gain their confidence quickly. I promise you we will arrange their escape, and the priest will bear witness for him with the traitors."

Fleeing to her chambers, she searched for ways to save Robert from the path he had chosen . . . and found none.

CHAPTER NINETEEN

". . . a loathing of all loose unchastity,
Then Love is sin, and let me sinful be."

—Astrophel and Stella, *Sir Philip Sidney*

Late August

WHITEHALL PALACE AND THE TOWER

The queen gave Frances leave to come to Whitehall Palace with her father. Frances, ahorse, was happy to miss the dust and tumult of Elizabeth's train of carts and wagons holding all the sovereign's furniture, bedding, and her two thousand gowns, which was even now leaving Greenwich behind.

It was unusual for the court to be in London during the late summer, but this was one season that had seen no late outbreaks of plague or sweat. The Thames did reek to the heavens, but noses were the only human part assaulted.

The queen had insisted on coming to her capital just in case the Spanish king dared send an armada against England now that Sir Francis Drake had attacked the Spanish settlement of St. Augustine in the New World. Mr. Secretary thought Philip II might take advantage, if not this year, then surely in the next. He urged Elizabeth to see to her fleet. Reluctantly, the queen had agreed with her spymaster, spending some of the Spanish treasure from ships captured by her piratical sea rovers. Captains Drake, Hawkins, and Frobisher contented her with one-third of all the silver and gold they liberated from the lumbering, high-castled galleons of King Philip.

Frances left the unpacking of her gowns to Meg and disappeared into her bedchamber, dropped to her knees, and sent heavenward a desperate prayer for Robert. She tried to erase from her mind the horrifying images of him under torture, but she succeeded only in growing them by denial.

Though Robert had made this choice, she feared he had done so for her sake in the hopes that his service to the crown would allow them some future nearness of company. Was this heart's pain heaven's payment for her unchaste behavior? Yet Philip had not paid for loving Stella, for still loving Stella. Did God really hold men to be favored above women, as she had been taught and had not wanted to believe?

Still, Frances prayed for heavenly forgiveness, though she was careful to make no future promises. She could not promise faithfulness to that hollow marriage and add another broken vow to her soul's burden. Philip had been able to live a lie, thinking love excused all unchastity, and having written that it did. Perhaps it did for him, for a man. Never for a wife.

She clasped her hands tighter. *Punish me, not my love*, she begged.

Frances searched her heart, looking for a better outcome for Robert. But she could find none, only the memory of cold, dank walls and the screams of the tortured. She was nearly faint when she tried to stand. She gripped the bedpost, demanding courage from her heart, enough to match Robert's in the bowels of the Tower.

———

*P*ushed along the corridor by the Tower guard using the butt end of his pike, Robert nearly stumbled into the priest. He shared his cell with Henry Garnet, who shuffled ahead of him, a victim of Richard Topcliffe's own invention, a device that had wrenched both his arms from their sockets. He must be in agony, having been tortured but yesterday, yet he had given up no names of Catholic families who would have hidden him in their priest holes in exchange for a Mass. He seemed intent on martyrdom and he would surely find it, if not now then one day soon. Walsingham was eager to accommodate such unwelcome traitor-priests.

Today they would force Garnet to watch, hoping to double his pain and frighten him into talking. Robert did not think the man would ever break, though every bone in his body most surely would. He was going to rescue the priest from that fate, at least for now, if his plan succeeded.

No matter how the walls of a filthy cell or these corridors closed about him, he would keep his purpose well in mind: He must be accepted by Babington and the other traitors. The priest would be his entrance into their number. Robert alone would bring them and the Scots queen to Walsingham's justice; his future would be secured. He had that hope and must keep it before him.

"Move along, papist dog," the guard growled, giving Robert a final push against the priest.

Garnet was whispering his morning office.

Robert knew he must prepare himself to suffer what was necessary for the queen of England and the queen of his heart. No intelligencer had ever done what he willingly did. If this day's act did not shake a preferment loose from the queen's frugal nature, nothing would: an estate at least, since he dared not hope for a knighthood. Yet his father had been granted a baronetcy by Henry VIII after service with the king in the French wars. He had a faint hope.

If he gained such status, he could be in Frances's company

without question. He could see her, by. God's grace; she would not be banished forever from his sight.

Just to see her would be . . . no, not enough, but it might keep him from madness.

As he lurched in chains onto the lowest Tower floor, now underground with no light except for torches, he came to a large room equipped as for hell. In one corner sat a huge vat of oil ready to boil to death the next condemned poisoner. That was the sentence for a wife who poisoned her husband, or a servant who served up arsenic crystals in the master's wine.

Although the Thames's damp near overwhelmed their warmth, hot fires burned in braziers set about the room, branding irons glowing red amidst the coals. The dark scents of blood, of burning flesh, vomit, and loose bowels were everywhere. He gagged.

"Courage, my son," Garner murmured.

"Thank you, Father."

Against the back wall, Robert saw a rack with its turning wheels and the iron cuffs on a side wall with its chain hoist and heavy cannonball to add weight as its victims hung helpless with their arms in manacles twisted behind them.

The priest, his lips moving, looked at the evil devices and did not shrink. He smiled. The priest was either a brave man or a lunatic.

Robert did not think himself a coward, but he had never been foolhardy. With a deep breath and his hands in tight fists, he recalled his courage, and the face of the woman he loved. He could go on; he could bear anything, even this hell, with Frances in his heart, her face as it had been in the inn a few nights gone, wanting him, loving him fully at last.

Garnet's lips moved in silent prayer. He looked up at Robert and repeated through trembling lips, "Courage, my son."

Robert nodded, praying for the same courage from the same God.

A hoary, decayed man of nearly sixty years approached Garnet wearing a strange smile, almost as if greeting an old friend. The priest did not shrink.

Robert caught his breath and swallowed hard. Richard Topcliffe, the queen's principal interrogator, was to be his inquisitor. He had seen the man many times in Walsingham's office, had listened to his bragging. He was an evil sadist who even had a torture chamber in his own home, where he prided himself that he could work faster and better than at the Tower. It was said he could neatly strip the skin from a man with his whip. Death came as a blessed angel to his subjects.

Topcliffe hated Catholics from his soul's depth and delighted in breaking them, either their bodies or their spirits, especially if he could get them to recant. Still, nothing saved them from Tyburn's tree.

The interrogator knew that Robert was no traitor, in the Tower on Walsingham's orders, yet he leaned close, leering a greeting, his foul breath roiling Robert's empty stomach. "I will make it look good for ye, sir, doubt me not."

Robert did not speak, wanting neither to encourage nor anger the man, if human man he could be called, nor did he want the priest to hear.

"Good day to ye, good priest," Topcliffe said, smiling with blackened teeth at Garnet. "We shall have ourselves a time"—he swept his arms wide—"gaming with all my toys."

A woman was dragged into the chamber between two guards. Her clothes were in tatters, her breasts exposed. She moaned on sight of Topcliffe, who liked to rape his female victims as part of his interrogation.

"Ah, my witchy succubus is here for another turn on the rack."

The man was mad, cruel for his own pleasure, fit for Bedlam, yet here he was with life-and-death authority over Catholics, because Elizabeth lived in daily fear of the pope's sanction of her assassination. "Bring my guest over here," Topcliffe ordered the guards holding Robert. "My apologies to ye, Master Garnet, but I will not have time for ye today. Observe so that ye may know what amusement you will provide me tomorrow."

Garnet did not speak, his gaze seeming to penetrate the arching stone ceiling, searching for God and finding Him. His smile was peaceful, almost satisfied.

God's grace, Robert thought. *The man seeks martyrdom.*

He had time to think no more. The guards shoved him roughly toward a chair bolted to the floor with dangling manacles and an iron band. He was soon in those irons, arms, feet, and head. He did not know how to prepare himself. He remembered the pain of his broken leg and of the lead ball in his shoulder, but those had come suddenly, without warning. How would he withstand torture from a madman who could easily forget that Robert Pauley was there for the queen's good?

Topcliffe leaned close to his ear. "Sir Walsingham gave me no orders about ye. Yet I know I must make of ye a convincing subject, or my reputation could be tattered. Her Majesty would not like that. My repute keeps Catholics in France, or quietly hiding in their holes." He leaned even closer, his stinking mouth almost brushing Robert's cheek.

Topcliffe stood back, peering at him like a painter ready to make a true likeness. "Ye are a handsome man, as once I was." He put his hand to his own cheek, wrinkled as old leather.

"Do as you must, Master Topcliffe."

"Ahhh"—Topcliffe sighed—"a brave man. I like brave men. They call me to my best work."

Robert planted his feet hard against the stone floor, pressing until the river damp came through his leathern shoes. He would not scream. He *must not* scream. Topcliffe might lose control and forget Robert's mission. It was said his manhood hardened and rose with a victim's screams. Such a madman could easily forget—would want to forget.

Topcliffe lifted an iron from the brazier, looked at it as if he'd never seen it before, and, shaking his head slightly, returned it to the glowing coals.

Robert had braced himself for the iron and now allowed his forehead to relax only the least bit against the restraints. Topcliffe was playing games. The man could not help himself.

"Now we shall witness how much you like playing with my toys, Master Pauley." He extracted another iron from the fire and, with a smile, his crazed eyes glowing in the heat of the rod, he brought it near Robert's cheek.

Robert jammed his feet against the stone floor, tight-closing his lips to hold in any sound that might escape.

The hooked iron came closer, followed by Topcliffe's grinning face.

Closer.

Robert thought himself prepared, but the heat melted his courage so that his fists tightened anew. He felt the skin on his cheek shriveling, though the iron still had not touched him. When it landed, he heard his own flesh sizzling and smelled the scent of roasting meat. The pain of it ripped through him, worse than the ball he had taken in his shoulder. Worse than his broken leg. Worse than both together. Worse than anything he had imagined. A scream roiled through him, churning about in his mouth, but no sound came forth from his tight lips.

He felt his head pressing back hard against the iron brace, but there was no escape even after Topcliffe removed the brand and stepped back, satisfied. "Ye won't be so pretty now." He leaned closer and whispered happily in Robert's ear, "Many have courage at first. It is the second time that I invite them to my fete that they lose all valor and beg for mercy. Do ye see any mercy in me, Master Pauley?"

Robert scarce heard his bragging. His flesh still sizzled and he was forced to prayer, wondering whether Frances would be repelled by his face. Had his desire to stay in her sight even after Sidney returned from his war made of him someone she could not bear to look at?

Then he lost any sense, ceasing to think, until a leathern bucket of icy Thames water hit him full in the face and he came out from his faint back to Topcliffe's nightmare. For a moment, he forgot his mission was to save the queen from Catholic plotters and was happy to think that Henry Garnet would escape this crazed man's further pleasure, though the priest would no doubt be recaptured and eventually returned here. His stomach rebelled at the thought. Could he ever allow this madman to torture Garnet again?

A guard approached at Topcliffe's summons and released Robert from the chair, though he remained in irons as he stumbled up the stairs to his cell. He could sense his cheek swelling as it throbbed mightily without cease.

While one guard was inside the cell securing the priest's shackles to the wall, the guard behind Robert whispered, "Tonight, late," then pushed his prisoner inside and did not chain him up to the wall.

The other guard kicked him, but not too hard. "This one will not move for his pain tonight," he said, chuckling.

The cell door clanged and the tiny space lost most of the light that had penetrated from the hall torches. The guards left, arguing loudly over who would pay for a bottle of ale.

"My son," Henry Garnet said softly, "pray with me and God will remove your pain."

Robert bowed his head rather than argue that God seemed to hold no sway in the Tower.

"Pater noster, qui es in caelis, sanctificetur nomen tuum . . ." When Garnet finished, he whispered, "I cannot reach you. Will you crawl to me?" With his foot, he pushed a vial of holy oil from under his straw pallet toward Robert.

"But you were searched," Robert said, wondering how Garnet had smuggled the oil into their cell.

"The true faith has believers in need of blessing, my son, even in such a place as this. Come closer."

Moving swiftly to the priest, Robert put the vial in his shackled hand to receive the sign of the cross on his forehead. The priest drizzled oil on his flaming cheek, soothing it at once. Perhaps it did have some heavenly healing properties.

"What was that fiend whispering to you?" Garnet asked.

"He thinks me twice a traitor, Father."

The priest shifted his arms, grimacing, but there was no way they would be comfortable. "Why is that?"

"Because I am a Catholic *and* a servant to Lady Frances Sidney. Or was until discovered."

"Walsingham's daughter?" Garnet's face hardened.

"Aye, the same."

Garnet's gaze was now confused. "But you are in this place under sentence of torture?"

Robert pointed to his cheek, careful not to touch the seeping wound. "As you see, Father."

Garnet stirred to take the weight from his arms, which must hurt him like Hades.

The man had shown him a kindness, trusted him. He whispered in the priest's ear, "Sleep now. You will need your strength later, when dark falls over the city."

Garnet raised his head, staring at Robert, sudden hope in his face. "Praise the Lord. Will we be delivered?"

"Sleep now," Robert repeated.

But neither man could sleep through his pain. They waited, looking up from the filthy straw at every guard who passed. It was very late when torchlight shone through the small iron grate and a key turned in the lock.

"Come swiftly," the guard said, his lantern lighting the way.

Robert helped the priest to stand, his arm about his waist.

Stumbling after the guard, who halted, cautioning them before turning every corner, they came to a small door where food was usually delivered, judging from the dried, shrunken turnips rolled against the wall.

"Out with ye. Leave and never return if ye know what be good for ye." The door clanged shut behind them, but not before the guard said, "And tell no one I be helping ye, or I will see ye dead."

The priest, his arms dangling useless, looked about, bewildered. "Robert, where shall we go? The watch will find us for sure, and there will be no escape again."

"Father, I have the key to Walsingham's house on Seething Lane, but a few steps from Tower Hill. Come behind me closely, keeping always to the shadows."

Garnet held back. "To that devil's lair? Are you mad?"

Robert smiled, though it set his cheek to throbbing more intensely. "And the last place anyone would look."

"You are too clever, sir, and sure to be daring, thus easily caught."

"I was clever enough to be in Walsingham's household without suspicion for many years. Come; follow me. Are you not out of the Tower?" He held to the priest's cloak and pulled him into the dark along Tower Hill and thence into Seething Lane, almost in the Tower's shadow. There was no watchman on his rounds in the lane. No doubt a cold wind blowing off the river kept him hiding in some warm inn.

Finding the gate to the garden open, Robert slipped inside and was surprised to see candlelight moving within the house. He went to a side door to be met by a maid and, from the look of the mixing spoon in her hand, also the cook's helper. Her mobcap sat over her dark hair, which was suitably untidy, though her familiar gray eyes looked a warning when Robert's gaze opened wide. She saw his branding mark, and though her lips grew tight and he saw her swallow hard, her eyes misting, she did not cry out or reach for him.

He could not help but be proud of her.

As Robert passed, he muttered, "What do you know of cookery?"

"I know how to eat it, sir," Frances answered, mimicking Meg's saucy language and quickly ushering them forward.

Robert glanced quickly at Garnet, but he was muttering prayers and seemed not to hear this exchange.

"Come to the dining hall, Master Robert. It be good to see ye again." She curtsied like a good servant. "Ye, too, sir," she said to Garnet. "Warm yersels while I fetch mulled wine and a pease pottage. It be a cold night for all it be August."

"Wine will do for now, girl." Though Robert did not smile, he appreciated her acting skill. The Christmastide play had scarce tested her.

Garnet's gaze followed the maid from the room. "You are known in this house, sir," the priest said in a questioning tone.

"Aye, Father, I have been here often in my mistress's company, though this house is seldom used. Walsingham does not come here, yet he keeps the maid and a day cook on hand to serve guests."

Garnet looked at him as if not knowing what to think. Robert decided it was time to move ahead before the priest's suspicions grew.

"I know a faithful barber-surgeon nearby who will treat your shoulders. It will cause you pain."

"Sir, I am no stranger to hurt. You see me in my own country, despised and hunted. What could be more wounding?"

Perhaps a brand to carry to your grave. "I will send the maid for the surgeon. He is but one street over, nearby Bakers' Hall."

Garnet nodded, his upper body held stiff.

Robert left for the kitchen below. The pain of his cheek was now almost a part of him. He could scarce remember when it had not been there.

Frances stood in the kitchen, tears tracking down her rather dirty face.

"Why are you here?" he said, taking hold of her shoulders and shaking her in his frustration.

Her chin went up, her attitude as defiant as ever. "There was no one for Phelippes to send who is not known."

"Phelippes sent you? He is begging for dismissal, if not banishment to the continent."

"Phelippes does not know."

"More measles?"

"Nay, an aching belly this time. I took my maid's clothes and the message from Phelippes's writing table and came with Will, then sent him back. Her Majesty will not miss me. She has another throbbing head and cannot bear light or noise . . . or her ladies."

In his frustration at her stubbornness, Robert shook her slightly again. "But you are known, Frances. Why must you be so—"

". . . much an intelligencer!" she said, bold as ever. "You must trust me once again with your life." She moved closer, her eyes wide at the sight of the swollen, seeping red wound on his face, and, standing tall, she kissed the cheek that was whole. "I must help you, be with you . . . while I can. Don't you know that?"

He turned his head away, then back again to see the truth of her answer. He motioned to his face. "You do not find me hideous?"

"I find you as I always have, brave and handsome and . . . and foolhardy."

"You name yourself, my lady."

"Dearest Robert, we are as alike as gloves. I need you, and you need me. Confess it again, as you did at the Falcon and Dove."

Robert held her tighter. "The priest needs a barber-surgeon to put his arms back into their proper place. Yet I dare not send you out on the dark streets, or leave the priest."

"The priest . . . yes, and I must tend your burn," she said, and she stroked his chest in a tender gesture he recognized well. "You have no choice but to let me go, Robert. We are coming to the end of our time together and of my days as an intelligencer. Do not deny me this. It must last me my life through."

He bowed his head. "I cannot argue further with you, but have great care. Wear your hooded cloak. If you are not back in a short time, on my oath I will come for you."

"There will be no need." She raised her skirt and pulled a folded paper from her hosen knotted above the knee.

He shook his head in dismay. "Will you never change?"

"When I am forced to it, and then reluctantly."

He knew she was right, but he did not wish to speak of it, or think of it. Opening the message, he read the lines:

> *Babington and his men are watching from the*
> *house across the lane. The Jesuit priest John Ballard*
> *is one of them in disguise as a soldier named*
> *Captain Fortescue. We must know his plan. He is*
> *an assassin.*
>
> P.

She nodded. "All true. While waiting for you, I have observed Sir Anthony and the captain at a window across the way. I will go through the garden and to the apothecary through the rear of Bakers' Hall. There is a narrow way around." She smiled at a memory. "I went there often as a child for sweet buns. The old night watch may remember me."

Robert worried still. "But Babington has seen you at White-hall!"

"He has seen a lady of the presence chamber, not an ashy-faced apron-clad maid."

"I have no choice. . . . You are my mistress again." He frowned.

"God's grace be with you, Frances. The streets are unsafe for a man, much less a woman, but I cannot leave lest I arouse suspicion in the priest and he flee."

"Pauley!"

They both heard the priest's faint, anguished call from the dining hall.

She pulled on a soiled cloak and picked up a blade from the table, slipping it into an inside pocket. When Robert's hand on her arm delayed her still, she said, "Please, sweet Robert, you took the hot iron for me—do not deny it—now I will chance this for you."

"Then I will not cease to worry for your daring all my days," he whispered, kissing the tip of her artfully smudged nose.

With a sob trapped in her throat, she whirled out the door.

"Wait!" he whispered hoarsely. "Do you know the surgeon's house?"

"Aye, Robert. Delay me no more."

"I would delay you for life."

She looked back at him, a tall figure outlined by lantern light, a most dear figure, then slipped into the narrow lane, her hand clutching the knife, her chest tight, her heart thundering.

Staying to the shadows, Frances hurried toward Bakers' Hall, stopping every few steps to listen for footsteps behind or ahead of her. When she came to dark places where no light penetrated, she moved to the center of the lane, straddling the gutter, lifting her gown to keep it free of the sluggish sewer waiting for a heavier rain to send it flowing toward the Thames.

Hearing a rustling ahead, she pulled the small cleaver from her pocket and held it before her, keeping her hand steadier with the other one. She had killed one man; she did not wish to kill another unless she had to.

She moved forward, looking from side to side and once, very quickly, behind her; then she stopped. A scraping, as of wool against stone, sounded to her left. She whirled, cleaver ready to kill, telling herself she could hit out again as she had plunged the knife on the road from Chartley. Her chest ached, crying for air. She breathed deep so her words would not squeak. "Come out!" Her voice was not at its usual lower note. "Out with you, or I will raise the watch!" She gulped, bile rising in her throat.

A large cat, its ribs showing through matted fur and carrying a kitten in its mouth, scuttled from the dark, and Frances laughed aloud in relief. "Stay well, little mother," she whispered.

At last, near Bakers' Hall, inching along the wall, she reached the rear door. *God's grace!* It was locked.

Renewing her grip on the knife, she rounded the corner and found the barber-surgeon's lantern yet lit. She pounded on the door, praying that all surgeons were not in their cups at night. The door opened. A young man dressed in well-brushed livery, shaved and freshly barbered, looked out.

"I be maid at Sir Walsingham's house on Seething Lane, sir. Ye be needed, quickly."

"Can it wait, girl? I am this hour to my guild's annual dinner on Monkwell Street."

"Nay, sir, a bad injured man . . . two of them."

"Two?"

"Aye, sir."

"Sir Walsingham sent you?"

She nodded dumbly, not giving voice to a partial truth, though she would if needs be. Let him think her an idiot servant.

"Wait," he ordered, and disappeared inside.

He returned quickly with an oiled sealskin-wrapped bag, which he slung over his shoulder.

"Lead the way."

"It be close, sir, but mayhap there be thieves about."

"I treat their wounds. They will not bother me."

This time Frances walked faster and without fear. Soon they reached the garden gate. "Come this way, sir." She did not bother to hide herself or the doctor. Let Babington or his men see them to increase their curiosity.

He followed closely, and Frances quickly led him through the side door and into the great hall. For a moment, she thought Robert would rush to her, but he clenched his hands together on the edge of the settle and nodded.

"What have we here, sirs? Ah, a cruel burn." His brows rose with a question, but he did not ask it. A surgeon must be known for his lack of meddling in his patients' affairs.

Robert pointed to Garnet, who had fallen insensible from pain. "This man needs your help more."

"Ah," the surgeon said, probably knowing very well what he was seeing. "And you are Sir Walsingham's men, are you?"

Robert answered for both. "Aye, sir, Robert Pauley by name, and Lady Sidney's man." He smiled, though Frances saw it become a grimace of pain. "You will be well paid for your skill and your silence. We are on the queen's secret business."

The surgeon bowed. "Thomas Vickery, sir, namesake to the barber-surgeon who gained a livery for our guild from Her Majesty's father."

"Then we are indeed fortunate, sir, to have one skilled by reputation and forebear. If you please, Doctor, to your work."

With light fingers, the surgeon stripped the shirt from Garnet and felt the priest's shoulders, causing the man to rouse. "I advise, sir," he said, "that you take some laudanum to quiet the pain, for as much as the dislocations hurt, they will pain you more when they are reversed."

"I will bear it, sir, to keep my wits," Garnet said, his eyes wide in fearful anticipation.

The surgeon shrugged, and Frances thought him well used to patients ignoring his advice.

Gently, Robert helped Garnet to the long refectory table used for dining.

Vickery pulled back the green velvet cover that protected the turkey carpet 'neath and bade Garnet lie upon it. Robert grasped his waist and helped him atop the table.

"Now, sir, I bid you again to take something for the pain," the doctor cautioned.

"Thank you, sir, but I have my own cure for all the hurts I suffer. I but think of Christ's suffering on the cross."

Vickery nodded grimly. "Then think hard, sir." The surgeon inserted a bandage roll between the priest's teeth. "To save your tongue, bite on this." He grasped his patient's right shoulder and upper arm and swiveled them quickly and sharply.

Garnet gasped, screamed, his body arching; then he fell back in a faint.

The surgeon nodded, a small smile playing on his lips. "Prayer is often healing, but for such pain, laudanum works much better. Now, Master Pauley, hold him while I work on the other shoulder."

It was quickly done. This time Robert heard the dull snap. Garnet groaned but did not scream, though green bile ran out the side of his mouth.

"Good that he does not have a full stomach, or yon maid would have foul work." Thoughtfully, Vickery added, "Tell him to keep his arms as quiet as possible and strap them when he sleeps, although he will always be troubled by the injury." Vickery looked up. "Now to you, sir, and I will be gone to my guildhall."

"Girl," he said to Frances, standing as close as she dared, her nails biting into her hands, "bring an onion and some salt from your kitchen."

She searched the kitchen until she found a moldy, sprouting onion in the back corner of a drawer, forgotten by the cook. After cutting away the bad parts, Frances ran back with it to the pewter salt dish sitting above the hearth. She scooped out a handful and moved to where Robert sat braced in her father's great chair.

Vickery salted the onion and placed it over Robert's burn,

pressing a bandage across it and, withdrawing an evil-smelling glue from his oilskin, secured it. "It will not blister or pucker if you keep it in place until the morrow. I warn you, do not be shaved for a fortnight, Master Pauley."

"Aye, sir."

Vickery began to roll his sealskin together.

Robert opened the street door, bowing. "Send your reckoning to Sir Walsingham at Whitehall."

"No bill for service. It is an honor to provide for his household."

"I will tell him of your skill and goodness," Robert replied, and bowed him from the front door, glancing quickly up at the windows across Seething Lane. They were dark, but a shadow moved by the opposing door. He opened his own door wider for a moment only, on the pretense of waving the doctor down the street, but giving a clear view of the priest on the table, who was stirring from his faint.

Robert quickly walked to where Frances stood, and pulled her into the dark under the gallery stairs. "Do you like onions?" he questioned.

Knowing he jested, she answered in kind. "As a stuffing for my Christmas goose," she whispered against his neck. "But I like my gingered bread even more."

He bent and kissed her earlobe.

She shivered and desire drove her to press herself against him until the priest groaned and tried to sit up.

"I must help him," Robert muttered reluctantly, and thrust space between them.

The priest was struggling to sit when Robert grasped him about the waist.

"I do not see the surgeon. Is it over?" Garnet asked.

"Aye, Father, but you must to bed and be strapped in until your shoulders are stronger."

"Get me to that big chair and I will rest there, but you must help me away from this place before morn."

"Such escape must be carefully planned. Every gate out of the city is guarded. Nothing hasty, lest you fall into Topcliffe's hands again."

"And you, Pauley. Since you are traitor to him, Walsingham must be most eager to take you."

Robert nodded, though somehow he knew he must get Frances away and back to Whitehall.

She approached with a wine cup. "Sir," she said, holding it for Garnet, "this will help you sleep."

"My thanks, girl." He took the cup and drank it thirstily, then lifted his head. "This wine is bitter, almost gone to vinegar."

"Beg pardon, sir, but my master does not use these cellars often." She ducked her head like a maid fearing a blow.

Robert looked a question and she nodded.

In a very few minutes, the priest was soundly sleeping. Robert strapped his shoulders with a heavy cord cut from an old tapestry. They both watched to see whether Garnet would awake, but he was deep in dreams.

"How much did you give him?" Robert asked.

From her pocket, Frances produced a small vial of dark liquid. "Near all of it. I pray the good surgeon does not need his laudanum this night."

"So you add pick-a-pocket to your many skills."

"I would add anything to get you from this dangerous game."

He enclosed her in his arms and her body trembled against his. "I cannot leave until I draw the plotters—"

A screech of hinges sounded from the rear entrance.

They jumped apart a moment too late. Sir Anthony Babington walked in, a pistola drawn and pointed at them.

CHAPTER TWENTY

✑

"Dear, therefore be not jealous over me,
If you hear that they seem my heart to move:
Not them, oh, no, but you in them I love."

—Astrophel and Stella, *Sir Philip Sidney*

Late August

Seething Lane and Whitehall Palace

Babington's handsome face held a smirk. "Enjoying the dusty charms of your pretty young maidservant, Master Pauley?"

Pulling Frances behind him, Robert bowed. "Whilst waiting for you, Sir Anthony, a man must take his pleasures as he can."

"Ah, I see a practical man before me, and you have our priest. However did you get him from the Tower and yourself as well? Topcliffe is not renowned for his mercy."

"A hundred gold nobles always serves to inspire clemency."

"I have heard so." Babington nodded, though he continued to swing his pistola about, his gaze darting to the darker corners. "Where would you gain such fortune . . . more than my yearly estate income?"

Robert leered. "There are many ways to gain wealth in the

Tudor court, as you yourself must know, especially in the service of the spymaster's daughter."

Babington lowered the pistola. "So you are a rogue whose loyalty can be bought for gold."

"Every man must set a price on his worth and work, Sir Babington, or be no man."

Losing his bravado in the face of Robert's boldness, Babington nodded, since this was his truth as well.

Robert spoke slowly and earnestly. "I beg you, call your men, sir. There is much to plan if we are to free Queen Mary from Chartley before Walsingham finds a way to persuade the heretic Elizabeth to sign the rightful queen's death warrant." Robert took a step forward and lowered his voice. "I have heard the same from Mendoza, the Spanish ambassador, who has promised sixty thousand troops if we free Mary."

Babington nodded. "You are unusually well informed, Pauley."

"That is my business, sir."

Babington stepped closer. "All the English Catholics must rise up in Mary Stuart's favor or the Spaniards will not risk their own men and ships from the armada."

Pauley nodded and baited his trap. "Englishmen of the true faith will not rise unless Elizabeth is taken down."

"Her death is our mission, blessed by the Holy Father in Rome."

Frances's breath trembled in her throat, as she busied herself playing the slovenly maidservant, sweeping about the hearth while Robert gave Babington much-needed surety as to where his loyalty lay.

Not totally convinced, Sir Anthony raised his pistola once more. "I would not have taken you for having Catholic sympathies, Pauley . . . for being one of us."

"We must all hide our true allegiance."

"Aye, by Protestant law we must," the man agreed, finally

placing the pistola in his belt, though his stance was not completely relaxed. "Indeed, your wound proclaims your allegiance."

Robert, perfectly at ease in appearance, thrust out his hand in welcome.

Yet Frances, moving aside, saw he was wound as tight as a crossbow, the pulse in his neck pounding.

He stepped forward. "Catholic, Puritan . . . I have no quarrel with either, Sir Babington. I have another, more personal reason to champion the Scots queen."

Babington pulled his pistola from his breeches and pointed it at Robert once more.

"Now you get to the truth."

Robert waved a placating hand. "Have a care, Sir Anthony. Truly, I hear Queen Mary is most generous to those who serve her well, not as the Tudor bastard, who never opens her purse. I would not stay in this station doing an ungrateful woman's bidding for all my life."

Babington smiled broadly, finally and fully understanding the persuasion of greed for advancement, and was convinced. He walked to the door and signaled.

The first man to enter was the Jesuit priest John Ballard in disguise, and it was a good one. A tall, dark man, Ballard was dressed as a swashbuckling soldier, in a fine cape edged in gold and a satin doublet with silver buttons. He bowed in a mocking way to Frances and she curtsied, keeping her mouth slack and her gaze dull. Three other men followed close, their hands on their swords.

"Sit, sirs; Pauley is just from the Tower and now known to me as a friend to Queen Mary's cause, having paid a price to that fiend Topcliffe."

Ballard went to the sleeping Garnet and lifted his eyelids. Satisfied, he made the sign of the cross on his forehead. The disguised priest then went to the long table, calling for drink.

The men sat to hear Robert's story, which he repeated, careful not to add new details, knowing he could be too clever only to be confounded later. Less was better in many things.

Far into the night, Frances served wine and ale from the cellars while they plotted how best to assassinate Elizabeth.

As they began to draw lots, Ballard, his dark eyes glassy, struck his sword and his crucifix on the table. "I demand the right to gut the petticoat bastard in the garden of her own court. Pope Sixtus sent me forth to rid England of this usurping queen, and I will do so or die."

He looked to Babington, who nodded his assent.

The priest's hands were clasped in a pious manner, which chilled Frances, all the more because there was no hatred in his face, only devout right. Her hands shaking, she was just able to fill the ale cups before happily escaping to the kitchen when the men called for food. To her amazement, she was able to start a fire under the kitchen spit and heat the cold pease pottage. There was bread, no longer fresh but not yet gone to mold, the same of a little cheese, just enough for so many men who favored their ale over food. They gloated over the opportunity to plan treason freely with a man so closely associated with the hated Sir Francis Walsingham. Her father had been right: They could not resist the idea of a double agent. Finally, they called only for drink.

As she served more and more ale, Frances saw the men ask, one by one, for Ballard's blessing. Then they all raised their cups. "To the death of the usurper!"

Babington added, "And so to hell with her!" and downed his ale.

Murdering traitors, everyone! Frances dared not appear too interested, making a quick exit to the kitchen, yawning.

"To your bed, girl," Robert called after her, his tone a warning.

"Can she be trusted?" Babington asked, as Ballard looked after her.

"A dull-witted girl," Robert answered, "she cannot remember a thing from one minute to the next."

Frances grinned as she hurried to the kitchen. Dull-witted, was she? Then he was twice a dullard for loving her.

Frances found a dirty pallet in the corner of the kitchen, but dared not lie on it for fear of fleas. She was fair to exhausted by the evil she had witnessed. She longed for Robert, but knew he would not come until he could.

Atop the scarred kitchen table, her head cradled on her arms, she slept until at last Robert woke her, a hand upon her mouth.

"Quiet," he said. "They are drunk or sleeping, gathering strength for tomorrow. Quickly," he said, reaching for her, "you must to Whitehall and tell your father to warn Her Majesty."

Her eyes opened wide and her hand flew to her breast, all thought of sleep gone. "Robert, how can I tell my father where I have been . . . what we have done here?"

"You must. Her Majesty's life is at stake! Ballard's blood is up and he can wait no longer."

She straightened her bodice, shaking her head to clear it. "Then I will do what I must, although it will mean Barn Elms for me . . . far from you."

He pulled her into his arms. "Barn Elms, the New World, the desert of Araby . . . sweetest, know you not that I will come to you where'er you lie?"

She nestled her head against his shoulder for a moment only, but it was a complete rest.

"Get your cloak. I will tell you their plans along our way . . . and we must leave with all haste."

"The priests?"

"Ballard prepares himself with prayer to kill a queen, and Garnet sleeps on from the draft you gave him. He is blessed to escape pain. He may wake only to sleep again." Robert's hand went to his face. The salted onion had fallen away, exposing a deep, reddening wound.

His voice faltered. "Do you find my face prevents you from—"

She ran her fingers lightly along his jaw. "Yours is the dearest face in all my world . . . always."

He grinned. "But, little maid, your world is the ashes on the hearth."

"Ssssh," she said, not for jesting. "My world is complete with you in it."

For a brief moment, his eyes shut against the reality that Frances fought so hard to ignore, though he knew she could push truth away for only a little longer, until Sir Sidney returned. "Come," he said, "we must away."

"What if Babington wakes and finds you gone?"

"If they wake, they wake. I will not have you in London's night streets alone again. Luck does not last forever. Get your cloak." His tone, even in little above a whisper, was commanding.

There was no denying him, as Frances knew, and truth be told, she wanted the comfort and safety of the palace. She loved acting as an intelligencer, but must she always be uncomfortable, dirty, and hungry while doing so?

Frances and Robert went quickly through the garden and into the alley, moving always west toward Whitehall.

It was misting again, early chimney smoke hanging low over the three-story houses and shops leaning one against another. He took her hand, kissed it, and pulled her along faster still.

They moved swiftly down Eastcheap and around St. Paul's, where early book stalls were being put in place by sleepy-eyed apprentices. They soon arrived at a place where the city wall was down for repair and thence beyond the Ludgate, always guarded.

Frances closed her eyes and shivered at sight of the quarter of a headless body hanging above the gate as a warning to traitors.

Gathering Frances closer, his gaze never ceasing to sweep the way ahead, Robert spoke in her ear. "The city gate guards would surely question our purpose to be abroad at this hour, but now we are without the walls and their protection. I will go first, and you hang to my cloak."

"I am not afraid."

"Aye, but I have this." He pulled aside his cloak to show a sword.

Frances pulled aside her cloak to reveal the small cleaver from the Seething Lane kitchen.

He threw back his head and laughed without sound. "You will always amaze me, my lady."

On to Fleet Street and past the Middle Temple they went, clinging to each other and the shadows, though even those often held menace. The night lanterns on each house mandated by the lord mayor had burned low or gone out, and Robert and Frances were engulfed in rain and darkness.

"We will soon come to King Street, where we'll have a clear path to Whitehall," Robert whispered, making a cautious way forward.

Yet from the next corner, several shadows moved, and shivering men in rags blocked their path, one menacing them with a sword.

Without thinking to be brave, only of escape, Frances pulled the cleaver from inside her cloak, ready to stand against them, but Robert stepped forward in front of her, sword at the attack. She was shivering, but from cold, she swore, not fear.

First light was just beginning to show in the fields beyond Barnard's Inn to the north when Robert sought the eyes of his opponent to see their every shift before the attack began. The thief seemed to have little sword skill, counting on the weapon itself to intimidate any so rash as to be on the dark streets outside the city gate.

The thief growled. "Throw yer purse, man, and spare yersel' and the maid."

Robert laughed. "We will be spared by your ill swordsmanship." He probed through one of the man's many weaknesses and drew blood from his hand.

One of the others hobbled around and ran at Frances, who held the cleaver at a menacing angle.

The men backed away, and the swordsman who was sucking on his wound whined, "So cruel ye be, sir. Can ye not spare a groat for a poor man's bread?"

Robert laughed, mostly in relief. "Poor thief is more like it. Perhaps if you had asked without such ill and threatening manners . . ."

Frances threw some coins in the gutter, and the men quickly left all thought of battle behind them to scramble for the money. "They need go to the thieves' school in Southwark to better learn their trade," she said, relieved to be beyond the rogues, who were now beginning to menace one another for the groats and pennies.

Holding hands, they hurried on down King's Road, which divided Whitehall into two parts. They soon came to a dark, unguarded doorway and quickly stepped inside.

"I must leave you, sweetest," Robert whispered against her cheek. "Go to your father and tell him what we've learned. The queen *must* be warned."

She looked up into his dear face. "You ask a hard thing, Robert, and you would do a hard thing." Her hands tightened on his doublet. "I beg you, do not go back to Seething Lane."

"I must. They would cancel everything, and Ballard would be afoot in London to preach and plot treason again. One of them now has the courage to try to murder Elizabeth to bring on an uprising. The queen must be guarded. She is too brave and takes chances." He smiled slightly, as a son for a mother who had grown cranky in her dotage. "You know her. She would want to take that rusty old sword of her father's and fight them herself."

Frances laughed. "You have the right of it, and I would save the queen, but—"

"No more, Frances. If you know the right, then you must follow it."

She clung to him. "Yet I need you. There is so little time before
Philip—"

Robert held her close, and despite his own warnings, the possibility of a passing guard or early stable boy, he crushed her to him.

Frances gulped tears and the choking fear welling inside her. "I
feel you slipping away from me already. Love me, before we are
parted, before others have your love."

He took her chin and tipped her head back, reading as much
as he could in the dim light. "Remember only this, dearest. It will
be the memory of you in them that I love."

Her face burning with desire, her body trembling, Frances
backed to the stone wall behind her and held out her arms for him
to step into. "Dearest Robert, love me now, while we can, before I
am sent away. I burn for you . . . burn . . ."

For the next few minutes, dawn crept slowly into the courtyard, as if the dark curtain of the sky had been lifted. She clung to
him as he lifted her, held her closer than ever before, her legs
wrapped about his hips, his lips bruising hers. She had never felt
such need for a man's love, nor felt any man so reach to her deepest
place, finding a new raging fire that he fully quenched again as he
had in the inn.

Frances pressed back her head, her maid's mobcap dropping
unnoticed to the ground, and then screamed without sound into
his mouth.

"My love, my love." He choked out the words. "No matter
how many leagues we are parted, this moment will stay forever in
my heart . . . and memory . . . as the happiest of my life."

He cradled her next to his chest, and though her hair brushed
his face and wound, he could not push her away.

Clinging to him fiercely enough to last all her life, Frances
knew she had broken her marriage vows again, and yet being with

Robert did not feel false, but like new virtue, the greatest truth she had ever known. And to think she could have never felt such womanly pleasure in her life without Robert. She had more than one reason to bless him.

Before she could speak of it, he set her upon the first step. "I must haste back to Seething Lane with wine." He was out the door, but turned back once. "Remember always, dearest: Love cannot be conquered."

Frances scrambled up the steps, a few times using her hands to hoist herself upward. She was tired to the depths of her soul, though her heart sang its song: *Robert loves me, only me.*

At the top of the stairs she realized that the spymaster's office was around the next corner. Panic rose along with her gorge, and she thought for an instant that she would not take the assassins' plans to her father.

What if he sent her this day to Barn Elms? What if she never saw Robert again? Was she choosing her queen over her love? Could she?

Taking a deep breath, she knew that if she did not go at once to her father, she could nevermore call herself an intelligencer, or even a true Englishwoman. Robert would despise her. And she could not even take the time to change from Meg's third-best gown!

She begged silently for God's help and announced herself to the astonished guards, who allowed her into her father's office, by this time well aware that she was more than Walsingham's daughter. Frances walked directly past the secretaries, who stood hesitantly at sight of her face and gown, their mouths slack with shock.

Sir Francis Walsingham sat at his writing table at the end of the long room, watching her approach, his face growing darker with each step she took toward him.

His voice was almost choked. "Daughter, what is the meaning of this . . . these clothes . . . your hair . . . and you here at dawn?"

"Father," she said, bowing her head, "give me your blessing, for I am in need of it."

When no blessing was forthcoming, Frances looked up at her father's candlelit face, his beard twitching as his mouth worked to form angry words. She did not wait.

"I have been with Robert Pauley at Seething Lane. He is much hurt from the Tower, but he has gained the trust of Babington, his men, and John Ballard, the murdering priest who is disguising himself as the soldier Captain Fortescue. . . ." She breathed deeply before more truth could be spoken. "And I helped Robert as a maid of the house." She hurried on while her father worked to form outrage into words, a problem he rarely had.

"Robert heard Ballard and Babington's men plot to murder the queen in her garden this very morn."

"Tell me all of what you know."

"They did not trust Robert completely with plans already made, but he heard that when the queen walks in her garden this morning—"

"How many men will come against her?"

"One. The priest Ballard claims the pope gave him the right to kill Her Majesty. Robert will hold the rest at Seething Lane until you send men to take them." Without taking breath, she dropped to her knees. "Do not send me back to Barn Elms, Father. You see an intelligencer before you. Though you may not want it, this is what I am become." She lifted her head with pride and was astonished to see a hint of admiration in her father's face, the first she remembered since her wedding night to a noted poet of great family.

He lifted her up, his hands light on her arms, and searched her face. "Indeed, for now I must think you have the right of it, daughter."

Though the words were sincere, Frances knew they were grudging and could easily be reclaimed.

Walsingham coughed. "But we will talk more of this later. At this time, I must call out the guard."

"Then the priest Ballard will be warned and escape to try again, or another assassin will come."

Walsingham closed his eyes and nodded without acknowledging the rightness of her advice. "My men will be hidden, lest they warn this Ballard by their presence." He tapped his quill on the letter he was writing. "My lord Essex is the man who would save Her Majesty and secure himself in her favor. . . ." He smiled slightly, pleased. "And perhaps earn your esteem at last."

"Aye," Frances agreed, "he delights in playing the hero."

Her father frowned. "Why have you so taken against this lord? He is your husband's friend, close to the queen . . . and speaks often of your beauty."

She could not help but think her father saw only Essex's youth, daring, and easy manner, not the man who had once sought to conquer his friend's wife.

Walsingham paused, his eyes sweeping her costume, his mouth pursed. "Though Essex has not seen you arrayed thus."

Her father stepped behind his writing table and bent to his papers. "Go, daughter, and prepare yourself to accompany the queen on her morning walk in her gardens. I will go to Essex myself before Raleigh gets news of this, as he always seems to, and rushes to throw his cloak at the murderer." Her father laughed . . . actually laughed.

"Haste, daughter." He fastened his starched neck ruff, which had been loosened for comfort.

"Will we talk again later?" she asked, knowing the answer.

"You may be assured of it. Now off with you."

Frances made her way to her apartment from shadow to shadow, as she seemed to do more frequently lately.

"Meg," she called as she latched the door and turned the lock.

A sleepy Meg came into Frances's bedchamber from her pallet in her small sleeping closet. Will followed closely.

So that was the way of it. It had not taken the minx long. "Dress yourself in livery, Will. I will have need of you soon."

He nodded and disappeared toward the closet.

"Watch that your belly doesn't betray you," Frances warned Meg, who yet rubbed sleep from her eyes, her lips still swollen from Will's kisses.

Meg hung her head for a moment, then lifted it and looked into her mistress's face.

"We wish to marry, my lady."

"I know you are of age, but does he have the lawful fourteen years?"

"Just, my lady, no more than three years my younger. I can teach him much."

"I have no doubt you have already played the teacher. We will talk more of it later. Now I must haste to wash myself and dress for the presence chamber."

Soon Frances was swathed in her usual kirtle, partlet, shifts, embroidered oversleeves, and a gown of shimmering white sarcenet that set her face and dark, sleepless eyes aglow.

Meg stood back from the polished-steel mirror. "Her Majesty will be jealous."

"Aye," Frances said, "and I would not have it. Bring my slippers without wooden heels so that I am not taller, and I will wear no pearls, and thus to the queen's eye be not too richly dressed."

Meg ducked her head, but not before Frances caught her knowing smile. The maid was too impudent for her station. She would either be damned for it or raised to a better one. Frances thought the latter more likely. She called toward the closet chamber, "Will, attend me!" and headed for the door, expecting him to reach it before her, and so he did. Perhaps he had already been well tutored in more than bed sport.

Joining the queen's procession into the presence chamber, Frances nodded to Essex, who tried to communicate with his darting eyes, but she, smiling with a somewhat forced friendliness, moved on toward the dais.

The dreary business of ruling took less time this day, Elizabeth being eager to reach her garden's fresh air, scented with spicy roses and small Spanish espaliered oranges to pick from her enclosed sun-warmed garden wall.

Frances congratulated herself for not wearing her pearls. Elizabeth appeared to wear every jewel in the royal jewel closet: triple strands of pearls swagged across her chest, table diamonds as large as thumbs lining her oversleeves, emeralds without number, and a large teardrop ruby pendant on her forehead.

When the procession to the royal apartments began, Frances moved to the queen. "Majesty, an urgent word for your ear alone."

"Well . . . what is it this time, Lady Frances?"

"Your grace, there is a plot to kill you—"

"There is always a plot—"

Frances interrupted. ". . . in the garden as you walk this morn."

"Traitors! They dare think to come against me in my own court! I do not fear them. I am King Henry's spawn and have his valor." She stomped to her hearth chair. Grabbing up her father's sword with both hands, she slashed at an imaginary foe. Looking satisfied, she held the weapon up in front of her. "This sword my father carried in France on the Field of the Cloth of Gold, with my mother at his side. Let them try to threaten me and they will rue it for the rest of their short lives."

Elizabeth straightened her back and drew herself to her full height. "Let us walk, Lady Frances. I have a desire for the fresh air of my garden. No traitor can keep the queen of this realm hiding in her bed!"

It was a sparkling morning, though the summer would soon come to an end, the rain of last night hanging like bright tears on the roses. It was not a morning for murder, and Frances vowed there would be none. She moved closer down the circling gravel path toward the queen, who was trailed by all her ladies. Her Majesty was on Essex's arm, of course. He was cloaked and wearing silk hosen, a russet shirt open at the throat to show his broad chest, and a silver embroidered doublet as befitted his rank, but with no sign of a sword or any weapon.

"Come, Lady Sidney," the queen said, "walk with your queen and my lord Essex the while."

"Gladly, Majesty." Frances moved up swiftly, her slippers not protecting her feet from the gravel.

Essex bowed. "Majesty, if it please you, let us stop here to admire your roses. I know you love the ones with the spicy scent."

"I do, my lord. Do you not like them as well, Lady Sidney?" Though she spoke normally, the queen's eyes darted everywhere.

Frances was looking about her and forward to the fountain at the end of the walled garden and back to where the garden opened into a long yew-covered walk, darker than it should be. She knew her father would have guards well hidden, dressed in forest green up in the trees and within the maze. Then she saw their shadows as two guards stepped out onto the top of the wall holding crossbows cocked, quarrels in place, while still hidden under overhanging branches. The queen saw them, too.

"My lady," the queen said in a voice that could reach to multitudes when she so desired, "you are not attentive!"

"Yes, Majesty," Frances said, curtsying quickly. "I, too, love the spice-scented roses, and have some in our garden at Barn Elms."

"Indeed," the queen said, her gaze darting everywhere.

Frances was more admiring of her than ever. Elizabeth had the instincts of her father, the great Harry. This was a joust to her, and she expected to win the prize.

"Yes, your grace," Frances said, "my father planted them for your enjoyment when you came upriver to honor us."

"Mmm," the queen said, a smile playing upon her mouth. "Let us move on to my oranges. I would break my fast with one while it is yet warm and juicy."

They moved toward the sun-soaked brick wall at the rear of the garden.

A small, seldom-used gardener's door was suddenly thrust open, and John Ballard stepped through, his face dark with purpose, a pistola in his hand swinging toward the queen.

Elizabeth halted to pull her sword from the scabbard hidden behind her gown. Without sound or thought, Frances stepped in front of the queen, only to be pushed away by Essex.

"Ballard," Frances said, "stop or you will get no more ale from me!"

She saw Ballard's eyes open wider in recognition of the maid of Seething Lane. Two shouts followed, both so close together that they were the same sound, spoken in the same breath.

"Majesty!" Essex yelled, lurching toward Ballard.

"My boy!" the queen cried.

In two loping strides the earl's long legs carried him toward Ballard, his knightly sword immediately drawing blood.

At that moment two quarrels struck Ballard; one hit his leg, bringing him to one knee, and the other removed an ear. The priest held to his pistola and tried to jerk it back into a line with Elizabeth, a longing for death on his martyr's face. *"Dabit dues his quoque finem!"* he groaned, as Essex planted a heavy boot on his chest.

Elizabeth was in a towering rage. "Traitor, God *will* bring an end to this. How dare you attack your queen . . . and quoting Virgil! To me . . . Elizabeth Tudor, who knew my Virgil by heart before you were born!"

Uncertain, Ballard seemed to slump into the earth at these words. This was an angry scholar before him rather than the hated Protestant queen. This moment of uncertainty was followed by another quarrel, this one shattering the arm that held the weapon.

Essex raised his sword to finish the assassin.

"Hold!" the queen said. She walked to Ballard and looked down. "My lord earl," she said, and the words that followed were bitten from great outrage, "have my guards take this traitorous priest to the Tower to wait for death, which will not be swift, I promise." At that she turned her back, took Frances's arm, and stalked from the garden, ending her spoiled morning walk.

Essex quickly caught up with them, sheathing his weapon, gravel flying from his boots. He offered his arm, and the queen grasped it lightly, as if she were strolling on an uneventful late-summer morn. "How will I reward you, my lord Essex?"

"Your life is my reward, Majesty."

A smile hid from her mouth, but lit her eyes. "Oh, I think not, Essex. Surely you will grant me the pleasure of a lesser reward . . . an estate, perhaps?"

Essex bowed and wiped blood from his sword carelessly on his cloak. "As you wish, your grace."

Walsingham came quickly from the yew path, with palace guards crowding in behind him.

The queen's blue eyes grew darker. "Ah, my Moor, who spoiled my own attack!"

His dark eyes held hers; then Walsingham waved to where the trees, preparing for fall color, overhung the wall. "You were never in danger, your grace. My men surrounded you, though we could not loose our quarrels earlier, lest they hit the Earl of Essex, who seemed always to stand in the way . . . though we would have if our queen was in more danger."

Essex did not seem happy to hear this information.

Elizabeth nodded to Walsingham. "Except for your marksmen, I would be in heaven, though even *there* you would no doubt still make outrageous calls on my purse."

Walsingham bowed as the queen stalked down the gravel path toward her private entrance into Whitehall. Frances caught her father's eye and winked. His mouth lifted on one side, as near a smile as he knew to make.

As soon as the queen was resting in the royal apartment, noticeably more shaken than she would ever admit, Essex offered his arm to Frances. "Allow me to accompany you to your chambers, my lady."

She could not refuse after his gallant conduct and her father's trust in his loyalty.

As they walked the long corridors, he made no attempt at the insinuating speech he had formerly used. *He is changed*, she thought, *grown in caution and perhaps regretful of his past conduct.* Yet how could the man change so completely?

At her door, he released her arm and bowed. "Rest now, my lady. You have been through an experience that would shake most men. You were admirably brave, but now you must to bed, lest a woman's weaker humors cause you serious illness. I know this would be the counsel of my friend, your husband, if he could be here, as I am." His face was almost gentle through his pride and male beauty, his curling auburn hair scarce disordered by his extravagant courage.

"No doubt it would be Philip's wish," she answered, meeting his gaze. "I thank you for your care.

"You have a cipher for me?" she asked, ever hopeful.

"Nay," he said, grinning. "Since we have the traitors' cipher, we just write it out in minutes and send it on. This one from the Scots queen at Chartley will not be delivered. Ballard and Babington and the rest will be taken and will suffer their sentence in a few days at Tyburn . . . as soon as Topcliffe has finished."

Frances shivered at that. "What of the Scots queen?"

"She will be exceeding desperate," he said, adjusting the light to better shine on the message. He tapped the vellum. "She may attempt to escape to France, or others could try, by some ruse, to gain access to Mary, perhaps by the plan Mary puts forward here in her last letter to Babington," he said.

Phelippes looked up at Frances, his face shining with the sweat of concentration, though the stone-lined room was always cool. "Mary must die, or these plots will go on and on until one succeeds." He pulled out another cipher. "Here the papist queen writes to the Spanish king asking him for troops to come against England, promising him that the north will rise in her support."

"Double treason," Frances said, breathing deeply, remembering the gentle-spoken queen with her little dog.

"My lady," said Phelippes, "Mary has here written in great detail a plan for her rescue, including firing the stables to draw off her guards, after which Babington's men could rescue the queen before they meet the army of the north and the Spanish troops."

Her father hurried into the long room where all his secretaries were standing and stopped at Phelippes's writing table. "Does she now call for our queen's death?"

"Not in those words, sir, but very near to it."

"Let me see." Walsingham reached for the cipher, reading swiftly.

His face hardened. "My dear Thomas. This may not make her treason plain to Elizabeth's eye! I had hoped for more."

Phelippes bowed his head and her father walked away. "There is room at the bottom for another line or two, and in other places for added phrases."

"But, Master Phelippes . . ." Frances got no further.

"I can write her hand as well as if born to it. If we are not rid of this women at last, our own dear queen, England, and the true Protestant faith are dead." He dipped his quill into an ink pot and bent to his careful task. Frances had no doubt that he would produce sentences so like Mary's that even she would be hard-put to deny them. Frances walked slowly toward the door, knowing that her life as an intelligencer would soon end. What of Robert Pauley?

The gates of London were already crowded with royal guards to prevent Babington and his fellow conspirators from escaping. They would all be in the Tower before nightfall. Mr. Secretary was already making long lists of recusants, assigning them to various prisons.

Mary's decades-long imprisonment was almost finished, but with a different release from the one she'd hoped for.

And Robert would return to Whitehall, his work almost done. She would see him soon. Perhaps even tonight.

As Robert hoped, Frances had left her door off the latch and waited for him on the settle by her hearth. A low fire burned off the night's chill, yet he could not cease his shivering.

"Have you heard about Philip?" she asked.

"Yes. I am sorry for him . . . and for you." It was not the whole truth, but he tried to mean his words.

She stood and took his cold hands in hers, looking into his face. "I see more in your eyes. What disturbs you in truth?"

"I accompanied your father to Tyburn to witness . . ." He swallowed hard, unable to continue.

"The death of Babington? Ballard?"

His mouth tightened as he nodded. "God's Son! It was . . ."

"You don't have to tell me. I can imagine."

"No! No, Frances, you cannot. It is beyond imagination except for a Bedlamite."

She clasped his hand and held it to her breast. He could feel her heart beating. Life. Enough life to bring him back to the balance that he had almost lost this day.

"Robert, you must forget. What you saw was the punishment decreed for traitors and regicides. They knew and plotted nonetheless."

"Aye," he said. "I would not excuse them, but . . ." He paused, taking a deep, shuddering breath. "Even the crowd, who called for their blood as they were cut down and quartered . . . was sickened at the slow butchery that followed. Some ran retching from the bloody scene." He shivered fiercely, unable to find warmth in the fire, gulping lest his stomach betray him. "The queen got such reports of troubled crowds and ranting preachers at St. Paul's churchyard that she ordered the rest of the traitors hanged tomorrow until quite dead."

He felt Frances leave his side, stand, and reclaim his hands. She led him to her bed. There she removed his doublet, untied his shirt and trunk hose, and gently pushed him down. She drew the bed curtains and lay close to him. She warmed him.

Robert did not speak for a time, seeking to quiet himself. As the cold left his body, he clasped her closer. "Are you always this kind to your servants?"

"Only to those who perform great service."

"Ahh . . . and am I one such, mistress?"

"I don't know yet . . . how you will perform, Master Robert."

"Don't you?"

His blood rose quickly, and he thought he would give a good account this night. He would remember her. Nothing else.

Before dawn, he slipped from the warmth of her body. "My love," he whispered, and quietly left.

Early October

"My lady, it is my sad duty to report to you that Sir Philip was wounded in the leg at the Battle of Zutphen a fortnight ago."

"Wounded?" For a moment Frances could not grasp the word's meaning, though Philip's tall, slender form and pale face were instantly clear to her for the first time in months. "How woun . . . ded?" she asked, a tremor breaking the word in two.

Essex tightened his mouth. "He took a ball in the thigh, Lady Frances."

"Is he calling for me?"

Essex paused, looked away, and did not answer.

Still, Frances knew her duty. Without hesitation, she said, "I must go to him."

"Nay, my lady, Sir Philip forbade it, saying it was but a scratch and would be healed before you could take ship. It is an arduous journey to a country divided by war. Capturing Mr. Secretary's daughter would be a Spanish prize, and they would use you to bargain for terms. I beg you take Philip's word that you are better here, as he is better there."

She knew not what to make of his words except to take them as they were. Philip did not want her to come for nursing. Perhaps he had called for Stella. She tried to dismiss the thought as unworthy and curtsied to Essex. "Thank you for your kindness, my lord."

"My lady, I must return to Holland for a short while with private dispatches for my stepfather, the Earl of Leicester, from Her Majesty. If the channel winds are favorable, I will return before the winter storms begin, with news of Sir Philip and to be of any service you desire." He opened her door wide to clear a way for her gown. He bowed and clasped her hand, kissed it, his lips barely touching her skin, then walked away without a look back. She watched him go, wondering how a youth could change so completely, though she did not doubt that he had. Such sincerity was not easily faked even by so skillful an actor.

When he was out of sight, she descended quickly to her father's office. He had not returned, but Phelippes motioned her to his writing table. If she could be of no use to Philip, perhaps she could still be useful in some way here.

CHAPTER TWENTY-ONE

"O fools, or over-wise, alas! The race
Of all my thoughts hath neither stop nor start,
But only Stella's eyes and Stella's heart."

—Astrophel and Stella, *Sir Philip Sidney*

October

ON THE ROAD TO FOTHERINGHAY CASTLE, NORTHAMPTONSHIRE

As the carriage bumped through the rolling countryside, the window curtains pulled aside so that Frances could catch the unseasonably warm sun, she stared out of her window to where the Earl of Essex was riding beside her on his great black mount. He was lean and tan, very much the soldier, returning from the battles in Holland with dispatches from the Earl of Leicester for the queen. He had brought Frances private word that Philip insisted he was recovering, and desired she not come to him. Bravely, he had lost much blood, having demanded that others be removed from the field first. Now he was mending and would soon return to her.

Why Essex thought he needed to accompany her to the Scots queen's trial, she could only guess. He had no part in Mary's trial, except, as he insisted, as an Englishman who longed for justice and for his sovereign's safety, and this particular Englishman's need to be at the center of the main events of his day. Her father had not refused him.

Despite Philip's desire to recover alone, Frances's father was determined that she soon leave for Holland. There was too much speculation in the palace; even the queen had suggested she should tend to her marriage.

Yet before Frances could leave for Holland, her father had insisted that she accompany him on his trip north to witness Queen Mary's trial . . . the fruit of her intelligencer labor. She knew that in her father's mind he was not cruel, but acting as any stern parent with an unruly child. He would never expose her, but in one way or another he would make certain that his family name was protected from any further strange behavior by a disobedient daughter.

Frances leaned from the carriage to smell the autumn air made of cottage smoke and falling leaves, to watch farm animals grazing midst rolling green pastures, and goldfinches darting to and from their nests, now empty of chicks.

In the carriage, Walsingham sat across from Frances, next to Robert Pauley.

"Master Pauley, I had news from the last rider from London that Archibald Douglas, the king of Scotland's ambassador, sends word that King James in no way minds that rigor be used against his mother."

Satisfaction lit her father's face, and Frances knew that her own son's disavowal was another nail in Mary's coffin.

"Daughter, I know it was not your wish to attend upon this trial, but since it was your wish to be an intelligencer, I believe you should see the results of your great efforts."

They were oft-repeated words, as if he thought she needed to hear them again and again.

Robert looked a warning to her, but her father felt he must win this battle with his obstinate daughter. And perhaps he had the right of it. This was the natural end of her part in the greatest intelligencer work of the age.

She was aware that Essex spent much time staring at her from atop his mount. Could the earl have any thought of keeping his eye on Robert? And on her? He was clever, if not of great intellect, but he seemed to sense something, as a hound on the trail of prey.

While Frances waited outside the great hall at Fotheringhay, she thought of Philip, wounded and alone, being attended by strange doctors. Why had he not called her to tend him? Even with a wound, he preferred to be nursed by his memories and not by his wife. Even more, she felt in the wrong for being secretly glad that she could stay near Robert for their last too few hours. Sitting across from him in the carriage all that way from London while not daring to meet his gaze had been a torture.

She longed to see Robert Pauley now, to hear his voice, to know that he was still her love no matter what the future held for them.

She took a deep, shuddering breath when she thought of the next days. Not only did Mary Stuart face an ending, but so did Frances and Robert. That she could not give all her loving thought to Philip made her head ache. She was now as poor a wife as he a husband. At least she had a letter from Lord Leicester via her father's diplomatic pouch assuring her that Philip had the best doctors in all Holland and would soon be ahorse and back to England. But the Earl of Leicester was known to paint roses on every calamity, and much of her anxiety remained.

Their carriage had crossed the moat and passed through the ancient gates with the sky darkening and rain clouds hanging across the half-moon. They rattled into the lower bailey at Fotheringhay, where Frances was quickly taken up the ancient high motte to the castle and now stood in the corridor outside the great hall. Meanwhile, her father conferred with the multitude of lawyers that he

and Lord Burghley had gathered. There was great grumbling, because the Scots queen refused to attend her own trial, insisting she
was a Scots sovereign and not subject to an English court. But
Walsingham and Baron Burghley were intent upon her facing and
answering publicly to the charges of treason against Queen Elizabeth. Without such a trial they would always be open to accusa-
tions of having falsely accused Mary.

Robert came from the hall and stood beside Frances.

She acknowledged his presence as any mistress to an attendant,
speaking low, as if delivering her wishes of the day. "There is a madness here, Robert."

"This day I am among the mad, my lady, for you have be-
witched me. Or should I not speak to you thus?" he said with a half
smile and bow.

"Why would you not?"

"Your husband lies wounded in another country, a hero to all
England."

"Yes," she said, "think you that I do not know and worry for
his recovery?"

"Frances, I know not what to think of you, of him, of . . .
myself."

"Think you this: I love you and will always. I have not
changed."

"But you feel guilty about us."

"Never that. Remorse, perhaps, that I could not love Philip
though he loved not me, but never guilt for loving you, never guilt
for knowing that which I will cherish forever."

As streams of lawyers, scriveners, and lords passed them going
and coming, Robert studied his hands, his lips scarce moving.
"There will be no time to meet or talk together at Fotheringhay, my
sweet."

She had to keep her face straight, indeed sad, since many had
heard of her husband's wound. She was in truth full of sorrow for

Philip, who had proven himself brave and not merely the impover-
ished poet of love sonnets, but this proof had come at the high cost
of a leg wound. Still . . .

"We must meet to say farewell," she said, the words torn from
her reluctant heart. "Our time together is near its end. Ro-bert."
She said his name haltingly, as if it were loath to leave her lips. "I
know my father plans to send me to Barn Elms on our return, and
Philip will be home as soon as he is healed."

Robert stared ahead out the oriel windows that opened the
corridor to what light there was on this rainy day. "Perhaps all will
be as you say."

"What other way could it be?"

"I cannot read our stars to foretell the future," Robert murmured, "but I will never feel parted from you as long as I breathe
life, no matter how true our parting. You are a branch of me,
Frances . . . forever."

"A branch of you," she murmured. Her eyes did not match
her hesitant smile. "As the ones we had for shade on the road to
Chartley?"

"Yea, those very ones."

Her father came then to escort her to her single chamber,
Robert bowing and following a few steps behind them.

The spymaster was in a fury. "That devilish woman refuses
to admit Queen Elizabeth's authority, even to confess she has ever
heard of Babington, whose head now sits impaled with the other
traitors' high over London Bridge."

Robert followed, with a lighter heart remembering that he had
helped the priest Henry Garnet to escape Babington's and Ballard's
fate and take ship for France at Dover.

Walsingham marched ahead, his face tight. "Mary even insists
she will not submit to the laws of England; nor will she answer any
question unless she stands before Parliament."

Frances bent her head, thinking of the handsome young face

of the oh, so foolish Sir Anthony, and how those fine features were now food for crows. "Father," she told him, her hand on his, since he needed calming, "you have done your work well. The Scots queen does not know what proofs are arrayed against her."

He lifted his head and came near to a smile. "Aye, daughter, thanks to my good Phelippes," he said, unable to grant her any credit as he closed her door, leaving her alone to light a candle, disrobe, and find her bed. She was happy that she had had no part in the forged evidence against Mary. Yet, as an intelligencer, Frances could not blame Phelippes for adding the lines that would condemn her. Nor could she blame Elizabeth for demanding the word *assassinate* before she could bring herself to denounce Mary Stuart. Elizabeth knew she would face the wrath and armies of all the Catholic kings of Europe and the pope, who had put a huge price on her head.

Frances's breathing echoed in the chamber, and she missed Meg, who was, no doubt, having a merry time with Will, now that her mistress was gone again. At last, Frances slept, wondering whether the Scots Mary might use her well-known charms to thwart her accusers, though they would not move Walsingham or Lord Burghley. Perhaps, when one was facing the executioner's sword, imprisonment became a sweeter fate.

The sun rose soon enough, and Frances dressed to go to the dining hall, able to dispense with the hot, itchy wig now that she was away from court, and coil her dark, now longer hair under her hood. The dining hall, though not near as large as the one at Whitehall, was full of lawyers breaking their fast. The scent of never-washed lawyers' gowns o'erwhelmed the food, though the smell was no worse than that of the overperfumed courtiers at Whitehall. A servant showed Frances to a small table where the Earl of Essex sat in lone blue velvet splendor, smiling up at her with his bright blue eyes. He rose and bowed while the servant pulled the bench aside so that she could sit.

"You slept well, I trust," Essex said politely.

"Very well, thank you, my lord."

"Your father tells me you are soon for Barn Elms."

When had Essex talked about her in such a way, and why? "That is his wish."

"Though not yours?"

"No, not mine."

"Perhaps, my lady, one day you could be at court for much of your year."

"I do not envision that happening, my lord."

He smiled as if he were the master of all secrets. "None of us can know the future, Lady Frances."

Bantering with the man, whose purpose she could not guess, near took her appetite.

"I thought to see my father here."

"Alas, no, Lady Frances. The Scots queen has agreed to appear after reading a letter your father brought from Her Majesty, in which the queen demands that Mary answer all questions as if it were to Elizabeth herself." He smiled on one side of his mouth. "I suspect that the Scots queen believes that she should not anger her cousin if she hopes for pardon, which she most certainly does."

Frances nodded, thinking he had the right of it. She sipped at the ale put before her. Why was she in conversation with a man who seemed to know more than she did? He could have no knowledge of her intelligencer work. She smiled at him. Ah, he meant to show how close he was to the center of things, although he was not. To this earl, what he thought was undeniable truth. He could allow for no other notion. Essex spoke on, perhaps had been speaking while she had not been listening. "I have heard—and I am truly sorry to report it—from my stepfather, Leicester . . ." He spoke tentatively, swallowed, and began again. "The Earl of Leicester tells me Sir Philip is not recovering as quickly as the doctors desire."

She gripped the table. "What is the delay?" She could not keep the worry from her face. "It matters not what the delay. I will go to him as soon as I can take ship."

"First you must eat, my lady. You will need all your strength," Essex said, cutting some still-warm manchet bread. He placed it on her pewter plate with a bit of cheese. She thanked him, though she preferred the steaming pottage.

"Perhaps I should not have spoken so plainly, my lady. If you would like, I will call a maid with lavender to ease your anxiety."

"You should not," she said, worried now that worse news was being kept from her. "I will speak to my father. Surely his couriers travel as fast as yours."

She rose and curtsied, already looking into a much changed future. She walked toward the door, her gaze darting everywhere without seeming to until she was assured that the dining hall did not hold Robert. Where was he? Was her father, suspecting their intimacy, deliberately keeping him away from her? No, her father was not coy about his suspicions. She must keep her mind from such wild thoughts.

Frances walked swiftly toward the great hall, knowing that her father would be there. She must hear the truth about Philip and see to her transport back to London and a ship to Holland. She must be a wife again. Her idyll of freedom, of being herself, of being truly loved, was over.

She entered the great hall, full now to bursting. The walls were lined with the nobility of the shire, the sheriff, lawyers in their dozens, Sir Amyas Paulet, Sir Christopher Hatton, and many others from court, all looking grimly important.

And Robert . . . he was there on a settle against the wall. It was natural for her to go to him. A man of her household would make a place for her. And she would tell him that she must leave at once.

When he turned his face to hers, she realized that he already knew. The knowledge was in his eyes, which lacked their usual bright greeting.

She was quickly seated, but others were too close for her to talk personally. "How did they convince Mary to attend the trial?"

"They argued for hours," Robert answered. "She is very clever and had answer for all urgings, but finally she agreed early this morning, after your father told her that if she dared not defend herself Elizabeth would think her guilty."

Robert looked away and spoke softly. "How did you find the Earl of Essex as you broke your fast?"

"You are yet an intelligencer, Robert." She smiled, though her lips trembled at the edges. "He had information that Philip's wound has worsened. I must leave for London and take ship from Deptford for Holland."

Robert looked shamefaced for his taunt, and his hands clenched against his breeches. "I am sorry, Frances." His face set in polite concern, he asked, "Will you be wanting me to accompany you to Holland?"

Frances looked down at her own trembling hands buried in the folds of her gown. "I would want it, but doubt my father would, or could spare you. My maid and groom will go."

"Of course, my lady." He nodded, not looking at her, and she saw his face was set into the servant's lines of obedience yet again, a pulse pounding behind his burn scar. It would always give away his true emotions to one who knew him well.

There was a hubbub in the room, people shifting, turning, looking up, and nudging one another. Frances followed their gaze to the doorway, where Mary Stuart stood. Her steward and physician, one on either side, assisted her with the stairs, and a maid of honor carried her train. She was dressed in black velvet with a gauzy white veil over her widow's cap, though she lifted it from her face before stepping down. A file of halberdiers walked beside the procession. As Mary descended, she winced with pain, her rheumatic joints obviously impairing her, not to be eased in this drafty, ancient castle.

Many in the room, peers of England, high magistrates of the land, and courtiers, all gasped. Mary's storied beauty had been part of her legend, but little of it remained. Instead, a very tall, fleshy, bewigged woman of forty-two with only a small vestige of her youthful attractions entered haltingly.

As Mary passed down the lines of onlookers, standing in respect though accusers all, Frances curtsied, bowing her head. Mary hesitated, and Frances looked up to see a small, sad smile of recognition and concerned lines form beside her eyes before she moved on to the center of the chamber.

Forgive me, Frances thought, watching Mary's retreating back.

Her head bowed, Frances knew that if she could live again these last months, she would change nothing. Duty and loyalty to one's own sovereign were a part of her, though she would always feel regret that this moment had to be. Intelligencers did not choose the punishment of those they exposed. And, thinking of Babington's end and possibly Mary's, she thanked the blessed Lord that this was so.

Queen Mary was escorted toward the center of the great hall, where a high-backed chair had been placed below a dais holding a throne covered by a gold cloth of estate, as if Elizabeth meant to sit there. Frances knew Her Majesty never would be a part of this, would keep her hands as clean as she could.

The Scots queen paused and looked up at the royal throne. "My place should be there," she said. "I am myself a queen, the daughter of a king, and the true kinswoman of the queen of England. As an absolute queen, I cannot submit to orders; nor can I submit to the laws of the land without injury to all other sovereign princes. For myself, I do not recognize the laws of England. I am alone without counsel or anyone to speak on my behalf. My papers and notes have been taken from me, so that I am destitute of all aid." Yet, after these words, she composed herself and sat in the smaller chair, looking about her. "All these councilors," she said, "and none for me." It was not a question, for the answer was plain to see.

Frances knew that Mary's protests would do her no good. Her complaints, her very regal presence were about to be erased by a mountain of evidence.

The sergeant-at-law laid out the details of the Babington plot, including the ciphers that had gone between the plotters and Mary.

Painfully, Mary rose to her feet and objected in her French-accented English. "I do not deny that I have earnestly wished for liberty and done my utmost to procure it for myself, but I knew not Babington. I never received letters from him, nor wrote any to him. If you have such proof, produce them signed with my own hand."

Both Burghley and Walsingham could not help themselves. They smiled.

Mary lifted her head into a stately pose and added, "It may be that Babington wrote them, but let it be proved that I received them. I say Babington lied. Other men's crimes cannot be cast on me."

The cipher letters she had written were now produced one by one and read out to the throng. Mary sat suddenly, her astonished expression revealing a sense of having stepped into a neatly laid trap.

Frances felt Robert's hand close about hers behind her billowing gown.

Mary looked about the room, arrayed with solemn lawyers and nobles, her judges all. She burst into tears. "I would never make shipwreck of my soul by conspiring the destruction of my dearest sister queen."

Frances wondered whether Mary knew that what she said was untrue. Or did she so desperately want to think herself falsely accused that she could make herself believe a lie?

Walsingham produced the ale keg in which Mary's messages had been sent to Babington and his to her. He placed it on the table in front of her.

The Scots queen's knees buckled, and her ladies helped her to be seated again. "I cannot walk without assistance or use my arms, and I spend most of my time to bed in sickness. Both age and bodily weakness prevent me from wishing to resume the reins of government. What ruler could fear me?"

Robert's hand tightened as he murmured, "She is coming to know that she is exposed . . . beyond saving herself with protests of sickness."

Frances took in a heaving breath. The only thing for Mary now was any pity she could gain from the judges, if such was to be had.

"I do not fear the menaces of men," the Scots queen protested as her silent accusers looked on. "I demand another hearing and that I be allowed an advocate to plead my cause."

For answer, Walsingham stood and read out her letter to Babington with the condemning phrase: "Fail not to burn this privately and quickly." Triumphant, Mr. Secretary said: "If you did not seek Queen Elizabeth's death, then why the urgency to destroy this letter?"

Desperate now, Mary sat forward and raised her arms toward heaven. "Mother of God, they wish only to destroy me!"

Walsingham's voice was heavy with scorn. "Heaven does not listen to assassins!"

"Nor to those who conspire against the queen of France and Scotland!"

This brought loud protests of honesty from Walsingham.

Mary, trying again to deny all, spoke in a voice that carried to the entire chamber. "As to the priest, Ballard, I have heard him spoken of, but I protest that I have never thought of the ruin of the queen of England and would rather have lost my life a hundred times than that so many Catholics suffer for my sake a cruel death at Tyburn." She drew in a deep, shivering breath. "And you, too, my lord Burghley, you are also my enemy."

"No," said Lord Treasurer Burghley, his voice firm and solemn, "I am enemy to the queen's enemy." He stared at Mary, nothing of compassion written in his face. "These proceedings will resume before Parliament to pronounce sentence."

Mary no longer asked whether she could plead before Parliament. She knew she was never to see London. But she had final words that caused many to avert their gaze.

"I have desired nothing but my own deliverance." Her doctor and ladies reached to support her. As she retreated, she said, "May God keep me from having to do with you all again."

Frances's father, intensely frustrated that he could not bring the Scots queen to confess, walked past her with no pity.

"I must to my father," Frances whispered to Robert, who went before and parted the crowd, all heads together, whispering their opinion and disappointment. Without Mary's confession, it was certain that there would be no beheading this day, though such a death would come as soon as her father and Burghley had Elizabeth's signature on a document of execution.

As Frances approached her father, he stepped away from Burghley and a group of lawyers. "I am sorry, Father, that you did not receive the sentence you hoped for."

Walsingham's tired face was also angry. "Delays, daughter, always delays. I fear I will die in my service before that woman dies for her treachery."

"Father, again I regret to add to your problems, but I must to Holland at once. My lord Essex tells me that Philip has worsened. It is my duty . . . and wish . . ."

"Yes, yes, Frances. I have a carriage waiting in the bailey now to take you to London. And, Pauley," he added, "ride on ahead and gain passage for your mistress on the next ship."

"Sir, am I not to escort Lady Frances to London?"

"Nay, Essex has kindly offered this service to his friend's wife."

Frances felt her future closing in on her. She bowed her head. "Then, Father, this is our parting and I ask your blessing." It was quickly given and she walked to her room, Robert following.

*H*e entered her small chamber and closed the door, standing there silent while she threw her belongings into her traveling chest. "I hope you find Sir Philip mending, my lady." His words were even, and he tried to make them sincere, because he had shut his mind to any thought of harm coming to Sir Sidney. Yet his chest had a sore ache, as if his heart were too swollen for its space. It fair hurt to breathe deeply.

She turned to him, anguish everywhere on her face, seeing him standing like a statue before her. "Why do I feel so suddenly a stranger to you?" she whispered.

"Because from now on we are but mistress and servant." Almost against his will his legs carried him forward.

She ran the short space to him. "Robert . . . Robert, forgive me. There is no other way. Our paths are laid for us by others and sad fortune."

He kissed her hair, which tumbled about her face as he liked it and would always remember it.

Her lips moved up to his and his mouth was hard upon hers. He sought kisses enough to last a lifetime. At last, gasping and flushed with need, she pulled back, then rose upon her toes to his cheek, kissing his wound, now pink and healing.

"I will always love you, Robert."

For one last time he crushed her to him, lifting her off her feet. Then he put her down, away from him. He needed the separation at once or he would not be able to allow it at all. He reached for her clothes chest, hoisted it on his shoulder, opened the door, and led the way to the bailey, his stiff leg suffering from the weight of the chest and his heavy spirit.

Essex waited with his horse tied to the rear of the carriage. "My lady," he said, and opened the door to hand her inside before following her to sit in the facing seat. "Pauley, put the casket above."

"Aye, my lord," Robert said. He bowed a moment later as the carriage pulled from the bailey, gathering speed just beyond the moat. He closed his eyes, listening to the horses' hooves pounding down the road, remembering that sound from the road to Chartley and the young lad sitting beside him . . . always beside him in his memory.

A short time later, after receiving letters bound for Holland from Walsingham, Robert took horse and headed for Deptford, taking faster lanes and roads too difficult for a carriage. Riding through the night and glad of the dark, he arrived the next day at the port of Deptford on the Thames south of London. He soon made arrangements for Lady Sidney's cabin on the merchant ship *Paul* swinging at anchor, a ship that still carried the faint impression of the word *Saint* before the name.

He inspected the tiny cabin, seeing the space that would hold her on her way to her husband. The scar on his cheek pulsed, and he knew that he was indulging in a form of self-torture. He must let her go. He must.

As quickly as he could, Robert rode from Deptford to Whitehall, hoping to see Frances before she took a barge for the ship, and berating himself for such a need.

*W*hen Frances arrived at Whitehall, tired and bone-shaken from the long carriage ride on roads already turned from dust to mud, she went immediately to her chambers on the arm of Essex.

"I will at once to Her Majesty and ask that I accompany you to Sir Philip's side, my lady." He opened the latch on her door.

"My lord, I thank you, but do not—"

He was gone before her remonstrance was fully voiced.

Meg rushed to her, worry making lines on her forehead. "My lady . . . my lady . . ."

"We must ready ourselves to leave for Holland within the hour. You and Will, too."

"My sweet lady, the queen calls for you to come to her immediately."

"What cause?"

"I know not, Lady Frances," Meg said, bowing her head, but not before the lie tightened her mouth.

With Will following, Frances quickly made her way to the royal apartments, wishing she could change to a fresh gown, not even knowing whether the one she wore had mud spatters or rain spotting.

"The queen waits," the liveried guard said, bowing.

Frances entered, making her three curtsies to Elizabeth, who sat on her throne chair with Essex at her elbow. Did she want a personal account of Mary's trial? Yet a different message was in the queen's face. . . . "Lady Sidney, I have sad news to impart. Comes this morning a message from the Earl of Leicester in Arnhem that the grievous wound of your husband, Sir Philip Sidney, turned gangrenous—"

Frances swayed and Essex rushed to her, clasping her in his arms. "Frances . . . Frances," he murmured, his lips near her cheek.

"—and it is my unhappy duty to tell you that he died of this wound." The queen stared, angry and unhappy, at Essex, but continued. "The people everywhere proclaim Sir Philip's courage. I will declare him a national hero and he will have a state funeral."

Frances heard Elizabeth's words as if from far away. She was overwhelmed with such a storm of emotion, of guilt and sorrow.

"My lord Essex," Elizabeth said, her face set hard, "you may leave us at once."

Essex looked startled, but bowed and obeyed.

When the door to the reception chamber closed, Elizabeth

said, "My lady, in your bereavement you may be seated in my presence."

"Very kind, your grace." She was glad of the chair, as her bones felt too soft to hold her upright.

"Do you have an affection for the Earl of Essex?" Elizabeth asked, her voice distant and hard.

"No, Majesty, none. I am . . . I was . . . a married woman."

"Has the earl expressed affection to you?"

"Majesty, my lord Essex was friend to my husband." Frances looked to the door, wishing to be anywhere but near a jealous, aging woman who was once a friend, but now might quickly turn an enemy. And over a man thirty-five years younger! But Frances saw more in the queen's face than her jealousy. Essex's desire for a younger woman forced the queen to face the lie behind her pretense that she never aged.

Elizabeth's eyes narrowed, and pieces of her Mask of Youth sprinkled onto the bosom of her black-and-white gown, the colors of which proclaimed her ever a virgin.

"My lady Sidney, you have the appearance of an innocent, but two men are drawn to you. I have heard of another, your handsome servant . . . and mine, Robert Pauley. Both these men are unsuitable to your station, one far too high and the other very much too low." The queen's eyes seemed to see into Frances's mind. "I forbid such attachments on pain of my great displeasure."

Frances rose and curtsied, not terribly surprised by Elizabeth's knowledge. Information flowed to her. No one could keep their secrets from her for long. Her own days as a lady of the presence were over. Indeed, most of her life seemed over. She would be a widow sitting by a window with her memories. "With permission, your grace, I will retire from court and my duties to you and begin my mourning at once."

Elizabeth's tone was angry. "Lady Frances, I have shown you favor, indulged your differences . . . your very great differences."

The queen lifted her head higher, looking down on Frances. "You have not been my lady of the presence so much as my plaything. I wish to see you no more."

Frances curtsied very low, then moved backward to the great doors of the royal apartment.

"Wait!" the queen said, her voice hoarse. "I admit that at times you have served us well . . . very well indeed, and most unusually . . . but your service is done here, all of it. I give you permission for immediate departure to Barn Elms."

"My gratitude, Majesty." Frances made her way to the great doors, somewhat stronger now for the quick change in tone from angry to peacemaking, unusual for this queen.

"My lady Sidney."

"Yes, your grace." She half turned.

"Since you did serve but two months of your second year of appointment, you will receive this year no annual pay."

Frances curtsied and hid a desire to laugh hysterically. The doors shut behind her with a final click, as if so ordered by Elizabeth. Frances knew that she would miss the queen who had looked on her with favor and with anger. Yet Elizabeth's favor, once gone, was gone forever.

This day Philip Sidney's widow walked slowly to her chambers, oblivious of those around her, indeed of Will following. When she faltered, she felt his hand on her arm, ready to assist if she should faint.

He was still to learn that she would never be given to the collapses of other women . . . if her courage held.

Later that afternoon, not daring to seek out Robert, and perhaps not able to bear another parting that might expose him to the queen's anger, she, along with her servants, was escorted by one of her father's secretaries to Barn Elms in her father's barge. All the way upriver in the misty rain, Frances watched the queen's swans hiding their heads under their wings. She sat huddled under a sealskin cover stretched overhead as the drumbeat of rain matched the splash of oars slicing into the Thames.

Frances forced herself to find a corner of her mind for Robert, a place to keep him and their memories safe and warm forever. She thought, too, of Philip. Had his last memory been of Stella, as God took him to his hero's place in heaven? Her heart did ache for him. But she had been mourning him all her married life. His body was now dead to her, as his heart had always been.

CHAPTER TWENTY-TWO

❧

"Woods, hills and river, now are desolate.
Since he is gone the which them all did grace:
And all the fields do wail their widow state,
Since death . . . their fairest flower in field that ever grew,
Was Astrophel . . ."

—The Doleful Lay of Clorinda,
Mary Sidney Herbert, Countess of Pembroke

———————————————— ❧ ————————————————

January
In the Year of Our Lord 1587

BARN ELMS

*M*ary Herbert, Philip's sister, had written a long poem eulogizing him and vowed to work on it until it was as perfect as Philip's own lines. Frances held the draft in her lap, proof again that talent and desire did not pass to sons alone.

Frances smiled, knowing that her father would never in this world agree, ever maintaining that if his daughter's work as an intelligencer were known, she would bring his name only great dishonor. Or did she find excuse for no longer being quite so fond of the name intelligencer? The queen of Scots' face at Fotheringhay, her proudly sad eyes seeing betrayal everywhere, yet haunted Frances and, perhaps, always would.

The lady widow, as the servants had named her, sat alone gazing from her bedchamber window onto the familiar snowy landscape. The winter afternoon had settled softly upon Barn Elms and upon Frances. These days she quietly mourned many people. She prayed for Mary Stuart awaiting execution at Fotheringhay; for Philip at rest in his casket while channel storms raged, preventing his body's transport to his homeland. She prayed for his grieving sister, bent so many days over his eulogy, and, finally, she silently pleaded for God's understanding of her own loss that could never be acknowledged.

Her room echoed with the voice of Aunt Jennet. "You do your duty, dear child, and that is ever the right way."

Frances's throat constricted at a familiar sight. Here came another rider in Essex livery up the road from Mortlake.

No doubt the rider brought more letters, more ponderous Petrarchan poetry from the Earl of Essex, extolling her every feature and limb in wearisome rhyme. Why? Why did the earl want her when he could have his choice of Europe's princesses and most of the unmarried noble daughters of England and perhaps even some married ones? She knew, or thought she knew. He was a conqueror. He had conquered Elizabeth, or so he thought, and now he would take the only woman at court who did not want him, and would make himself her master. Her reluctance was her allure; it enticed him and always had. That was not love. To be taken first by a famous poet in need of escaping his failed love and his debts, and next by a man who dared not lose was neither love she would ever choose. Yet the love that thrilled, that contented her in every way, was impossible—nay, more than that, lunacy. A common man of no station against a high noble of the kingdom . . . Why couldn't her heart follow the path her father and all custom had laid for her?

She gripped the arms of her chair not for the first time that day, glancing at her writing table, where she had placed a number of letters from Essex, which arrived now most every day, sometimes one in the morning and another before an early winter's night made the roads too dangerous for horse or man.

In a smaller and quite separate stack were letters from Robert tied round with a blue ribbon, but they'd been read and reread almost to tatters. He had promised to come as soon as the Thames was clear of ice, and her hands clasped tight to think of it. She had not seen him for near two months; her father had kept him busy, almost using him as a courier, as if to keep them apart. She doubted her father had any such thought, except an instinct he did not want to own.

She heard a servant answer the door and waited while the rider from Essex was invited to rest with mulled wine to warm him for his ride back to Mortlake a few leagues away. Then, as if in a play of Lord Leicester's men being performed every afternoon to the penny groundlings, Frances heard the servant wearily climb the stairs, waited for his knock, and, when it came, called out: "Enter and place the package on my table. There will be no answer."

Waiting for the rider to take horse and return to Mortlake, she stood and brought the package to her chair to open in the light. If it contained another jeweled necklace or earring, she would return it with the next rider.

Unwrapping the long package, she lifted a narrow full-length portrait of Essex standing by his horse, looking heroic enough for a hero's widow, which was no doubt his intention. She held the frame at arm's length, the winter light falling on his long, lean body and handsome face. It was obviously a copy of a much larger image he was having painted. How thoughtful of him to have rushed a duplicate to her.

She closed her eyes and breathed deeply. This gift was difficult to return. Jewelry, unsuitable for her mourning, was one thing; to reject his portrait was too much a rude rebuff of the man himself. Surely there was a dark corner at Barn Elms that could hold it.

A note under the portrait read:

> *My dearest friend Lady Frances,*
>
> *I stay with my fellow soldier Sir Andrew Petty at Mortlake, resting from my service in Holland and ready to offer you my protection. Call on me any hour, day or night, for any possible need you might have.*
>
> *E.*

He offered himself. There it was, written plainly. She had heard other widows speak of such kind offers from gentlemen who thought once a woman was a wife, she would always be in need of bed sport. God's grace, he would find none in her widow's bed!

Feeling as if her chamber were closing in about her, Frances stood and wrapped herself in her heavy cloak for a walk in her desolate garden. As she trod the lane of poled elm trees, she missed their summer shade and pruned symmetry. Her roses, similarly, were trimmed to bare sticks for early bloom. All was as winter-bare as her life. No, no, she was too morose, a burden to herself. She forced her head up and widened her mouth into a semblance of pleasantry.

At the end of the gravel path, the Thames flowed sluggishly toward London. She saw some ice chunks near the banks where the water shoaled, and pulled her cloak tighter. She was surprised to hear a drumbeat. It was a raw day for any but the most determined traveler to be abroad from London. Could it be her father? Or another lord come to soothe a grieving widow? Or a kind neighbor seeking to cheer her?

Pray God, no!

Yet, she did grieve for Philip's painful death. From his friends, she had heard much of his last hours and his bravery, along with some gossip of Stella. Had she come to him, or had he called for her in his final delirium? Only the men close about him knew, and they would soon enough tell the story, which would be carried to her. It would get out, as all secrets eventually did, and she would see it in the hands raised to hide the whispers.

She gazed hard through the fog toward the steady sound of oars splashing. The oarsmen were not coming from Mortlake in Essex livery. If not Essex, then who? Gradually she recognized her father's official barge. A man stood in the prow by the lantern pole . . . something her father would never do because of the pain to his sore joints.

Her legs started moving toward the pier as the man's clear outline, his dear outline, came from behind the foggy shroud. Could he hear her above the sound of oars rasping in their locks and the beat of the drummer? "Robert!" she called, caring naught for the gardeners raking the last of the fallen leaves into piles for burning.

*R*obert heard her call his name and saw her as he had imagined her almost since taking leave of Whitehall hours before. Her cloak swirled about her; her skirts were pulled by the breeze surging upriver from the channel as her hair was whipped about her face, the face that had dwelled in his night dreams and filled his mind from one day's break to the next.

The barge came alongside the Barn Elms pier and he leaped to the landing with a mere trifle of stiffness, not waiting for the men to ship their oars. He knelt at once and bowed his head. "It is ever good to see you well, my lady." He looked up, seeking to read her face, to see in it what he had seen that last day at Fotheringhay: the desire, but more, the desperate hope that fed his own. Until he saw that face, he would not embarrass himself by assuming that her feelings had not changed in the two months of her mourning. And

with Essex lurking nearby . . . Oh, it was the talk of the palace that
the earl hoped to bring the young Lady Sidney to love him, if not
immediately to his bed. Some malicious enemy of the earl's had
informed the queen and she was furious, raging or crying, which-
ever suited the moment, demanding his return to her side, though
he pleaded an ailing back related to much riding on bad horses in
his country's wars abroad.

"You have grown a small beard, Robert."

"Aye, I sought to hide my scar, but hair will not grow on it.
Howsomever, I hope to distract the eye of the ladies." His mouth
teased.

"You have succeeded in that last particular. Yet I like it. It gives
you authority, if you needed it."

He grinned, then sobered. "Madam," he said softly, and shivered, "with you, I am always in need of the last word. May we go
near to a fire? I will show my beard to you in light so you can judge
for yourself how well it suits me."

"Indeed, sir, I will be happy to advise." She smiled fully. "Come
this way."

*I*n the hall, where a huge fire was roaring and the scents of
clove and cinnamon were strong, the servants were busy
hanging berries and holly to add good winter cheer.

Frances ordered mulled wine and led Robert to cushioned
settles by the fire.

While they waited, she was amazed that she had not remembered his every plane and muscle, which were so obvious to her
now as she took in his features. How could she have forgotten? Or
was it a tender God giving her possible happiness in forgetting?

"Frances, you are wondering why I am here."

"Not so, Robert. I am wondering why you did not come
sooner."

He lowered his voice. Servants were always eager to know what their masters said. "It was impossible to come without official reason. And the queen made certain that your father gave me every long trip possible."

"The queen?"

"Aye, did you say aught to her?"

"Robert, no one needs to tell Elizabeth anything. Her eyes see through you and into your heart."

"Not every heart. She could not see into Leicester's when he hid his marriage to Lettice Knollys for longer than a year."

"She did not want to see; Robin had always been hers . . . and still is. Her eyes are not closed to us."

"Perhaps that is the reason she has not seen fit to reward me."

"With nothing?"

"Nothing."

Frances asked the question that plagued her. "Robert, has Her Majesty decided the fate of Mary Stuart?"

"She has signed the order for execution, but she cannot bring herself to dispatch it."

"Will Mary escape?"

"Your father and my lord Burghley will manage to bring this to an end. If Mary lives, Elizabeth dies, and with her all who serve her . . . and they know it. So does our sovereign."

She nodded. Now her eyes begged him to agree, though her voice was loud enough to satisfy the servants. "You must dine and rest the night before returning to Whitehall, Master Pauley."

His gaze was on her face. "My lady, I am yours . . . to command. And I bring greetings and a letter from your father. He awaits your answer."

"Yes," she said, trying to keep from showing a too obvious joy. "I will need time to compose my reply. There will be a chamber made ready for your rest this night."

"My thanks." She could tell that he wanted to reach across the space and touch her, take her hand, pull her to him; she wanted it, too.

He stood and bowed as she left for her chamber, telling Meg to arrange food and accommodation for Sir Walsingham's courier.

Meg dipped into a saucy curtsy.

Later, Frances and Robert were served supper in her father's library, with Will in livery attending.

"What will Mr. Secretary's servants think if we sup as equals?" Robert asked.

"You work closely with their master, and they know to treat you well."

While Will carried in dishes to a table before the hearth, Robert walked about, looking at the chests of books and manuscripts, wanting to open them. "My father had many books when I was a lad. I don't know what happened to them. My half brother did not love them as I did."

Robert sat down and relaxed, winking at Will, who was fast growing out of his new livery and had a hint of beard on his chin. "You have grown to near manhood since the Falcon and Dove."

The lad answered with a grin. "Aye, sir, in many ways." He bowed and served the hot boar soup and a coffin of partridge stuffed with wrens. Soon they were ready for their gingered bread and a steaming minced pie smelling of currants and spiced meats.

Frances dismissed Will to wait outside, and as soon as the door closed, she asked, "Robert, do you know what my father wrote?"

"Do you wish to tell me?" he asked, his eyes dark and unreadable now that the candles had burned low.

"I do not wish it, but there is no avoiding it." She pulled the letter from her bodice, the wax seal hanging loose, and handed the paper to Robert with a slightly shaking hand.

He opened it and read aloud: "'Daughter, I have wonderful news. My lord Essex has asked for you to be his wife. . . .'"

Robert's voice caught on an indrawn breath. He paused, looked at her, though she turned away. He began again:

> *. . . to be his wife after a short mourning. His*
> *request for your dowry is very small, since his love*
> *for you is great. This is beyond my dreams for you,*
> *and I have consented most gladly. He does you and*
> *our family great honor. Never in my life had I*
> *thought to see you a countess, our family allied*
> *with the greatest in England. I am beyond joy and*
> *I know, though you grieve, you join me in this*
> *happiness.*
>
> *Your father*

> *The earl has agreed to help me pay Philip's debts,*
> *which you know reach to fifteen hundred pounds*
> *spent for his service to the crown.*

Robert refolded the letter, pushed it toward her, and looked up, his face as blank as he could make it, though his heart thundered in his ears. His voice was low, dull. "Your father has the right by law to give you in marriage to Essex."

"None can give my heart. I *will not* marry Essex. Two loveless marriages in one lifetime! It is too much to ask of any daughter. I love you . . . only you." She rose, her body straining forward as if ready to run. "We could escape to France, the Palatine, Italy!"

He went to her and clasped her arms without pulling her body to his. If he did, he knew he would agree to anything to be with her, his better self surrendering to desire. "Frances"—and, God forgive him, he shook her slightly—"we would be hunted down and it would go the worse for us. There is no country where your father could not reach us and have me murdered. Then you would be given to a man you had humiliated before the world, if he would yet have you. What life would that be?" He shook her again. "Dearest, you know how quickly word of Essex's offer will spread about the court. Walsingham would never recover from disgrace if you refused the earl."

She was shaking her head, blindly denying his words. "There must . . . must be a way."

"Have you forgotten the queen? It could be the Tower for us. Remember the queen's lady Katherine Grey, and my lord Hertford, who married against Elizabeth's will. They were kept in the Tower, then banished to the countryside . . . never to see each other again. I mind not for myself, but for you. . . ."

She opened her mouth in protest, but he could not listen. She was pleading for what he wanted with all of his being. All his strength of will had gone into that one denial. He could not make another. He dropped her arms and went blindly to the door, leaving it open behind him.

That night, Frances, knowing well how to walk the shadows, went to the chamber that had been given to her father's courier, opening and closing the door in complete silence.

"Are you awake?" she whispered as she bent over the narrow rope bed on which he lay.

"Think you that I could sleep, knowing you are above me in your chamber?"

"I did not know for a certainty that where I slept would trouble you."

He laughed softly and pulled her down atop his body, aroused even before she came to him. "You knew, Frances. You have always known. It was yourself that you had to overcome, not Robert Pauley."

Laughing lightly with him, she asked, though with a tremor in her voice, "Will this night change our circumstance?"

"No."

"The days of the troubadour are very much . . . over," she murmured, her tone rueful, breaking. "You are . . . too honest to be a lady's lover."

"My lady, you have discovered my fatal flaw, which I promise in every way to overcome . . . but not until after this night." His hands found her breasts and she bent to press her mouth to his, stretching atop his long body, and he, increasing his pressure on her lips, sent his tongue searching inside. She felt her face blaze and the fire make a searing trail down her belly and below, to where he was ready for her.

Holding her tight, he turned her onto her side in the narrow bed, the ropes creaking, and pulled her leg over his hip, moving ever slower and stiffer, deeper inside her until she stuffed a hand into her mouth to keep from screaming out her craving for him to go deeper still.

Again, he reached to her melting core, as only he had before or ever would. Irresistible love was the only fuel that could feed a fire so deep. She knew that she would endure another man's love, but never this way . . . never this. . . .

*R*obert woke Frances before dawn and shook her gently. "Go to your bed now, my sweetest."

"How will I ever sleep again without your love?" she whispered, putting a foot on the cold floor, her body bent in anguish.

"Know this," he said. "My love will always be with you in your dreams, and during the mornings in your garden. Even when you are an elder countess sitting at your embroidery, you will remember your youth when you realized who you were. Know then that I have been with you forever. Sweetest, love can never be conquered. Never." He drew in a shuddering breath. "Now go from me while I still have reason enough to save you from yourself . . . and from me."

Still, she could not move.

"Quickly, Frances, while I can send you away from the certain ruin of your life."

She did not turn to look at him as she fled. And later, at dawn, when she heard the barge oarlocks creak, the drum begin and fade to nothing, and knew he'd gone, she buried her face in the bolster to hide from the emptiness and silence of her world.

CHAPTER TWENTY-THREE

✺

February 17

LONDON

*F*rances pulled her fur-lined cloak tight against her body as an icy winter wind howled from the Thames down the east London streets. Holding her Bible against her breast, she nodded to the crowds as the queen's open carriage came into a new street in the Minories on the way to St. Paul's for Philip's funeral. Silent crowds, their heads bowed, lined the way to mourn their newest hero, the brightest flower of English knighthood.

Essex and Sir Walter Raleigh marched beside the royal carriage horses, leading the long procession of London notables. Leicester, who had returned from Holland before Christmastide, now strode on the queen's side with little left of the young gallant he had once been.

Elizabeth Regina continued to acknowledge her people,

speaking to Frances without looking her way. "I must warn you, my lady . . ." she began, but paused.

What now? Frances wondered. "Yes, Majesty?"

"The Earl of Essex is altogether too young and unsuitable for a hero's widow. I forbade him to marry. And you, Lady Frances, must retire to your country manor and mourn for at least two years, after which I will find a suitable husband of rank for you . . . neither too high nor too low. Nay, express no gratitude; I honor your secret service to me."

So, Frances thought, the queen did not know that her father had given Essex permission to marry her. Perhaps she would stop it. Her heart grew more lightsome, as much as it could this day.

The queen nodded to her subjects, who were both sad for Philip Sidney and happy that the hated Scots queen Mary had lost her head but a week earlier. They had lit bonfires and danced in the streets to celebrate. "It took three blows to sever her head," Elizabeth murmured, her hand resting on her neck.

Though she did not explain her change of subject, Frances knew the queen was haunted by Mary's death.

"Three," the queen whispered. "And her little dog crawled from her skirts to lie in her blood."

The words were barely perceptible, so that Frances had to bend close to hear them. The queen seemed unaware she'd spoken.

"I did not order her death. My faithless councilors tricked me, and now all Catholic Europe comes for *my* head," she said, her voice rising. After a deep, shuddering breath, she pressed her lips together and spoke no more.

Frances had heard as well that after the sheriff's men made Mary's death mask, her head was buried in a secret place, lest it draw Catholic pilgrims.

The carriage turned down Ludgate into Paul's yard. Elizabeth spoke again in a softly understanding voice, looking at Leicester. "As a woman, Lady Frances, I know that at times, in full youth, the heart speaks louder than the head. Yet as queen I know that my duty lies, as does yours, in obedience to God's order of being."

Frances nodded. *Not too high, not too low.*

The queen was speaking of her old love for Leicester, Frances knew, and that kept her from screaming out, *My heart is not with Essex, but with Robert Pauley.* She dared not say the truth aloud, dared not name her love, as Elizabeth did not. Were women made silent by their forbidden emotions?

The carriage stopped, and Frances, carrying her Bible, put one foot forward and then the other. Her heart was gladdened by the chance to pay due homage to Philip. She had not been the wife he wanted in life, but she would not disgrace him in death.

Her head high, she walked down the wide stone aisle of the empty nave. The queen went first toward the chancel arch, which was illumined by a thousand candles to chase the dark into the far, dusty corners. The rose window cast its many colored lights over the pointed arches and clustered pillars. To honor Philip, the Chapel Royal choir sang sweetly the solemn music written especially by the queen's composer, William Byrd.

Frances caught her breath at sight of Philip's casket before her. She stopped by her chair, feeling some faintness. Always when in need she looked for Robert, but this time she did not see him.

Now the endless procession of public mourners began. First came thirty-two poor men, one for each year of Philip's life; then nobles carrying Philip's sword, spurs, and armor; then high men of the guilds, the lord mayor, and many other dignitaries.

Amongst the nobles walked Lord and Lady Rich. . . . Stella, as Frances had known, would not ever miss the prospect of excited notice. Or was she truly mourning the man who had made her immortal? Frances would never know.

Frances sat, her head erect, unable to wish Stella gone. All who loved Philip, all whom Philip had loved, should be with him now, though his soul had long since departed for heaven.

She heard little of the service, the long praise of Philip's worth as a courageous soldier of England, his bravery in giving his leg armor to another, his generous act having made him vulnerable to the bullet that smashed his thigh and eventually killed him. She saw him again as he rode away from Barn Elms, hoping in vain to have left a son behind to keep his name alive.

She had lived so many emotions of late that she felt numb to more when she should have felt most. Her gaze wandered across the tombs of ancient kings along the far walls and lifted to follow the jackdaws and pigeons as they flew near the high crevices that held their nests.

Eulogy followed eulogy until, finally, the service was over and Frances moved toward her husband's casket to kneel, her hand on the crypt.

As her fingers came to rest on the cold stone, her discarded faith flooded back into her soul. Now that she loved Robert, she understood Philip's love, and her love of God was no longer blocked. The moment she forgave Philip, God restored her faith. She whispered what was in her heart, what she could never have said if Philip had lived. "I know now, sweet husband, what you suffered married to a woman you did not love and leaving your true heart elsewhere. Rest, brave Philip, at last." She rose, her legs trembling. "Astrophel, dear star lover, I will bring your star to you at last."

Retracing her steps down the nave aisle, Frances stopped next to Lady Rich, whose lovely face glowed even in the dim light. Frances held out her hand to Stella, who hesitated but took it, linking her arm with Frances's and returning with her to the casket. Frances had no words, so, placing Stella's hand on the casket, she gave Philip over to her, leaving her there. Returning to Paul's courtyard, she stepped into her father's carriage . . . where Essex was waiting.

He was magnificent in a silver breastplate and helm and held a sword across his lap. "Philip's sword," he said, caressing it. "He gave it to me . . . as he gave you to me, dear Frances."

She said nothing.

"The queen has called me to her," he went on, his mouth set. "I will tell her that I will marry you immediately. If we wait, she will work her will on your father. I have seen it too many a time. My stepfather, Leicester, advises that she would forgive me quick enough . . . and you, though it will take her longer and she'll never accept you back in her service."

Frances could scarce breathe at such news. "Yet, the queen . . . Her Majesty may send us both to the Tower."

He laughed. "I know her well. She loves me and cannot have me from her. She keeps her youth in me." He was still smiling. "She may threaten, but one tear from me . . ." His low voice trailed away, suggesting he was not as certain as he wanted Frances to think, as he himself wanted to think.

Frances knew that would mean all would be done in haste.

*R*obert was at the door when Meg opened it to a knock. Frances sat before her sea-coal fireplace, yet was bone-chilled from the penetrating cold of London and St. Paul's.

Meg answered with the haughty air of a countess's maid. "I will ask whether my lady may see you, since this is her husband's funeral day."

Frances called out, trying to make her tone normal, as her heart beat against her bodice. "Of course I will see Master Pauley."

He was swiftly there, kneeling before her. "Robert," she said softly. "I could hope for no better end to this day than to see you."

"You may hope for better, sweetest."

She saw then that he was dressed in a newly cut suit, richly embroidered, and wore a single earring. She gave a small, tremulous smile. "I have never thought to see you play the fine courtier."

"Think it then, Frances. By the queen's order and own hand this very hour, I am made Sir Robert Pauley by Henry the Eighth's own sword of state, to honor my distinctive service." He put a hand to his burned cheek. "It is the real reason I suffered this, in hopes of having the right to claim you as my wife."

"You could not have known. . . ."

"I hoped . . . always hoped. It was my only path to you."

"But I am asked for and promised—"

"I know Essex has sought your father's agreement, but the queen does not look kindly upon the match. In fact, she forbids it outright." He took in a deep breath. "Her Majesty also kindly provided me with a small estate once belonging to a Catholic traitor. She has decided that I am more suitable than she once thought." He grinned.

"An estate—"

His eyes shone and his scar nearly disappeared in his proud smile. "It will bring me an income that, while not large, is enough to care for a wife with the simple needs of a former brewer's apprentice." He stood and held out his hand to lift her up, his eyes shining brighter yet.

Frances was in his arms, her head quickly on his shoulder, his mouth hard on hers. She half cried, half laughed, while he yet hungrily kissed her. "This cannot be happening," she murmured.

"It can and it *is*, sweetheart." His entire face smiled. "Come, we will haste to your father before Essex can escape Her Majesty's close attention. Walsingham *will* want your happiness on this day of all days."

She was swept along the corridors, her hand in his, avoiding the shadows, seeking the light. Within minutes, they were passing the halberdiers and walking swiftly down the long office, lanterns aglow, past openmouthed secretaries toward her father's writing table. Walsingham pretended not to see her, and spoke only to Robert.

"Yes, sir knight, I have heard." He handed Robert a pouch with a red seal hanging from it. "Here is the queen's appointment for one Sir Robert Pauley as secretary to her ambassador in Paris. You are to depart immediately . . . and alone."

"No!" Frances cried out before she could stop the word. Elizabeth had worked her will after all. No lady of her court was to find the happiness that had been denied the sovereign.

Walsingham was not finished. "Here are also orders from me to report on the ambassador, who may be in the pay of Spain and France."

"Sir Walsingham, I cannot accept the appointment—"

"It is not yours to accept. It is yours to obey, or rest in the Tower for your life long." His voice softened. "I value you, Robert, but I value my family's good name more. Go now, before I call my guards and your skills are lost to me and to the queen."

Robert half turned to Frances. . . .

"Now," Walsingham said, with real menace. "Do you want to ruin the lady Sidney's good name on the day her husband finds his last rest?"

Robert's hand reached for the pouch in Walsingham's hand, the orders for his posting and the end of his dream. "I will do what is best for you, Frances."

"No, Robert," she said, her voice trembling, a tear falling onto her lips, her tongue reaching to take it in.

He looked at her, his gaze seeming to see forever. "Remember what I said."

She whispered, and though her father obviously strained to hear her, he could not: "Our love can never be conquered."

Robert bowed to Walsingham, then to Frances, hesitating, his gaze memorizing her face, and marched back down the long room and out the door.

"My barge waits for you," her father said, not looking at her, his dark-circled eyes on his many papers. "I myself will escort you home, daughter. You will marry my lord the Earl of Essex in one week's time at Barn Elms. Set your mind to it; you will have him and bring honor to our family. . . ."

"Rather, Father," she replied, her words bitter, "I feel certain such haste will confirm my disgrace."

February 24

BARN ELMS

*I*t was a small, very quiet wedding. Until the final words were spoken, Frances was never quite sure that the queen would not send her royal guards to break down the door and stop it. She did not. When she wished to know nothing, she made nothing truth. Everyone—Walsingham, Essex, and all who knew—agreed the queen would soon forgive her handsome young favorite.

As Frances repeated her vows, it was to the remembered image of Robert Pauley's face that she made her promises, though she knew he was on a ship braving winter storms on its approach to Calais on the French coast. She spent the wedding feast treasuring again every moment that they had spent together . . . and most especially in the secret knowledge that she carried his son below her heart, Robert with her forever.

She raised the cup Meg gave her and smiled at the guests, including Essex's sister, Penelope Rich . . . *Stella* . . . who was part of her life again. Above all she toasted her father's pleased face. Finally, she was the daughter he'd always wanted.

For herself, she would fill the empty days ahead with her son, who would be an earl, with all the privileges and more that his true father had been denied.

It would be enough, she knew, taking a deep breath. She would make sure it was enough. Their love would live on, every day to come, in their son.

EPILOGUE

⤬

February 25
In the Year of Our Lord 1601

THE TOWER

The winter's morn, made colder by the sodden wind whipping off the Thames, greeted Frances, Countess of Essex, as, heart pounding, she stepped through the postern gate of the Tower, leaving the last of her former life behind. Looking up, she saw the queen's standard being raised above the Bell Tower, Elizabeth triumphant.

Facing a pale sun beginning to light the sky to the east, Frances knew this would not be a sunny day in any sense. Spring would not come for many weeks yet. Even the recent plow day had not brought husbandmen to the fields.

There was a palpable hush in the streets, where vendors of every kind usually jostled and sang out their morning wares. It was as if all London prepared to mourn her husband, the long-ago hero of Cádiz. No Englishman had forgotten that Essex had burned that enemy city and the Spanish fleet in the harbor. The queen had not been pleased when he had missed the treasure ships returning from the New World, but she had forgiven and favored him . . . until he defied her orders and made peace, losing the late Irish War and emptying her purse. She had sent him from court to house arrest and stripped him of his honors and his income. He would not have been lost had he not led a rebellion through the streets of London. Treason was the one crime Elizabeth could never forgive.

Behind Frances, she thought she heard the thud of the ax on the Tower Green block. She was certain of it when a faint cheer rose from behind the ancient walls, and, though she was warm under her cloak, she shivered, swaying.

I have nothing left but that which I must pay the queen, he had written to her from his cell. Now he owed Elizabeth nothing. He had given her everything.

Frances was twice widowed now, first by Philip Sidney and now by Essex, both men who sought glory, only to find bitter death.

Faintly, she heard the street rhymers already hawking the earl's imagined last words.

> *Upon my death, at my good night,*
> *Farewell, Elizabeth, my gracious queen!*
> *God bless thee and thy council all!*

Had it been his good night? Essex had refused to see Frances, his heir, Robert, or his young daughters, Frances and Dorothy. Instead, the earl had clung to his chaplain and so maniacally desired heaven and God's forgiveness that he had had no time to beg hers. She doubted he had thought it necessary, though she had borne him five children. Only three had lived, her firstborn son beside her now, his dark head high and his step firm, the strongest of them all, speaking to his good blood. Young Robert would be a comfort to his sisters, playing their games and distracting them with his good humor. He had always spent more time with them than their father had.

Once in her life Frances had been loved for herself, and the memory was yet part of her, well hidden but utterly alive and breathing. It was that remembered love that warmed her now, as it always had and ever would.

The tall boy striding beside her clasped her hand tighter and spoke in the croaking voice of one near thirteen years. "Do not fear, Mother; I will have a care for you, always."

She tightened her grip. "Yes, Robert, we will care for each other and your sisters as we have done." It was true. Trying to smile at him, she felt her lips quiver and gave it up. She had never wished a traitor's death for her husband, but he had not sought her advice. He had thought to force her love, and when he could not, he had turned for opinion and caring to his sister Penelope, Lady Rich . . . *Stella, again and always* . . . a tragic mistake. That lady had advised him to rebel, then counted too much on Elizabeth's former love for her brother and went to beg his life. The queen had denied her entry, though Penelope had pounded hard on the great doors to Her Majesty's privy chamber. They remained unopened. Like her brother, Penelope never understood that the queen loved her throne more than any man, always had and ever would.

The carriage waited, her old horses Quint and Claudius restless in their traces, the golden crest of the Essex arms on the door spotless as the weak light glinted on it. The footman held the door open.

A movement in the shadow of the draper's shop across the cobbled street caught Frances's eye and stole her breath. Even after so many years, she knew him, and when he stepped stiffly toward her, his stride proved his identity. When he removed his hat, he was little changed, though she saw that white had sprouted in his hair.

"Come, Robert," she said to her son. "I wish you to meet a worthy gentleman of old acquaintance."

"Countess," the man said, approaching, "I apologize for such an untimely intrusion."

She looked up into the same steady, dark eyes, the same beloved face that had haunted her dreams these many years . . . so little changed . . . so dear. This meeting, this longed-for meeting, was almost too much on such a day. To lose a husband and to find her love again in the same hour.

"Robert," she said to her son, "this is Sir Robert Pauley, a very old friend of my father's . . . and of mine."

"Good day, sir," young Robert said, looking curiously at the man's face. "I have many cousins. Are you one?"

"No, my lord, not a cousin."

"Your face is familiar to me, sir. Have we never met?"

He smiled at Frances. "I have seen you at a distance, my lord, but . . . no, we have never met as we do now."

Young Robert drew himself to his full height, his mouth, which started to tremble, held firm. "You do not have to call me 'my lord,' sir. The sons of executed traitors lose their titles and estates."

"Yes, I do know that, young Robert." His gaze rose to Frances's face, and he spoke as much for her as for the boy. "But what is lost can be restored. I have lived long enough to believe that truth."

"Thank you, Sir Pauley. I will remember your words." He climbed into the carriage, on his face his clear need to be alone.

Frances swallowed hard. Was Robert saying that they might yet be together? Pray God it could be true. "I did not expect to meet you here, Robert."

"It takes no great skill in cipher, such as yours, to know some things."

She almost smiled, remembering the days when deciphering the Scots queen's messages had been her own triumph.

"Did you not know that I would be near?" he said quietly. "I have never been far from you, Frances."

She bowed her head, shy and at the same time wanting to lean into him as she once had. "There were times when I needed to know such was true."

"I hoped you knew it, Frances."

"How could I? You have never written or approached me at court."

"That was not possible. I wanted you to find your happiness."

"Happiness?" The word almost choked her. "I knew such once, but now young Robert and my two daughters are my only happiness." She turned her face away from the carriage and her son. "I never expected to have more."

His voice was proud, his gaze telling her that he knew the boy was his. "Young Robert is a fine lad and must bring you much joy."

"Yes."

"You want more than you have?"

She stared at him, keeping all hope from her eyes. "What more is there for me?"

He looked long at her. "You did not believe me all those years ago, or do you not remember?"

She laughed, a small and bitter sound. "Believe what? Remember what?"

"All I once told you, all you once knew: Armies are vanquished, countries overrun, but . . ."

"I remember now," she said, repeating the long-ago words he had planted in her heart. "Love is never conquered."

Author's Note

_⤸_

This is a work of fiction. Although it is based on real people and events, the love story and adventures come from my imagination. Some dates have been changed, but wherever possible I kept to historical fact.

First, my sincere apologies must go to Sir Philip Sidney, magical poet of love and hero soldier. I took great liberties with his life for the sake of my story. There is little evidence that he was anything other than a good and loving husband to Frances Walsingham . . . except for one troubling find in 1964. An original manuscript by George Gifford, a clergyman who was present in the room in Holland when Sidney died, differed from its published version. This sentence, describing those gathered about the deathbed—"It was my Lady Rich . . ." —was deleted. I have to ask: Was Stella with him at the end and, if so, could that mean this work of my imagination might hold more truth than I know?

Sidney did not fall deeply in love with Penelope Devereux until after her forced marriage to Lord Rich in November 1581. He left court and over the next summer wrote 118 beautifully sad sonnets after realizing that he had lost the love of his life.

> _I might!—unhappy word—O me, I might_
> _And then would not, or could not, see my bliss;_
> _Till now wrapt in a most infernal night_
> _I find how heav'nly day, wretch! I did miss . . ._

He never meant them to be published, but, as with so many secrets, they were passed about and eventually printed and handed down to us today.

Robert Pauley (or Pooley, Poley, or Poole; spelled many ways in records) was a real Walsingham agent and attached to Lady Sidney's household. He was described as "the very genius of the Elizabethan underworld" and was involved in breaking the Babington plot to assassinate Queen Elizabeth. His name also appears on a list of prisoners in the Tower. From these few facts, I wove my adventure and Robert and Frances's love story. Pauley surfaces again in history in 1593 when he is placed at the scene of Christopher Marlowe's stabbing death at the Bull tavern in Deptford. Since Marlowe was also one of Walsingham's agents, the men would have known each other. What involvement Robert had in Marlowe's death, if any, is unknown. During the later 1590s, Pauley served as a spy for Robert Cecil and Elizabeth's Privy Council in France and in the Netherlands, where he was jailed briefly for spying. After that, he disappears from written history.

In my story both Dr. Dee and Frances try unsuccessfully to break Johannes Trithemius's *Steganographia* code, a complex number cipher book written by the German scholar/monk around 1500 that claimed to be a way of delivering messages in a single day. At that time of slow travel, the book seemed to call on demons and was banned by the Catholic Church. There is no shame in Frances's and Dee's failure. The code was not broken until the 1990s.

And, yes, Dee was the original 007 and signed himself so in his communications with Elizabeth. My sense is that he was an internal spy, keeping abreast of what was going on within the court and nobility, for Elizabeth's eyes only.

Did Thomas Phelippes really add incriminating lines to Mary, queen of Scots' secret message to Sir Anthony Babington? No one knows. It was suspected at the time and Mary voiced her suspicions at her trial, but all was denied. There was no doubt that Mary thought herself the true queen of England and longed to claim her rightful place. She even thought that if she could only meet with Elizabeth, she could talk her way free. Since they never met, we'll never know.

Mary greatly overestimated her powers of persuasion and underestimated Elizabeth's determination and sense of her own destiny. She was threatened on all sides during most of her reign, but she was Henry VIII's daughter and would not be intimidated. Elizabeth was the supremely strong ruler that Henry thought only a son could be and she remains an icon the world round. Anne Boleyn, beheaded because she did not bear the longed-for male heir, had the last laugh. For all things Tudor and Anne Boleyn, try www.theanneboleynfiles.com.

Although one source claims that the sheriff of Northamptonshire took Mary's head from Fotheringhay Castle and buried it secretly so that it would not provide a place for Catholic pilgrimage, there are several death masks claiming to be the real one. You can find one here: www .news.bbc.co.uk/2/hi/uk_news/scotland/edinburgh . . . /5236154.stm.

Queen Elizabeth was right to worry about the repercussions of Mary's execution. Philip of Spain sent his huge armada against England in the following year. It failed spectacularly, thanks to Sir Francis Drake, John Hawkins, Lord Howard, and the God-sent English wind. "God blew and they were scattered" is a phrase used on commemorative medals. But Philip didn't give up, sending three more armadas during the next decade until he died and Spain was bankrupt.

Frances Walsingham Sidney did not have a happy marriage with Robert, Earl of Essex, although she bore him five children, three of whom lived. I think Essex was too selfish and involved in his schemes of glory to really love anyone but himself. He thought he was fit to sit on Elizabeth's throne, a flight of fancy that eventually led him to rebellion and the executioner's block in the Tower with his enemy Sir Walter Raleigh looking on. He "touched her scepter," as Elizabeth famously charged, and that was unforgiveable.

Frances's life was not over with the loss of her second husband. She married again, to Richard De Burgh, Earl of St. Albans and Clanricarde. They had a son and two daughters; altogether, she had ten children, including two with Sidney. Frances lived out the rest of her life in Ireland and died a Catholic in 1631. What would her father, the great Catholic priest hunter, have made of that?

Of all my characters, that leaves Stella, Lady Penelope Rich. But she deserves a book of her own.

ABOUT THE AUTHOR

Jeane Westin began her writing life as a freelance journalist, then wrote a number of nonfiction books, and finally came to her first and true love, historical novels. She published two novels, with Simon & Schuster and Scribner, in the late 1980s, and after a long hiatus is once again indulging her passion for history. She lives in California with her husband, Gene, near their daughter, Cara, and has been rehabilitating a two-story Tudor cottage complete with dovecote for more than a decade. You can reach her at www.jeanewestin.com.

The
SPYMASTER'S
DAUGHTER

~∽~

Jeane Westin

A CONVERSATION WITH
JEANE WESTIN

Q. What intrigued you about Frances Sidney and made you want to write a book about her?

A. The intrigue lies in what might have been. The personal details of Frances's life are little known. We do know that she was the daughter of Francis Walsingham, the mastermind of the greatest spy network of the Tudor age; that she married the wildly popular poet of love Sir Philip Sidney; and that she was the wife of Elizabeth I's last love, Robert Devereux, the Earl of Essex. But who was she apart from these towering male figures?

Frances has been most often cast by historians as a shadow behind these men and little worthy of note. Since I was a cryptographer at the Pentagon during wartime, I put myself in Frances's slippers: She must have overheard plotting, been aware of important secrets, seen the supreme urgency of her father's work. It is unimaginable to me that she would not have been caught up in that excitement and wanted to be part of the spy business . . . just to prove she could. This kernel of an idea eventually became *The Spymaster's Daughter*.

Q. In your last three novels, you've combined historical and fictional characters. How do you decide which historical figures to include and which characters you need to make up?

A. Choosing historical characters is determined by the story I'm writing and the people actually involved. The choice of new characters depends a great deal on the evolving story's needs. I did not imagine Lady Stanley until I thought that Frances Sidney, who so obviously had Queen Elizabeth's favor and the interest of the handsome young Earl of Essex, would have aroused jealousy among the other court ladies. Aunt Jennet served to illustrate how serious it was to have Catholic sympathies in Elizabeth's England. Meg and Will, Frances's servants, also evolved from the story's need for minor characters that had roles to play in her adventures.

The animals who inspired Quint and Claudius, the Percheron horses who pull the dray to Chartley, are currently living at my daughter's Percheron farm in California.

Q. Can you describe the international espionage network set up by Frances's father, Francis Walsingham? How did it compare to royal spy networks from earlier and later periods?

A. We know that spies and secret writing were used from earliest history. There is evidence that cuneiform tablets from ancient Mesopotamia disguised city names to confuse the enemy. Egyptian hieroglyphs were altered, and a Greek commander coated his message with wax so that it looked like an empty tablet ready for the stylus. Later, the Romans had twenty different kinds of secret writing, as it was known then. Individual legion commanders even had their own codes. There was cryptography of every kind, using colored beads and pebbles, and messages wrapped about cylinders that could only be read by wrapping them around the same size cylinder. Alphabet reversal and disappearing ink have been in use since writing began. In every time, we have needed covert forms of communication for state, military, and even private purposes.

For its time, Walsingham's network was a marvel, so extensive that it reached into Asia, every European court, and even into the Vatican. It set a high bar for subsequent spying operations. The breaking of the German Enigma code by Alan Turing at Bletchley Park, England, during World War II marked the beginning of modern code breaking and led to the complex computer codes of today.

Q. How do the codes that Frances cracks compare to codes used at other times in history?

A. Frances's ciphers were complex for the time, but many systems were still based on earlier substitution systems: one letter standing for another. Double substitution was also in use and agreed-upon nulls—meaningless letters meant to confuse—made messages more difficult to break. Some systems were based on ciphers known to both sender and receiver. There was danger of discovery in having an agreed-upon code in two or more places. Mary, queen of Scots was actually trapped by one and lost her head.

Spies in the field might also use disappearing messages, quite often written in their own urine, which became legible when held close to a candle's flame.

Q. You make it sound as if popular poet Philip Sidney was the equivalent of a modern-day rock star—a celebrity of the Tudor period who incited a frenzy of emotion among readers. Is that a fair comparison?

A. He *was* a rock star! After his death in 1586 from a leg wound suffered at the Battle of Zutphen in Holland, during which he gave up his leg armor to a friend, he was celebrated as the perfect English knight. The popularity of his love sonnets to Stella and his brave death at the age of thirty-one inspired a cult following that lasted until 1700. It then diminished only to roar back during Queen Victoria's reign, at which time he returned to even greater cult status.

For a fascinating flash reenactment of Sidney's funeral procession, go to http://wiki.umd.edu/psidney/index.php?title=Main_Page.

Q. The novel suggests that well-born women had almost no say in whom they married. Was that uniformly true or were some parents more lenient with their daughters? How did this compare to marriages made between members of lower classes?

A. Children were legal property. The purpose of marriage for the well-born was to increase the family's property or title. This held true for sons as well as daughters. The lower classes had less to gain from marriage, but the primacy of a father as head of the family was still the rule. I can easily imagine that a farmer with a pretty daughter wishing to add to his property would have his eye on the son in line to inherit the neighboring farm.

Of course, there were favored daughters and sons for whom the rules were set aside.

Q. You depict Elizabeth I as a notorious skinflint. Did her efforts to keep government spending within what it could afford have any long-lasting impact on the country? When she died, was England a wealthier or poorer country?

A. Elizabeth watched her purse and spent nothing without good reason. What about her extravagant dress and jewels? These were necessary to reinforce her regal position, both at home and abroad. True, when she died in 1603, England was poorer in its treasury. There had been years of too much rain and poor harvests in the 1590s; Spain had sent four armadas against the country; and Irish uprisings were continuous and ruinously expensive. But England had a foothold in the New World and Elizabeth had signed the charter forming the East India Company. The island nation was about to become a world power, while Spain was bankrupt.

Q. You suggest that the Earl of Essex pursues Frances because she rejects his overtures. Do you think he had any genuine affection for her or were his reasons for marrying her as self-serving as one might expect?

A. Essex was very young and, though strong-willed, he was emotionally needy. I believe he had to have constant reinforcement of his self-image. He may have married Frances to defy the queen, who objected to all her handsome young courtiers marrying. When one took another woman, it destroyed the romantic attachment for the queen they all pretended to. It is also rumored that Sidney left his sword and his wife to Essex, passing the torch, as it were, to the next perfect English knight. Nobody really knows. Essex did reject a last meeting with her and his children before he went to the block, as I have noted in the epilogue.

Q. You portray Mary, queen of Scots as a woman who did, indeed, plot to assassinate her cousin, Queen Elizabeth. Is that how you really see her or did that portrait simply fit the needs of this story?

A. Yes, I think she plotted to escape every minute of the eighteen-plus years she was imprisoned in England by Elizabeth. Mary always considered herself the rightful queen, even quartering her arms with the English coat of arms. By 1586, after so many years of foiled attempts, in ill health and growing old, she must have become desperate to escape, and agreed to Elizabeth's death, thinking to take the throne. This was the one plot that could and did condemn her.

Q. In your novels, Elizabeth I's ladies-in-waiting almost always fall in love with someone they meet at court, yet they feel estranged from most people there, unable to trust the people around them and beset by traps and trickery. Yet the court was supposed to be a place where top-notch entertainments were available to be enjoyed. Did anyone have any fun there?

A. Many families sent their sons and daughters to court to gain an advantageous marriage, hoping that Elizabeth would arrange or at least allow one. The costs of court life were huge, so sacrifices had to be made.

Of course, the court was full of traps and trickery. Follow the money and the power was as true then as now. Think of it as Washington, D.C., only with better clothes.

Q. Do you ever wish you could have lived during the Tudor period?

A. Absolutely, although I would hope to bypass the odors of open sewers and unwashed bodies and clothes. When I'm walking along the Strand in London, I'm not seeing the double-decker buses and modern shops; I'm seeing York House and Leicester House, the Thames with a winter frost fair and boys on bone skates and Whitehall sprawling on the opposite riverbank. Not a one exists now except in my mind's eye. When I'm in London, I always stay at the Royal Horseguards Hotel, which sits atop the site of Elizabeth's palace.

Q. Are your own interests still firmly fixed in the Tudor period or do you find yourself reading about other eras? If so, what books have recently captivated you?

A. I read in many historical periods. I've recently finished all of Rosemary Sutcliff's Roman Britain trilogy, starting with *The Eagle of the Ninth*, and am beginning her Saxon period novels. I read many new Tudor period novels and nonfiction books, especially the work of Karen Harper. *The Queen's Governess* and *Mistress Shakespeare* are on my keeper shelf, along with all the nonfiction written by Anne Somerset. I like World War I novels and am reading *The Somme Stations* by Andrew Martin, short-listed for the CWA Dagger Award, while also listening to Margaret George's *Elizabeth* (in my car). George captures that queen's droll wit to perfection. I'm also reading Jeri Westerson's Crispin Guest novels about a disgraced medieval knight turned "tracker." For a change of period, I recently finished *The Paris Wife*, which is about 1920s Paris and Hemingway's first marriage.

Usually, I have about four novels ongoing, not including three or more nonfiction research books. One novel rests by every TV set. I'm a frequent user of the MUTE button. Unfortunately, life is too short to write about every historical period I'd like to explore.

Q. Last we heard, you were renovating your Tudor-style home. Have you made any noteworthy changes?

A. I'm always changing or adding details for authenticity. Last year, I adapted an iron courtyard gate based on famous designer Gertrude Jekyll's design. My most recent and most delightful addition is chimney pots on both chimneys, just like the ones you see in old English villages. My husband and I spent three years searching for them and finally found them in Ohio. A mason with an assistant in a cherry picker drew a sizable neighborhood crowd while installing the 350-pound pots. They are a delight to see from a distance when I return from my daily walk in the park. You can see them at www .jeanewestin.com/bio.

Q. What would you love to write about next?

A. I have several ideas, but Stella, Lady Penelope Rich, continues to intrigue me. There's more to tell about that lady . . . much more.

QUESTIONS FOR DISCUSSION

1. What did you most enjoy about *The Spymaster's Daughter*?

2. What character did you like the most? The least?

3. Are there any details about Queen Elizabeth that you find particularly intriguing?

4. Would you have liked to live during the Tudor period? What about it would you have liked the most? The least?

5. If you'd been part of a family that Queen Elizabeth intended to visit on her "progress," would you have gone all-out to host her, even to the extent of bankrupting yourself, or would you have quickly left town and pretended to know nothing of her impending visit?

6. Mary, queen of Scots is portrayed in a mostly negative light in this novel. Have you read other books, or seen plays or movies, in which she comes across as a more appealing and sympathetic character?

7. What do you think was really going on in Elizabeth's relationship with the Earl of Essex?

8. Elizabeth I is generally considered to be a great queen. How does her behavior in the novel support or undercut this idea? What qualities do you think a great ruler needs? Does a woman ruler need different qualities than a man?

9. What do you think happens to Frances after the novel ends?

10. Which actors would you choose to play the major characters in the movie version?

11. How does the book compare to other Tudor-set novels you've read?

On the night of her greatest triumph, England's naval victory over the Spanish armada, Queen Elizabeth I suffered her most devastating loss: the death of her lifelong companion and lover, Robert Dudley, Earl of Leicester. Overcome with grief, she locked herself in her room for days with Dudley's last letter to her.

This is the story of that great love. . . .

His Last Letter

by

Jeane Westin

Available in paperback and ebook
from New American Library.

An excerpt follows . . .

ELIZABETH

September 1588
Whitehall Palace, Westminster

*B*right explosions of fireworks arched over the Thames from Baynard's Castle near the Strand to Billingsgate downriver, sending flashes of light through the tall open windows of Whitehall's presence chamber. The shouts of Londoners could be heard as they wildly celebrated with gunpowder mixed with strong English ale. Their virgin queen Elizabeth's glorious victory over Spain's invincible armada had come in answer to her prayers.

Trumpets and drums announced the queen's approach from her privy chambers.

Lord Treasurer William Cecil and the queen's philosopher, Dr. John Dee, in court from his home in Mortlake, moved through the crowd of courtiers toward the chamber doors. Cecil produced a rare smile on his sober face. "I have seen Her Majesty in moments of triumph before, but none to match the glory of this victory, the jewel of her reign."

Dee nodded, his mouth scarcely visible within his full white beard that came to a point at his waist. "My lord, the victory was foretold in her stars . . . and in my lord the Earl of Leicester's. It was inevitable."

"Good Doctor, although God commands the winds, perhaps Lord Howard and her majesty's sea dogs, Hawkins, Drake and Frobisher, with their new naval guns and fast ships, aided the Almighty," Cecil said in his slightly amused way, which showed a little of his disdain for Dee and all necromancers. Still, his gaze never left the chamber doors.

Dee, in defense of his art, refused to yield. "I would have to cast the captains' natal charts to determine what was written in their stars."

Before one could give further offense to the other, the huge double doors of the presence chamber opened and red-and-black-liveried yeoman guards entered, their tall pikes rigidly upright.

Trumpeters and drummers marched in and stepped to the side, followed by a retinue of lords, ladies and gentlemen pensioners, and at last by the queen. Elizabeth paused for a moment just inside the chamber, dazzling in the torchlight from her jeweled scarlet slippers, past ropes of pearls looped about her white brocade gown, heavily embroidered with silver thread, to the great ruby-and-diamond crown glittering on her head. Her thoughts blazed through her eyes and were read by every courtier who knew her well: *I will remember this day as the best of my life; my great triumph when Spain was no longer master of sea and land!*

She straightened her already near-rigid back, her corset allowing no real respite, nor did she want it. Although she loved her flowing gowns and dazzling jewels, her flower scents and the line of lovely ladies-in-waiting behind her, she never forgot that she was a queen before she was a woman.

Elizabeth stopped near Cecil, who bowed, since he had her permission to stay on his feet and save his old knees. "My lord treasurer, today England takes its rightful place in the world."

"Your grace, it is a day your realm will remember and celebrate down the ages."

"My lord," the queen announced in full voice, as much for her gathered court as for Cecil, "Philip of Spain claimed all shipping lanes from east to west." She tossed her head and laughed. "Now he knows that the seas are no longer a Spanish pond!"

Rough shouts and approving laughter spread throughout the chamber as Elizabeth moved on down the double line of uncovered and kneeling courtiers, who shouted, "Huzzah! Huzzah!" At the foot of her canopied throne, she saw Sir Walter Raleigh waiting. He was not on his knees. The handsome rogue took unusual liberties even for a man who thought himself a favorite of his sovereign . . . and who had from his elegant boots to his perfect face every bit the look of a favorite. *Robin never makes such a mistake; he observes all court protocol, bless him.*

Raleigh, not to have his achievements forgotten for a moment, took his pipe and lit it, drawing every lady's gaze. It was said that he was growing rich on the tobacco he had brought back from the New World. Perhaps she should consider a tax.

"Sir Walter, we have seen many men turn gold into smoke, but you have managed to turn smoke into gold."

The jibe was greeted by polite laughter, enough to reward the queen and yet not offend a rising courtier. She watched him brave it all with ease. He needed a small reprisal. "Are you then so much a hero after your voyage to Virginia that you need not be on your knees to your sovereign?"

"Majesty, forgive me," said Sir Walter Raleigh, choking on his weed a little before falling to his knees as Elizabeth mounted the dais to sit on her canopied throne. "Each burst of victorious light from the city brings added beauty to your perfect face and I am dazzled."

She laughed at his very pretty excess, admiring his quick recovery from her rebuke. Planned or not, she believed him. What courtier was not a little in love with Elizabeth Tudor? Still, she knew she could not play this game of courtly love with her usual zest. Not on this day. Today she was in love with her country. England was her husband, the people her children, and she had given them their greatest victory since Agincourt.

Sir Walter, sensing her heart's distance, stepped down and bowed low so that she could see the perfect dark waves in his hair and how at the bottom of his tanned sailor's neck his hair curled up—probably pomaded to do so—in the arrogant way of a handsome young man who was determined to heat every woman he saw. And almost certainly succeeding with most. *And perhaps, at times, with me.*

Elizabeth could not help but erupt into gleeful laughter at her own private entertaining thoughts, since she had seen many handsome young men determined to catch her eye and favor—perhaps a grant of land or a better title—though she gave the ever-watchful court another reason for her obvious delight. A loud burst of gunpowder and flash of light brought her to her feet, her fist raised in victory imitating the Greek goddess of war, Pallas Athena. She regretted not wearing the breastplate and gorget she had worn at Tilbury last month.

The court cheered. "Down with all Spanish papists! Up with our good Queen Elizabeth!"

Raleigh raised his voice and it rang through the large chamber above all others. "Majesty, it seems your loyal English people would sink Philip's armada . . . a second time!" He bowed with a flourish of his hand, no longer callused from the sea, but soft as any courtier's.

"Nay, Sir Walter, we think that King Philip's fleet, his 'Great Enterprise of England,' is already well sunk, or soon will be in the storms off the Irish coast. He must be content to creep about inside his Escorial palace and hide from us. We did more than singe his beard in the channel. We left him hairless as a babe!"

The court erupted into laughter and Elizabeth knew that her every word would soon be repeated in the streets of London and shouted back at her when she rode down Cheapside on her way to St. Paul's for the service of thanksgiving. Even more, one foreign ambassador or another, seeking to curry Philip's favor, would report every word to him, probably sending the Spanish king to his knees again to beg God to strike Elizabeth down. But God was listening to her and not to Philip. She shook with silent laughter.

Raleigh bowed again, undefeated as always. "Madam," he said, his hand over his heart, "my only regret is that my lord Leicester could not be here to witness this celebration. He left court two weeks ago to take the waters at Cornbury. I long for news of his recovery. A man of his years cannot be too careful."

The chamber hushed.

Two weeks only? It seems longer. But how dare Raleigh? Elizabeth was tempted to slap his perfect face for giving Robin his sly backhand, but such a cocksure court rival needed different handling. She would have him take care of his words, but not beaten down. Still, there was bitter reproof in her face that she did not bother to remove. He must learn that Elizabeth was the only person in the realm who could challenge Robert, Earl of Leicester, not a lowborn sailor from Devonshire . . . no matter how a queen might favor his too-handsome face, well-turned calf and artful love poetry.

She waved Sir Walter away, giving him the back of her hand in curt dismissal. "Your love and care for the earl are well-known to us, Sir Walter."

Immediately, she signed for the musicians in the gallery above to begin playing to cover her own dismay. "Let us have one of my father's galliards. 'Time to Pass with Goodly Sport,' if you remember it." She and Robin had danced it for Henry when they were yet youngsters in the palace school. Whirling about with Robin at Greenwich Palace in front of her father's throne was like yesterday in her mind and always would be.

How could she have reveled for an hour, even for a minute, while Robin was sick these many weeks with his old fever? He had suffered a recurrence in the swampy land around Tilbury in July and August, while waiting to lead her faithful troops against the Spanish armies if they landed at the mouth of the Thames. Everyone had thought they would wait to make an assault on London and try to capture England's queen alive. They had planned to take her to Pope Sixtus to be tried for heresy. Ha! God had other plans for His anointed Elizabeth. He had sent a great storm to douse the heretic's fire that Rome would have lit for her.

The queen tapped her foot to the galliard. How she had danced it with her sweet Robin, who now even in his middle years was still the most manly, most well-favored man, never to age in her eyes and heart. The world may have seen them change, but they had never changed to each other. She was sure of that. Robin was the one man in her world of whom she could be in no doubt. Always.

Cecil stepped forward again, unusually merry. Would he be smiling if he knew what she planned? What she hugged to herself? She wanted to see his face when she announced that she would name Robin Lord Lieutenant of England and grant him the title of duke, ranking him above every other peer; indeed, he would rank next to her as sovereign. In spirit, he would be her heir.

Cecil bowed. "Majesty, it does my heart good to see you so triumphant."

"My thanks, Spirit," she said, using the nickname she had given him on her first day as queen. She turned her gaze from him. If he thought to read what she was thinking, he would be confounded.

She had told no one of her plans, especially not Cecil, who would most certainly disapprove, perhaps threaten to resign again. Such power for Robin would gall her lord treasurer, all her council, and the rest of the country's peers. Sir Walter would be most unhappy, having expected a peerage for himself. She would give him a manor in his native Devon with enough sheep and wool to ease his pain.

"Play another galliard, master lutenist," she called to the gallery. "We command that there be no gloom here this day. Let us be lively and dance so that King Philip will hear we held revels as the last of his defeated, starving sailors and soldiers struggled toward home, their ships broken by good English shot and God's gales, heaven and earth against him."

Drums, pipes and guitars accompanied the sound of the court's laughter, as she saw Dr. John Dee weave his slow way among the dancing couples and bow, his long beard tucked neatly into the belt of his doctor's robe. *Why do old men grow huge beards as if to proclaim a manhood that has long since fled?*

"What news of Lord Leicester to explain the melancholy I see behind Your Majesty's joy?" he asked, keeping his voice confidential.

"Do you look in my face as into your scrying glass, good doctor?" she answered softly. "There is no news, though I have sent to know."

"No news explains melancholy, Majesty," he said, his breath blowing the long hairs of his mustache that drooped over his lips. "And yet Sir Walter is here for your merriment."

The queen frowned. "Good Dr. Dee, you are a man of travel and learning. You talk to spirits and angels and yet you cannot see to Rycote and tell me when the Earl of Leicester will return."

"Your Grace, only God sees all. I see only the little he allows me to see in my magical glass."

His face was somber, but Elizabeth's voice nearly shook with anger. "Jesu, good doctor, tell me what is the little that you *do* see."

She had her answer in the next moment, though it was an answer that came not from Dr. Dee, or from an angel in heaven, but from hell.

A gentleman pensioner walked toward her holding up a dusty lad, his thin legs unsteady, nearly staggering from fatigue.

A message from Robin at last. Elizabeth sighed with relief, eagerly motioning the boy forward. "Young Tracey," she called aloud down the length of the hall, "what news from my lord Leicester?"

Cecil took the lad's arm and led him to the throne, where the boy dropped to his knees in both exhaustion and courtesy, breathing hard.

"What news of my lord Leicester's health, lad?" The words crowded past a full throat, her heart beginning to beat faster.

"Majesty, I am sent to tell you that—"

He took a shuddering breath and, Jesu help her, she yelled at the used-up boy. "Tell us what!"

"The Earl of Leicester is dead, Majesty, these two days gone."

She opened her mouth to shout down his lie, but at that moment came a great boom of cannon from the Tower and what the queen howled was neither heard nor understood by anyone in the presence chamber, least by herself. It was a cry of denial from the deepest well of her heart.

Cecil hastened forward and offered his arm. "Majesty, please you, come at once out of this crowd into a private place."

She said something, but it was lost in a swift-moving red pain that filled her and became a sound . . . a name. . . . *Robin . . . my long love. How could I have forgotten you for a moment, even in my greatest triumph,* our *greatest triumph?*

"Majesty, you should come away to your chambers. I would not have the court see you thus. A queen does not—"

"Does not!" she shrieked at her faithful advisor of thirty years and more. "Does not feel agony, does not . . ." She lost the words spilling from her heart, if she had ever had words instead of shrieks of disbelief. It could not be. Not Robin. He had promised never to leave her.

Cecil took her arm and spoke on determinedly: "A queen does not allow her subjects to see her shaken so."

She had no more strength to dispute him; she could scarcely lift her legs, though she stumbled into the hall from the presence chamber, her gown weighted with heavy embroidery and pearls suddenly pressing her down, her arms almost too weak to hold on to Cecil's arm so that, with the aid of his cane, he must hold them both upright. Her body was empty as death.

"And yet," she croaked, "my people know I am a woman born with a woman's heart."

"You are a queen first, Majesty. That is what you have always been from the cradle and must remain until . . ."

"I die. Oh, God above, let me go to Robin." It was a howl that rang through the hall, bringing her yeoman guards to greater attention, their pikes trembling, for what they did not know.

"Majesty," Cecil said as they reached the privy chamber doors, "you must go on. Lord Leicester would hav—"

She turned to rage at him. "What do you know of what Robin wanted? He wanted life . . . life with me, beside me. I could not give him more than a little . . . what I could, but never enough. . . ." Now she shook and sagged once more toward the floor.

"Majesty," Cecil urged, his tone reminding her of herself just enough to keep her from a faint.

Once inside the anterooms, Cecil beat on the doors to the royal apartment, loudly calling for her ladies of the bedchamber.

The doors opened on the large privy bedchamber and she could see the flashing victory explosions from London City through her mullioned windows and the fire in her fireplace that burned day and night in this damp old palace beside the Thames. She saw the arras tapestries that covered her walls and the intricate Flemish lace on her bed bolsters. She feared madness. *I can see only things. I have no sense of myself. I can't think. I can no more believe.*

She croaked a question as her ladies helped her to her bed and bent to her. "Did you know, my lord Cecil?" she cried.

"No, Majesty. Not for a certainty. I have this for you from young Tracey."

He held a letter in front of her eyes so that she could read. It was Robin's handwriting, shaky, scrawled in his illness with fading strength.

His last letter.